D0982057

black bird *of the* gallows

black bird of the gallows

MEG KASSEL

This book is a work of fiction. Names, characters, places, and incidents are the product of the author's imagination or are used fictitiously. Any resemblance to actual events, locales, or persons, living or dead, is coincidental.

Entangled Publishing, LLC
2614 South Timberline Road
Suite 109
Fort Collins, CO 80525

Entangled Teen is an imprint of Entangled Publishing, LLC.

Visit our website at www.entangledpublishing.com.

Edited by Liz Pelletier and Jenn Mishler
Cover design by L.J Anderson at Mayhem Cover Creations
Interior design by Toni Kerr

ISBN 978-1-63375-814-8
Ebook ISBN 978-1-63375-815-5

Manufactured in the United States of America

First Edition September 2017

10 9 8 7 6 5 4 3 2 1

For my mom and dad, who always knew this would happen someday.

1

the boy and the bees

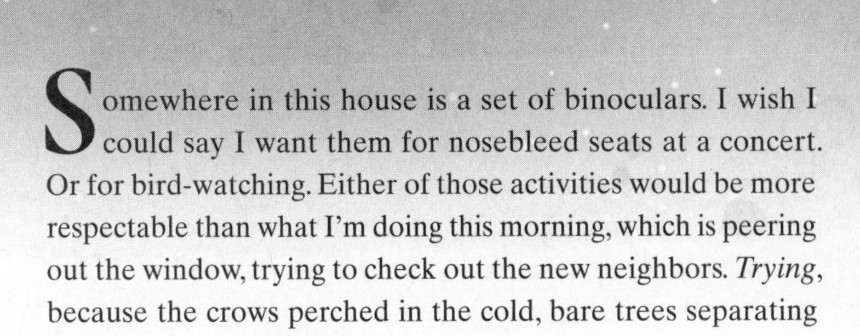

Somewhere in this house is a set of binoculars. I wish I could say I want them for nosebleed seats at a concert. Or for bird-watching. Either of those activities would be more respectable than what I'm doing this morning, which is peering out the window, trying to check out the new neighbors. *Trying*, because the crows perched in the cold, bare trees separating our houses are impeding my snooping efforts.

An adult female voice filters through the woods, directing the location of a leather sofa, asking to please be *very* careful with *that* painting. Through the screen of birds, I glimpse a woman directing a battalion of brawny movers. Even from a distance, she makes an impression, with long black hair and buff cashmere, but I completely forget about her the instant a boy with a backpack comes outside. He's tall, about my age, and moves with a smooth, confident stride. From a distance, he's seriously cute, and I suspect the view is even better up close. Nice shoulders. Something vaguely familiar about the tilt of his head.

I shift for a better view and watch the woman give the boy a quick hug. He kisses her cheek and then starts down the driveway, out of sight. Not for long, I hope. Maybe he's walking to the bus stop where I am headed shortly. Curiosity sends a flutter through my belly. *What's he like? Is he nice, or will I be stuck living next door to a jerk?* You couldn't tell these things by watching a boy walk. They only come out when he opens his mouth and words come out. Cute or not, I'll be reserving judgment on New Boy. I finish off my glass of orange juice and turn at the sound of footsteps.

"Morning, Angie." My dad strides into the kitchen, followed closely by our dog, Roger. Dad is decked out for their morning run in designer sweatpants and one of his tight running shirts in a retina-piercing shade of highlighter yellow. Still, he manages to look dapper and sophisticated, even first thing in the morning and, well, *in that shirt*. Roger's eyes are glued to my dad, as if the powers of his dog mind will make Dad pick up the leash faster.

"What are you doing?" Dad asks.

"Watching the new neighbors move in," I reply. "Where are the binoculars?"

Dad joins me at the window. "In my bottom desk drawer."

Eh. I'm not running upstairs for them. Especially now that the boy's gone.

He shifts, tries to angle for a better view. "Binoculars won't do you any good with all those crows in the way."

"I know it," I mutter. "So who are these people, anyway?"

"Fernandez, I think their name is," Dad says. "I ran into the realtor a few days ago. She gave me the lowdown of the sale." He scratches his freshly shaved cheek and squints harder. "The lady is from Spain. Bunch of kids. No *Mr.* Fernandez," he adds. "Probably a good thing, considering what happened with Mr. Ortley. Sick bastard."

What happened with Mr. Ortley is still a matter of distress to the neighborhood and our entire small, southwestern Pennsylvania town. It's not every day a man returns home from a business trip and kills his family and then himself.

Although they kept to themselves, the Ortleys were our next-door neighbors, and we saw it all when the police arrived and the bodies were removed. The local news media didn't linger on the incident—just a rich businessman who snapped. But the sprawling, Tudor-style home seems to hold on to the grisly events that happened there. At least a dozen hopeful realtors had planted signs in front of the house over the past year and a half as weeds grew up around the three-car garage. Even priced rock-bottom cheap, no one wanted to live in that house. Potential buyers looked but left quickly. Some wouldn't even go inside.

I don't believe in ghosts or hauntings or any of that, but even I have to agree that the house makes me twitchy. It's as if some creepy melancholy had soaked into the bones of it, making it unnerving to be near. But maybe that would change with new owners.

Roger wags his thick yellow tail and lets out an impatient whine. It's *past* morning run time, and he doesn't care for a delay in his favorite part of the day.

My dad rubs a hand over the dog's blocky head. Our big, happy yellow lab wasn't always ours. He'd belonged to the Ortleys. After their passing, Dad had offered to take Roger, and the police were only too happy to turn the orphaned dog over to the neighbor and his kid rather than call animal control. It was one less hideous thing they had to do that day. And so, Roger became ours.

Dad takes out a pitcher of lumpy, green liquid from the fridge. It smells faintly of parsley and strongly of garlic, but he pours a healthy glass and downs half of it in one chug. To his credit, he winces only a little. I don't understand why he does this to himself.

"Okay, *okay*. We're going," he says to Roger, whose whines are now accompanied by a tap dance on the hardwood floors.

"You could try eating normal food." I grin and put my breakfast dishes in the sink. "Lots of people do it. You might like it."

"Working with doctors, you learn what 'normal food' does to the body. No thanks." This is the way all these conversations end. My dad sells medical equipment to hospitals, clinics, and doctors' offices, so he knows all the ways people can die. His job is to sell equipment intended to keep them alive. The result is, he's all in on the "prevention" end of things. I can say with authority, it's not easy being the offspring of a health fanatic. Last year, everything he—make that, *we*—ate was gluten-free. The currently banned food item is dairy. Living without pizza is miserable, but the milk thing is near unbearable. I dream about eating ice cream.

"I'll see you tonight, Dad," I say.

He points to his cheek. I give him a kiss and scoop my backpack off the counter. Weird food aside, living with my dad isn't a hardship. I could have been dumped on a far worse doorstep five years ago.

I pull on wooly, fingerless gloves and head out to catch the bus. Yes, the *bus*. For the record, I have a car—a ten-year-old Civic. It's so generic, it's virtually invisible, but I don't drive it to school. There's a cool, quirky explanation I hand out readily: I can do homework or study or fold paper cranes while riding. I tell people it's like having your own personal chauffeur. But the darker answer is, I worry obsessively about leaving my car unattended in the lot all day. Anyone could break in, steal it, or just do something to it. And yes, I'm familiar with the word "paranoia." I come by it legitimately. A big chunk of my childhood was spent in an old VW van that was broken into all. The. Time. Occasionally, while my mom and I were sleeping in it.

So I ride the bus. Aside from the part about standing on the corner in bad weather, it's not a terrible way to start the day.

I walk gingerly down our very long, very steep driveway, crunching on the mix of salt and ice. Mount Franklin Estates, otherwise known as my neighborhood, was built into the side of Mount Franklin itself, in the foothills of the Allegheny Mountains. As far as mountains go, Franklin is less of a "mount" and more of a pretty, wooded hill with some expensive houses on it. Still, the roads can be steep and, because I shun practical footwear in favor of aesthetics, I have to watch my step.

The bus will arrive in eight minutes. Mrs. Pierce is as exact as an atomic clock. I pick up the pace when I hit the sidewalk, which is scraped right to the concrete and gritty with sand. Sure enough, the house next door is bustling with activity. The forlorn For Sale sign is gone and a champagne Lexus SUV sits next to the moving truck.

I pass big, gracious trees, driveways twisting off toward large homes, until the bus stop comes into view. I slow down. I've had the corner to myself since sophomore year, so it's jarring to see two boys standing there. One is backpack boy—my new neighbor—and a quick glance confirms that he is, indeed, binocular worthy. The other guy is… I can't tell. At first, I think there's something wrong with my eyes. He looks a little blurred, like I'm viewing him through a smeared lens. His lack of a bag of some sort tells me he's not waiting for the school bus. Also, his attire—wool cap and puffy coat—is ordinary enough, but not high school-style. He holds himself in the way one would if he were about to bolt. Even from a distance, something about him sets off my finely tuned creep meter.

It's obvious that backpack boy and creepy guy are not friends, although they appear to know each other. There's tension in their stances, underlying the hum of their low-pitched voices—it's like they're squaring off. I slow my pace and look for something to duck behind, but their heads turn toward me at the same time. I falter, feeling like an intruder. Silly, considering this is public space.

Puffy Jacket takes a step backward. Closer up, he comes into clear focus, and I can see he's young—twenties, with a hooked nose and thin lips that turn down at my approach. The inexplicable scent of warm honey cuts through the late February chill. It should be a pleasant smell, but there's a sharpness to the aroma that makes the hair on my neck stand up.

I feel Backpack Boy's gaze on me. I'm still trying to gauge the other guy when, impossibly, his face changes. Not his expression—his actual *face*. Instead of a hooked nose and thin lips, wizened eyes peer back at me. His nose is small, almost feminine, and a mustache scruffs his upper lip. His gaze turns to mine with a cold intensity that makes my footing falter. He pulls his lips back over clenched teeth in what is perhaps meant to be a smile, but it's just not. My heart rate picks up. I drop my gaze, disturbed by what looked like hunger and menace and an unnatural familiarity in that strange guy's face. Caution escalates to the first prickles of actual fear.

It's okay. Don't freak. Mrs. Pierce will be here in a few minutes, and that baseball bat she keeps next to her seat is not for an impromptu game.

Puffy Jacket turns away. He mutters something to Backpack Boy and starts off down the street in the opposite direction.

Relief—that he's leaving, that I don't have to look at him anymore—eases my racing pulse, but already, I'm doubting what I saw. That couldn't have been real. I mean, it's impossible for a person's face to take on a whole different set of features without a ton of plastic surgery. There's a better explanation—

deceptive lighting. Sleep deprivation. Too much sugary cereal.

Yeah. One of those things.

I turn my attention to Backpack Boy, whose face has *not* appeared to change, thankfully. My head is still a little fuddled, and I get stuck staring at him. Worse, I find it impossible to get *un*stuck. He's got more than a nice walk. He's got a nice everything—high cheekbones, straight nose, and expressive eyes to go with a tall, athletic body that just screams *I play all the sports*. Not my type, but the only thing I know about my "type" is that it hasn't been any of the boys at Cadence High. Except for this new one, apparently. It's irritating, because I could do without a hot neighbor. An attractive boy living next door adds a pointless layer of nerves, like stress about wearing my ratty sweatpants to the mailbox, and I don't want to be tempted to spy on him with my dad's binoculars. It's an exercise in futility. A waste of perfectly good energy, as in my experience, the noisy boys who play the sports don't notice the quiet girls who play the music. And that's fine. I have no problem with the natural order of things. I have no idea what a girl like me, who spends most of her free time in the basement with laptops and sound mixing software, would talk about with a guy who throws balls and runs for *fun*.

An amused light sparks Backpack Boy's dark eyes, as if he had heard those last few thoughts. One hand is wrapped around the strap of his backpack, the other is tucked in the pocket of his black wool coat. He wears cargos with a lot of pockets and black Chucks. His hair is a floppy chestnut mess. "Hi. I'm Reece Fernandez." The cold morning has put a chilled flush to his cheeks. He nods in the general direction of our houses. "My family is moving in to number forty-one."

I scramble for something interesting to say. Maybe even something witty. "Yeah, I saw— " *No!* Do not admit you were peeping at him from your window. "The truck." I clear my throat and shove my fidgeting hands in my pockets. "Moving day. Exciting."

Reece squints in the direction of his new home, then turns to me. Our gazes stick and hold, and for a moment I wonder if I've seen these eyes before. And those are some nice eyes, even though...*wow*, they aren't just dark, they're black from iris to pupil.

He blinks to the ground then laughs, but it sounds forced, like he's digging for an appropriate response. "Exciting is one word for it."

I nod and smile like we *didn't* just stare at each other for several strange whole seconds. "So, I'm Angie Dovage. My dad and I live next door to you. Number forty-three. I hope I didn't..." *Stare at you like a brain-hungry zombie.* "Interrupt your conversation."

"You didn't." His lips quirk up at the edges. "Thanks for running him off."

"Do you know that guy?"

He shakes his head, shoulders hunching. "Some freak asking for money." Dark eyes shift to squint down the street. Not the body language of someone telling the truth. After having lived with a drug addict until the age of twelve, I know fiction when I hear it.

I glance down the street with a shiver. The guy in the puffy coat is gone. Just...gone. He must have ducked off the street and into the woods, as there aren't any houses or side streets on that stretch. If that guy tries to break into any of the fancy homes here, he'll be greeted by a shrieking, top-of-the-line security system, but I don't like the thought of some "freak asking for money" lurking in the woods of my neighborhood.

If that's really what he is. I doubt it, but I won't press. The guy could be Reece's relative—a cousin with a drug problem—and I know all about that type of pain and humiliation.

As for the face-changing thing, it must have been my imagination. A trick of the light or something. People's faces are what they are. They don't change like that.

"My car won't be delivered for a few days. Once it arrives, I can give you a ride to school, if you like." His voice betrays traces of a New England accent when he says the word "car." It comes out sounding like *cah*. Kind of cute.

"I have a car," I say, surprised by the offer. "I just...prefer the bus."

Reece's gaze moves over me. It's a general perusal of the curious, non-leering variety, but my cheeks warm. "You a junior?" he asks.

"Senior." *Here we go.* He's the one with the creepy friend or relation, but *I'll* be the weird one because I take the bus.

"Oh, right. I should have kn—" He cuts off, eyebrows lifting in the middle, like he can't find the right word. "I didn't mean—"

I have no idea why, but his momentary fluster charms me, and I smile at him. "It's no big deal."

It earns me a grin. "I think it's cool that you take the bus. Sort of like getting chauffeured around, you know?"

Aw hell, now I'm smiling at him too much. "That's kind of my thought, too." I clear my throat when the silence stretches past a few seconds. "So, where did you move from?"

"It's more like, where *haven't* I moved from," he replies with a flashing grin. "We've lived all over."

"I thought you were from up north," I say. "Your accent. It sounds like Massachusetts or something."

"Really?" He starts to say something else, but wherever our conversation was headed cuts off with a sudden incoming flap of black wings and rasping caws. I look up as a throng of crows swoops in low and fast.

"Get down!" I drop into a crouch and cage my arms over my head. A mass of feathers and beaks heads right for us. It's called self-preservation, a trait I assumed everyone possessed.

Not so. Reece Fernandez remains standing. I peek up and watch in horror as he closes his eyes and lifts his face to the mess of curved talons and flapping wings.

"Reece!" I cry out, but he doesn't move. He continues to stand there as they surround him like a writhing cloud. These are not little, dainty birds, but big and solid and *organized.* However, as inky wings beat all around him, Reece remains unscathed. I swear one of them tweaks his sun-streaked hair with a shiny beak. It looks almost...playful. Then, as fast as they arrived, they soar away. Reece watches them depart with a quiet smile. Miraculously, he is unharmed.

"What the *hell?*" I gasp. "They could have taken your face off."

"Nah. They wouldn't have."

He's unnaturally calm about this. Emphasis on *unnatural.*

"Really? You know that much about wild birds?" I sputter. "They were all over you. You're lucky you weren't ripped to shreds."

Reece tugs his backpack higher on his shoulder and shifts his weight a little awkwardly. A little defensively. "We were safe. Haven't you seen those nature shows? If you stand up and don't act scared, they'll leave you alone. See? It worked."

I get to my feet and brush snow off my knees. "I'm pretty sure that advice is about bears," I mutter, heart still racing. "I don't know what shows you're watching, but—"

Reece draws in a sharp breath. "Angie!"

What now? My gaze snaps to the sky, expecting another round of crows, but no, he's pointing at my coat sleeve like it's on fire. What's he worked up about? The only thing out of place is a bee, resting on my coat sleeve. "Oh, it's a honeybee."

His lips draw tight over his teeth. "That's *not* a—" He snaps his mouth shut. "Just hold still." Teeth clenched, he raises a gloved hand.

I rear back, alarmed that maybe he's looking to swat *me*, but his gaze is riveted on the bee. "Hey, it's not hurting anything," I say. "What are you doing? It's not—"

He whacks the bee to the ground and proceeds to stomp it. Really, *really* stomp it.

I watch this, wondering if I missed a key scene here. In eighth grade science, we'd spent a whole unit learning about bees, so I thought it was common knowledge that honeybees aren't naturally aggressive. They die after they sting, so they don't tend to let loose without good reason. Reece must have missed that lesson.

"Yeah," I say. "I think it's dead."

He's breathless. His hands shake. "Just making sure."

"What's with you?" A clanking rumble announces the approach of the school bus. "A bunch of crows dive-bombing you is fine, but *one bee* is the end of the world?"

He swallows hard. "Thought you might be allergic."

"I'm not. Are you?" He shakes his head as I blink down at the pulverized bee, a smear in the snow. "That was weird."

"Trust me, you haven't seen weird."

I glimpse his face before he turns away. I wish I hadn't. What I see there sours my stomach. His features are stretched taut with grief. Reece looks as if his soul itself had been cleaved. As if he has to stitch it up every day just to keep what's left of him together. The sight sends a shiver burning down my spine because I know how that feels. My dad said there was "no Mr. Fernandez." Maybe Reece lost his father tragically. My heart bumps unsteadily against my ribs. *This boy knows grief. He knows that isolating ache that doesn't quite ever go away.* It's right there, laid bare for anyone who cares to look. How many would, in the halls of Cadence High?

The bus grinds to a halt and the doors wheeze open.

Reece pauses on the first step, looks at me over his shoulder.

"Angie, stay away from the bees."

"But—" I fall silent as something raw flashes in those dark, haunted eyes.

Eyes as sharp and black as the crows who touched his skin and played with his hair.

He wasn't afraid then, but he is now.

2

the lunchroom

Cadence High has the smallest cafeteria in the history of cafeterias. It's cramped, uncomfortably warm, and smells like thirty years of deep-fried things. Narrow tables are arranged in long rows and spaced close to one another. Pull out your chair too far and you'll bump into the one behind you. It's impossible to sit alone, even if you wanted to.

My friend Deno drops his tray next to mine with a heavy clunk. It's heaped with the cafeteria's dubious fare. He seems to enjoy it, so I check a snarky comment about how troughs would be more efficient than trays in this cafeteria and try to disentangle my congealed pile of french fries.

"Check out the new kid." Deno jerks a chin to where Reece stands in line.

"That's Reece," I say. "My new neighbor."

Deno's brows rise above the thick aqua frames of glasses he doesn't need. "No way. Dead family house?"

"Can't call it that anymore." I wag a soggy french fry at him. "New family is very much alive."

"Sure, until Ortley's ghost shows up and scares the piss out of them."

I roll my eyes. "The house isn't haunted." *But the boy living there might be.* The memory of Reece's anguished expression is warmer and fresher than the food in front of me.

Deno grunts then scoops a spoonful of soup. "Dude broke in on his first day. 'Course, he looks just like them. Maybe they don't realize he's new."

Deno's right. Reece is *in*. I watch him from my designated spot at our table. Most of the school band, as well as a strong contingent from the Arts and Literature Club, sits at this long row of tables. *We* think we're cool, but the rest of the student body doesn't necessarily agree. It's the next row of tables over, which I have a perfect view of—packed with varsity jackets, pretty hair, and vapid conversation—that's supposedly the one to be at. I don't see it. I can't imagine wanting to sit anywhere else.

There is little doubt which table Reece will be sitting at. He's still in line and has rendered himself nearly invisible among the pack of Cadence High's athletic stars. He laughs easily and a little too loud, like the rest of the boys. His grin holds on the edge of a perpetual smirk. His eyes are greatly transformed—banked, heavy-lidded, and disinterested, they render him unrecognizable from the boy I met at the bus stop. Reece's gaze slides to me, then away, without a flicker of recognition.

Seeing him like this makes my belly sink with disappointment. Bus-stop Reece was interesting, someone I related to on a pretty deep level. I thought we had a little bonding moment this morning, but School Reece belongs to a different species than me. Still, as I sharpen my gaze, I think I see signs indicating which is genuine and which is fake—his fingernail picks the seam of his shirt. His smirk holds like it's superglued in place. It's like he's wearing camouflage, designed to render him indistinguishable from the rest of the socially well-to-do. It may fool them, but not me, who has always been different. You can paint black-and-white stripes on a horse, but that doesn't mean he belongs in a zebra herd.

Deno shakes his head. Not one strand of hair budges from the retro-wave thing he's got going on up there. "Too bad you didn't get someone cool moving in next door," he says with a mischievous smile. "We really could have used a decent keyboard player."

Lacey Taggert, my closest girlfriend and the most gifted pianist I've ever met, sits down across from me. She purses her full lips and sends Deno a condescending sniff. "Oh yes. It's never the *drums* we have to record a hundred times to get right."

I laugh and angle a finger at Deno. "You set yourself up for that."

Deno shrugs. He knows he's not a great drummer. He is, however, a genius sound engineer and the best musical partner I could ask for. Our friendship fits around music, filling in the cracks and gaps like mortar.

"Angie, how do *you* feel about that boy living next door?" Lacey studies me with serious brown eyes that tell me she caught me staring at Reece. She's horribly observant.

Deno ignores that the question was meant for me and frowns at her. "What kind of question is that?"

I know *exactly* what kind of question that is. Lacey and I have been friends since I showed up at middle school band practice, clutching my dead mom's battered acoustic guitar that still stank of pot and, shaking so hard, I dropped all my picks in the sound hole. She pried the guitar from my hands and shook the picks out, saying only a real musician would come out to play when they were so scared. Lacey, coming from a Very Serious Family of Musicians, held to the belief that "real" musicians are rare persons to be treasured. I know that she also treasures Deno, although in a different way than I do. That difference makes it a bad time for an honest answer to her question. Not with Deno studying my face like he's looking for Waldo in one of my pores.

Yeah. I should mention that Deno and I made out once. Yes, I made out with a guy who likes to be called *Deno*, though his name is really Daniel Steinway. I can't fault the guy. I go by the name "Sparo" when I DJ at the local club. So, Deno and I made out once, last year, after a particularly magical recording session. I'm not sure how it started—swept up in the moment, I guess. He enjoyed the encounter more than I did, but didn't make a big deal about it when I politely declined another go. We never spoke of it again, meaning we never *addressed* it, so I don't know how he'd react if I announced that I like another boy. I don't want to possibly hurt him over such a nonissue as Reece, who I just met today under strange circumstances. I haven't decided what I think of Reece Fernandez, but I've *got* to stop staring at him like he's parading around in skivvies with gallons of mint chip ice cream on his broad shoulders. Although that's a really nice vision.

Lacey's lips curve. "What *are* you staring at, Angie?"

Crap. "Nothing." I take a deep drink from my water bottle. "I'm not staring at anything."

"Mmm. Okay." Lacey raises one dark eyebrow, and I'd like to tape her mouth shut. But I get it. Despite a romantic streak she'd like to deny, Lacey has a thing for Deno. Something about him works for her, and it's more than his good looks. She didn't even seem to mind when he started doing doofy things with his hair and calling himself *Deno*.

Lacey *might* not know about the make-out episode from last year. I suspect Deno had a chucklehead moment and spilled. *I* never mentioned it.

"Seriously?" Deno's chest deflates. "You're checking out the new guy, Ange?"

Yes, I am. I flip my hand. "Pfft. New bug in the jar."

Sitting directly across from me, Lacey has a better view of the lunch line. She tilts her head. "He's cute." She says this like she's noticing for the first time, and maybe she is. Lacey's never gone for the sporty type. Neither have I, come to think of it. It's a day of surprises.

Lacey's eyes widen. "Oh, *oh*. He's coming over here."

A french fry sticks halfway down my trachea. "No, he's not."

Oh, but he is. I feel a presence behind my right shoulder and my senses go on high alert.

"Hey, Angie," says a voice with a New England accent.

I turn and look up slowly, trying to ignore the hot burn of curious eyes on me, on *us*. But the way Reece stands there with his lunch tray is transitory. He's not here to sit. Has no intention of trying. That's a good thing. And it kind of bums me out.

"Hi Reece." I paste on an easy expression, complete with a courteous smile. "What's up?"

Tension in his features takes me by surprise. Maybe he thinks I'm going to blow him off in front of everyone. Or he's worried I told people about the crows. Or that creepy guy. Or any of the other weirdness he managed to pack into the six minutes we spent together while waiting for the bus.

"My mom would like to ask your dad about a few things—like who plows your driveway and stuff." He shifts on his feet. "So I was wondering if I could get your house number or your dad's cell. To give to my mom."

"Uh, sure," I mumble, a little confused. A little more embarrassed. I rip out a scrap of notebook paper and scribble down both numbers, but not mine. He very clearly didn't ask for that one.

At the table behind Lacey, a strawberry blond head pops

up. "Over here, Reece."

Ugh. Kiera Shaw. Her squeaky voice makes my molars grind. No one here has put more effort into making me miserable than Kiera.

He gives her a smile—a charming one—then looks back at me. Balancing his tray on one hand, he takes the paper from me. Our fingers brush. I pull my hand away, surprised by how tuned in I am to his touch. It's a zing to the senses. Suddenly, the world seems a little more vivid.

"Thanks." He tucks the paper into his front jeans pocket. His eyes look darker than they did this morning.

"Sure. No problem." I squeeze my tingling hands together under the table. Why couldn't I have felt this with Deno? That would have been so much more convenient.

Kiera calls his name again. "Saved you a seat." She touches the empty chair next to her. I wonder who was ousted to free up the spot.

He smiles at her, but there's weariness to his movements, in the set of his shoulders. And again, that strange whiff of despair. It clings to him like the after-stench of cigarette smoke. No one else seems to sense it.

He straightens his shoulders and walks back around my table to Kiera's. Her smile turns megawatt as he heads for the seat she saved for him. I watch from beneath lowered lids as he's sucked into the abyss of highlighted hair and varsity jackets.

Lacey lurches over the table. "What was *that?*"

I shove a cold french fry into my mouth and chew without tasting. "It was nothing."

"Nothing?" Lacey's eyes are shining. "He asked you for your number. That's *something*."

I rip the crust of my sandwich into little pieces. "He asked for my *dad's* number. There's a difference. Sort of a big one."

Lacey shakes her head but drops the subject. A little too

late, I remember Deno sitting next to me.

He adjusts his glasses and peers at me intently. "Which one did you give him?"

"Which what?" I ask, unable to keep an edge from my voice.

"Which number?" His brow furrows. "Did you give him your cell?"

"No," I reply slowly. "I gave him my dad's cell and the house line. Those are the ones he asked for. For snowplowing purposes."

"What's wrong with him?" Deno's brow smooths out, but he looks confused. "You go up to a girl to ask for a phone number, and you ask for her *dad's cell* but not hers?"

Does he *have* to rub it in? "And the house line," I murmur with a glower, but part of me is relieved Deno's more puzzled by this than anything else. Of course, I don't know what his reaction would have been if Reece *had* asked for my cell.

I'm not surprised he didn't want it. I shouldn't be disappointed.

"Daniel," Lacey says, using his real name to irritate him. Which it does. "Let's drop it, okay?"

"Fine," Deno says with a shrug. "But the dude's weird, if you ask me. And I wouldn't sit so close to Kiera, if I were him." He leans toward us and lowers his voice. "She poisons her boyfriends."

I smack Deno's arm. "That's the dumbest thing I've ever heard."

He rubs his arm and sighs gustily. "It's not. Reece better not piss her off, or he'll find out for himself soon enough."

"Deno, please stop it," Lacey says tartly. "That's not true. I'm sure Kiera Shaw did *not* poison anyone."

"No?" Deno raises a brow. "Brayden McKee broke up with her two days ago, and he was sent home this morning with a suspicious ailment."

"*Not* suspicious," Lacey says. "Brayden got stung by a bee in the parking lot and his tongue swelled up. The nurse gave him an epinephrine shot, then his parents took him home."

"That's what they *want* you to think," Deno says around a chicken finger. "He's not allergic to bees."

"How do you know?" Lacey asks.

"Because almost all of us got stung two years ago at that school trip to Thomas Lake, remember? Brayden didn't need any shots."

"I don't remember that."

Deno turns his gaze to the ceiling. "Geez, Lace..." The rest of their argument fades out.

Stay away from the bees.

I glance up, peering around Lacey to Reece's back. He's having an intense, animated conversation with Cody Knox about what I can only assume is hockey, since that's the only topic Cody talks about with multi-word replies. To look at Reece now, nothing about him appears strange. He's as normal as a teenage sports fanboy could be, grinning and nodding with no pretense whatsoever. I was probably reading into the entire bus-stop thing with the bees. Some people are really afraid of them. Even big, handsome guys who like hockey are allowed to have phobias.

Just then, Kiera Shaw lets out one of her high-pitched giggles and taps Reece on the shoulder. He turns to her.

"You should come out with us on Friday night." Kiera leans into him, brushing her shoulder against his. "There's a local club—The Strip Mall—that has an awesome DJ on Friday nights."

"The Strip Mall?" Reece asks. "Is that seriously the name?"

She tosses her head. "I know. Dumb name, right? But it actually *was* a strip mall. It sat empty for years until this lady bought it and gutted the whole thing and made a club out of it. It's actually pretty cool."

Reece shrugs. He has the nerve to remain unconvinced, despite Kiera's declaration of The Strip Mall's coolness. *Amazing.* "What kind of music?" he asks.

A grin pops up on my face. Even just watching their backs, I can see Kiera struggle to regroup. "It's like..." Her finger circles the air as she digs deep for a sophisticated term. "Electronic music," she says, finally. "But not techno. Well, maybe *some* techno. It's just cool remixes and chill tunes. Friday night is all ages, but you have to be twenty-one to drink." She waves a hand. "Someone usually brings a flask. But it's no big deal, either way. The DJ, Sparo, is so *city*. She seriously rocks."

I morph a bark of laughter into a noisy cough. People look, but I don't care. This conversation is a gift from the gods. I'm betting Kiera made up the term "city" to sound cultured, but it's such a gem, I file it into long-term memory. I'll remember that bit about the flask, too. Maybe the bouncers should take a closer look in those sparkly little purses she and her friends carry.

Deno thumps me on the back. "Hey, you okay?"

"Yeah, fine," I choke out.

Deno pumps me on the back again, this time pitching my face within inches of my pile of soggy fries. "Good. No hemlock maneuver, then," he says.

"Stop hitting her, you Neanderthal. And it's *Heimlich* maneuver, not hemlock," Lacey says, probably wondering why she's so hung up on this guy. "But *you'd* kill a person by giving them either one."

Deno gives my back one last thump that sends me into

another round of coughing. I draw more looks, including Reece's, who swivels to look at me. His expression is unreadable. Concern or annoyance—it could be either. Or neither. For one reckless moment, I meet his gaze and smile. I know it's a mistake the instant my lips curve.

Kiera's brows rise in twin arches of condescension, and my stomach dips. "What's your problem, little freak?"

My bravado is tremulous, but I take a sip of water, then give her a level look. "Is that a rhetorical question?"

She stares me down, and the air around me thickens. My face warms. My gaze drops to my tray. You would think, after all I've been through, that I would be tough as bricks, but my defenses are membrane-thin and easily shattered.

"Don't let her get to you," Lacey hisses. "She's hot air."

My cheeks burn and my hands fist at my sides, and it's all magnified because of the boy sitting next to her, staring at me with a look I can't interpret.

"That's right. Look away." Kiera's sugar-sweet voice drips with disdain. "Poor Angie. How do you get by without your mother's pervert boyfriends around to keep you company?"

The air rushes from my lungs. That was a low blow. The *lowest*. And the worst part is, I don't even know *why*. Our school is pretty small and chilled out. For reasons unknown, Kiera singled me out to torture.

Our corner of the cafeteria goes quiet. Just our corner, thankfully.

"I mean, I'm sure you had your hands *full* with—"

"Stop it," Reece clips out. "Seriously. That's messed up."

Kiera gives him a well-practiced *down, boy* look, but her cheeks flush. "It's okay, Reece. Angie knows we're just playing." She aims a pinched smile my way. "Don't you, sweetie?"

Reece frowns at her, eyes narrowed, like he finds her as filthy as the thing she just implied about me. Then, he looks at me, and the weight of his gaze is breathlessly intense. He doesn't blink, doesn't shift his attention away. Cafeteria Reece is gone. The boy from the bus stop, with all that hidden pain, looks back at me. For a second—*just* a second—Kiera blinks out of existence. So does everything and everyone except for me and the boy with those deep, dark eyes.

"What's your problem, Kiera?" Deno's voice crashes into my head. "You don't *say* stuff like that."

Suddenly, the intensity of everyone's attention is too much. I close my eyes, shuttering Reece, Kiera, my classmates' stares. I can't take it. I push away from the table. The room closes in around me. I grab my bag and head for the door.

"Get over yourself, you hipster wannabe," I just barely hear Kiera reply. "She's a tabloid freak show and everyone knows it. Or they *should*."

I don't hear anything else. I exit the cafeteria as tears blur my vision. The miserable truth is, I *am* a tabloid freak show. The way the police found me and returned me to my father, my mother's death—it made national news for a whole week: *Private Investigator Finds Man's Daughter Living in Van; Girl Reunited with Father After Seven Years; Woman Charged with Drug Possession and Child Abuse, Dies from Overdose; Witness Says Girl Abused by Mother's Boyfriends.*

The headlines went on and on. Each one more outrageous than the next. I know what some people think: I was abused, a drug mule, a child prostitute. They don't care that none of it was true. Stories are so much more interesting than the truth, and interesting sticks.

I lean against the locked stall door in the bathroom and ignore Lacey's calls for me. Later, we'll spend some therapeutic time bitching about Kiera, but right now…that just *hurt*. Most of the time, I can take what Kiera dishes, or ignore it, or stay unnoticed. Most of the time, I can count the months until graduation and let it roll. But now, the thought of facing Reece again makes my stomach turn. I'm sure Kiera is filling him in on the sordid details of my past, and some of it *won't* be lies. My mother was an addict. I did fight the police when they took me away from her. She did die from a drug overdose.

I wipe my eyes and count the reasons why this. Doesn't. Matter.

Screw Kiera. I have a show three days from tonight, and maybe Reece will be there. Maybe he'll find Sparo more interesting than little Angie Dovage. Maybe more interesting than Kiera Shaw.

Maybe I'll find out Friday night.

3

the dark way home

Deno drives me home from school in his 1999 Chevy Venture minivan. It's rusty, smelly, and makes an ominous front-end rattle that Deno willfully ignores. What had once been someone's kid-shuttle is now gutted and sticker-covered, used primarily for hauling musical equipment. He drives Lacey to school since she doesn't have a car. She bought a hundred-year-old violin, instead.

I sit in the one remaining back seat, thankful that they're not making me talk. Lacey has the sense to not deconstruct the cafeteria scene. But Deno has difficulty with silent spaces. He likes to fill them with sound—*any* sound. Even now, his fingers tap the steering wheel to a beat in his head, because the radio stopped working six months ago. I curl up and press against the threadbare seat. *Tomorrow will be better. It always is. How long until graduation? Four months and eleven days.*

"That was decent of your neighbor," Deno says. "He didn't have to say anything to Kiera."

I close my eyes, wishing the radio worked. "No, he didn't."

"Risky, too. Being his first day and all."

"What's your point, Deen?" Lacey asks.

"No point." Deno shrugs. "Just saying he might not be an asshole, that's all."

A harsh breath hisses from Lacey's teeth. "You might have spoken too soon," she murmurs, pointing to an old black sedan turning down the street toward my neighborhood. "Isn't that Kiera's car?"

My eyes fly open and snap to the window. Kiera *does* drive an old black sedan, along with about a half dozen other kids, but she doesn't live in my neighborhood. The only reason she'd be here is to give Reece a ride home.

"Nah." Deno turns into my development right behind the sedan. "See the hockey mask sticker on his bumper? That's Trevor Bent's car."

Lacey squints. "Oh. You're right."

"Angie." Deno swivels, shoots me a curious look. "Am I driving you home today because the new kid saw Kiera's ugly in the cafeteria?"

Lacey smacks his arm. "I *told* you, she's upset."

"Over the new kid?"

"Over the whole awful thing," Lacey says. "You are *so* dense sometimes."

I relax into the seat with pointless relief. So Reece is getting a ride home from Trevor. That doesn't mean he isn't into Kiera. It doesn't mean anything.

"Geez, Angie." Deno leans forward to look up through the windshield. "What's with all the crows in your neighborhood? Someone not bagging up their garbage?"

"What?" I sit up and look out, pulled out of my sulk. Sure enough, there are about a dozen crows flying around the van and the black car in front of us. "There've been a lot, lately." I say it casually, but I don't like this. I'm very happy to be inside a layer of metal and glass right now.

"They're quite large for crows," Lacey adds. "I think they're ravens."

"What's the difference?" Deno asks, braking at a stop sign.

"They're different species."

I am about to agree with Lacey, when one of the crows—or ravens—flies up right alongside the minivan. It hooks its claws on the window frame and squawks at me.

"Whoa!" I jerk back, even though I know it can't get in. The crow cocks its glossy black head at me, as if peering inside. It blinks a round eye and, even through the tinted glass, I can see the bird's eye is not black, but garnet red. It glitters like a cut gem in the cold afternoon light.

It's got something—a speck of gold glints in its closed beak. I lean forward to take a better look.

"What the hell is that?" Deno hits the gas and the crow loses its tenuous hold on the window frame. The bird takes to the air and soars into the trees with a rough *kraa.*

I keep a death grip on the seat, gaze locked on the birds, flying circles around the cars. The sedan pulls into Reece's driveway. Rock music burns through the seams of Trevor Bent's car.

Something's up with those birds. Something not entirely natural. The bunch of them diving at Reece this morning could be explained—the birds might be tame. But the red eyes on that one were too strange to ignore. I'd still like to know what it had in its beak. I didn't imagine it. I'm beginning to think I didn't imagine the man with the changing face from this morning, either, and I don't know what to make of that.

Deno puts the van in park in front of my three-car garage. Lacey gets out to open the sliding side door for me because the handle on the inside is broken.

"Thanks for the ride," I say to Deno.

"Sure thing," he says, shaking his head. "You should try driving your own car to school. This hill you live on kills my gas mileage."

I give Deno a mock salute, and he grins as I climb out of the minivan.

Lacey pauses before getting back inside. She glances at the border of trees between my house and Reece's. The branches are thick with crows. "There's something wrong with those birds," she says in a quiet voice. Her eyes are troubled. Unlike myself, Lacey is a believer in things like omens and signs and superstitions. She likes to think she's tuned in to the vibes of the world, or something like that.

"They're birds," I say.

Her dark eyes narrow. "Well, yeah. I'm just not sure that's *all* they are."

I nod, wishing I could argue with her. "What else do you think they could be?"

"I don't know. I'm just saying it." She tilts her head toward mine. "So. Are you okay with what happened at lunch today?"

"Yeah." I hunch my shoulders against the chill and thoughts of Kiera Shaw. "Nothing some time in the basement with my guitar can't fix."

She hugs me, a little too tight, then pulls back and turns a leery eye to the sky. "It's going to rain."

Not today, it isn't. "I'll take anything but more snow."

Her brow knits. "No, this is different."

Overhead, the sky is blue. One dark cloud tumbles in amongst the white puffy ones. I stifle a shiver and tug my coat tighter. I have no clairvoyance. I'm not tuned in to the vibes of anything, but I can't deny the uneasy feeling uncurling through the air like a dark ribbon.

Also, there are facts. Since the Ortley family murders, the neighborhood has been quiet. Nothing strange has happened until the Fernandez family moved in. Along with vibes and omens, I also don't believe in coincidences.

Upstairs in my room, I toss my backpack on my bed and go to the window. I have a partial view of Reece's house and notice a few lights illuminate windows as a quiet curl of smoke winds from the chimney. Trevor Bent's car has left.

My gaze catches on something small, gleaming in the dirt of the flower box outside my window. *Gold.* I unlock the window and shove it and the sliding screen up enough to reach for the object. Cold air pushes through the narrow space and bites my hand. The begonia stems, which had bloomed there in the summer, look like brown veins trailing over the soil. I reach out and pluck the thing from the dirt. It's a small gold earring, missing its back. The tarnished setting once held a stone but is now empty. I close the window, locking the cold back outside, and peer at the earring in confusion. It's not mine. I'm sure of it.

A low *krahhh* sounds from the deck below. I glance down to see a crow sitting on the railing, looking up at me. It tips its head up and cocks it to the side. It looks *pleased* with itself, if that's possible. Logical answers are usually the correct ones, but here, the logical answer is that someone dropped it there. But...who? The only other person who comes to my room with pierced ears is Lacey, and as far as I recall, she has never even looked out my window, let alone *leaned* out of it.

I swallow hard and glance at the crow. It's starting to make a racket down there. Um, didn't that bird have something shiny in its beak when it came to the van window? The crow flaps its wings a few times but doesn't fly off. One of its wing feathers is pure white. *Red eyes and a white feather.* That's... different. I stare down at the bird, working to make sense of this. I suppose it's possible—*remotely*—that it put the earring in my flower box for me to find.

With a scowl to the crow, I yank my curtains closed and turn away from the window. I move to throw out the earring, but I hear that gentle *krahhh* again and drop the gold stud into a glass dish on my dresser. A shiver wiggles down my spine. It may not be wise to throw away gifts from this bird. It's clearly trying to communicate something.

I collapse on the bed and fling an arm over my eyes. What if that really is an earring of mine I forgot about? I don't remember owning any gold studs. All my jewelry is silver. Also, I only got my ears pierced four years ago, but hell—I don't even *know* anymore. Maybe this is all in my head. I groan into my pillow, because if I'm imagining these things, it's very bad news for me. What if the mental demons that plagued my mother have finally come for me? She didn't survive them. Would I?

4

the music

The music thumps fast and deep and loud. It's an amped-up Zero 7 remix that most people here haven't heard but I'm particularly fond of. Mel, owner of The Strip Mall, gives me a lot of leeway to play what I want. Over the past six months, I've proven that the place won't empty out if the people can't mouth along to the songs. Quite the opposite, actually. Friday night attendance has increased, from what I hear. They keep me on the schedule, so I must be doing something right. A bunch of my classmates come, and the club has become popular with the Somerset College kids who think anything played on the radio is garbage. They think I'm "enlightened," which I think is hilarious. All I do is play music I like.

I hold one half of my headphones to my ear and queue up my next track. The songs transition seamlessly, thanks to a swirly filler beat I put in between songs that shifts and builds to the next. Transitions are when everything could go wrong, and the only part of my set that's *all* me. I move to the pulse of music, filling up those empty, hungry parts of the night, of me.

The energy of the packed dance floor floods my veins, pounds through my bones, but there's a weird agitation to the floor tonight, as if everyone is dancing slightly off beat. The clientele is usually docile, but two guys have already been kicked out—one for threatening the bartender and another for punching a guy who bumped into his girlfriend. A few others got stern warnings. None of this is typical. The Strip Mall's bouncers usually stand around bored out of their minds. Tonight, they're prowling the floor, watching the crowd with sharp eyes.

My gaze flickers over the unsettled floor as I fade in a six-minute house remix I made myself last week. I signal Deno, who works the booth with me, to adjust the pre-amp settings. There's some weird feedback going on.

Aside from Deno and Lacey, no one knows I am Sparo, the Friday night DJ. It blows my mind, honestly. I never let anyone near enough to look at me closely, but just in case, the lighting is set up to make it hard to get a good view at the girl in the booth. Plus, my outfit is pretty intense. Six-inch platform boots make me super tall, and my transformation includes an array of wigs, massive green sunglasses, and about three pounds of makeup. If my dad saw me in full Sparo gear, he'd die. Thankfully, he's given up asking to see my set. "A lot of teenagers," and "very loud music," were both effective in deflecting him. Instead, I make him playlists for his iPod.

Most patrons are looking more at one another's asses than at me, but I thought someone eventually would see through my disguise. I figured Deno would blow my cover or people would figure it out, since we're together so much in and out of school, but no. It helps that Deno is *always* here. The Strip Mall is his second home. He assists three other DJs and fills in whenever the owner has an empty shift. He could have his own set if he didn't prefer working behind the scenes.

Someone appears at the booth for another song request. I glance over and see Kiera Shaw, writing her song on the Post-it note Deno gives anyone with a request. She would lose her mind if she knew Sparo is me—Angie Dovage—the "little freak" she likes to spew verbal bile on. It's been three days since her lunchroom humiliation. I'm over it, but I cannot wait until I don't have to see her face every day.

Kiera hands the yellow Post-it over and tries to peek around him to get a look at me. Deno deftly blocks her view, but I'm not worried. Sparo looks way older than seventeen and nothing like me, anyway. My shoulder-length hair is hidden under a vivid purple wig and huge headphones. Angie doesn't wear lipstick, but Sparo's lips are slicked up Blow-Pop pink. Sparo's clothes are flamboyant, weird, colorful, while Angie wears dark, don't-notice-me clothes. I like to think maybe somewhere in between Sparo and Angie *is* me.

Deno hands me Kiera's request with raised brows. It doesn't matter what she requests or how many Post-its she hands Deno—I'm not playing her requests. I ball it up and flick it to the floor, and Deno firmly waves her off. She makes a pouty face, says something to Deno, and then huffs away. A smile tugs at my lips. It's not nice of me, but I do enjoy denying her. She shouldn't get *everything* she wants.

She returns to her group of friends. A guy comes up behind them with a cup in each hand. He hands one to Kiera, and the smile falls off my face.

It's him. Reece. *Here* with Kiera Shaw. We share a few classes and lunch, but we haven't spoken since his first day. His mom, or someone, drives him to school, I guess, because that champagne Lexus rolled by while I walked to the bus stop every day. It had been a relief and a disappointment to not face him every morning. I wasn't sure if he was giving me space after the lunchroom incident, or if he decided I was too much of a social liability, or if he was just *busy*. Whatever the reason, I must have misread him. Maybe that connection I thought we had was another thing my head invented.

Still. I hadn't thought he'd want to hang out with Kiera after what she said. He'd appeared upset at that. But that's the problem these days: few things are what they appear.

My teeth gnash. I guess Kiera *does* always get what she wants. She sips her drink and starts to dance, like *on* him. He does shift away, but whatever. He's *here* with her. The next song I was planning on was a chill tune, perfect for slower dancing, but instead, I queue up something angry and fast. Probably not going to ease the edgy vibe in here, but I won't make it easy for Kiera.

Deno notices the change in the playlist and gives me a puzzled look.

I shake my head, but Deno can see my scowling brow above my glasses. His gaze traces the general path mine had just been on, and his brows go up. *Kiera. Her friends. Reece. Obviously, Reece.* Deno is thick sometimes, easily distracted, but can tune in at the most inopportune times. He leans in close. "You can't play techno for the next hour and a half just to keep those two from dancing."

My face burns. I should have hidden my reaction better. I shouldn't have reacted at all. Denial isn't an option with Deno. "Watch me," I say.

But instead of frowning, he lets out a chuckle. "My-oh-my. I'd say it's confirmed that our little Angie has finally found a boy she likes. A *sporty* boy." He sighs. "I just lost a bet, you know."

It's on the tip of my tongue to ask who he made a bet with, but it's undoubtedly Lacey. I start up the next track, a sexy downtempo tune that's impossible to *not* slow dance to. "Fine. Now we can stand here and watch them make out. Happy?"

He looks out on the crowd again. The smile on his face twists with mischievous delight. "Not about losing a twenty-dollar bet, but cheer up, kid. Your boy's not making out with anyone. He's headed straight for you."

I wobble on my platform shoes. "What?"

Deno stretches. His grin goes Cheshire wide. "I need to take a piss. Be back in five. Or ten."

"No! Don't you dare—" I grab for his arm, but he skips out of my grasp.

"Thank me later," he tosses back, just before disappearing.

Reece doesn't come around the side like he's supposed to and, with Deno gone, there's no point. He's so tall, he doesn't have a problem leaning over the speakers and mixer to get my attention.

"Hey," he says—shouts.

I hold up a finger, finish setting up a transition sequence that totally could have waited, before tilting my head at him. Even with my big, green glasses, he's got a pretty good view of me, which makes me nervous. I *will* kill Deno when he returns.

Reece's eyes are amused, like he knows I'm stalling. "I want to make a request."

Without speaking, I hand him the Post-it pad and a pen. His fingers brush mine, and I swear he does it on purpose. He wouldn't be the first guy here to do it, but he's the first to send tingles marching up my arm.

Reece scribbles something on the pad and hands it back to me. I stare at him, jaw slowly hinging open. In the six months I've been a DJ here, no one has requested this song. Given what I experienced with him at the bus stop a few days ago, his request is more than a little unsettling. The song on the Post-it, sprawled in slanted Sharpie, is *Black Wing*.

"You want me to play *this*?" I look at him, unable to hide my surprise.

A smile plays at his lips. "Do you know it? It's a little obscure. The guys I came here with said you had an extensive library, so..." He gives a slight, self-conscious shrug.

The guys I came here with. So he didn't come with Kiera. My heart does an uncomfortable flip in my chest. I have this song. I *love* this song. I've remixed it twice myself. It *is* obscure, and one of my favorites. But still...

"Black Wing."

I really hope this song isn't some sort of message. I swallow thickly. "Do you want the original or one of the remixes?"

"Which remixes do you have?" He grins. "Never mind. You choose."

I nod and turn away from him. This is usually when the civilians—even the odd ones—move along, go back to the dance floor, but Reece leans closer and cocks his head at me. He smells like Pepsi and fresh air and all I want to do is lean in and breathe deep. "Hey, you look kind of familiar," he says. "Do I know you?"

What? We're done here. If he sees through my disguise... I'm not ready for that. I wave him off, trying to keep my voice from revealing my jumpy nerves. "Go. Play with the other kids."

He backs up, but his black eyes continue to study me like I'm a weird vanity license plate he's trying to decode. I swing back to my laptop with gritted teeth.

Sloppy. I almost missed the end of the song. Almost had dead air. My fingers fly over the mixer, fading in a makeshift beat to bridge to the next song.

Deno returns, making a show of adjusting his pants. He grins, eyebrows raised and palms out as if to say *Where's my thank-you?*

"Yeah. That was great," I snap at him. "Very professional."

"Admit it. You're secretly thrilled I did that."

Maybe I am. I'm also relieved that Deno isn't being weird

about it. It's pretty obvious now that I *am* interested in Reece. Seriously, I couldn't have bungled that more. "Don't *ever* do that again. Or you're fired."

"You can't fire me."

Damn it, he's right. He's the one who talked the owner into giving me a shot here. If anything, he could probably fire *me*.

"I still think he's weird," he says.

He's not *wrong*.

"Hey, you must have done something right. He's not dancing with Kiera."

I don't look up. I can't. *Won't*. "What's he doing?"

Deno's brows draw together in confusion. "Why don't you just look?"

He's not being a smart-ass this time, so I do. Reece is no longer with Kiera, and it's disturbing how happy I am about it. He's on the other side of the room, talking with a couple of seniors on the hockey team. Kiera glances at him once, twice, then flips her hair and doesn't look at him again. She's never worked for a boy's attention. Eventually, he'll come back to her. They always do.

But Reece Fernandez doesn't appear interested in getting Kiera's attention. He mimics the other boys' loose postures, leaning back against the bar. One of them raises a cup and laughs at something Reece says.

My mouth is dry and my hands shake a little, but I queue up Reece's song. It's something I never do—play a request right after receiving it—but here I am, sending a message to *him*.

Reece tips back his Pepsi like it's a beer and splays his fingers over the rim of his cup. I puzzle over some bizarre hand gestures between him and the guys he's talking with until I deduce the topic is sports—hockey, naturally.

His song starts. Reece's head whips up. He looks at me from across the room, and I feel it like a touch. His teeth flash white in a smile that sends a pleasant tingle straight down to my toes. It's all I wanted, his eyes on me. His smile, for me.

In that moment, there's nothing else. Nothing but flashing black eyes and a slow smile and the hectic thud of my pounding heart.

But prowling in the back of my mind is another scene.

Reece surrounded by inky feathers and curved talons. Long, sleek beaks caressing his cheeks, playing with his hair, plucking gently at his coat.

"Black Wing."

He smiles then, too.

5

the watcher

The small employee parking lot behind The Strip Mall can be creepy. Anyone could be lurking in the thick trees behind it, and although no one ever has been, my paranoia is always wondering if someone *is*. The peeling white and red paint and the big loading doors where trucks once backed up to are the only reminders this really was once a strip mall. What had been a moldering eyesore is now a lucrative exercise in building revitalization. If I remember what Deno told me, the main dance floor was an office supply store. The stage was the custom printing lab.

Deno and I break down our equipment in companionable silence. I'm not mad at him anymore. In fact, I would consider thanking him if he wasn't so likely to gloat. On the floor, the under-agers filter out and the over-twenty-one crowd gets fresh drinks. I run some ambient music through the house speakers while Anton, the DJ for the eleven p.m. to two a.m. slot, sets up. Deno hauls the equipment to his van while I wrap up cables and tuck little, expensive bits of equipment into their cases.

"All packed up." Deno meets me by the door to the parking lot. "I'm gonna collect our money." He tosses me the keys.

This is what we've done all winter: Deno packs the van and I warm it up while he gets our pay. Since he's the only one who knows this labyrinth of a building well enough to actually *find* the owner in her back office.

Maybe it's because of the vibe tonight, the tense bouncers, or Reece, but this night feels compressed, thick with something other than air. I'd rather wait inside. The words are there, coiled on my tongue, but I swallow them back. Deno doesn't seem to think anything is off. Maybe I'm overreacting. "Okay," I say. "See you in a few."

I step through the metal door and into the parking lot. Cold claws through my coat like icy talons. No surprise there. It's eleven thirty at night in February. The dumpster smells like vomit. The lighting is terrible—just one yellowish lamp and far too many shadows. A dark shape shifts on the dumpster's lip, and I suck in a breath and tense up. A puffed-up crow stares back at me, eyes like shiny red beads. It tosses its beak in the air, like a greeting, and stretches its wings. One long white feather gleams among the inky plumage. I'd bet anything it's the same one that left me the earring.

Crows are everywhere these days—lined up on telephone wires, sitting on the sign at school. This one, with the white feather, seems way too attached to me. I don't *like* this—this crow hanging around all the time. This feeling of being watched. I shiver, but not from the cold. My rubbery fingers fumble through Deno's key ring.

It's a bird, Angie. I purposefully ignore it. The van's only ten feet away. I head for it, but my wildly impractical shoes hit an icy patch and I go down hard, glasses flying. My hip and shoulder take the brunt of it. Nothing's broken. That's all I should be worried about, but I'm suddenly and acutely aware that I'm in a vulnerable position and I'm alone. Instincts turn my senses sharp and blunt at the same time. I scramble to my knees and grope for the van's bumper. Damn these platform shoes. They're like stilts, and they render me as agile as a newborn giraffe.

The crow opens its shiny beak and shrieks as a strong hand closes on my upper arm. Adrenaline numbs the pain from my fall. Blood rushes to my head. I'm *not* alone out here.

I turn to see a guy in a wool hat and a puffy jacket. He looms above me, silhouetted by that one crappy light, but I can see well enough. It's *him.* The guy Reece talked to at the bus stop three days ago. He's wearing the same clothes, giving off the same pungent smell of honey, but his face is different. Again.

My bones turn to rubber. Fear punches my lungs inside out, robbing my ability to scream. "You," I say on a gasp.

The crow begins to caw. Its noise is grating, repetitive, scratching the inside of my skull.

He pulls me upright with such speed and force, pain shoots through my shoulder. For a slender man, his strength is immense. He turns, setting his face in the light, and my whimper turns into a gurgle of fear.

Like a mask that can't decide what it should look like, the man's face is morphing, constantly. *Thin nose, broad chin, narrow face, brown eyes, broad nose, pointy chin, wide face, green eyes…* The shifts are subtle and blurry. Sometimes the features are female. Mostly, they're male.

The slightest of smiles curves his mouth as he holds me still and waits as I watch the horrors of his face unfold. He wants me to see this. Wants me to know I'm not being held by a human being. To know I could die by his hand at any moment.

Reece knows this thing. He knows, he knows, he knows. And in this moment, I fear him as much as the creature holding me, because surely Reece knows what this man-thing is and what it can do. Knows there's no fighting free of it. Anger breaks through my paralyzing fear just long enough for air to charge into my lungs. I let out a pealing scream that would impress Alfred Hitchcock.

Changeable brows draw together. "No one's listening, my dear." His voice is low and garbled, as if run through distortion software.

My heart twists with the truth of his words. Anton's set is in full swing, and angry techno pounds through the concrete walls. Rivulets of cold sweat slide down my back. I can't stop shuddering.

Where is Deno? If this guy wasn't impossibly strong, I'd be willing my friend to come bursting through the door and help me out. Aside from the hair, there's nothing delicate about Deno. He's big, tough. He was a force to be reckoned with in the few schoolyard scuffles I've seen him in, but this man holding me is clearly not a man at all. I don't want Deno near this creature.

"Wh-what are you?" I ask. Not that it matters.

The grip on my arm loosens. He glances at the shrieking bird, then angles his head toward me in a way that suggests I should know its significance. Of course, I don't.

"*He* watches you." My question is ignored. His voice sounds as terrifying and wrong as the rest of him.

"W-who?" *Who!*

The face, or faces—whatever the hell it is—smiles. "*He:* scavenger, cleaner of bones, a black bird of the gallows." He leans his terrible face close. *Way* too close. "He watches you. Why?"

My heart smashes against my ribs. His nightmare face is inches from mine, but no breath comes from that changing mouth. No puff of white in the cold darkness. Only the disorienting scent of honey and a skin-crawling drone that sounds an awful lot like bees. *A lot* of bees.

"I don't know w-what you're talking about." Tears ice my cheeks. I'd like to wring that bird's neck. It's screaming like *it's* the one about to die. Between the crow and this awful buzzing sound, I'm going to lose my mind. "Please, just…"

I fall silent as a new mouth and nose appear on the creature's face. They're female, and familiar in a way that makes my ribs contract around my heart. Full pink lips and a delicate nose with a little mole under the right nostril. The eyes are someone else's but…

I know that mouth. I know that mole.

I saw it every day for the first twelve years of my life.

"*Mom,*" I rasp. Pain, fresh and devastating, unravels throughout my body. This is madness—fear driving me to hysteria, or some perfectly logical nonsense—but no. Those are her features. I know them as well as my own.

Without realizing what I'm doing, I reach for her mouth on this creature's face. He rears back, and the instant before my fingers brush skin, my mother's features fade and morph into a stranger's. The mole disappears. I'm staring up at this creature who, frankly, looks as confused as I feel.

The face-shifter parts his lips and something crawls out. It's a bee. From his *mouth*. More and more come. Dozens. Hundreds. They engulf the lower half of his face in a writhing, buzzing mask. He doesn't blink. I let out another scream, but not because I expect help. This scream is a reflex, an expulsion of primal fear, as impossible to stifle as breathing.

Footfalls slap on the chunked-up pavement, fast and sure, approaching from the long rear wall of The Strip Mall. The man-thing's head turns. His grip on my arms goes tight. Bees slither back into his mouth.

"Hey!" a male voice shouts. "What the hell are you doing?" It's not Deno. It's not a bouncer. But I know this voice.

The face-shifter's hands fall away so fast, I stumble backward onto the pavement.

The crow goes silent.

I look up at my rescuer and juggle an ugly mix of unease and relief. There's the chestnut hair, the high, chiseled cheekbones.

Reece. Of course it's him. He came all the way around from the front of the building—no small feat for The Strip Mall. *But how did he know?* Anton's earsplitting volume ensured no one heard me scream.

Reece stops a few feet away, his body a tense line. "Get away from her." His voice is firm, lacking fear. Lacking negotiation. *I knew it*—he knows this creature. I dread to think what that makes *him*. I shrink away from both of them.

My attacker backs up a step, but he sneers at Reece. "I have as much right to be here as you."

Reece bares his teeth. "I'm here because I have to be. You're here because you choose to be."

"*None of us* are here because we choose to be," the man snarls back, spitting bees into the air. "This town is marked, making *her* marked. Both are fair game."

"Are you unhinged?" Reece asks him. "That's not how it works."

"How much time is left?" it asks.

Reece looks far older than an eighteen-year-old boy should look, and not at all civilized. "I don't know."

How much time for what? This is like listening in on one side of a phone conversation.

The face-shifter laughs, a terrible, warbled sound. His eyes tilt toward me, then back to Reece. "You know you are not permitted to interfere. Look what happened to the last one who tried." The creature chuckles, a leisurely sound. "You cannot save her, *harbinger*."

Color drains from Reece's face. His nostrils flare as his

black eyes bore holes through the creature he's squared off against. "Just stay away from her," he says through clenched teeth.

The face-shifter seems unconcerned with the malice being leveled at him. He gives me a mock bow, complete with a grotesque smile, then slinks into the dark trees behind the dumpster. Bees follow him in a lazy, disorganized cloud.

Reece releases a breath. His face clears of anger, but his features are still pinched. The crow flaps its wings, but remains silent, watchful. It starts preening its feathers.

Reece rubs his eyes, a weary gesture, or maybe a resigned one, and turns to me. "Are you okay?" He squats down, places a light hand on my shoulder. "Were you hurt?"

I pull my shoulder away from his touch. "I'm fine."

Reece withdraws his hand, tucks it against his ribs. "Can you stand?"

I feel liquefied and shaky. Drained of everything that made me solid. I use the van's bumper to push myself to standing. Still, my shaky knees buckle the instant I get upright.

He slips his hands under my armpits and catches me before I crumple to the pavement. "I'm sorry," he says gruffly. "I don't want you to fall."

One hand slides to my waist—no, *Sparo's* waist. We stand there, his hand a warm pressure on my waist, steady and chaotic at the same time. I don't like him touching me, but I like the way his touch makes me feel—like listening to good music. Our mouths are close.

"You shouldn't be out here alone," he says. "It's dangerous."

"What was that thing?" I ask. "Don't say you don't know."

"Okay, I won't say it." His hand falls away, and I sag against the van. "What did he want from you? Drugs?"

Is *he* on drugs? He's so obviously evading, it's insulting. If he said he couldn't talk about it, for whatever mystical, made-up reason, I might have respected that. For a while. *Maybe*. But drugs?

"No! You...that-that *thing*—" I stick my finger right at his chest, making contact with firm muscle. "What is he? He's not human." My voice heats, along with the rest of me as I replay my conversation—if you want to call it that—with the creature. Even my own freshly made memory looks false. My mind stretches for an explanation, aches when a rational one doesn't surface. "And the bees... My God, those *bees*." I press my hand to my mouth to stifle a sob. I *hadn't* imagined this. It was as real as the bruises I'd wake up with and the ache in my shoulder where it was wrenched. That was... I can't even comprehend what I just experienced. I want to go home *so* badly.

Reece bends down. So calm. He picks up Deno's keys and my green sunglasses. I tense up with a new sort of panic. Oh crap, I'm exposed. Even with the wig and the makeup and the extra six inches in height, he could recognize me now. I hold my breath as he studies the keys, then hands them back to me without a flicker of recognition. I nearly gasp in relief.

"I'm glad you weren't hurt." His eyes are tight, restless, and they don't meet my gaze. His words are final.

"Hey! What was that thing?" I rasp, but he's already heading back the way he came.

"Be careful, Sparo," he tosses over his shoulder. "Stay away from the bees."

6

the dark of the mine

Saturday morning. I climb out of bed slowly, feeling like gravity has more pull than usual. A headache gnaws at my temples, and my shoulder seizes when I sit up. I gasp from both the wrench of pain and the memories of the previous night. I could write them off as dreams, maybe, if not for the physical proof that it happened. A glance at my upper arm reveals bruises made by the grip of a strong hand. I look away with a shudder and pull on leggings and the old, frayed U2 sweatshirt that I'd rescued from my dad's Salvation Army box.

I open the drapes, letting watery morning light pour in my room. There, on my windowsill, is a coin. It's just a quarter, but its presence makes me hug myself with apprehension. My gaze sweeps the deck below, the trees beyond. Crows are tucked in the branches. None on the deck. None on the railing looking up at me with red, far-too intelligent eyes. I crack open the window and take the quarter. It goes in the glass dish with the earring.

My hands move to the jewelry case beside it. I open it and remove a white envelope, which I stuff in the large pocket of my sweatshirt. It contains photos of my mother. The only ones I have.

Downstairs, my dad sits at the kitchen table in his fancy bathrobe (and matching slippers) and eating a bowl of cereal. He glances up from the game he's playing on his iPad. "Morning. How was the show last night?"

"Strange."

"Strange good or strange bad?"

Strange very bad. But I can't say that unless I want to tell him what happened or make up a lie. Neither is a wise option. "Just strange. I'm going for a walk." Roger prances around me, all simple hope and longing.

Dad just nods, watching me in a thoughtful way. He can tell I'm upset about something.

"Put on a hat," is all he says, and because I'm in such a precarious place with my emotions, and because I'm grateful he didn't pry, I kiss his cheek and tell him I love him. He looks surprised—maybe a little alarmed—but I smile and ask him to not use up all the almond milk, that I want cereal when I get back. I clip Roger's retractable leash to his collar, and he surges toward the back door. The envelope rustles noisily in my pocket. Dad doesn't ask me about it. I grab a wool hat from the basket on the counter and pull it on my head.

"Be safe," he says.

"I will."

One of the selling points of this development—according to the brochure—is the hiking trails behind the houses that weave around Mt. Franklin and down the side of it into land bordering the shuttered coal mining operations. The mines are long dead, but some of the roads still exist and are kept as trails. They're rarely used. I can count on one hand how many times I encountered another hiker back here. Roger angles an eye at me. He knows where we're going. We turn up our street and head for the dead end where the forest begins.

The trees are thick, although the path is wide from decades of trucks coming and going. My breath comes hard as we traverse up, then down, then sideways along the slope. Finally, we arrive at a chain link fence, overgrown with vines and rusting at the joints. I curl back a loose section, and Roger and I duck through.

I found this place in the first year I moved here. My dad and I utilized the hiking trails as "bonding exercises," as prescribed by my therapist. I spied this side path during one of our walks and followed it once when out on my own. I've kept coming back ever since. The entrance to the Burnham mine is a high, wide concrete dome. A wooden-slat wall was built to close it off, with a door, sort of. The whole thing is fairly rotten, but you'd know that only if you went up and touched it. The decaying padlock is just for show. You can open the gate and prop it open with a rock. That's what I always do. It's what I do now.

Temperate, musty, moist air wafts from the entrance. The air is always the same, no matter the season. It warms in the winter and cools in the summer. It's a constant thing, unchanged by seasons or time or weather.

I sit just inside the mine entrance, on a natural ledge of rock, back and feet braced on either side of the wooden frame. Sunlight slants an angle across my belly. To my right, there is only blackness as the mineshaft twists deep into the rock below. The tunnel holds no allure for me. Fear of collapse, of getting lost, of poisonous gases, keeps me in the pool of sunlight that reaches a few feet inside the mine.

I remove my envelope of photos and open the flap gingerly, as if the pictures may bite me. It's not comfortable to look at these. In a few of them, she's sober. In most, she's not. The one on top of the stack is of the *nots*. Her half-lidded eyes gaze blankly at the camera as she flashes the peace sign and a vacant smile with me perched next to her, beaming a wide grin. I might've been four. Those were the days when I was too young to understand my mother's illness.

But I'm not looking at the photos to reminisce. I'm looking to examine, and that purpose gives me strength. I angle the photo into the sun and focus in on my mother's mouth. She's smiling, and kind of far away, so I can't accurately compare this image of her mouth to the one I saw on the creature from the parking lot. I flip through them quickly, scanning for a close-up, unsmiling image of my mother. I find it in an unremarkable candid shot of her sleeping. I lean close, half hoping, half dreading that her features match the ones I saw on Friday night. There's her mole. *Her nose, her lips, her mouth.* It's all there. Her features are exactly as they were on the creepy bee-guy's face.

I rub my eyes, trying desperately to make sense of the events that transpired at The Strip Mall the previous night and the gifts in my window box. Either they happened as I recall them, or I am losing my mind. I prefer option number one, despite knowing that if the face-changing man is real—if I am really getting gifts from red-eyed crows—it means I am dealing with things I can't comprehend. Things likely dangerous.

The scratch of shoes on gravel snaps my attention. A figure steps through the chain link fence. Roger is on his feet in an instant, sniffing the air.

Reece.

I fumble the photographs, hastily gather up a few that drop, then tuck everything in my pocket. He doesn't see me yet. He's maneuvering through the brush, dealing with the fence's sharp edges. Plus, he has headphones on. His phone is tucked in his coat pocket. I have a bad moment wondering what to do. He'd be easily confronted here. I could find a stick or something and—*look asshole, you will tell me what that thing was last night, or I'll—*

—give away my Sparo identity; that's what would happen and it's not an option. I have so many questions. I'm afraid that the guy with the shifting face will return. I'm afraid of the crows. Of the bees. Of the dread growing in my belly. Of liking this boy.

Confronting or threatening Reece won't get me what I want. Befriending him may, but I don't know if I can pull that off. It's impossible to be friends with someone who has answers you desperately want. I could try to get out of here before he sees me.

Roger has other thoughts. He strains at the leash, tail wagging furiously. He lets out a friendly yap. Reece looks up, sees us, and his eyes widen. He tugs off the headphones.

"What are you doing here?" he asks, not terribly friendly.

"I could ask you that." Unlike my encounter with Kiera Shaw last week, I don't feel at risk of crumbling. Maybe because I don't believe he's cruel. "This is my spot."

He comes forward, stops right in front of me. "Is not."

I point at the thick beam just above where my feet are braced. "My name's on it."

He leans down and squints at the letters I carved there with a sharp rock a few years ago. "So it is." But he makes no move to leave. Instead, he braces one foot on the low, flat stone next to my hip. "May I join you?"

"I'd rather not, if you don't mind." Here I am, trying to be polite. I pick a stone out of the rocky ground, annoyed with how unsettled he makes me feel. There's so much swirling through my head. The horror of last night still sits fresh and vivid in the forefront. This place has always been somewhere I've been able to think clearly, and now it will be imprinted with a memory of *him*.

"Why?" he asks. "Of all the places to go, an abandoned

mine is kind of creepy."

I gaze up at him, full of skepticism. "You don't get to lecture me about creepy"—I have to be very careful what I say—"when you're the one who snuggles with crows."

His eyes turn amused. "They're highly misunderstood animals."

"Sorry, not buying it." I pick up a sliver of shale and flip it between my fingers like a coin. "So, how did you find this place?"

"I followed the trail," he replies.

"This mine isn't on the main trail."

"Then I followed a trail of death and destruction."

"I'm being serious."

"So am I," he insists. "I like to do research when we move someplace new. I read that about sixty years ago parts of this mine collapsed, killing some miners, trapping a bunch more."

"That's true," I say. "What are you, some kind of history buff?" It wouldn't surprise me. He appears quite interested in Mrs. Bryan's U.S. History class.

"Yeah." He takes a headlamp on a strap from his pocket. "See? Nothing diabolical. I like local lore stories. Just came to check this one out, being it was so close to home and all. Want to go inside with me?"

I peer into the tunnel. Although I know the miners died deep, deep inside, the tunnels are a tomb. "No. Thank you."

"You're terribly sensible." Reece drops into a crouch and scratches Roger behind the ears. The dog melts into his touch with a pleased grunt. "Is it true this dog belonged to the homeowners before us?"

"Yeah," I say, resisting the urge to tug Roger back. "Who told you that?"

"Do you always have so many questions?"

"For you? Yes. Do you ever answer them?"

"Not without motivation." He raises one brow in what could

be a challenge, or a joke. I can't tell which.

Maybe I should have gone after him with a stick. "We took Roger after the Ortleys…passed. We didn't want him going to the shelter."

"He's a lucky boy, then," Reece murmurs, delving his fingers into the thick rolls at the dog's neck. His eyes go soft and heavy in a close mirror of Roger's blissful expression. The dog leans in to Reece's scratching fingers, lifts a hind leg, and scratches the air. "He's not sad about them anymore, by the way."

"Who?"

"His dead family. He's over it."

I blink slowly. "Now you're a history buff *and* an animal psychic?"

"*Tsk, tsk.* No, Angie." He raises one eyebrow. "He's just clearly happy. That's all I'm saying."

That is *definitely* not all he's saying. "So are you going to explain the crows?"

"There's nothing to explain." He squints into the woods. "I told you—the nature shows say not to display fear to the wildlife."

"Oh, you are so full of—"

"We aren't going to be here too long," he blurts. "My mom is a consulting doctor at the hospital. A month, maybe a little more, and we'll be gone." He runs a hand through his hair, knuckles tense.

"Why are you telling me this?" My mouth goes dry. *Leaving?*

He angles into the sun, throwing the shadows under his cheeks into relief. "Just thought I should."

The headache I woke up with had subsided, but it rattles back to life. It's as though we're having a conversation about something that's really about something else, but I'm too dense to grasp the subtext.

Suddenly, I can't stay here another minute. If I do, I'm

going to blow my cover, tell him it was me in the parking lot last night—if he hasn't figured it out already—and bombard him with every question backed up in my mouth. I get to my feet, giving Roger a tug. The dog reluctantly moves to my side. Face-to-face, Reece's eyes are as soft and as sad as they always are when it's just him and me. He sighs. "I didn't mean to chase you off," he says. "I'll leave."

I shake my head. "It's okay. I need to get back. Just tell me one thing, if you can."

His gaze moves over my face. He steps closer. I can smell him—fresh pine and clean air. He swallows, pushes his hands deep into his pockets. He's hard to look at right now, with the light turning his hair to gold and those smoldering eyes gazing into mine. It's like looking into the sun.

"Okay. One thing." His soft voice clashes with the intensity of his gaze. "You're adorable when you're trying to be mad at me. You needn't work so hard at it, though. We aren't meant to be adversaries."

"I, um…" My thoughts disband, leaving nothing for communication purposes. I'm *adorable*? Adorable has many definitions. I think Roger is adorable, for example. "That… wasn't what I was going to ask you."

He inclines his head. "Okay, then. Ask."

But that "adorable" echoes through me, clinking around like a penny down a well. "What are we meant to be, then?"

His lips curl up at the corners. "That wasn't your question, either."

I swallow with effort. If Lacey were here, she'd be subtly pinching my arm right now. *Get a grip, Angie!* "Am I in some kind of danger?"

Reece's mouth tightens. He sighs and turns toward the gaping blackness of the mineshaft. "Of course not. Someone's always watching."

7

you already know the answer...

Thank God for Google.

Seriously.

My father says that all the time, and I roll my eyes because he's usually looking up gross health things, like cancer moles or how headaches could indicate a brain tumor. But here I am, hunched at my laptop, engaged in the world's most unproductive activity: an internet search without knowing quite what you're looking for. It's eleven thirty on Sunday night and instead of studying for my test on the War of 1812 tomorrow, I'm looking up every term I can remember from Friday night. *Scavenger. Black bird of the gallows. Cleaner of bones. Harbinger.* It's difficult to describe a man with a transforming face into a search engine. The results have varied from strange to deeply disturbing. It's amazing how creative the porn industry is.

The only phrase that got a meaningful result was *harbinger*. The old-fashioned definition is *someone who is sent ahead to secure lodging*, but the modern meaning sends a shiver over my skin: *one who comes ahead of a major change. One who foreshadows an event yet to come. Usually, a bad one.*

There are other sites—ones run by people who are into conspiracies, the paranormal and whatnot, but I stumble across one with an author who documents facts and writes with clarity. Despite the dubious online moniker of *ShadowMan43,* his entry on harbingers pulls me closest to the screen.

Ravens and crows have long been called harbingers of death by many cultures.

These opportunistic birds rarely deserve the distinction, but some early cultures tell tales of roving murders of crows who feasted on more than just the bodies of the dead. These creatures are said to perform some sort of grim reaper role, where they took human form and sucked the souls from the dying.

Good grief. Is *this* what I'm dealing with? Grim reapers lurking around Cadence? It simply couldn't be. And didn't explain the existence of creepy guy with the bees. The article continues:

It's important to remember that early cultures did not always bury the dead, especially in times of war and widespread sickness, so it was not uncommon to see crows feasting on human corpses. Mainstream historians will say the shadowy figures seen lurking around the dead were thieves, but many theories of impending evil persist. The Greeks, especially, believed crows were a bad omen, often forecasting death.

I scroll down, past a poorly scanned painting of St. Benedict with a crow at his feet, and continue reading.

Crows' preference for carrion and perching in graveyards and near gallows has wrongly associated them with evil, but many ancient peoples saw the crow as a divine creature, existing in two planes of existence—the Earthly plane and the magical one.

The face-shifting man mentioned gallows and called Reece

a *harbinger*. Not a normal thing to call a teenage boy. Unless the teenage boy is something other than he appears. I'm not comfortable with the idea that magic is involved. It brings to mind rabbits in hats and Halloween, neither of which have ever interested me.

My fingers curl tight, digging shallow half-moons into my palms. Reece knows what this thing is. It drives me up a wall that *he knows*.

The bee guy said the town was marked, whatever that meant. It doesn't mean anything *good*, that's for sure, considering the rest of the conversation. It sounded like something bad was going to happen in our town. If Reece knows what that is, I need to find out, too, for the sake of my dad, my friends—heck, everyone who lives here. But clearly, Reece isn't going to give up his secrets easily. He can try to distract me with the—admittedly, interesting—attraction that sometimes sparks between us, but his chilling words linger.

Fear has become a baseline emotion, sitting low in my gut, but I don't know what, exactly, I should be afraid of. I don't feel safe. Not at school, not in my own home, with its insane home security system. I need to know if that strange bee-man is going to come for me again. I need to know why my mother's features were on his face.

8

the bus stop

It's a little jarring to see Reece at the bus stop Monday morning. He looks so normal standing there, leafing through his U.S. history book like he's perusing a catalog. He's wearing jeans under his wool coat. The morning sun glints off hair that appears still damp from a shower. He hasn't been here since his first day, last Tuesday, but I'm surprised yet pleased to see him. Today begins my official surveillance of this boy. Considering the encounters I've had with him, it won't be long before something bizarre or scary happens. I'm prepared for either.

The lone crow with that one white feather perches on the lamppost across the street. It's beginning to feel normal, seeing it around all the time. However, if I'm dealing with harbingers of death, like I read about last night, it's not a good sign that I'm being followed by one. The crow lets out a sharp *caw*. I startle at the sound, but Reece doesn't so much as twitch. My palms go cold and damp. I don't even know how to stalk anyone.

He finally looks up when I'm standing right in front of

him. His face is pinched, his skin pale. Shadows sling under his eyes, as if he didn't sleep well. That's only fair. Thoughts of him ruined *my* sleep all weekend. His brows dip low, just shy of a frown. "Hey, Angie."

"Hello, Reece." I'm determined to keep this casual, light, despite the beady-eyed crow watching me. Despite the nerves crawling up my throat. "Cramming for the history test today? It'll probably be multiple choice. Mrs. Bryan usually alternates essay and multiple choice, and the last test was essay, so…" I shut my mouth. *Shut it, Angie.*

He looks up again with narrowed eyes. "I'm prepared. Are you?"

No, not at all. "Yes."

"Good." A tight smile pulls at his mouth. "It's good to be prepared. Quite an interesting mine you have back there. I went exploring a bit after you left. Brought you something." He digs something out of his pocket and holds up a deep purple amethyst, smoothly faceted and wide as a quarter. Light fractures through the translucent stone as he turns it in the sunlight.

"It's beautiful," I say, genuinely charmed by the thing. "You found that in the mine?"

"Yeah." He takes my hand and places it in my palm with a wink. "You like purple, don't you?"

My fingers close around the crystal. I've been receiving a lot of interesting "gifts" lately. I'm not sure I want them. I drop it in my pocket. It's going straight to my glass bowl with the other goodies I've been given. "It's lovely. Thank you."

I don't think I'm imagining the knowledge curling in the set of his lips, the glint in his eyes. *Do I like purple?* This is ridiculous. He knows exactly who I am. He's deduced I'm the purple-haired DJ he saved from the man with the shifting face. He saw me close up, without my glasses. He called me Sparo, not Angie, but that just means we're playing an elaborate game of psychological chicken, and he's waiting for me to crack. This gift—like everything else about this boy—holds double meaning.

"So." I take a deep breath, frantically groping for the rules of this game. This is beyond my skill set. "What did you think of The Strip Mall?"

"You were there?"

I roll my shoulders. *Keep it casual.* "Everyone goes there."

"If *you* had been there, I would have noticed."

What does that mean? That I stick out or that he finds me noticeable?

Maybe he really *didn't* recognize me. It's possible, I guess; maybe he has bad eyesight. "My friend Deno works there. You may have seen him. He was assisting the DJ. I stopped in to say hi." My words crackle like plastic to my ears. I can only imagine how fake they sound to him.

"Oh yeah. Deno." He shrugs. "The show was okay, I guess."

"*Okay?*" My pride thins like an overinflated balloon. "People say Sparo is the best DJ around."

"She was *okay*." He enunciates into his history book. "But compared to some other clubs I've gone to, her set was missing something."

My throat closes up tight—a clear signal to stop right there. *But, no*. "Missing what?"

"I don't know. Originality? Authenticity? It doesn't take a genius to spit out other people's music. When I go to a show, I like to hear something new, be surprised. That didn't happen." He snaps the book shut and glances over my shoulder. "The bus."

I turn to see Mrs. Pierce's yellow monster turn the corner and begin lumbering up the hill.

Warning bells clang in my head, but my mouth still opens.

Words come out. "You know, I *know* Sparo, and I can tell you she works hard on her sets." My voice is full of sharp, personal affront. The opposite of casual. The opposite of normal. "Her original music is good, too. She's just waiting for a better venue to debut it."

"Oh, you know her, do you?" He laughs and shakes his head. "Look, your friend's problem isn't the venue." Reece's lips tilt into a crooked grin. "Or her talent, I'm sure. And she's hot up there on stage—*seriously*. The stuff she played was just… limited, you know? She plays it safe."

The crow caws again. It sounds annoyingly like laughter. But honestly, I ceased coherent thought after—*She's hot.*

Okay. He actually said that. And "hot" has a very clear meaning in that context, unlike the "adorable" I got on Saturday morning. My mouth feels stuffed full of cotton. My heart pounds like a kick drum. I grasp the handrail and get on the bus.

What do I do next? Oh yeah, find a seat.

I must look off, because Mrs. Pierce's eyes narrow on me. She flicks a suspicious look at Reece's retreating back and leans toward me. "That boy bothering you, honey?"

I blink at her, surprised and—*oh hell*, embarrassed. "Uh, no."

She raises a brow and shuts the door behind me. "Must've been running, then. You're mighty flushed."

From the corner of my eye, I see Reece swing into a seat. He looks up at me. His mouth isn't smiling, but his eyes are.

Fantastic. If my face was red before, it's in flames now. I duck my head and practically dive for the first empty seat. It's a three-seater, diagonally in front of his.

Reece Fernandez thinks I'm hot. I heard him say it.

Just then, the boy in question leans forward and taps my seat. "Hey. Angie."

My stomach flips over. What now? "Yeah?"

"Tell your friend Sparo to watch it outside that club at night. I saw a sketchy-looking dude hanging around."

Is he serious? I open my mouth, but some last remaining shred of sense closes it. "Sure."

He gives me a wide grin. "Thanks. Hey, maybe one of these days, you can introduce me. She kind of blew me off on Friday."

And...that's all I can take. I turn away and clamp my hand over my mouth before hysterical laughter bursts from me like a geyser. Reece retreats to the safety of his own seat with raised eyebrows.

Despite my aborted laughter, *nothing* about this is funny. There's an inherent problem here. Unless he's pretending to not know I'm Sparo—very, *very* possible—Reece would like me to set up an introduction for him with *myself*.

Maybe he really *does* have bad eyesight. He does squint a lot. Or he's not as smart as I thought.

Either way, I had not anticipated this little wrinkle.

And it's not even the worst part.

I don't even know for certain if the boy I'm trying to stalk is a human being.

9

the visitation experiment

Surely this isn't healthy behavior. I am at my kitchen table, partly doing homework, mostly peering out the window at the house next door. Reece and I got home about fifteen minutes ago, and the only thing he's done is collect the mail and go inside. I turn my attention to my physics homework and eat an apple slice. The only two living things who can see what I'm doing are Roger, who is snoring on the floor next to me, and the white-feathered crow cleaning itself on the other side of the window.

I've started thinking of this one as "my" crow, and there's no getting around it—all the crows at the Fernandez house are more than just crows. That's not a pleasant truth to acknowledge. It makes it even more imperative to learn Reece's secret.

Movement draws my attention up from my notebook. Reece has come outside as two little kids run up the driveway, backpacks swinging behind them. I snatch up the binoculars from the counter next to me and focus on the little group. Reece kneels down for hugs. My chest tightens to see them throw arms around him and hug with such force, he tips over backward. I can hear their shrieks of laughter from here. He's *so* cute like this, being a good big brother, that some of my annoyance with him and his secrets thaws. The kids toss their backpacks on the lawn, and one of them digs a soccer ball out from behind a bush. A three-way passing game ensues, with lots of wayward kicks and more laughing. Seeing this, it's hard to imagine this family is anything other than what they appear. But I know better.

It's a perfect time to take Roger for a walk. I scoop up the leash. The sound of the clasp jingling propels the dog from sound sleep to prancing at the door in under three seconds. I throw on a hat and an old coat—what I always wear for walks with Roger—and pop earbuds in my ears for good measure. We start down the driveway. Roger's good on the leash, but today he hears the noise of children from his old home, and his nose is raised, feverishly smelling the air. I slow down only a little as we pass Reece's house. It's enough to give Roger encouragement to pull toward the children and for them to notice *him*. Which is what I want.

"Look!" A little girl with warm brown skin points at us. "A dog! Hi doggie!" She runs toward us, waving, followed by the boy. Trailing behind them both is Reece.

"Easy, Fiona," he calls out. "Remember what to do around dogs you don't know."

If Fiona hears him, she's pretending she can't. She does, however, approach the wiggling Roger with caution. She looks up at me with a sweet little smile. "Hello, I'm Fiona. May I pet your doggie?"

I can't help but smile. "Of course," I say, half smitten with her already. I crouch down, get a good grip on Roger's collar in case he decides to show his affection too enthusiastically. "He's very friendly. Sometimes, too much so. You may get kisses."

"That's okay." She pulls off a glove and extends one small hand for Roger's inspection. He complies as respectfully as he can, but he can't resist licking, which sends her into a peal of giggles. "That tickles! What's his name?"

"Roger."

She peers up at me from beneath thick lashes. "Are you Angie?"

"Um, yes. That's me." I'm a little surprised but manage not to show it. *This kid knows my name?*

She leans forward, cupping a hand over her mouth. "My brother talks about you," she whispers conspiratorially.

"Oh." Well. That answers that. "Really?"

She giggles again. "Yup." Just then the little boy joins us. "Look! That's my other brother, Paxton."

Paxton is a pale, blond, serious-looking boy who appears to be about the same age as Fiona. He greets Roger without smiling, presenting his hand to be sniffed, but he lets out a laugh when his fingers also get a lick.

"Very nice to meet you, Angie," says Paxton in a formal, important voice.

I can't help but grin at him. "Likewise, young sir."

"This is Roger," Fiona informs him. "Angie said we could pet him."

Reece jogs over then, as I expected. White teeth flash in a quick smile. "Hi, Angie. I'm sorry about these two. Are they behaving?" He uses a serious voice, but his lips twitch in amusement. "Using manners?"

I'm still eye level with the children, and it's them I address. "You two are the most well-mannered kids I've ever met. Roger here thinks you're great, too. He loves new noses to kiss."

Fiona wrinkles her nose and brings it close to Roger, then rears back when he tries to lay one on her.

Paxton scratches Roger in the rolls of his neck, exactly

where he likes it. "May we please play with him?"

I hesitate, look up at Reece. This is exactly what I want—a reason to loiter around this house. To observe and see if anything seems off. Roger, who is a good judge of people, is clearly telling me everything is *fine*, but I'm determined to find answers. "I can let him off the leash, but it's up to you. We were headed for a walk in the woods, so he might leave a present on your lawn."

Reece shrugs. "That's okay. If you're sure he won't run away."

Perfect. "He won't." I unclip Roger's leash, and he bounds across the frosty lawn in unbridled joy. Paxton runs to the garage and returns with an old tennis ball—which was probably originally Roger's—and hurls it as far as he can. My dog leaps after it, gloriously happy.

"They're your siblings?" I ask.

"Yeah. We're adopted." He says it in an automatic sort of way, probably used to curiosity about the differences in skin color between the children. He watches the children fondly. "There're five of us including our older sister, Brooke, and our little brother, James."

My brows go up. "That's quite an age range."

"It is," he replies. "It's been hard since our dad passed away."

"When did that happen?"

"A few months ago."

His words—the remote coolness of them—scratch through me like flat notes in a song. As someone who *has* lost a parent, I know there's no way to *not* have feelings about it. If his father died a few months ago—even if the man was a monster—discussing his death would evoke *something.* But Reece's voice is hollow. His words sound rehearsed. No emotion, but I've *seen* Reece with emotion and he's quite expressive. I've seen him frightened and sad and angry and surprised. I've seen him confront a creature with a mouthful of bees and a face that transforms every thirty seconds or so. So I'm not sure I believe him, and that's an uncomfortable thought, considering my own history.

I eye him closely, searching for a physical tell to reveal sadness, hidden grief, *something*, but there's nothing. No slight pinch of the mouth, no tightening of the hands. Not a glimmer of the grief he revealed the first time we met at the bus stop. His voice sounds painfully empty. Painful only to me, apparently, as he seems perfectly at ease. I swallow heavily, searching for the right response. I won't call him a liar—that's just unthinkable.

"I'm sorry for your loss," I say quietly.

"Thank you. Everyday life is the hardest part. Just...going through the motions of it all."

Now *that* was the only part that felt like the truth. The rest of his words sounded like poorly delivered lines, read from a script. The implication that he's not telling the truth about the death of his father makes me a little light-headed. Why would someone *do* that?

"Is it?" I'm seriously questioning the wisdom of coming here. Who *is* this boy? Who are these people? I may not want these answers. Whatever illusion I had been weaving about this being a normal family can't be true. This is a family, yes, but one putting on an elaborate show to appear to be something they are not. "Everyday life can't be so bad," I say lightly, eager to change the subject before I start luring myself down a hole. "You have a beautiful home, a nice family. You're popular at school. Kiera Shaw certainly likes you."

He turns his gaze to me, slowly. "Kiera Shaw? You think I like her?"

"I don't know what you like." I don't blink. I don't look away. "I know only what I've seen."

Reece leans close, gently entering my personal space. Close

enough to put me on edge, but not close enough to intimidate. His voice is silk on gravel. His narrowed eyes glitter down at me. “And what, exactly, have you seen, Angie?”

Shivers race up my skin. I want to defuse this so badly, but I feel like this is a challenge I can’t lose. “I’ve seen and heard things that don’t make sense. Things I can’t understand.” I shift my gaze to my crow sitting on a branch above my head. It watches me with an intensity that would scare me if I wasn’t accustomed to it. “Tell me about the crows.”

He shakes his head. “Sorry. Either you know about them or you don’t.”

My jaw tightens, even as I step toward him. I can feel his body heat. His clean, guy scent fills my senses with a unique magnetism that draws me close. Closer still. “I *will* find out.”

His gaze sweeps my face, lingering on my lips. “I hope not.” His breath warms my temple, sending a shiver under my skin. “There are worse things out there than a few watchful birds.”

“Like what?” I’m breathless, damn him. My words are barely audible.

His lashes fan low over his eyes. The narrow space between us crackles with tension. “Oh Angie, you don’t want to know.”

It’s exciting, frustrating, *and* exhausting, this coded language we speak. Worse, I may be the only one speaking it, and it’s hard to keep my thoughts coherent when he stands so close. The boy is overloading to the senses, but maybe that’s his intention—to get me so flustered I can’t ask the questions I want. Of course, I really *can’t* ask many questions, since Angie Dovage wasn’t in the parking lot behind The Strip Mall on Friday night. That was Sparo, who is cool and arty and free of the baggage that Angie carries around. Sparo, whom he finds attractive. Sparo, whom I want to claim so badly, I have to clamp my lips together to keep from blurting out my secret.

“Reece!” Fiona calls out. “Roger pooped on the patio!”

He steps away from me slowly, hands spread. Cold air replaces the zinging warmth on my face. "Duty calls," he says, backing away.

"This isn't over," I hiss, to remind him that his charm hasn't zapped all my wits. If anything, I'm more determined than ever to figure out what his deal is.

"Yes, it is." His voice is low and edged with frustration.

I whistle and Roger runs from the back of the house toward me. Except, he doesn't come to me, he goes to Reece, bumps his head into the boy's hand. Reece pets him, scratching behind one floppy ear. He considers me. I know my jaw is jutting, my expression mulish.

"Leave it alone, Angie. I don't want to see anyone get hurt when it can be avoided."

"Is that a threat?"

"No." His eyes widen in surprise. "It's… I just want you to stay safe."

"I see." I run my tongue over my teeth. "Message received." But I'm not leaving this alone. I feel like I've stumbled into an altered world, and I won't spend the rest of my life wondering what I saw, what I *know* I saw.

10 the stalking experiment

This is lunacy. It is six something on a school night. I should be locked in my basement music studio or doing homework.

But no. I'm following Reece Fernandez. If my strategically timed walk with Roger yesterday was a little questionable, this surely qualifies as stalking. It is shameful, and by far the dumbest thing I've ever done. My heart pounds. My hands shake from an overdose of adrenaline. When I got it into my head to see where he went after school, I didn't think it would involve slinking around Cadence's east side.

After going home, I employed Dad's binoculars *again*. Pathetic, yes, but I was able to see when Cody Knox—one of Reece's new hockey buds—came by and picked him up. I had just enough time to grab my keys and purse and jump into my car to follow them. Reece had not yet seen my car. What a perfect disguise it was. Reece and Cody stopped at Shopmart, after which they exchanged friendly good-byes. Cody left in his car and Reece started off on foot.

So did I. I was feeling pretty proud of myself. He couldn't know I was following him. I'm good at disguises. I wore a boxy black coat, loose jeans, and I tucked my hair up under a short-brimmed wool hat. The idea was to disguise my gender somewhat. If, at quick glance, I could look like a boy, he'd be less likely to recognize me. It was possible. I gave him a decent lead.

It was all going just fine. Until it became evident where he was walking to.

Cadence, which sits in a wide valley, is a decent-sized town. Certainly big enough for no one to know everyone. It also didn't entirely bounce back after the mines were closed, so there exists the east end of Cadence, which is a small, downtown section, not-so-affectionately nicknamed The Dredge, named after its main drag of Dredge Street. Every effort to "revitalize" The Dredge has failed. It remains one of the only areas of Cadence that doesn't sport pretty coffee shops and boutiques with water bowls set out for dogs. However, if you're looking to purchase an illegal substance or sell something you shouldn't have, The Dredge is your go-to. The few remaining open storefronts are pawnshops and seedy bars.

It's getting dark. The shadows are making it harder to see Reece, dressed in dark jeans and a gray coat. At first, I think he's going back to The Strip Mall, which is a few blocks away on the outskirts of town, but he doesn't. He seems a little aimless. Maybe he's supposed to meet someone. Is he here to buy drugs? My stomach sinks at the thought.

I'm about to turn around and head back to my car when Reece veers into a parking lot. We're at the Mountain View Gardens, an apartment complex that's in the local news way too often, and never in a good way. The four-story structure looks more like a postapocalyptic ruin than a residence. There *is* a view of a mountain, but it's hard to avoid them around here. Even the town dump has a mountain view.

Reece stops at the curb, next to the dented guardrail dividing a mostly empty parking lot from the highway. He looks so casual, standing there.

I flatten against the building, about thirty feet from him. I pull my scarf over my mouth to hide the white puffs of my breath. My heart beats, fast. Something about this feels off-kilter. I can't place it, can't define it. Time has sped up and slowed down at the same time.

What are you doing here, Reece?

And then—

A set of wobbling headlights wrenches my attention from Reece. The sound of screaming tires makes me jump, and a brown sedan skids into the shoulder. It slams hard against the guardrail. Metal screeches, shooting sparks into the darkening evening. The tires catch, and the car flips. A scream lodges in my throat as it smashes upside down in the parking lot. One wheel spins like a rolling eye.

I can't move. I'm like a frozen computer—processing, processing. I feel like I'm choking on my own tongue. Sound won't leave my mouth.

Reece stands there. He just *watches*. Then, with the laze of a stretching cat, he pushes off the mangled guardrail and ambles toward the crashed car. It adds to the surreal quality of the moment. Makes me question what I'm look at with my own eyes.

Forget it—I'm done stalking. My legs are shaking terribly, but I lurch forward, pointing at the car. Someone is in there. Someone is probably hurt. Terror coils in my gut at the prospect of what carnage lies inside the car, knowing I lack the skills to help, but I have to do *something*.

Reece crouches down next to the smashed side window. He pulls out his cell phone and so help me, he had better be calling

911. He speaks rapidly, then places the phone on the ground. He tries to wrench open the driver's side door, but it doesn't budge. With a heavy sigh, he kicks broken window glass out of the way and reaches inside the car. Checking for a pulse?

I jog up alongside him. "Reece." My voice a strangled croak.

His head snaps up. His eyes are wrong. They're solid black, like empty sockets. I suck in a breath, and he ducks his head. Hair falls over his eyes, shielding them from view. The movement is immediate, like a reflex.

Dawning horror slides over his features. Horror at seeing *me*—arguably the least horrible thing that he has witnessed in the last five minutes.

"Angie?" His voice is incredulous, edged with anger.

"Did you call 911?" I point to the phone on the ground.

He nods. "Not that it matters for this guy. What are you *doing* here?"

He frowns, squeezes his eyes shut, and when he looks up again, he looks normal—*or did I imagine that?* Maybe he's in shock. That might explain why his reaction seems so wrong.

I move closer, gulping air and steeling myself for what I'm about to see. He holds up a hand. His fingertips are dark with blood. "No, Angie," he commands. "No closer."

Anger floods my head with a set of chemicals far different than the fear that had momentarily paralyzed me. "Let me help." I come to his side and yank on the door handle without looking inside. "I *want* to help." It's immediately apparent that there's no opening this door without special equipment. Still, I yank again, bracing my feet and pulling with all my strength. Reece is on his knees next to me, silent and still.

"Help me, damn it!" I shout at him, even though I know why he's not helping. It is too quiet inside this car.

"Angie, stop," Reece says quietly. "Just...stop."

The high whine of a siren cuts through the crisp night air.

It's in the distance, but coming closer. Coming here.

My hands unwind from the door handle. I look inside.

I will forever wish I hadn't. Some things, you just can't unsee. The man inside the car is crumpled against the roof like a pile of laundry. Blood pools against the broken window and spills onto the pavement. The pungent smell of alcohol wafts from the car interior. It mixes with burned rubber and death for a stench I can't describe.

It will not take the police long to piece together why this man lost control of his car.

I spread my hands on the pavement and swallow back a wave of nausea. I've witnessed many awful things, having lived with a drug-addicted mother. I have seen exactly two people die—this one makes three—and countless others who were already dead inside, but waiting for their bodies to catch up. It takes a piece of you, seeing death. Every time, it rips something away. I don't want to lose any more of me. I'm terrified there isn't much left to spare.

Tears fill my eyes. I cover my mouth with the back of my hand. Suddenly, the origin of Reece's sadness is obvious—this isn't the first time he's seen someone die.

Reece's hand touches my arm. "Are you…okay?"

I jerk back and turn to him. He's breathing hard, but his face is flushed to the point of glowing. A light sweat shines on his cheeks. A very weird reaction to what we just witnessed. He looks almost rapturous, as if…

"Oh *God*." I draw back in horror. "Are you enjoying this?"

"No!" Grief twists his features. "No, it's…" The fingers of his clean hand press to his temple. "I can't explain this to you. You aren't supposed to be here."

"*What* are you?" The question slips out—suddenly, vitally relevant.

For a moment, we just stare at each other, our mingling

breath making white puffs in the cold air. He drops his gaze. I know, then, the answer is horrible. He's kept his secrets for a reason, and that reason may be as scarring as the scene before us.

"Get out of here, Angie," Reece grinds out. "Before the police come. We'll talk. But not now."

"I witnessed this," I say, waving to the car. "I have to stay."

He closes his eyes. "This wasn't a crime." He draws in a long breath through flared nostrils. "It'll be better for you if you go. I'll meet up with you."

"But..." The sirens are louder. If I stay, I'll have to answer questions about why I—a girl from the fancy Estates—is down here in The Dredge. The assumption will be drugs. Not a stretch. I surely *look* strung out right now. "What about you?"

"I'm new here." His voice sounds sluggish, weary, even though he looks the opposite. "I wandered into a bad neighborhood. Got lost."

I get to my feet. "I'm parked on Second Street, in the Shopmart parking lot. Tan Civic. I'll wait for you there."

His shoulders drop in resignation. There will be no avoiding my questions this time. He turns back to the dead man in the car. "Fine."

I walk back toward the street, away from this horror. Stalking Reece had been a *bad* idea. The worst. Only then do I see it—my crow. Its single white feather winks, nestled in its black plumage. A silent sentinel, perched atop a telephone pole. A dark shape against a dusky sky. It turns its head slowly, following my progress up the sidewalk. I tug my coat tight around me, but nothing can chase away this chill. The crow watches, holding something in its beak.

11 the harbinger

The moment I hit the sidewalk on Dredge Street, it's a struggle not to break into a flat run. But that might draw unwanted attention. Every step puts distance between me and Reece. Me and answers.

Me and the entrance to a rabbit hole I may not find my way out of.

I let out a few ragged sobs once I'm back in the safety of my parked car. My forehead tips against the steering wheel as I pull in long, deep breaths. The familiar smells of Jolly Ranchers and the vinegar potato chips stuck between the seats unwind my nerves. My car. Safety.

I should drive home right now. I *shouldn't* be sitting here, waiting for Reece. Hell, he might not even show up.

The minutes tick by and collect. *Ten. Fifteen. Twenty*. I'm beginning to think he ditched me until the passenger door wrenches open, and he throws himself inside. He slams the door and turns to me with hot, furious eyes.

"What the hell are you, a stalker?" he asks without preamble.

Why, yes I am. "No, I just—"

"What were you thinking, Angie?" he snaps. "You could have been killed tonight."

It takes me an extra second to respond because—*whoa, he's in my car.* "What were *you* doing there? Don't tell me you were sightseeing in The Dredge."

"Maybe I was. It's none of your business."

"I'll tell you what's my business." Fury curls through me like a ribbon of heat, squashing good sense like a bug. "Seeing my mother's features on that-that *thing's* face on Friday night. You know what he is."

There. Done and done.

He draws back. "What did you say?"

My vision tints red. My stomach clenches to a tight knot. I hadn't known I was going to show my hand like that—I hadn't *intended* to—but there's no walking it back. The truth is out, and I will find out very soon if the biggest risk I've taken in my teenage life will also turn out to be the biggest blunder. "You know very well that was *me* in the parking lot with the purple hair and the glasses. *I'm* Sparo. I'm the girl you 'rescued' Friday night from that guy with the-the…" I circle my hand impatiently. "Changing face and the bees."

The corners of his mouth lift. "Yeah, I knew that was you."

"You *did?*"

He rolls his eyes. "How could I not?" He leans toward me, crowding my space. I press back into my seat. "I was *this* close to you, Angie. Makeup and wigs don't change your face."

"Why the pretense, then? Why not just call me out on it?" *Good grief, why does he have to be this close?* "Why be all manipulative and fake about it?" I ask with full knowledge that this is *not* the question I should be asking right now, but my thoughts swirl like dry leaves in the wind. My cheeks burn at the thought of all the times we spoke and he knew the truth.

He probably had a few good laughs over it.

His gaze dips to my lips. "I was curious why you seemed so determined to hide such an amazing part of yourself."

"It's none of your business," I say, tossing his words back at him.

"Touché." He nods. "You're amazing up there. Powerful. So beautiful it's impossible to look away from you. So completely different from the quiet girl in school." His thumb brushes my cheek, unleashing a spray of tingling nerves. "I wanted you to admit it was you," he says quietly. "The only question is, why the disguise?"

If he's trying to distract me, he's doing an epic job of it. "Sparo and I are separate." *For reasons too complicated and fragile to explain to you.* "I want it to stay that way."

He frowns. "I have no choice but to keep a part of myself hidden, but I don't understand why you do."

My defenses rise into full protection mode. Deno and Lacey—my dad, too—have asked me why. I've never said. "My music is *separate*. It has to be." I say it again with finality. "Reece, who was that man?" I whisper. "And what is with the bees?"

Reece lets out a long breath but doesn't pull back. "Angie, that's not an easy question. The answer is…"

"What?" I counter. "Too much for me to handle? Me and my little, simple human mind can't grasp it?"

He blinks at me. "Angie, it's a lot for *any* mind to grasp. That man you saw isn't a human being—not anymore. Not for a very long time."

My fingertips are ice cold. I curl them on my lap. "What do you mean, 'not anymore'? How does someone stop being human, Reece?"

"I mean, he was changed into what he is by powers in the world that are now dormant, but once wielded incredible destruction." He watches my face closely, maybe to see how much I *can* grasp. "He's one of the last remnants of a time when people lived under a very different set of rules. When certain people possessed powers that no one could comprehend now."

"What kind of…powers?"

He sighs. "This was a bad idea."

I turn toward him in my seat. "Look, just give it to me straight. Don't take it down to a kindergarten level or be all evasive. That makes it worse. Just…tell me. I promise, I can deal with whatever. I just want the truth."

"The truth…" He runs his tongue over his teeth and turns his gaze to the cloth roof of the car. "Fine. Here's the truth. The man you saw is a being called a Beekeeper. He's many centuries old, and he goes around with a hive of bees in his chest. *Yes*, I know how made up that sounds, but those bees are deadly. Their sting infects a person with a venom that causes paranoia, delusions, and violent urges. It strips away reason and decency in favor of base impulses. Get stung by one of his bees and you'll go dangerously insane."

Okay. Deep breath, Angie. I gave my word. I said I could deal with whatever. This is a bit more than I'd bargained for, but then again, maybe it isn't. Some part of me knew that the truth about the man with all the faces and the bees would be something outside the realm of the normal world. I'm also aware that of the sea of knowledge on this topic, Reece has offered me only a single drop.

I take another deep breath. I *can* do this—talk about the impossible. "So was that guy in the car…stung?"

"Maybe," he replies. "I don't know. I couldn't see very much of him."

A shiver slides down my spine. "That's why you freaked when that bee was on my coat."

"Yes." He drops his forehead against mine. Soft hair fans my skin. His fingertips brush my cheek. "Angie, I wish you hadn't followed me today."

I swallow with effort, through the desert in my throat. "He called you a harbinger. What is that? Are you...like him?"

"We're not the same, but we're both cursed. What he is—what *I* am—is..." He leans back and rakes long fingers through his hair. "It's really complicated."

"We're veering back to evasion here," I say in a warning tone. "What about my mom?"

"I don't know what to say about that." Reece's voice drops low. "Each feature that appears on his face belonged to a person who died with Beekeeper venom in them. There's no surviving a Beekeeper sting. You'll kill yourself, or someone else will take you down. Did your mother go on a shooting rampage in a shopping mall? Did she ever try to kill you or anyone else?"

"No..." She died a sad death under a highway overpass after years of drug abuse.

"Then you couldn't have seen her features on the Beekeeper. You saw someone who looked like her."

"No. It was her. I know what I saw." Without photographic evidence, which I'm not getting, he won't believe me. "Whatever. Forget it."

He rests a hand on my shoulder. "Facing a Beekeeper in true form *is* terrifying. Why *wouldn't* you see a familiar face in all that madness?"

He makes it sound so reasonable. So excusable. "Reece, what were you doing here tonight?" I ask. "I want the truth."

"The truth," he says again, drawing it out as if saying it for the first time. "You won't like it."

"Tell me anyway."

He stares blankly out the windshield. "I went there because I knew someone was going to die there and I—"

A rap on my window makes us both jump. A frowning

police officer shines a light inside. He makes a rolling motion with his finger. *Oh great.*

I turn on the car to lower the window. "Good evening, officer."

He gives me a quick survey. No clothes out of place. No stink of alcohol or glassy eyes. No heavy breathing—well, maybe a little. "What are you kids doing out here?"

Reece leans over and nods at the officer. "Just talking, sir."

"Uh-huh." He narrows an eye. "Windows are steamed up. You two aware this is a public parking lot?"

"Yes sir," I say with my best smile. "We were just about to head home."

"And where's that?"

"Mount Franklin Estates." Reece's tone borders on pompous, as if declaring our neighborhood excuses us. "It's a little after seven p.m. Have we violated any laws?"

We haven't, and the officer knows it. He grunts something about know-it-all rich kids and backs up. "Get going, then. Do your 'talking' at home. And be careful," he adds. "The drunks are out tonight."

"Yes sir. We're going," I say with an earnest nod. "And thank you."

My fingers can't put the car in gear fast enough. I pull away with a little wave and hope he doesn't follow us home. He doesn't. I merge into the light town traffic, jaw clenched and hands tense around the steering wheel.

Reece's face is turned away. All I glimpse is the illuminated line of his cheek and the curve of an eye. He stares out his window like a passenger on a bus. The policeman snapped him out of his open, sharing mood. I'm sure he thinks he came to his senses, but… "You were saying you came out to The Dredge because you knew someone was going to die?" I ask.

"Yes. My kind are drawn to death, but you already know that," he replies coolly. "Just ask me already. Get it over with."

His *kind.* That's pretty much the answer right there. "You're a…harbinger of death?" I ask it anyway, hardly believing I'm saying the words out loud.

He nods slowly, holding my gaze. My heart beats in the palms of my hands, the soles of my feet. My suspicions are finally confirmed. My stomach twists into knots. I would rather the first boy who makes my heart beat like this, who makes my senses come alive, be a normal, human one, but I shouldn't be surprised. "Normal" hasn't exactly defined much of my life.

"It's my fault the Beekeeper noticed you," he murmurs. "Did he have all the faces when you saw him at the bus stop?"

"I thought I was imagining it."

"Hmm," he says after a pause. "That's interesting. It's unusual for a normal human to see a Beekeeper's true face."

"What do they usually see?"

"They see a man so perfectly generic, so unremarkable, he's essentially invisible."

"Only guys?" I ask.

"I don't know the full story on them." He waves a hand. "They were prisoners, or something, but yes. All the Beekeepers I've ever seen or heard about are male."

"Why is that Beekeeper watching me?"

"He's watching a lot of people. Try not to worry. *We* are also watching you."

There's that "we" again. "Who's 'we'? The crows?"

"Yes." No pause that time.

"Are you seriously telling me you're a *crow?*" I draw my top lip between my teeth and try to make that compute. "How does that even work?"

"Like I said, it's complicated." He turns away from me to the dark trees flickering by. "*I* don't even fully know how it works. You'd have to ask those who cursed us. Unfortunately, they've been dead for a thousand years."

"A *thousand* years?"

He shrugs. "Give or take."

If that last bit was supposed to blow my mind and shut me up, it works, for a little while. I switch between thinking he's messing with me again or he's delusional. "I can't believe this. You're *not* a one-thousand-year-old crow."

"No way, I'm much younger." His voice is without a trace of humor. "But the magic that made me this way *is* that old."

"Oh, sure." My voice pitches high. "Magic."

"Hey, you asked."

I pull the car to the shoulder just inside the entrance to our neighborhood. The car idles in park. I'm not ready to take him, or myself, home. "I have more questions." *Way* more than I'd like.

"I've told you everything I can." He presses long fingers into the center of his forehead. "Which is already more than I should have."

"You can't just drop magic crows in my lap and leave it at that."

"I just did." His voice takes on an edge. "Angie, I answered the questions relevant to your safety. The rest is curiosity, and I'm sorry, but I can't indulge it. I have more than just my own selfish wants to consider."

"I'm going to keep following you until you answer me."

"I strongly advise against that." Reece's eyes narrow to glimmering slivers. "Go home. Make music. Study for the geometry test tomorrow. Be a normal teenager." His features take on that grief-stricken look again. "This isn't how I wanted things to go with us, Angie. I wanted…" He clips off his words with a terse head shake. "Forget it."

"No. Don't do that." My voice is barely above a whisper, but he hears it.

Reece's gaze drops to my mouth. His own lips part and his gaze darkens. He leans toward me and for one giant, breathless moment, I think he's going to kiss me. Wait. *Kissing?* This had not been on the radar when I set out on this absurd mission a hour or so ago. My senses fly into high alert. He braces a hand on the dash, then lurches back. He flexes the fingers of his right hand with a wince.

"Hey, are you hurt?" I reach for his hand, but he folds them over his chest.

"No. I'm fine." His voice is rough. His face is a mess of conflict.

"Reece—"

"No. *No*. I have to go." He opens the door and gets out as if the seat is on fire. "Don't follow me again, Angie. Death is never far behind me. I don't want it to catch you."

He slams the door and takes off at a run, disappearing through Mrs. Garrett's backyard. He must be truly desperate to get away from me if he's willing to set off her motion lights *and* her Rottweilers to take the direct route home.

I let my car idle at the stop sign. Someone honks and steers around me, and it barely registers. My head is a buzzing mess of unanswered questions, unnamed fears, unbelievable thoughts. Slowly, I lift my leaden foot off the brake and drive the remaining half-mile home. Nothing looks the same as it had when I left for school this morning. Even these streets, my own home, seem foreign.

I pull into my driveway. A crow swoops low over my car, wings silhouetted in the floodlight. And I wonder…

Magic.

If you had asked me a few weeks ago, I'd have said magic is impossible. Irrational. Just considering its existence in this world is insane. But I saw bees crawl out of a man's mouth. I saw him change faces like pages of a book.

I hold my breath and watch the crow glide away. It melts into the blackness, silent as a ghost. Lonely as the night.

Dark as a boy's eyes.

12

the ride

"It's no good, Angie. Timing's off." Lacey clicks the mouse with a flourish, ending the frustrating, twenty-second attempt to record a simple fourteen-note sequence. We're in my basement music studio having zero fun at an activity which is usually pure enjoyment. She spins in my desk chair and faces me with a puzzled frown. "What's going on? You know how to play this."

I rub the spot where the strap of my electric guitar digs into my neck. In the two nights since I followed Reece into The Dredge, I've slept badly. My dreams have been plagued with crows and boys with writhing faces. Bees. Swarms of them that are always on the verge of encircling me. In others, Reece is there with gruesome, all-black eyes. I'm running from him, too, but always find myself in his arms and inexplicably relieved to be there.

"I don't know." I tap my foot, encased in my favorite slippers—little ballet flats covered in tiny skulls. "I'm off tonight."

"You're more than off," Lacey replies. "We recorded Deno's vocals in less time, and he's partially tone-deaf."

"I am *not* tone-deaf." Deno scratches Roger's ear. The dog presses against Deno's hand and grunts in appreciation. "Are you nervous about seeing your hockey boy at The Strip Mall this week? I thought that worked out well for you last time. I can schedule another pee break, if you like."

I lean back and stare at the drop ceiling. "Do that again and I'll strangle you with one of your own power cables. I'm just…" I close my eyes.

There are no words. None that would sound even remotely sane to them. "I'm just not feeling this right now."

I'm so confused. When I returned home from The Dredge, I found a wilted red carnation on my window box. Seeing it didn't surprise me, but the smile it brought to my lips did. I'm starting to look forward to my crow's gifts. Almost as much as I'm look forward to seeing Reece again.

Deno kicks off from an amplifier and rolls his stool my way. "Does your being 'off' have anything to do with that neighbor of yours?"

Oh yeah. I make a face. "*Pfft*. No."

"You are telling an untruth," Lacey declares.

Deno rolls his eyes at her. "Can't you say things normally? Like, Angie, you're lying?"

"That would sound harsh." Lacey's brows go up. "My way is prettier. And Angie is not a *liar*. She's telling an untruth, maybe because she doesn't want to tell us what's really bothering her."

She's right, of course. Lacey has an uncanny ability to almost always be right. Deno has the uncanny ability of not ever picking up on this. He pulls his knitted beanie low over his brows, muttering how lying and telling an untruth are the same damn thing.

I look between the two of them and wonder how it is *they*

haven't made out yet.

"Angie, by all accounts—meaning Deno's report—the encounter at The Strip Mall went well." She laces her fingers together. "You talked to Reece. Learned you have compatible taste in music. Made a connection. He's *not* interested in Kiera; that seems obvious."

"Good thing," Deno gives Lacey a smug look. "Aiden Moore's mom works at the hospital and he said that Braydon was admitted a few days ago after trashing his house and threatening his parents or something. He attacked a doctor and had to be restrained. He's been on the psych floor ever since."

Lacey looks down with a frown. "I heard that, too."

"Ha!" Deno cries. "I *told* you it was more than a bee sting."

She sneers up at him. "Daniel, Kiera Shaw did *not* poison Brayden. Mrs. Lowsen, the assistant nurse, hit her husband over the head with a wine bottle, then tried to kill herself. Did Kiera make Mrs. Lowsen do that, too?"

I listen with increasing nausea. I'd heard whispers about Brayden and chose to write them off as rumors, but I didn't know about Mrs. Lowsen. She seemed nice. Definitely sane.

Stay away from the bees.

The Beekeeper. It's the only explanation. Unlike Brayden, who was treated for a bee sting, I have no way to know if Mrs. Lowsen was stung by the Beekeeper's bee. Given the circumstances, I can assume she was.

But what are they doing here? Why is Cadence such a hotspot for…hell, I'll say it—*magic*—all of a sudden?

"Angie?" Lacey waves a hand in my face. "Earth to Angie. So did something happen between you and Reece to make you sad?"

Deno raises his brows. "All that fancy way of talking, and you come up with *sad*?"

"Fine." Lacey's brown eyes flash. "Unsettled, conflicted,

and yes, she looks *sad*."

For a brief moment, I consider telling them *why* I'm unsettled, conflicted, and sad, but I don't. Can't. It may be irrational, but I feel like I'd be betraying a confidence, even though I owe Reece nothing. Well, except maybe my life when he intervened with that Beekeeper. There's also the fact that they would never believe me if I told them about the supernatural goings-on around Cadence.

I give them the easier-to-swallow answer. "It wasn't *me* he had the connection with. It was my colorful alter ego, Sparo."

Lacey leans forward and rests a hand on my knee. Her eyes are very earnest. "You do know that you and Sparo are the same person, right?"

"Yes." I run my fingers through my hair. There's about an inch of my natural dark roots, grown out from when I tried out being a dark blonde a few months ago. I pluck at the guitar strings, wishing I were alone. "And so does Reece. He saw through my disguise."

"He knows?" Deno sits up straight. "You're just telling us this now?"

I grind my teeth and pluck out the simple fourteen notes I'd been screwing up for the past half hour. "Yeah, so?"

Lacey smacks my leg. "You make us jump through hoops, tell a thousand lies to keep this alter ego of yours secret because of some social phobia you have. Then, this new guy shows up and you're fine with him knowing. I get that you have the hots for him, but— "

"It's not *some* social phobia. My music is a separate thing." *Why* must I keep explaining this? "You've never been national news. It's traumatizing."

Lacey gives me a stern look. "Sparo is *not* national news."

"But *I* was." Sweat breaks out on my palms and I crack, just a little. Enough to finally admit the truth. "I don't want my music to be listened to in the context of the girl with the dead junkie mother. My music is untouched by all that. Don't you understand? I don't want those stories—my life with *her*—to infect it."

"Angie, your mother isn't a disease," Lacey says, nose scrunched. "She can't contaminate your music. Or you."

But that's what I'm terrified of. Half afraid it's already happening. "Just forget it. It's done. Reece knows, and I didn't just *tell* him. He accidentally saw me Friday night in the parking lot. I didn't have my glasses on." I slice a hand through the air. "Not that it matters. He wasn't all that impressed."

It shouldn't bother me so much. Reece has far bigger issues than me or my part-time job.

Deno, who had been carefully—and wisely—quiet, appears relieved the conversation is steering back to a safe topic. "The music must be too complex for him."

"I don't think it's that, not that it matters." I fiddle with the knobs of my guitar pickups. "I'm sure Kiera told him some lovely stories about my mother and me. The 'prostitute' one is always a fan favorite."

"Anyone who listens to Kiera Shaw isn't worth your time," Deno declares. "So there's your litmus test for Reece."

A smile curves Lacey's lips. "Litmus test. Nice, Deno."

"That's right." He tosses back his head. "Who's the Neanderthal now?"

If only it were that simple. If Deno and Lacey knew what I know about Reece, they'd agree that Kiera's blather is the least of my concerns with him. If only he weren't so complicated. And interesting. And possibly not human. If only I didn't know things about him that no one else does. And there's that sadness that drapes over him like a cloak. Those lost, broken eyes that no one seems to notice but me.

Roger's ears prick up at the sound of footsteps on the

basement stairs. It's my dad, and there's a spring in his step. He's excited about something, and it's not the ginger-carrot smoothies he's been pounding lately. He knocks on the door, sticks his head through. "Hi Deno, Lacey." His face is flushed. "Angie, there's a boy here."

I'm not sure, but I might be a little offended by the surprise in his voice. "Okay. Who is it?"

His gaze flickers to the stairs, and he drops his voice to a whisper. "It's the kid next door, I think. I don't know his name."

By some miracle, my friends keep quiet as my dad delivers this news. I, on the other hand, instantly turn into a jumble of nerves. "Did he say what he wanted?"

"He didn't. He just asked to speak with you." Dad's voice is still incredulous, and yeah, I *am* a little offended.

A dozen thoughts crowd my head at once. Very few of them are good. He came here, to *me,* after clearly telling me to leave him alone. "Okay." The word exits more evenly than the breath pulled in to form it. "I'll be up in a minute."

Deno lets out a low whistle as soon as my dad is gone. "And you didn't think you left an impression."

"Go, Angie." Lacey wiggles her brows. "This is exciting."

"It's not. I don't know what he wants." I place my guitar on its stand and chew on my bottom lip. I'm not sure I want to know why he's here.

"Well, go find out," Deno says. "And use complete sentences, instead of your usual grunting."

"I don't grunt." I fiddle with the choppy ends of my hair. "Anything else?"

"Yeah. Make eye contact. So he doesn't think you have social anxiety."

"I *do* have social anxiety."

"He doesn't need to know that."

Probably too late for that. I go to the door and look back.

"I'll be right back."

Lacey smiles beatifically. "Oh, I hope *not*, Angie."

Reece is in the foyer, alone, pacing. My dad is nowhere in sight, but I guarantee he's not far. Reece's hands are stuffed in the front pocket of a hooded sweatshirt. He pulls them out when I come into the room and rubs them on his thighs. "Hey," he says, looking so very normal in a well-worn baseball cap.

"Hey yourself." I cross the foyer on the balls of my feet—a nervous habit I *hate*—and uncross my arms, at a loss of what to do with them. "What's up?"

"I'm sorry to show up like this." He peeks up at me, his face solemn. "I hope I'm not disturbing you."

Disturbing. A fine word choice. "Nope."

"I need a favor."

"I got the clear impression you wanted to keep your distance." I *don't* feel bad about the frost in my voice. "You're sending *very* mixed signals."

"I know. It's messed up." He looks down at my skull slippers and amusement slides across his expression. "You have no idea how much."

"Oh, I have an idea." I cross my arms again. "What's this favor?"

"I was wondering if you'd mind giving me a ride to the ice rink."

"The ice rink?" I ask. "Isn't the hockey season half over?"

"Yeah." His shoulders jerk into a shrug. "But Coach Radley saw my last season stats and agreed to let me try out tonight at practice. He lost a center to bad grades and, if I make it, he said he can swing a special circumstance waiver, letting me join the team mid-season. My car arrived, but it's in the shop, and my mom is out, so I was wondering—hoping—you'd be willing to give me a ride."

"None of the puck heads felt like picking you up?"

His voice and eyebrows lower. "Fine. I wanted to talk to

you, okay? Without an audience. I didn't know how else to do it."

He wants to talk. I let out a breath. "We have a terrible hockey team."

A grin flickers, quick and bright. "I suspect that's why Coach is letting me try out mid-season."

I glance back toward the basement stairs. "I don't know. I have friends over."

"Oh, I didn't know." His eyes widen. "Didn't mean to interrupt." A flush brightens his cheekbones.

"That's okay," Lacey pipes up, appearing behind me. "We were just leaving, weren't we Deno?"

Of course, they wouldn't just stay in the basement.

Deno looks baffled. "We're leaving? But our equipment—" Lacey cuts him off with an elbow to the ribs. "*Ow*. Okay, yeah," he says. "On our way out. See you tomorrow, Angie."

"Wait," I say. "You don't have to."

"Sure we do," Lacey chirps, eyes darting to Reece. "It's a school night."

The whole scene is ridiculous, with Lacey and Deno exchanging looks and trying—but not succeeding—to make a smooth, non-obvious exit.

Lacey lets out a peal of laughter as soon as the door is shut behind her. Reece cocks his head, eyebrows raised in bemusement. "What was *that* about?"

"On Earth, we call it embarrassing." I rub circles into my forehead.

"I *am* from Earth."

"Are you sure?" I roll the ball of my foot over the tile. "So you want me to drive you."

"Or we can fly. Whichever is easier."

"Funny. Okay, fine, since you've run off my friends. Get your stuff."

His "stuff" is a small mountain of gear already piled up on the front step. My jaw locks at the sight. Presumptuous of him to assume I'd drop everything and dive for my keys. As if my deepest desire on a Thursday evening is to drive his butt across town to the ice rink, but he's pretty confident. Probably not used to the word "no."

I find Dad in the kitchen, pretending to be busy, and let him know what I'm doing, then make Reece haul his load of hockey stuff through the house to the garage, where my dad's BMW, my car, and my mom's old Volkswagen Bus are housed.

Reece drops his hockey gear at the Civic's bumper and makes a beeline for the VW. "Oh, wow, Angie. *That's* cool." He lets out a low whistle and spreads his hands before the mint-blue paint. It looks good. I don't know why my dad had it restored. Probably because it was stinking up the garage with the skunky reek of weed. Maybe he just wanted to.

But Reece is right. The Bus *is* cool. At least, I can see how someone other than me might think so.

He leans close, runs a hand over the thick white stripe along the side. "What year?"

"1962." I resist the urge to rush over and slap away his hand. "Can we go now?"

"Does it run?"

"As far as I know," I reply. "Aren't you going to be late?"

He shrugs. "Can I sit inside?"

"No." It comes out sharper than I intended, but not nearly as sharp as I feel. He's too close to the van, and we're very much alone in this dark garage. Both things make my nerves jangle like loose change.

He looks over in surprise and holds out his hands. "Okay. No problem. I love old cars. Is it your dad's?"

"Mine, technically."

His black eyes find mine and widen. "*This* amazing beast

is yours, and you take the bus to school?"

I take a breath and chew on my bottom lip. My mother died in this car. It's been here since the Philadelphia Police Department released it to my dad five years ago. He had it completely restored, but I can't imagine driving it. I also can't imagine getting rid of it. So here it sits.

I tap a finger on the Honda's doorframe. "Do you want a ride or not?"

"Yes." He stands there for a moment, gazing in the Bus's window with a puzzling fascination. When he turns around, his eyes are bright. He's *really* into weird old cars.

And crashed ones with dead people inside.

Something cold skitters down my back. He *did* admit to being attracted to death, but he's on crack if he thinks I'm ever going to let him drive my mom's van. He flashes me a wide smile and reaches for his discarded gear. "You're a puzzle, you know that?"

I roll my eyes and hit the trunk button on the key. He must be joking. Of the two of us, *I* am not the puzzle. "I'm sorry, *who* is the harbinger of death here?"

Reece grins. "Good point." He dumps his hockey stuff in the trunk and climbs into the passenger seat. For the second time this week, he fills up the front half of the car with the smell of pine and clean air on a spring day. Smelling nice doesn't cancel out my nerves, though. I'm wound tight as a coil. My hands keep a death grip on the steering wheel, and I'm not even driving yet.

"Do you know where the ice rink is?" he asks.

"I've lived here for five years," I reply. "I know where everything is."

He lets out a sigh. "You're angry with me."

"Angry is a strong word," I say, sounding an awful lot like Lacey. "More like frustrated."

He nods. “I understand. I should never have told you those things then taken off like that. I apologize.”

So formal. So stiff. Fine. Two can play at that. “You can’t basically admit that you’re not human and not expect follow-up questions.”

“I know it.” He slants me a look. “You shouldn’t have followed me, but after what happened at The Strip Mall, I should’ve expected you’d want answers.”

“You said you were cursed. That magic was involved. *Magic*.” I shake my head. “How am I supposed to process that?”

“I get it. The present world has a specific view of reality, but it wasn’t always like that. Magic used to be as ubiquitous as wifi. It was everywhere, a part of everyday life. These days, people have been well conditioned to disbelieve magic, even when they see it with their own eyes. Tell me, what do you think the Beekeepers are, if not magical creatures?”

“Well, why isn’t it still around, then?”

He sighs and takes off his baseball hat. “It is. There are a few remnants of magic remaining from a far earlier time. You happened to come in contact with one. Or two, if you include me.”

“And the rest of it just…went away?”

“It was purged, but that’s a long, complicated story for another time. Maybe.”

I want to hear it, but my logical mind still really doesn’t like the word magic and reality used in the same utterance.

He rubs his chin and gives me a considering look. “Maybe it will help to put a name to the Beekeeper’s face, or rather, faces.” He grins, but my mouth stays flat. I do *not* see the humor. “So, the Beekeeper who approached you at The Strip Mall is named Rafette. He follows my family around. Most harbinger groups have a Beekeeper attached to them to one extent or another. Rafette’s been around a long time. He…has weird ideas about things sometimes. He likes to spy on people—good at it, too. He may have noticed how often I look at you and got curious."

Um. I don't like the idea of anyone spying on me *at all*, but the idea of that guy watching me without my knowledge twists my stomach in a knot. Also, I look at Reece plenty. This Rafette creature surely would have noticed that. I clear my throat. "Curious about what?"

He blinks a few times, as if the answer is so plain, he can't fathom why I'm asking. "About whether or not I'm interested in you."

"Hmm." Okay. *Don't ask, Angie*. Do. Not. Ask. "So, are you...?"

He looks straight out the windshield. "I really can't make it more obvious."

Yeah, he could. "You avoided me all week."

"This is confusing for me, too." Reece waves his phone with the time displayed. "I don't mean to rush, but practice starts at six, and I can't be late tonight." A flush rides his high cheekbones. He looks at me and away, as if he's unsettled. Or possibly nervous. Meanwhile, my nerves are riding so high, they're making me want to laugh. The boy likes me. *This* boy. This harbinger of death who has already told me that my town is going to be hit by some sort of disaster and he'll be leaving in a month or so after this happens. The giddy rush slipping around under my skin is so unbelievably irrational, it *is* funny, in the most screwed-up way possible. I clamp my teeth on my bottom lip until it hurts and back out of the garage wondering what the hell is wrong with me. Reece is one big walking complication. I still don't really know what his feelings are. He may think he's "obvious," but the boy is about as clear as a wood door.

He fiddles with his phone. "I won't let Rafette near you again. One of my family members, Hank, keeps an eye out for him when I can't. I just…thought you should know."

Hank. My mom dated a guy named Hank once. He was nice, something I can't say for any of my mom's other boyfriends. He'd left, of course. Or we had. It was an on again, off again type of thing. Either way, the end result was the same.

I force my shoulders down and back and steal a glance at Reece. He's got a killer profile. Angular and strong, like it belongs on a coin. Or leading an army to battle. *What has he been through?* Remembering Hank brings the past surging into the present, and suddenly something about Reece feels achingly familiar. A memory just out of reach, or perhaps I've thought about him so much this past week, I think I know him better than I do.

He looks down and there it is again—profound sadness. Deep hurt, hiding just beneath the veneer. I know it's there. It answers an ache within me like a haunting echo.

The illuminated blue-on-white sign for the ice rink comes into view. I pull into the parking lot and find a spot. Practice doesn't start for a few more minutes, and a handful of guys are waiting in the covered vestibule. I don't turn off the engine, expecting him to grab his stuff and go. But he doesn't. He just sits there, looking at his hands.

My own hands drop away from the steering wheel. "Hey, Reece—"

He glances up suddenly, with alarming intensity. He wants to say something. *Badly*.

"What is it?" I ask.

His mouth opens but closes with a sigh. He rubs his thumb over the opposite palm.

That's when I see them—three deep, ragged scars running the length of his palm. They start at the web of his fingers, trace between the bones of his hands, and converge at the wrist.

I reach for him without thinking, pulling his hand into the

dim light of the parking lot lamp. "What happened to your hand?"

His fingers curl into a fist, but he doesn't pull away. "Nothing. Just an old scar."

"It's not nothing. These look deliberate." My eyes snap to his. "What happened to you?"

He lets out a laugh with a sharp twist in it. "What *hasn't* happened to me?" He tips his head back and closes his eyes. Long, dark lashes on golden cheeks. "Oh Angie, I can never tell you it all. And this isn't the time or the place to tell even a little of it."

"Then why did you want to talk to me?"

"To apologize. To— " He rolls his head toward me, gives me a vague smile that doesn't match the hunger in his eyes. "Angie, I will answer your questions. There isn't enough time right now, but soon. I have one request."

"What is it?"

"That you'll hear me out." He draws in a breath through his teeth. "That after you hear what I have to say, you'll try not to be afraid of me."

I wrap my arms around myself on a chill. "I already am a little afraid of you, Reece. In more ways than one." The words tumble out, more breath than voice.

He swallows hard. "A harbinger of death isn't the same thing as a Beekeeper, but not altogether different, either."

Reassuring words stick in my throat. "I want to know."

He lowers his head in a resigned nod. Wavy chestnut hair falls over his furrowed brow.

I squeeze his fist, still clasped between my hands. There's a hum, almost a vibration, between us that gets stronger the longer this goes on. It may be my freak-out meter busting out of the red zone. Slowly, I release his hand, and just as slowly, he retracts it. I drag my gaze up to his.

"Hey, maybe you can come inside, hang out until practice is over?" His voice is rough-edged. "It's not long. We have only forty minutes of ice time."

I feel like I just swallowed a rock. Sitting in the stands during a guy's sports practice is a galaxy away from my comfort zone. And not something I think I'm ready for. Plus, watching any sports practice sounds awfully boring, even with Reece playing the sport. "Oh, I don't think—"

"Damn it," he hisses through his teeth. His gaze narrows on something outside, in the darkness.

I scan the parking lot but see nothing. "What is it?"

Slowly, he raises a finger and I see him—Rafette, the Beekeeper who grabbed me outside The Strip Mall—standing at the edge of the parking lot, nearly in the trees. I was just looking there. It's as if he materialized.

Fear unrolls through me like a ribbon of ice. "What do we do?"

"Nothing. I go play hockey and you go home." Reece unbuckles his seat belt and pulls his baseball cap back on. "Pop the trunk, okay?"

"I'm not leaving you here with…him."

He smiles faintly. "Oh, Rafette can't hurt me." He nods to the boys hanging out in front of the rink. "But he can hurt them."

My stomach dips. "You're *staying?*"

"If Rafette releases bees on those boys, they're dead. I won't let that happen." He leans close. *So* close, I should be able to see the line where his iris ends and his pupil begins. But it's solid black. "I want you to go straight home, okay? I will make sure he doesn't follow you, although I don't believe that's his intention tonight."

"What is his intention?"

Reece sighs. "I have to go, Angie." He reaches over and

hits the trunk button on my key fob. "I'll see you tomorrow at school."

He gets out of the car, hauls his hockey equipment out of the trunk, and strides straight into the pack of boys. I watch him meld into their sea of mismatched gear and backward caps. Their teeth flash, but not in warning. He's welcomed into their tribe with backslaps and fist bumps. He doesn't glance back. Not once.

I look back to the edge of the parking lot.

The Beekeeper is gone.

13

the dead beat

There is no groove tonight. Nothing that works. No matter how high I push the volume, how deep I drive the beat, I'm separate from the music. It's not in me, but around, over. I can't flow with it, and that is the mark of an unsuccessful DJ.

People are still moving. The floor is active, but if I can feel the forced vibe, others can. Deno has worn a frown all night. He monitors the sound output on his laptop, displeased by how loud I'm making things tonight. I usually play a mix of strong beats with spaced-out remixes, but tonight is all in angry techno. Tonight, I am not comfortable in Sparo's clothes. The makeup itches my eyes. The shoes pinch and make me clumsy. I undo the buckles of my platform boots and step out of them. My breath goes shaky and my head goes giddy from the act of releasing those six inches of height and easing my sore feet to the carpeted booth floor. I feel incredibly naked, curling and uncurling my stockinged toes. My hands move over my tablet, monitoring the music I'm playing. Other people's music. Other people's talent and work. And here I am, hiding behind a disguise that, at this moment, feels ridiculous. I have made music. Dozens and dozens of songs, locked away on my hard drive at home. I never play them. If I do, I may have to admit they're mine. I'd have to do more than play them—I'd have to own them. And myself.

Lacey, folded in a corner of the cramped booth, extends a leg and pokes me in the butt with her toe. She points to the discarded boots on the floor with questioning eyes. I wrinkle my nose and try to communicate through my face that they hurt, but she looks out to the floor with a frown, as if my act of shoe shedding is another sign that something just isn't right tonight.

I have to agree. Lacey came along for fun, but she is not having any, either. I glance at the time on my tablet: 9:16. Never before have I actively wished for a set to be over. Usually, it's the total opposite.

Reece is not here. I'm relieved about that. If he wasn't impressed with the last show he attended, he'd be sorely underwhelmed by this one. When we spoke before homeroom this morning, he told me his hockey coach wanted him to attend the team's game tonight before playing in the next one. Without him nearby, I'm scanning for Rafette everywhere. I *think* I see him everywhere. Slipping around corners, walking through crowds. Even at school, turning down corridors, slinking into classrooms.

And so, here I am, playing skull-splitting music to a room of people who mostly know my style well enough to forgive me and come back next week. Artie, the guy who does the lighting for all the sets, has set the room at pulsing red with stabbing spotlights on the dance floor. He's doing his best to create a mood, but I'm not giving him much to work with.

Tom, one of the bouncers, comes up to the side of the booth and motions to Deno. They talk for a moment, then Deno turns to me.

"Trouble's brewing in the parking lot," he tells me. "Tom asks that you ease things up, Sparo. The testosterone runneth over."

I feel terrible about contributing to any issue the bouncers are having. Tom's never interfered with a set before. Violence on any night is bad, but on all-ages night, with the place packed with teenagers, a fight would be disastrous.

I bite my lip and switch up the tracks on the fly. Next up will be a chilled-out remix of a Lana Del Rey tune. A tricky little transition takes the beat from hard and driving to slower and melodic.

The song is in line with Sparo's usual vibe, but the abrupt shift in tone seems to throw the energy off even more. No one is moving, except toward the walls. I watch from behind my tinted glasses. The reason for the sudden shift becomes clear, and it's not the music I'm playing. A young man is acting strangely. He pulls at his hair, muttering to himself. The patrons have gone tense, on edge. They move away from the man like a school of fish, instinctively sensing that he is volatile.

He makes his way toward my booth, cutting a meandering, weaving path through the parting crowd. My pulse spikes. This has never happened before. *Where the hell is Tom?*

All at once, the double doors burst open, and a knot of men explodes through. Tom and his fellow bouncer, Justin, are hard at work, trying to break up the fight, but there are more fighters than peacekeepers.

Lacey is on her feet, hand curled around Deno's forearm. He sends me a sharp look and slashes his hand in front of his throat: *cut the set.* I couldn't agree more. With a flick of a few controls, the music abruptly shuts off, throwing The Strip Mall into silence. Artie hits the houselights, and the room goes white and bright.

"Show's over, folks," I say. "Time for everyone to just chill."

But the tussle is still raging by the door, and that muttering guy is now right in front of the booth. I rear back as he flattens his hands on the mixers and leans forward.

"It's coming," the guy rasps out. His eyes are wide and wild, the whites livid red. "Demons. Coming for all of us. A great wave will swallow us whole. You'll see!"

Deno shoves Lacey and me behind him and leans over the mixers toward the guy. Despite the fussy hair and glasses, Deno is quite a force when physically threatened. He stands over six feet tall, and despite never working out (that I know of), he's a muscular dude. "Get lost," Deno snarls.

I can't drag my gaze away from the advancing guy's eyes, though. They're vacant, lost to some unreachable place. On the side of his neck is a red welt that looks as if it's been scratched at. It *could* be a beekeeper's sting, but I've never seen anything like it—red, but with strange white striations radiating out from the center.

Then the guy's countenance changes completely at Deno's order. His face twists in rage, and he swipes at Deno. "Did you hear me? We're going to *die*. You, me, your girls there." A demented smile spreads across his lips, which he licks. "*Crack your bones and eat the marrow, snap your spines like broken arrows,*" he sings, and I'm sure I've never heard anything more disturbing in my life.

Even Deno looks unsure of what to do—he doesn't want to be bitten by this guy. Luckily, Tom appears behind the man. He plucks up the raving guy and pins him to the floor where he can restrain him. Tom looks up, sweaty, with a fattening lip, and shrugs. "I better get a raise after tonight."

"I'm so sorry," I say. "I had no idea—"

"It wasn't you." Tom glances around with a grimace. "Something's just...wrong these days. Been like this every night for the past four I've worked." He rubs a hand over his jaw thoughtfully, and I'm amazed at how composed he is, after just breaking up a six-man bar fight. "Telling you—it's because our water comes from that lake right next to the old mines. Not good, with all those heavy metals floating about. What are they—arsenic? Mercury? Makes people not right in the head."

I hadn't heard of either of those things making people act like this. Deathly ill, yes. But I don't need to be a doctor to know the water didn't cause this. Suddenly, the danger Rafette poses to the community feels horribly real. *Anyone* could be stung. Anyone could be infected with this poison and turned into a dangerous, paranoid person. Even someone I love. "Thank you, Tom."

The police have arrived. I can't run away from this one, though. Deno's phone vibrates. He looks at the screen and turns to Lacey and me. "Let's pack up and get out of here. Mel's closing The Strip Mall for a couple of weeks."

"*Weeks?*" Lacey asks.

Deno nods. "Seems Tom isn't the only one who thinks something bad is going on in Cadence." He shrugs. "Maybe there *is* something in the water."

14 the house next door

School is canceled Monday. It snowed a few inches last night before turning to rain. Then the whole thing froze solid and turned the outside world slippery and crystalline.

So, no bus stop. No Reece. Probably a good thing, since I'm still trying to work my head around harbingers of death and Beekeepers. Magic and reality. A hot boy who thinks I'm "adorable" and a possible impending apocalypse.

I sigh over my breakfast choices, longing for Lucky Charms or something equally sugary and brightly colored. The decision goes on hold as my dad flies into the room, iPad in hand. He thrusts the thing at me. "Read this. I think the woman in the article is our neighbor."

Oh boy. My gaze falls to the news article that got Dad all worked up.

Deadly Crash Kills Three

By Kali Blake, *Staff Writer*

A four-car pileup in Windsor County has left three dead and five injured. Two of the injured were brought to Fisher Memorial

Hospital and are expected to recover. High speed and ice appear to have been factors.

Crash survivor Lucia Fernandez, who was the sole occupant of her vehicle, told The Star Press *that avoiding the jackknifed tractor trailer was not an option. "There was no escaping it," said Fernandez, a forty-four-year-old resident of Cadence, who sustained a broken arm...*

I look up at my dad. *Keep calm.* "This Lucia Fernandez is the lady next door?"

"It could be." Dad perches on the stool next to me. "That's about her age. I don't see their vehicle in the driveway."

My stomach bottoms out as cold sweat covers my suddenly shivering skin. *The sole occupant.* So no one else was with her. Those sweet little kids, Paxton and Fiona, weren't hurt. *God*, Reece wasn't hurt, but he could have been. He told me once that death is never far behind him. He was not just being dramatic—he meant it, literally.

Dad pulls back the iPad with a determined look. "I've been meaning to go over and introduce myself in person. We've spoken on the phone, but this may be a good time to see if they need anything." He glances at the clock. "It's nearly ten a.m. Not too early to stop by, right?"

My gaze falls to the other headlines on the screen. My heart jumps into my throat at the headlines alone:

Two Dead in Unprovoked Attack

Kent Taylor, forty-seven, a Cadence resident, attacked Mike Miller, the attendant at Cory's Cleaners last night in Somerset. Police shot and killed Taylor after he attacked two officers, and Miller died while en route to the hospital. Taylor, a member of the school board and respected businessman, showed no previous signs of psychosis, and witnesses say the attack on Miller was completely unprovoked...

Police Called to Popular Area Nightclub

Police were called when a six-person fight broke out at The Strip Mall, an area nightclub popular with all ages. Another man, Andrew Pence, was taken to Somerset General Hospital after suffering a psychotic break and instigating the fight…

Good thing my father didn't finish reading the news. I'd be facing a hundred questions right now. And banned for life from The Strip Mall.

"You're right. We should go over there." The words rush out, a little too fast.

Dad stares at me in surprise, then nods. "Yeah. Okay. Let me get dressed and…" He narrows an eye. "By the way, is anything going on between you and that Reece kid?"

Whoa. I freeze in the act of closing the web browser. "Going on how?"

"Don't even start," he says mildly, brushing crumbs off his shirt. "You know what 'going on' means."

I grin, because he looks so *darn* uncomfortable. "The other night you seemed pleased that a boy came calling."

"The other night you didn't seem so eager." A flush creeps up his neck. "I'm not trying to be nosy. I just— I'm your father," he says, because that explains it all.

"He's a neighbor. Maybe a friend," I say. "I don't know yet."

It's all I've got. I don't know what's "going on" with Reece. And I won't until he tells me the truth about himself.

"Okay." Dad's shoulders relax. "I'll go get ready. You put some boots on—real ones. Not those things you wear to school."

Right. Real boots. He means the sassy, zip-back number he bought me for Christmas last year. They're white with pompons, but I'll wear them.

I reopen the iPad's browser and scroll through the local news. The headlines alone make my skin crawl. Violent incidents are increasing in Somerset County, with Cadence appearing to be at the epicenter. The county jail is extraordinarily busy. So are all the area hospitals' psychiatric units. Ordinary, everyday people are having full-blown psychotic episodes. There is a petition going around to have the drinking water tested again. The whole county gets water from Lake Serenity, which used to be a river that ran through the valley. It was dammed and a hydroelectric plant put in, but it borders Mount Serenity. Tom isn't the only one worried that waste from the past mining activities may have contaminated the water.

Test away. The water's not causing it.

Tucked very tiny, at the very bottom, in the "Our Environment" section, is an article on how the bee population seems to have come out of hibernation early this year. It's one paragraph. No comments at the bottom. I doubt anyone has even read it.

But there it is. The bees. *That's* causing it, and no one would believe me if I told them. Not my dad. No one.

We walk through the ice-encrusted snow, which breaks like thin glass under our feet. I wear the white boots. And the matching down ski jacket. Had to pull the tags off the jacket, but I must admit, it's warm. My dad looks like a Macy's ad in his black double-breasted cashmere coat, leather gloves, and Burberry scarf. So refined. In contrast, my mother was all long, wild hair with wilder eyes. Cigarettes and tattoos. Dad catches my expression and raises his brows.

"What?" he asks.

"I just don't see it—you and Mom, that is." I gulp down cold air. "You're like, different species."

Dad tries to hide a smile. "Your mom and I met at a Lollapalooza concert. She was sitting up on some guy's shoulders, arms in the air, blond hair everywhere. She was *so* beautiful. I was living on a friend's front porch at the time. Unemployed, with a few bad habits I will never discuss with you." He raises an eyebrow. "So you see, I wasn't always so respectable. I caused Grams and Grampa many sleepless nights."

I can't imagine him that way *at all*. "So what happened?"

He smiles, full and wide. "You."

"*Me?*"

"Yes, thankfully. And the realization that sleeping on Egyptian cotton was preferable to my buddy's nasty couch."

My tongue is heavy in my mouth. "But you lost her. She couldn't do"—I sweep my hand back toward our house—"this."

Dad lifts up a pine branch for me as we pass from our lawn into the wooded buffer between our property and the neighbors'. "Your mom was a true free spirit. Too trusting. Selfish. Unstable. But not…destructive. That came later. I've spent too many nights wondering why we were always on again, off again and why she took that bad turn after you were born. It crept up on me, on her, and nothing could fix her. The drugs were more than an addiction. There was no way to separate her from them." He spreads his hands, drops them. "The truth is I didn't lose her. I never had her." There is no sadness or reproach in his voice. Just fact.

The words bump through me, scraping raw spots, touching secret, hidden bruises. "I never had her, either."

Dad puts an arm around my shoulders. "You have me."

I shove my hands under my armpits and force a grin. "Grams and Grampa are proud of you now."

His brows go up. "They said that?"

"No," I admit. "But they did say your car was pretentious."

"Hmm." He scratches his chin. "That's progress. Maybe I should trade it in for a new model. A red convertible."

"Grams would *die*," I say with a giggle. We cross onto the Fernandez's property laughing, but immediately sober as we step onto the wide driveway. No one has been outside yet today. The untouched snow glistens like a sheet of diamonds. My gaze catches on the unused doghouse in the backyard. Two crows perch on the peak, watching us in silence.

"Been seeing more crows around lately," he says. "This must be part of their migration or something."

Or something. I give the crows a knowing look before we slog up the steps to the front door. They are *not* just birds, but he wouldn't believe that, either.

Dad glances down with a grimace. "I should have brought the snow shovel. Could have at least dug out their steps for them."

I roll my eyes. "A teenage boy lives here who's perfectly capable of such manual work."

The door opens at the first knock. The woman answering the door is so beautiful, so vibrant, Dad and I both back up a step. Her black hair flows in loose waves past her shoulders. Her figure is a curvy hourglass, and her smooth skin fairly glows. All I can think is, *wow*. I want to look like this when I'm, you know, old.

Dad's recovery is decent. After an initial fumble, he yanks off his glove and extends his hand. "Good morning. I'm Bradley Dovage, your next-door neighbor. We spoke on the phone. Once. About snow removal. And this is my daughter, Angelina."

Angelina? I don't think he's used my full name since telling the doctor to put it on my birth certificate. He must be nervous.

The woman smiles. One of her arms is in a sling, but she shakes his hand with the other. My poor dad's Adam's apple rocks up and down.

"Ah, it's a pleasure to meet you at last." Her lovely accent has an immediate effect on my father, who starts fidgeting with the fringe on his scarf. "I'm Lucia Fernandez, but please call me Lucy. Come in, come in. You're just in time for breakfast."

"Breakfast?" My dad's eyes go wide. "Oh no. We couldn't. We just stopped by because we heard about the accident and—"

Lucy smiles sadly. "My arm will heal, as arms do. I am blessed beyond words to be alive. Others in that accident were not so fortunate." Her mouth turns down at the corners, before she opens the door wider and steps inside. "Today, we celebrate life. It's easy to forget how precious it is. Come, come inside. My Brooke makes the best pancakes you will ever eat. And enough to feed an army." You cannot refuse that kind of invitation. A *celebration of life* makes polite retreat impossible.

My dad is no match for this woman. He goes right in like a corralled cow, but I'm not so easily herded. And I'm suddenly not so eager. Reece said it himself: death follows these people, and it's soaked in the bones of this house. My mind draws up the images released to the media of blood-spattered floors and smeared handprints scrabbling for doorknobs. A crow on the roof above me lets out a noisy *kraa*. A wave of dizziness washes over me. My dad shoots me a pointed *get in here* look, so I drag myself inside.

Lucy studies me with interest and knowledge. "Angelina—or do you prefer Angie? We have heard so much about you." Her gaze lingers, assesses. I can't imagine what Reece told her about me. Maybe she knows that I know they're not quite what they seem.

"Nice to meet you, Mrs. Fernandez," I say. "I do prefer Angie."

Her smile is warm, lacking even the slightest threat or warning. "And I *do* prefer Lucy. Now, come inside. Before breakfast gets cold."

These people are not entirely human. I must try to remember this, even though standing in this house, hearing the sounds of a typical family, the thought is surreal. It's difficult to feel menaced here. One look around and my nerves ease. What did I expect? A moldering house with peeling paint and graffitied walls? Not a chance. The sounds of living people pour through the walls. The smell of fresh paint mingles with coffee, maple syrup, and hot butter wafting from the kitchen. The two young children I met with Roger race past. Their footsteps pound down the hallway, until they spot us and stop abruptly.

"I believe you've met Fiona and Paxton, Angie, but Mr. Dovage has not," Lucy says. "How do we greet guests?"

The children blink up at us, gap-toothed and flush with energy. Paxton nods his regal little head. "Hello, Mr. Dovage. It's nice to see you again, Angie."

Fiona looks around me, mouth turned down in disappointment. "You didn't bring Roger?"

I grin at her. "No, but I'll let him know you missed him."

She nods, serious and satisfied. "Okay, but bring him next time, okay?"

"What did we say about manners, Fiona?" Lucy asks.

"Oh, sorry." The girl rolls her eyes theatrically. "*Please* bring Roger."

I grin at her. "It's a deal."

She leans toward me, conspiratorially. "Reece *still* talks about you, you know. *All* the time."

My face heats with the mother of all blushes. Dad gives me a raised-brow look that says, *are you* sure *there's nothing going on?* "Oh, well." I fumble for words. "We go to school together."

Fiona rolls her eyes again, and the two children run off.

Lucy looks after them fondly. "My late husband and I have five. All adopted." She takes our coats and hangs them on hooks next to the front door. Then, her gaze moves to the staircase behind us. "Ah. Here comes another one. Good morning, sleepyhead."

I turn around, and my breath catches. Reece halts midway down the stairs. Loose gray sweatpants hang perilously low on his hips. And I'm pretty sure that's *all* he's wearing.

He rubs his puffy eyes and squints. "Oh."

I'm staring. My throat is suddenly bone dry and I'm *staring*. There is no looking away from him. Reece Fernandez shirtless is making me rethink the merits of hockey players. He's hiding a ripped bod under all those layered shirts. Dad and Lucy are probably aware of my staring, but I can't summon the will to care.

Reece stares right back at me in a bleary, *are-you-really-here?* sort of way.

Lucy clucks her tongue. "Reece, for Pete's sake, say hello to our guests."

"Oh. Um, good morning, Mr. Dovage, Angie." His voice is still sleep-roughened and absurdly cute. He scratches his head, where the hair is flat on one side and sticking up on the other.

"Well done," Lucy says drily. "Now kindly take yourself back upstairs and put on some clothes."

Really not necessary on my account, but my dad is twitching. As if I've never seen a shirtless boy before. In case my dad's spidey-sense is going haywire, I do the polite thing and drag my gaze to the floor until Reece's retreating footsteps sound on the stairs.

Lucy leads us to the kitchen, where the smells are mouthwatering. It's organized chaos in here, noisy with laughter and argument, joy and conflict. A toddler introduced as James sits in a booster seat wearing a large plastic bib. An older woman, Aunt Jean, wipes a wet cloth over his food-smeared face and tells the two kids, Fiona and Paxton, to sit on their backsides, not on their feet. They do as they're told without pausing a heated debate over whether elephants peel bananas or eat them whole. Or eat them at all.

A young woman, Brooke, stands at the stove. She looks older than me—maybe college-aged. I am completely envious of the funky space-print apron she's wearing. My dad eyes the ingredients set out on the counter—*all* the forbidden foods—and winces but says nothing.

Lucy nudges us into seats and sets plates full of pancakes in front of us. They're made with buttermilk, I'm sure of it, and is that actual *butter* melting on top of them? With more on the table to smear on top. I check myself from devouring them like an animal. *Use the fork!* My dad looks conflicted for a few seconds, but he, too, picks up his fork and digs in. Smart of him. He'd sound like an ass trying to explain his dairy boycott to these sensible people.

I close my eyes and savor a bite of pancake. *Oh,* yum.

There's a shadow and a little breeze to my right, and I open my eyes as Reece drops into the seat next to me. He's still wearing the sweatpants, but his hair is smoothed down, and a wrinkled blue T-shirt covers his torso. I'm left to speculate about the underwear as I chew a blissful bite.

Brooke brings him a full plate and tousles his hair. "Morning, asshole."

"Thanks." He turns the grin to me and hooks a thumb over his shoulder. "She makes *amazing* pancakes."

"Yes, she does," I agree fervently. "They're the best *ever.*"

Dad frowns. "*I* make good pancakes."

I give him a level look. "Sorry, Dad. You make them with whole wheat flour. And no milk or butter."

My dad straightens and prepares to launch into his healthy-body speech, but Lucy sits down next to him, and he thinks better of it.

Reece leans toward me. His breath brushes my cheek, and I forget to chew.

"No milk *or* butter?" he asks.

"No dairy in any form." I lower my voice to a whisper. "He thinks dairy impedes the body's immune system and causes inflammation."

"Inflammation of what?"

I let out a chuckle. "I don't want to know."

He smiles back, and his eyes go warm and heavy. They're still a little sleep-puffed and there's an intimacy in seeing him like this, freshly woken, carrying the smells of fabric softener and toothpaste. His arm skims mine. *Zing!* What *is* it about this guy that obliterates every coherent thought in my head?

Thankfully, my incoherence is brief. The heavy cloud of Reece's secret is always there, scratching around in the dark corners of my mind. I wish we could just be friends like normal people. But Reece isn't normal. I'm beginning to think I'm not, either.

James smiles and points a sticky finger toward me. Reece's black eyes flicker to Brooke, who sits across the table with her own plate of pancakes. They exchange a look I can't interpret, but as I glance from one to the other, then to the other Fernandezes, I notice something that raises the hair on the back of my neck.

All these people—*every single one of them*—have the same black eyes, even though none of them are related by blood. The curse that makes them harbingers of death must affect them all the same way.

"Are you finished?" Reece asks me.

I jolt at his voice, but nod. Reece rises and puts our plates in the sink.

"I'd like to give Angie a tour of the house, if that's okay." He directs his words to my father, which is smart of him, but everyone pauses and stares at us. Even the toddler quietly watches with strange, thoughtful eyes. Too intense for a person that young. Too *aware*.

Reece offers a crooked smile and a shrug. "She must have some bad thoughts about what happened here with the previous owners. I thought she'd like to see how changed it is."

I hold my breath as Dad gives Reece a very *dad* look. My father is not used to dealing with me, dealing with boys. He's never considered Deno anything to be concerned with, but Reece is not a boy to be dismissed. Dad takes his time before nodding. "Sure. Of course." He gives me a meaningful look. "Don't get lost."

"I won't." I rise with a little too much bounce, so eager to get out of this room. Away from that toddler with the too-intelligent eyes.

The moment we're away from the kitchen, Reece's hand wraps around mine. His fingers are warm and strong. My mouth goes dry as dust.

He tugs me forward. "I'm showing you my room first." He grins at my instant hesitancy. "Not scared, are you?"

15

the rabbit hole

My dad would not be thrilled with this turn of events. Reece leads me to the stairs and straight up. My pulse pounds, my palms are clammy, but I go with him.

Because I am curious, and attracted, and excited. And a little scared.

I'm in the rabbit hole. I want to know where it leads.

He pulls me into his room and shuts the door behind us. All of a sudden, my back is against the door, and Reece is right in front of me. If I inhale deeply, my chest will touch his. Our fingers are still tangled. Our breathing is chaotic. I didn't expect this. I don't even know what *this* is.

I open my mouth to say something, but he closes the space between us and kisses me.

My legs are mush. My mind goes haywire, then blank, and I'm kissing him back as if the world is coming to an end. Who knows? Maybe it is.

He threads his fingers into my hair and we break apart, breathless. "I wanted to do that last night." His voice is soft against my cheek.

Smiling, I push him away. "That was really nice, but I don't kiss guys who won't tell me what planet they're from."

He braces his forearm on the door above my head, a cocky grin on his lips. "I told you before. I'm not an alien."

"Well, you sure as hell aren't human."

"Yeah, I am…sort of."

My fingers splay on his chest. His heart pumps wildly beneath my hands. I can't take my gaze away from his lips, which are still flushed from our kiss. I can feel the tension in him. How much he wants to kiss me again. I want it, too, but I need know a little more about what I'm kissing. He didn't completely contradict me when I said he wasn't human. "Sort of" doesn't count.

With regret, I remove my hands from his chest, letting them slide over his abdomen a little and enjoying his shudder in response. "Reece," I say. "Is that Beekeeper—Rafette—stinging people in town, making them violent? There was an incident at The Strip Mall last night, and I read there was a murder at that dry cleaners. Did he—"

"Yes." Reece drops his voice. "It's what he does. He stings."

"And the man who lived in this house before you guys—Mr. Ortley. He murdered his family and killed himself. Was that also a Beekeeper sting?"

His eyes flicker. "We did a little investigating. Ortley was in Miami right before Hurricane Viola hit. He likely got stung, boarded a plane, returned home and…" Reece sighs. "It's the way it goes sometimes. We get great real estate deals on houses the Beekeepers have broken."

I jerk back. "That's *horrible*."

"Oh, I'm well aware of that, but we've lived this way for a long time. Eventually, tragedy loses some of its impact on you. It has to, or you lose your sanity." He steps away and rakes both hands through his hair. "Look, my family and I talked. We decided that you should know the truth. You're too close to this in more ways than you realize."

"You needed permission?"

He shrugs off my skeptical look. "When you're in a group like mine, decisions like this impact everyone. So I *wanted* permission. It would be hugely disrespectful if I hadn't discussed it with them." He glances at the door. "There's not enough time right now. Your dad is probably freaking out as it is. What are you doing tonight?"

"I… Nothing. Why? Do you want to go somewhere?"

"Yeah," he says. "I want to come over."

My heart bumps hard in my chest. "I don't really think my dad will go for that."

"He lets that Deno guy come over."

I roll my eyes. "Deno is different."

"How?"

"We've been friends for five years. He knows there's nothing going on between us."

Reece raises a brow, but I wave my hand before he starts asking more questions about Deno. I would rather not reveal too much about the dynamics of that friendship.

"The problem is, I think my dad knows that I-I…" I swallow the burn of nerves in my throat. "I think he knows I like you. He'll keep tabs on us, and I doubt this is a conversation he should overhear."

"It's definitely not," he says, then pauses. "Okay, what time does your dad go to bed?"

"Around ten, most nights."

He nods. "Leave your basement door unlocked. That's where your music studio is, right?"

"Yeah. Hey, how do you where my studio is?"

He rolls his eyes. "Well, I know it isn't in your garage. And anyone can see the basement light on at night when the rest of your house is dark." He grins and releases my hand, opening the door behind me. "Is ten thirty too late for you?"

"No, but— "

He presses his lips to my forehead and gently pushes me out of his room. "Look annoyed and tell your dad I got a phone call. It may lessen his worry that I'm attracted to his daughter."

My brows pop up. "You're *attracted* to me?"

"Very." His hand curls around the back of my neck, and he pulls me into a quick, hard kiss that leaves me breathless. "See you tonight."

He steps back, and the door closes gently, but firmly, in my face.

Well, *wow*. A pleasant warmth uncurls in my belly and sends a current straight down to my toes. I stand there for a moment, heart beating like a drum, staring at his door. Resisting the near-crushing urge to open it again.

I'm in trouble. No question. That rabbit hole is looking way too appealing for my own good. And ten thirty is twelve long hours away.

16

a boy in the basement

For the first time I can remember, the basement is not my solace. The fluorescent lights are buzzier, the drop ceiling lower. My music equipment sits there, silent and untouched. The fact that my dad is still up does not soothe my nerves. Of course, tonight *would* be the night he stays up late.

It's 10:26 p.m. Reece should be sneaking into the basement in four minutes.

My knee won't stop jiggling. I press a hand to my stomach, but there's no calming the jittering mess. I'm nervous. For so many reasons.

Roger always comes down with me when I'm in my studio, so I couldn't shoo him off. He's sprawled in his usual spot on the floor, but he'll react to Reece's arrival. The question is, how loudly? He *does* bark.

I lift my acoustic guitar from its stand and pluck out a random melody. I don't even know what I'm playing. It's just noise. I can barely hear it over my pounding heartbeat.

10:32 p.m.

He's going to stand me up. I know it.

I strum my guitar pick over a flat chord. *God*, this was a bad idea.

Then the doorknob turns. The door opens.

My breath catches as a tousled chestnut head pokes in. He looks at me from beneath raised, inquiring eyebrows. I wave him in and the guitar pick slips from my fingers, clatters through the sound hole and into the hollow body of the guitar. *Very smooth.*

Roger's head comes up. He cocks it as Reece gingerly clicks shut the door behind him. The dog gets up, stretches, and comes forward, nose out and tail wagging.

Reece flashes me a quick smile and greets Roger, who flops down and rolls to his back. My dog is clearly infatuated. I may not be far behind.

"It took me six months for him to greet me like that," I say.

Reece pulls off his gloves and scratches behind the dog's ears. "Well, he was sad."

I cock my head. "This again? How did you know the emotional state of my dog?"

"I just do," he replies. "There's a certain scent when someone or something is full of grief. Dogs feel it, too. Roger knew something terrible happened to his owners."

Did I hear that right? "He *smells* sad?"

"You asked." Reece releases Roger and stands before me, arms folded, eyes full of question and challenge. "Are you sure you want to hear what I've come here to tell you?"

I abandon the pick and put the guitar back on its stand. "Yes. I need to know."

"You say that now..." He tilts his head toward the ceiling and the faint jingle of the TV. "Your dad is still up?"

"He won't come down here." *I hope.* "I blame your mom for his wakefulness. She left him completely spellbound."

He offers a crooked smile. "She has that effect."

"My dad ate butter for her. I'm afraid he's smitten." I gnaw on my lip. "I um, had a nice time, too."

"I hope I didn't scare you."

"You scared me long before this morning."

"That was not ever my intention."

He shrugs off his coat, and we stand there for a moment in awkward silence. I'm out of smart comments and so is he, it seems. He shifts on his feet. Maybe he's second-guessing his decision to come here. It's strange to see him appear unsure of himself. He circles away from me. The distance doesn't feel like rejection, but rather like protection. For him or me, I can't be sure.

I lick my suddenly dry lips. "So, what's with the crows?" Not graceful of me, but it gets the job done.

Reece sits cross-legged across from me on the floor. Roger rests his blocky yellow head on Reece's leg. "The crows are my family," he says, running long, idle fingers over the dog's fur. "Part of it, anyway. You met the ones in human form this morning."

"So...you're a crow?"

He flashes a crooked grin. "Not at the moment, obviously."

I breathe deep and dig deep for patience. "Reece, are you telling me you...transform into a crow?"

"That's exactly what I'm saying." He spreads his hand. "Angie, I'm a harbinger of death. My family and I travel our territory as a murder of crows. When we scent out a place where disaster is soon to hit, some of us change into human form and...wait."

"Wait for what?" I prompt. "People to die?"

"We feed on the energy people give off when they die. That's why we're here in Cadence. That's why I was at that car crash you saw and Lucia was at the one yesterday," he says. "We don't make anyone die, but we do need death to live. Our bodies absorb death energy like a recharge, but it works best if we're in human form." He shakes his head and damp, wavy hair falls into his eyes. "It sounds horrible, I know. I can't imagine what you..."

Recharge. "So you...put yourself near dying people to sustain yourself?"

He looks up and holds my gaze. "Angie, this is not a lifestyle choice. It's a biological need. I can't *not* do this. You asked me what I was, and I'm telling you." A blotchy flush creeps up his neck. He splays his hands. The scars on his palm stand out in sharp relief. "These scars appeared the day I awoke with the curse. They are always there. I didn't *choose* this."

I take a long, deep breath. "Are you like a-a vampire?"

He snorts out a laugh. "No. I don't stay young forever. I can die as easily as you. I have no superpowers and, despite how often I must see it, I do *not* enjoy the sight of blood."

"It didn't look that way the other night."

Pain slides over his features, making him look older, weary. "It's survival. And living like this is not pleasant. We have an extra sense that foretells where death is coming and we go there to meet it. We're always moving to the next disaster or massacre or whatever. And we die a lot. *That's* not fun at all."

My mouth goes dry. "So after whatever terrible thing happens in Cadence is over, you'll just leave, if you...survive it?"

He nods. "We'll turn back into crows and seek out the next marked town or street or building." He pauses, shrugs. "Of course, some of us in human form *will* possibly die. When our human form dies, we sort of...respawn as a crow, and we stay that way for a while. The time frame varies—sometimes a week, sometimes a year—before we can change back to human form. But when we regain human form, we're at a younger age. James, Fiona, and Paxton all died in a fire we were at last year.

They just regained their human forms a few months ago. James came back unusually young, which is inconvenient for all of us. We have to grow up from childhood over and over again. It's pretty awful." He notices my slightly gaping mouth and cocks his head. "What? You're the one with all the questions. I'm just obliging the lady."

"*Obliging the lady?*" I raise my brows. "What century *are* you from?"

"That term isn't *that* old." He frowns at the floor. "Or maybe it is. It's not easy, keeping current on everything. The decades sort of, well, blend."

He sounds impossibly old now, contemplating the passage of time. For the first time, I get a sense of all he's seen, all he's experienced, much of it through the eyes of a child. "That toddler, James?" I ask. "Is it typical to come back that young?"

Reece shakes his head. "Nah, we usually don't come back *that* young. James has been a harbinger for the longest of us—almost five hundred years. That could have something to do with it." He looks at me intently, as if searching for something. "Last time I died, I returned as a six-year-old."

My poor spinning head. The worst part is, the thing that's sticking pins in my heart is that he'll be *leaving*. I should be focused on the dying part. I should be much more interested in the disaster that's soon to hit Cadence. But no, I'm worried about a broken heart. So selfish.

So much like my mother.

I shiver at the thought. Can't go there. Not now.

Reece leans forward, reaches for me, then drops his hand. "I'd give anything to be a normal boy. To stay. Go to prom with you. But even one of the reasons why I'm drawn to you is because I'm attracted to death."

My skin chills. "What do you mean?"

He pauses with a resigned sigh. "Death, tragedy, has a

certain vibe to it. It makes people uneasy. It's why no one wanted to live in the Ortleys' house, but it's exactly why we feel so comfortable there. Death has a distinct...aroma to a harbinger of death. To us, death is life. In the same way, you wear the misery and tragedy of your past like a second skin. Suffering has a very strong...scent."

I jerk back. "I *smell*?"

"Yes, but in a good way." His eyes widen. "Don't worry."

I don't see how that's possible. "What does it smell like?" Good grief, why am I asking this?

He pauses. "I really can't describe it."

"You mean it's so bad you don't want to."

"No!" He reaches toward me when I cover my mouth, then drops his hand. "As I said before, it drew me to you. But it's only one reason."

The first prick of tears burns my eyes. *No! I will not cry!* "So, you want to be around me because I'm...*miserable?*"

"You're not miserable," he says quietly, urgently. "There's a difference between enduring hardship and absorbing it. You've endured. You experienced more sadness and pain as a child than most people do in their whole lives. The odds you've beaten are astronomical. You have no idea how strong you are." He smiles, faintly. "Maybe someday you will, and you won't hide your greatest talent behind a disguise."

I shrink back, away from him. From *this*. I don't want insights into my soul. It's intrusive, poking dangerously close to wounds that don't heal, reminding me of aches I've lived with for so long, they are my state of normal. I don't want to remember them. *Ever*.

My shoulders jerk in an awkward shrug. "I have to admit, it's a lot to take in." My voice is forced air, higher and lighter than this conversation deserves.

I tuck my hands under my legs. They're shaking, and I

don't want him to see. If not for my experiences in the past few weeks, I would be suggesting he find a psychotherapist with a thick prescription pad.

But the things I saw were real. And Reece is deadly serious about them.

"How did you become this way?" I ask in a whisper.

Reece's eyes darken and turn unreadable. "I don't want to say, considering your feelings regarding magic."

"Sorry. Mystical stuff was my mom's thing. She made money reading palms and tarot cards and auras. She used to say we were always safe because she could see the people who were truly dangerous and avoid them." I let out a breath. "Honestly, I don't know what I believe anymore."

"Was she right?" he asks urgently. "Were her readings accurate?"

"I don't know," I admit. "I never paid attention. Her clients seemed happy enough. They *paid* her." Not that she spent the money well.

He shrugs. "True psychics are rare. They're the descendants of magicians. Maybe your mom had a touch of magic as well."

"Then she may have been better at predicting her own death."

Reece rolls his shoulders in a leisurely shrug. "Death doesn't require a prediction. It's an inevitability."

"Not for you," I say.

"Not so. I've died many times." He lets out a resigned sigh. "It just doesn't stick."

"How long have you been a harbinger of death?" This question sounds surreal coming out of my mouth, like I'm reading lines from a movie script. "You weren't born this way."

He pulls in a breath and drags a hand through his hair. "No, I was born a normal person, just like you. I've been a harbinger of death for almost two hundred years."

Two hundred years! I must remember that he hasn't always been eighteen, otherwise this would feel weird. Well, weirder than it already is. Having the hots for a harbinger of death does *not* qualify as normal. But Reece grew up, lost baby teeth, learned to read and write, went through adolescence, just like I did. Only, he did it a bunch of times, and I've done it once. It's like he was reincarnated but remembers all his past lives. That does not sound appealing. "So can you ever *really* die?"

"Eventually, most of us unravel from experiencing so much tragedy, pain. When one of us gets to the point when their mental state threatens the whole group, everyone gets together and-and…" He swallows with a grimace. "Look, we congregate in crow form and peck them to death, okay? It's called the *mortouri*, and it's the only way for one of us to actually die. It's not pretty, everyone hates doing it, and all it does is release the magic so it can possess some other poor person. *The curse* doesn't go away. So you've got to be pretty far gone in order for that to happen," he says defensively. "We do it, though. Comes a day when you just can't live like this anymore. You just can't stand to look at one more dead body. Your mind breaks."

I stare at him, fully aware that my mouth is hanging open. Nothing I can do about that. "I'm sorry, I just can't imagine you *pecking* someone to death."

"Trust me, it's a blessing to the peck-ee," he says. "I've participated in only one execution, and I didn't contribute much." He rubs his palms over his face with a light groan. "Not that it matters. *Ugh.* I don't want to know what you think of me right now."

"All this makes me think of fourteen-sided dice and magical dragons."

"You mean twenty-sided. There are no fourteen-sided dice." He raises his brows. "Don't give me that look. I've gone through puberty nine times. Maybe ten. I can't remember."

Nine times? I wince. Once is enough, thank you. "Okay, Mister Know-it-all." I give him a look anyway. "So can't someone undo this…what, curse? Can't it be broken?" It's getting easier to say the words "magic" and "curse" without cringing.

He shakes his head. "The way to dispel the harbinger magic was lost when magic was systematically obliterated prior to this age. Long before the harbinger curse found me. However, traces of that magic escaped the extermination. Us. The Beekeepers. Other beings that are very good at staying hidden. Dark, terrible creatures that can create evil and corruption with a single touch. These things exist but go unnoticed by most modern people." He cocks his head at me. "You noticed, though. Most don't see the Beekeepers for what they are. Yet you did."

Lucky me. "Why? Are there more of them out there besides Rafette?"

"There are. They don't work together like harbingers. Each Beekeeper is its own swarm. I think there're two more in the area, but they likely won't interfere with Rafette." He studies me. "As for the 'why,' maybe there's a remnant of magic flowing through you—like your mother—that allows you to see what most can't." He shrugs. "Like I said, there is still magic out there, hidden. Waiting."

I suppress a chill. "So you aren't friends with the Beekeepers?"

"We don't exactly socialize with them, no," he says with a grimace. "They just follow us."

"Can you talk to them?"

He sighs. "We do, but we have no authority over them. They're stronger, faster than us. They aren't fans of harbingers, even though we are the ones who lead them to each marked place. Plus, to make it worse—" He shakes his head. It's a weary gesture, but I lean forward and touch his knee.

"No, go on," I say. "Finish your thought."

"There's word going around that if a Beekeeper could convince—or manipulate—a harbinger into accepting the Beekeeper's curse into himself, the Beekeeper would be released from his curse. As in, allowed to die."

I tap my fingertips to my lips. "So Rafette's increased stinging is his way of putting pressure on you, to get harbingers to take their curse? So they can be free? That doesn't make sense."

"No, he stings to generate chaos and fear, because Beekeepers consume that. We need death energy, but they need negative energy from the living," he says. "As for freeing himself from his curse, there's no proof of any curse being broken. It's a false rumor." He shakes his head. "I'm sorry. All this is hard to explain. It must be nearly impossible to understand."

"It is a lot to take in." I look up. "Am I ever going to see you turn into a crow?"

His eyes go wide. "No."

"Why not?"

He looks slightly ill. "It's not a pleasant thing to view or experience."

"But it must feel good to fly."

That gets a small, but brief, smile. "Oh, it does. But it's at such a cost."

My first thought is, I can't imagine how awful it must be to live in such conflict, but that's not true. "It's not exactly the same, but I know what it's like to need the thing you hate."

He looks up in surprise.

"My mom." I look down, pick at a ragged fingernail. "My childhood with her was pure misery. School was sporadic and we moved a lot. I was made fun of for reeking of smoke and wearing the same clothes every day. I hated the drugs, the constant moving, the weird men. You were right when you said I experienced sadness and pain. And death." A shudder trembles through me. I clench my teeth to keep them from chattering. This is so much emotion—so much stuff just tumbling out like an overpacked suitcase. Feelings crammed in boxes and stacked in the attic of my mind, falling over, spilling their contents. I've never known what to do with it all.

But this boy can't judge me. He's got boxes, too. Bigger, heavier, weirder ones. "My mom's one real boyfriend was nice to me—without, you know, being creepy about it. He probably saved my life by telling the police about me." I continue. "They came for me and were pulling me away from her. She was screaming and crying, and I clung to her like she was the best mother in the world. When they finally separated us, it hurt like my skin had been ripped away. She overdosed only a few weeks later." My breath comes in short, ragged breaths. I look up, meet his dark, liquid gaze. "Am I defective because I didn't want to leave her? That I hated the police who took me away from her?" I choke back a sob. "That sometimes, I miss her still?"

He's quiet for a moment, then a gentle smile softens his face. "You are the opposite of defective."

I screw up my face in disbelief. "Don't even think of telling me I'm perfect."

"Oh, you're totally not," he says with a grin. "But you see the good in people, even your mom. You forgave her, and you clearly love your dad. I just told you I consume the energy of dead people, and you haven't kicked me out. That makes you pretty amazing."

I have a snappy retort all queued up, but it fades away. "Thank you," I say, surprising both of us.

He tells me about his life—hurricanes, tornados, terrorist attacks. Mass shootings, ravaging fires. And then there were the wars… His harbinger family made the trip across the ocean to experience World War II. There was so much horror, the largest harbinger groups converged on either Japan or Europe and stayed there for about a decade.

I let out a shaky breath. "So what's the earliest thing you remember? You said you've been like this for two hundred years."

He shakes his head. "My first memory as a harbinger is the Civil War. You have to be dying at the same time a harbinger crow is executed or dies. The curse finds only the dying, and my memories before that are fuzzy. No one clearly remembers their real life after the change, but I looked myself up after the fact. I totally shouldn't have."

"Why?"

He grimaces. "Because I was hanged for stealing a horse."

"Oh." I let out a giggle, not that this is funny. At all. "You were a criminal."

"Apparently." A grin creeps around his mouth. "Are you going to judge me now?"

"I'd say you've served more than a fair sentence." I scoot a little closer. "So, are there any records of you in history? Could I look you up?"

"Not likely," he says with one eyebrow raised. "We change our names regularly. Lucia isn't really our 'mom.' Whoever happens to be of parental age gets to play that role, and we make sure we stick to our roles when outside people are around. It's very important that we can pass as a typical family. Sometimes, however, the family structure gets unconventional, when more than one of us are grown. Lucia is up as the parent this round so we've taken her last name. A few times we've taken my last name." His lips pull into a wide, devilish grin. "I'm not ready to tell you what that is."

"I thought we were done with secrets," I reply with a grin of my own.

"I have to maintain my air of mystery." He reaches out, tweaks a lock of my hair, before letting his fingers slide through the strands. My breath catches. "I wouldn't want to bore you," he murmurs.

"Sure," I say with an eye roll. "That's a valid concern. So can you tell me what's going to happen in Cadence? A raging wildfire? Nuclear war? Or is that another secret?"

He shakes his head. "Not a secret, just an unknown. We're drawn to a place where death is coming, but we never know *how* death will come."

"Maybe it was for a different reason," I say hopefully. "Maybe it has nothing to do with…with—"

"It *always* has to do with death."

"Oh." I swallow thickly. My words feel sluggish, as reluctant to come as I am to hear the answers. My whole life is here—everyone I care about. Just the thought of losing them makes my breath stop, my stomach knot. I wrap my arms around my middle and lean forward. "Do you know…*when?*"

His expression goes sympathetic, edged with frustration. He gets it, but he's as helpless to change anything as I am. *Knowing* can be a curse in itself when you can't stop something terrible from happening. "Can't be sure. My guess is, we have a few more weeks." He rolls his shoulders up and back, but the movement does not appear to relax him. "The scent will intensify and change. You need to be out of here before then."

"Ha. Yeah. I can see that conversation: 'Hey, Dad, the people next door are harbingers of death, and they say we're going to die if we stay in Cadence, so can we move out for a while?'" The thought is so ludicrous, I laugh. "Guess how that chat will end."

"That may not be the best approach," he says seriously. "But we'll have to think of something. You *need* to be out of here."

"And what will you do after the…bad thing happens?"

"The same thing we always do—we'll put our things in storage and leave. Start scenting out the next impending disaster." He looks up, eyes turbulent, anguished. A muscle flexes in his jaw. "I'm sorry, Angie. We have so little time."

His words squeeze my heart. I have so many more questions—loads of them, but they're suddenly not as important as this charged beat of quiet. Time holds still. Neither of us moves. Neither of us breathes. The air between us snaps, compresses, pulls us toward each other.

He moves forward on hands and knees at the same time I do. His hand slips around the back of my head, into my hair. He pulls me close as I reach for him. My hands land on his warm chest, curl against the rapid beat beneath.

Unlike our last kiss, I know this one's coming. I have a sudden, unbidden worry if I'm any good at this—kissing, that is—then his mouth is on mine and coherent thought blasts into a billion tiny pieces. Blood roars in my ears. A soft sound comes from one of us. It could be me. Right now, there is only *this kiss*. And, oh man, what a kiss it—

"Hey, Angie, just wanted to..." A familiar voice breaks in, then trails off in a quiet expletive.

Reece and I separate in a disoriented tumble. I goggle at my father, who stands open-mouthed in the door.

17

the ones you love...

My father's face is a mask of horrified bewilderment. "Say good night," he finishes in a strangled voice.

"Dad, I..." This is it—worst. Case. Scenario. "It's not... We were just—"

Dad's face floods with color. "*You.*" He aims a finger at Reece. "Go home. Now."

This looks bad. Hell, to my dad, this *is* bad. On the other hand, neither of us is terribly mussed. One less reason for my dad to have a coronary.

"Ah, yes sir, Mr. Dovage." Reece gets to his feet and gropes for his coat. He spreads his hands in a soothing manner, as is he's dealing with a feral dog. Or a lunatic. "I-I'm sorry you— I mean, I apologize for—"

Dad's eyes narrow to dangerous slits. It's so strange to see him like this. "I *will* hurt you, son."

Reece wisely ducks his head and shuts his mouth. He shoots me a sympathetic look and turns to the door. "Good night, Angie. Mr. Dovage."

Dad watches Reece leave in silence. He stares at the closed door for a moment. When he turns to me, it's not anger I see in his face.

My stomach flips over. I've hurt him.

"*Angie.*"

My shoulders drop. I'd prefer anger. "I'm sorry, Dad."

He sinks onto one of my music stools. "I don't understand. I've never told you not to date. In fact, I was beginning to worry a little that you *weren't* dating. I have no objection to that boy—at least I *didn't.*" He scowls at the door. "Why did you sneak around behind my back? Am I an ogre or something?"

My chest squeezes painfully. "Not at all. You're…" *the best father I could have.*

"You could have told me the truth." He sighs. "I wouldn't have forbidden you from seeing him."

"I know." It's hard to talk choked up like this. "I-I really am very sorry."

"Just…*why*, then?"

The full truth isn't an option. "Honestly, I-I wasn't expecting… We were just talking."

"You could have 'talked' on the sofa in the den."

No, we really couldn't have. If he had overheard even a snippet of our conversation, he *would* forbid me from seeing Reece—except maybe during visitation hours at the psychiatric ward.

I need things to be good between my dad and me. And I need him to forgive Reece and not do something catastrophic like ground me. I bite my lip and consider my options. The most surefire way to defuse this is to break out an excuse I haven't pulled on him in years—my mom.

I take a deep breath and gulp back the pinch of shame at what I'm going to say next. I'll atone later, with interest. "I don't know what I was thinking." I pitch my voice high. "Don't be mad at Reece, Dad. I invited him here, but I didn't know I *liked* him. And then I realized I did, but I thought about Mom and how she thought she was falling in love with every guy she met, and I just felt so *confused*." *Oh man, if there's a hell, I'm going straight to it.* And I would deserve every flame. "I mean, how do you know when you like someone or if it's *more* than like?"

Dad blinks at me with deer-in-headlights glaze. "Um."

"And I hurt you, and that *kills* me." These tears, words are real, and they are what melts his scowl. He comes forward and pulls me into a warm hug.

"Look, I get it. You're growing up. But…easy does it with the neighbor kid, okay? Slow down. You guys have plenty of time to figure things out."

I *so* wish that were true.

He sighs. "I love you, kiddo."

I rest my head against his shoulder. "I love you, too."

My eyes close, and we just sit like that for a while. When he says he loves me, he just says it. He doesn't follow up with, *I met this guy at a bar last night and, get your things! We're moving in with him today,* like my mom often did. It's good, living with my dad. He's steady. Safe. Inherently decent. He's probably better than I deserve.

"As for knowing when it's 'more than like'?" His words are hesitant, but there's a smile in his voice. "Trust me. You'll *know*."

18

a shift in the air

A drizzle falls from a leaden sky. It's mid-March. The day begins warmer than normal for southwestern Pennsylvania. It's raining, but that's not all. The air feels different. I am not a harbinger of death, but even I scent something is off.

Something is *changing*.

Much of the snow and ice melted overnight. The world on my side of the mountain is all fog and mud and rain. I stand alone at the bus stop, in a too-thin sweatshirt and a zinged-up set of nerves. I got here early so I could talk to Reece, but he's a no-show. I still have so many important, practical questions, but my primary one is: What. Are. We. Doing?

Dating? If so, is it casual or serious? In public or secret? Or is he regretting our kiss last night and wants only friendship? Again, same earlier questions apply. And if we are dating—big *if*—how does his status as a supernatural being affect that? I know it does. It *has* to.

I turn at the sound of an approaching car. It's a green

Mustang—one of those muscle cars from the 1960s that's old but still super cool. It stops next to me. Reece sticks his head out the window and grins. "Hey you."

I look in his window. "Is this the car you've been pining for?"

"Yup. She's pretty, isn't she?" The grin falls off his face. "Are you allowed to ride to school with me?"

I have no idea about my dad's policy on rides to school with boys who he's kicked out of the house. I go to the passenger side and get in. The car smells like Reece—clean air and the woods. "My dad said I can see you. Just not in the basement or in secret." My face goes warm. "That is, if you—I mean, we—"

He leans over and captures my lips in a quick, hard kiss that leaves them tingling and the rest of me a little less coherent.

"I, um...okay. And yes, your car is very pretty."

"Thanks." He pulls away from the curb. "I'm glad your dad is letting us see each other. I didn't want our time together to be limited to lunch at the cafeteria. Or more secrets."

I press my lips together. Okay, so we *are* dating. I'm fine with that. *More* than fine. And he doesn't want it to be a secret. I'm not sure how I feel about *that*. I've worked hard to fade into the cinder blocks. To stay off the radar. Strolling into Cadence High on the arm of Kiera Shaw's intended boyfriend is going to wipe that.

We arrive at school a little before the rush. The high school shares a parking lot and some facilities with Somerset County College, but there are plenty of spaces. Reece pulls into one a little farther away. We sit there for a moment. The drizzle has changed to a steady light rain. The droplets make a rhythmic pattern on the car.

Reece leans forward, glances skyward. His expression turns pensive, and he sniffs the air in a manner that's distinctly animal. "This rain isn't going to stop."

"It always rains this time of year."

His brow knits. "This is different."

Déjà vu causes the hairs on the back of my neck to stand up. I remember a very similar conversation with Lacey a few weeks ago.

"I've never heard of spring rain showers being fatal," I say, more fiercely than I'd intended. "Unless the water turns to acid. Or radioactive fish."

He gives me a stern look. "Calamities are a riot until they happen to you."

I look him in the eye as my fingers curl into the seats. "Reece, do you know if *I'm* going to die? Or my dad?"

His jaw hardens. "No, but I plan to get you both out of the area when I sense the disaster is close. When it's time, I'll come to you and say good-bye." He sends me an earnest look. "I won't just leave. I promise."

"So in the meantime…"

"I don't know what to say." He spreads his hands, lets them fall to his lap. "The only way I know how to live is to enjoy good moments as they come. I don't think about the future, because my future is never enjoyable."

"I get that." I *do*, but it doesn't stop the growing hollow in my chest. "I don't want to feel something for you only to have you leave."

He thinks for a moment. "This is why I usually avoid close relationships with people outside of my group. The leaving is awful. But you know, people leave relationships when neither member is a harbinger of death, too."

"Sure, but in this case, it's likely neither of us will *want* to leave. It's not usually like that in breakups."

"I know." He lowers his gaze. "This is all I have, Angie. I'm sorry."

The car falls into silence. The rain-streaked windshield

casts his face in gray. His gaze rises past the weedy edge of the parking lot to the distant college. I close my eyes, press my hands into my thighs. "We should get to homeroom."

"Yeah. Okay." He unclips his seat belt and leans over. Fingers on my cheek turn my face to his. Lips brush mine, and my breath catches. Every kiss with this guy feels like a first kiss. And the last. "Walk in with me?" he asks.

I draw in a breath. "Yes."

We both sense someone standing in front of the car, watching. I look at the same time as Reece.

Rafette. I would recognize him anywhere. His face may change, but his clothes are the same: puffy coat. Wool cap.

Fear uncoils in my gut, even though the Beekeeper isn't so menacing in sunlight. There is a weary solitude to him. A desolation that bleeds through his shifting mask of features. It doesn't matter whose eyes he wears, they are tight with a despair that makes my chest ache.

My crow lands on the curb across from the car. Its one white feather gleams like an opal in the morning light. It puffs out its feathers and lets out a long, warning cry at Rafette.

Reece reaches for the door handle. "Stay in the car."

"No." I unclip my seat belt. "I want to talk to him."

Reece frowns but nods. "Don't get too close to him. And if you see any bees…run. Whatever happens, don't get stung."

We get out of the car. I edge my way to the front. Reece's body is long and taut. His eyes are hard and black and undeniably birdlike. Never before has he appeared less human to me.

The Beekeeper lightly bows in my direction. "I have not properly introduced myself." His voice lilts with an accent I don't recognize. "I am Rafette, although I imagine you know that. It's a pleasure to meet you, Angelina."

Tension radiates off Reece. "You agreed to keep your

distance," he says to Rafette in a deceptively calm voice.

The Beekeeper addresses Reece with a sigh. "You do not direct me, scavenger." The Beekeeper opens his mouth and a bee escapes to buzz aimlessly around Rafette's head. I try not to stare at it.

Every nerve in my body is on alert. Sweat slides down the small of my back.

"Why are you here?" I ask. "Why are you hurting so many people?"

Rafette looks at me. "It is my nature, my dear. I create chaos."

"But bees are orderly creatures," I say. "They sting only in desperation."

His eyes, currently heavy-lidded and lined, blink. "Have you known desperation, Angelina?"

My breath is shallow, my palms slick and cold. "Yes."

"Remember that, and multiply it by ten thousand. Only then could you know *my* desperation." He tilts his head. "It's interesting that you see my true face so easily. The curse I bear is designed to prevent that. The others in this parking lot—those who are looking—see the two of you speaking to a perfectly forgettable young man."

"I don't care," I whisper.

"It doesn't matter to you that only those whose bodies hold traces of the lost magic can see me?" He smiles, wide and terrifying. "You would resist the venom of my bees longer than most. But never forget, the queen's venom is deadly to all."

Reece pulls in a sharp breath through flared nostrils. "Don't."

"I don't care why I can see you," I tell him, heart pounding icy blood through my veins. It's hard to pretend you're not scared when you *are*. "I care that innocent people are doing sick, terrible things because of you."

Rafette's features turn distinctly feminine. I hold my breath, afraid I'll see my mother's features again, but it's another woman's mouth, another woman's eyes.

"No one is innocent, least of all those chosen by my bees. They target unbalanced minds, those already edging toward darkness and madness," he says softly. "People have always done terrible things. They always will. With or without my involvement." His eyes narrow. One side of his mouth curves upward. "I cannot help but think we have met before, Angelina. You look so familiar."

Reece's hand slips around my arm. He angles me slightly behind him. "She has one of those faces," he says.

Rafette gives Reece a slow, knowing smile. "No, she does not." A mustache briefly appears on the Beekeeper's upper lip before folding back into its skin. "And neither do I, yet she can see it. I see you have found someone worth saving, *scavenger*. Eventually, all of your kind will find something, someone, you want to save. And we will be there. To help, of course."

Every remaining bit of color drains from Reece's face. His eyes take on a lost, hunted look. "I don't want your form of 'help.'"

The Beekeeper calmly holds Reece's gaze. "You will." His mouth opens wide. Bees crawl over his teeth and lips, just as they did that night in The Strip Mall's parking lot. His tongue crawls black and yellow with them. I take back my previous assessment—he is *much* worse in daylight. I gasp and shift backward, bumping my calves against the Mustang's bumper. Reece's arm snakes around me. His body is tight as a bow.

"I will tell you a story, Angelina. It is a short story, for a life so long as mine." Rafette's words are clear despite the bees in his mouth. "In the old language, we were called the *Mothe*, which means *maker of chaos*. We were all young men, before we were captured, changed by sorcerers and their corrupt magic into this." He gestures to his face. "Our queen wanted a creature engineered to enter enemy lands and weaken their defenses. When we were sent into service, we could fracture any army, shatter any siege, all with the power of our bees' venom. We served our queen, because we had no other purpose. And when the great purge of magic happened, we—like the original group of harbingers—escaped annihilation in our animal forms. We no longer had purpose, but we were compelled to continue on, doing what we had been created to do. My curse is as endless as the Earth itself. It is an agony you cannot comprehend. It is unendurable in a way no living creature should ever know."

His voice reveals his pain. It soaks through his words. This creature was not always evil and perhaps still isn't. He is desperate, which makes him far more dangerous. The bees crawl back into his mouth and disappear. All but one. It buzzes a lazy, random path near Rafette. "I promise few things, Angelina, but I promise you this: you will be safe when death comes to this town. *I* will make certain of it."

There is nothing reassuring about the Beekeeper's promise. It fills my veins with cold dread.

Reece bares his teeth. "Nice story," he says. "But Angie doesn't need your assistance. She's got my murder of crows watching over her."

I startle at the use of the word, murder, used like that. His *murder of crows*. His group. There is no difference. Just a more accurate, and darker, way of saying it.

Gravel rumbles as a red pickup truck pulls into the parking spot next to us. Corey Anderson, neckless wonder of the wrestling team, spares us a brief, speculative glance. He grunts, sticks earbuds in his ears, and trudges across the rapidly filling parking lot.

I gape after him. "He really didn't see..."

"It's true—the Beekeepers' curse keeps their true faces

hidden," Reece murmurs against my ear. "So they can move around without notice."

Rafette flicks a finger and the bee meanders into the parking lot, toward school.

Reece yanks me behind him. "What are you doing?" he snarls at the Beekeeper. "You can't do that *here*."

Rafette's eyes narrow. "Harbingers are not the Beekeepers' masters." Suddenly, the bee's course turns deliberate. It bumbles a path toward Corey Anderson, who walks across the parking lot oblivious to the danger he's in. Normal honeybees don't target people to sting. *This* is no normal honeybee.

"No!" I gasp, as the bee disappears down the back of Corey's jacket. I don't like the kid—he's a mean-spirited bully—but he doesn't deserve whatever he's about to get stung with. I lurch forward to help or *something*, but Reece holds me back, tucking me against his chest.

"Don't," he warns into my hair. "You will only make it worse."

"Ow!" Corey slaps the back of his neck. He swipes the bee to the ground and stomps on it with a few foul words. And keeps walking.

We watch in silence until Corey disappears through the school doors.

"That's it?" I turn to Rafette, but he's gone. "Where did he go?"

"Gone," Reece grinds out.

"Gone where?"

"Just gone. Beekeepers move differently than others," Reese says roughly. He flattens his palms on the still-warm hood of the Mustang and drops his head between his arms. "One of their many interesting gifts."

"What was he talking about, that I'm protected?"

"It means he won't let you die."

"I got that part," I say. "But why? He wants something in return."

"Of course he does." Reece gazes over at me with hot, dark eyes. "He'll take nothing less than my soul as payment."

The gravity of his words drops on me like bricks.

Nothing less than my soul...

"That's *not* going to happen," I breathe.

He shakes his head, lips twisted in contempt. "You're right. I'm already damned. Not going to make it worse by forfeiting my humanity. Besides that, it *can't* happen. No one's ever broken a curse. Or transferred it." He taps the side of his head. "Rafette's getting a little scrambled after being around for nearly a thousand years."

I swallow through a tight throat, trying to swallow my unease. Reece may not believe Rafette could alter their curses, but the Beekeeper seemed *very* confident that he could. The parking lot is packed now, but the curious stares and fizzy voices barely register. Twenty minutes ago, I was breaking out in hives just *thinking* about walking into school with Reece. How trivial those worries are now. "What will happen to Corey?"

"He was stung," Reece says. He slings an arm over my shoulders and nudges me toward the entrance.

"I saw." I adjust to the warmth and feel of his muscled arm, looped so naturally up there. For once, I'm the perfect height for something. "What's *going to happen* to him?"

"Probably the same thing that happens to everyone who is stung." Reece nods to a few guys from the hockey team, standing by their cars, gaping at him with me. "I advise staying far away from him."

19 the announcement

Corey Anderson got a nosebleed in Geometry class. I was there. I saw it. He went to the nurse. The nosebleed stopped. He came back to class. All was good until PE two periods later, when he slammed a volleyball into Steve Collier's face because of a bad serve. It went downhill from there. He received a two-day suspension.

That volleyball part I hear secondhand from Deno. At lunch. The meatball I'm swallowing changes its mind halfway down my throat and tries to come back up.

Deno thumps my back. "What's with you lately? I had no idea you had such a personal interest in Corey Anderson's attendance."

"I don't," I choke out. "I'm having trouble swallowing today."

"Distracted much?" Lacey raises a brow and grins at me. "New boyfriends will do that." She glances over her shoulder at Reece, who is sitting with the hockey guys at their table. He agreed—reluctantly—for us to sit at our respective tables. No force on this Earth could get me to sit over *there*, and the thought of trying to integrate him into my table made me feel vaguely ill.

I grin, pleasantly disturbed by the terms "girlfriend" and "boyfriend" and baffled by how the act of walking into school with a boy's arm around you automatically bestowed the official title.

Deno shoots me a look. "It's *still* surprising."

"I know." I don't pretend to misunderstand him. Everyone is talking about the hot new hockey guy and a weird band girl getting together. We are not a logical pairing. Kiera Shaw laughs with her friends as if nothing is different. She hasn't looked at me once, thankfully. She hasn't acknowledged Reece, either, even though he's still sitting just a bunch of seats down from her. Obviously, she's not going to compete for his attention with someone like me, who she considers far beneath herself.

Lacey leans forward and lowers her voice. "Oh! They're talking about you now, Angie."

The three of us fall into silence. My breathing goes shallow as I strain to eavesdrop on Reece's conversation at the table behind Lacey.

"You're seriously with Angie Dovage when you could have Kiera Shaw?" Mike Gordon, another hockey player, an asshole one, doesn't care who hears his conversation. "I don't get it. Kiera was all about you."

"Whatever, dude." Reece's reply is muddled by whatever he's chewing. "Have you ever actually *looked* at Angie? She's beautiful. Talented. And really nice."

Quiet. "Oh, Angie," Lacey twitters. "I wouldn't look if I were you."

I'm *not*. My gaze is firmly fixed on my spaghetti, but I can hear the scrape of metal chairs shifting on concrete floors, and I can feel the curious eyes on me. My cheeks start to burn. Okay, I'm not a fan of blatant objectification, but the lunchroom is not the place for deep, meaningful talk with this particular subset of the hockey team.

The chairs squeak back around, followed by grunts of agreement.

Wow. *Seriously?*

"Besides," Reece continues, quietly. "Kiera yells. A *lot*."

"Kiera does yell," Mike says, loud enough for Kiera to hear. "That's true. But a band geek, Reece? Really?"

"Yeah, really," Reece says. "She's a killer performer."

Deno shoves his turquoise glasses up his nose. "Where's he going with this?"

I'm tense as a rod, wondering the same thing. He totally wouldn't out me. He *wouldn't.*

The loudspeaker cuts off whatever Reece might have said next with a loud crackle. The principal's voice fills the cafeteria. "Students are to immediately report to their homerooms. Under no circumstances are staff or students to leave the building. I repeat, students report to your homerooms…"

This is not Principal Henderson's usual bored drawl. Her voice squeaks like a sneaker on the gym floor. I look up sharply at Reece. He shrugs back at me, then yawns.

No one else seems to share his blasé attitude. Kids shove a few last bites into their mouths, gather up their things, and make for the exits. There's a sense of curiosity, of worry. Some excitement. My harbinger boyfriend is the only one bored by the whole thing. Reece finds me in the packed hallway. His hand curls around mine. "Maybe it's just a drill."

"You know it's not."

He pulls in a deep breath, nostrils wide. "Nothing to worry about here."

"Really? You can just…smell that?" I wrinkle my nose.

"Yup. Hey, you're the one who wanted no secrets."

"That's right, I did," I say. "Speaking of which, what were

you going to say to those guys at your lunch table about me being a good performer?"

"What?"

I suppress a sigh. "You were talking to the hockey guys about me before Henderson's announcement. It sounded like you were going to tell them about my…part-time job."

"I wouldn't do that."

My stomach jumps. "Thank you. It's not for you to tell."

"No, it's for you." He dips his head, swipes hair from his eyes. "If you don't free yourself of that secret, you'll always regret it."

"Oh yeah?" I turn narrow eyes up to his. "Adding clairvoyance to your skill set?"

"No," he chuckles. "I've been around a while, Angie. I've seen a lot of regret—felt a lot of it, myself. It's the kind of thing that will eat holes through you. You should show these kids the true you."

"It's my decision."

We stop in front of my homeroom, lean against the lockers. He takes my hands in his and leans in close.

"Agreed. But at this point the only one judging you by your mother's flaws is you." He glances at the thinning hallway crowd. "Do you have your cell on?"

I nod. "Text me if you hear anything."

"Okay. See you in a bit." Reece's homeroom is two doors down. He drops a kiss to my forehead and breaks away. I file into my homeroom last as Mr. Dougherty closes the door behind me and locks it. He motions for everyone to sit, and we do, waiting with fresh alarm to hear what's going on.

Before our teacher begins, Anne Brighton springs from her seat. She holds her phone aloft and lets out a panicky cry. "My dad just texted that there's some guy at the college shooting people!"

20 the preshow

Anne's huge blue eyes just about bug out of her head. "My parents want to pick me up *now*."

"No one's leaving." Mr. Dougherty dabs a handkerchief over his forehead. "Everyone stay calm. This is not happening inside the school, but a block away. We're to stay right here and keep the door locked until the police say it's safe."

Half the room erupts. Even the tough guys go high-pitched. The other half are hunched over the phones we're not supposed to have in school. Poor Mr. Dougherty tries to settle everyone, but he's got to be the most high-strung chemistry teacher ever. On our *best* behavior, we make him nervous. I don't know how he'll survive being locked in a room full of panicked students.

I stay in my seat and text Reece. *Shooter at the college parking lot? Your sister there?*

His response is immediate. *Yes*.

Is she safe?

Depends.

What kind of answer is that? She's either safe or she's not.

Is this it? I text. *Is this THE catastrophe?*

So eager to be rid of me? ;-)

I let out an annoyed sigh. *Is it*????

He responds, *No.*

The *pop-pop-pop* of gunshots somewhere outside prompts a few of my dimmer classmates to rush toward the window and start yanking up the shades. Mr. Dougherty leaps for them, face red. "Get away from that window!" he bellows. "In your seats and quiet. *Now*."

Amazingly, everyone listens. Seats are filled. The room goes silent. Honestly, it doesn't sound like the gunfire is a block away. It sounds like it's right outside.

We can hear the unintelligible garble of police speaking into megaphones. The blare of sirens. Then, the lights go out.

Whimpers. A few whispering prayers. Suddenly, this is real. *This is happening* and I'm scared. We all are.

A thought slams into me with the force of a bullet—if I die here today, Reece would be right.

I would regret hiding behind Sparo. I would regret hiding my music.

My dad sends me a frantic text, and I respond that I'm okay, safe in a locked classroom and this is all happening outside, away from us. Deno and Lacey, in other homerooms, send quick texts. They're scared, too.

For the first time, I notice the details of my homeroom. The creamed-corn walls. Blue smeared whiteboard. Sun-bleached periodic table of the elements, peeling off the wall behind Dougherty's desk. I don't want these things to be the final images I see.

My heart pounds through my entire body. My phone is locked in my sweaty grip, but my hands are shaking too hard to text. What would I say, anyway? Should I tell my dad again that I love him? No, that would only make him worry more.

Don't worry, Reece texts. *No one in this school is going to die today*.

I believe him—of anyone, I guess he'd know this—but I still can't unbend my fingers enough to text back. The reality of it all rushes at me. Disaster. Catastrophic event. This thing is coming, even though it seems impossible.

Suddenly, noises erupt outside. I wrap my arms over my head and squeeze my eyes shut. Glass shatters somewhere, followed by a screaming car alarm. Orders are shouted. Sirens wail. A man yells. It's a horrible, wrenching sound that makes my stomach twist.

The gunfire stops.

My phone vibrates.

Reece texts: *Are you holding up ok?*

I nod numbly at the phone, then remember I have to type. My fingers are stiff and shaking, but I manage: *Yes. You?*

There's a pause, then, *So fun to be trapped in a room with twenty frightened kids*.

I automatically recoil at the words. *Are you feeding off this?*

Course not. Everyone's alive here.

I pause, bite my lip. *Are you worried about dying?*

I stopped worrying about that years ago.

Of course he has. This is a breeze for him. Probably nothing can scare him.

I peek up to see Aidan Moller unfolding off his desk. His face is inches from the face of his cell phone. "My dad's on the police scanner. They said the police shot and killed the shooter." His voice cracks through the middle of it. "It's over."

More than half the room is crying to varying degrees, but it's sobs of relief now. I vaguely wonder why *I'm* not crying. Have I seen so many bad things in my life that I'm impervious to this kind of thing? No, I've never been through a gunfight. It was Reece's calm assurance that no one in the school would die today. I believed him.

Mr. Dougherty moves to the window and peeks around the window shade. "Yes, it appears to be very much over—*no!*" he says when a few students move toward the window. "There's nothing to see. Stay in your seats until the police come and escort us out."

No one argues with Mr. Dougherty. Cell phones light up, including Mr. Dougherty's. I text my dad and assure him I'm fine.

We get word that one bystander was killed. Two more people are on their way to the hospital, but are likely to make it.

Reece texts me. *U hear the news?*

Yes. Brooke okay?

Yup, he replies.

I'm not crying. Is something wrong with me?

There's a pause before he responds. *You're the opposite of wrong. But you also know who caused this.*

The Beekeeper?

Yes. And this was only the preshow.

I respond, *Huh?*

Sick knots of dread clench my stomach as his words scroll down my screen.

Today was nothing. A tiny sample of what's to come.

21 the connection

School is closed Friday, the day after the shooting, and so is The Strip Mall. It's a good thing, since my dad isn't letting me out of his sight. We spend Friday and Saturday hanging out on the couch, playing video games, eating ice cream straight from the container—*yes*, Dad decided that life was too short to live without dairy after the awful events at school—and watching the news. The ice cream is glorious. The news is not.

The shooter was a twenty-three-year-old guy with no previous problems with the law. The network flashes his picture on the screen every five seconds and really, you couldn't find a more everyday-looking guy. I mean, he really did *not* look like a psycho. He wasn't from Cadence, but from a rural town farther east in Appalachia. The shooter's red-faced parents cry to the reporter that their boy was a *good* boy. They never saw this coming. And no, they didn't know about any guns. They don't know why their son tried to kill all those people. None of the smart people on the news know why, either.

The sad thing is, there is no *why*. The shooter probably *was* a good boy before he was stung.

Dad shakes his head, drilling his spoon into a pint of rock-hard mint chip. "I don't get what makes people do these things," he says. "I'm just so glad you're safe."

The number of times he has told me how glad he is I'm safe this weekend is in the double digits. I pat his arm. "Me, too."

I'd been trying to find the right time to bring up a possible temporary exit from Cadence. To get myself and Dad out of town, in case that *really bad thing* happens. With the recent violence, now seems to be a good time to try. "Hey, Dad, what do you think of taking a trip?"

"Hmm." He nods. "I could see about taking some time off in April. When's your break?"

"I was thinking like, next week? We could check out a few of the colleges I applied to. In Philadelphia and New York? We could make a road trip of it."

"Can't do it. I'm closing a huge sale of equipment to the hospital and will be in Pittsburgh part of the week to train the techs on it." His brows knit. "Besides, you can't miss school for a road trip. Don't you have midterms coming up?"

"Right. Okay. Just a thought, with all the stuff that's been going on around here, I thought..."

He shakes his head. "You're not missing school. I understand what happened scared you, but Cadence is still a safe place, Angie."

Nope. He's not biting. A trill of panic traces up my spine. I'm not getting out of Cadence, but my dad will be in Pittsburgh. That's something. I could get really hysterical, tell him a catastrophe's coming and we're going to die, but I suspect all that would do is make my dad cancel his appointments in Pittsburgh and stay home with me. I'd rather he get out of here and be safe.

"You know, they're going to be testing the water," he says.

"Folks think it's contaminated with heavy metals from all the mining back in the day."

I study him from the corners of my eyes. "What do you think?"

"I don't see how mining from sixty years ago is suddenly affecting us *now*, but hey, I'm not a scientist." He nods toward the kitchen. "There're three cases of bottled water in the pantry. Use that for drinking and brushing your teeth until all this is figured out."

"Okay, but I seriously doubt Lake Serenity is contaminated. They test it all the time," I say. "The dam has been there for decades, so the water is nowhere near the old mines."

He shrugs. "What else could it be? Decent people don't turn homicidal for no reason. Don't worry. I've got us covered if it's the water. We're getting a new water filter installed next week." His eyes go bright with excitement. "You should have seen the demo of this thing. It turned urine into drinkable water—"

I hold up a hand. "I'm not drinking my own urine."

"No, no, of course not. But you *could*, if you had to. They use a reverse osmosis filtration…"

I stop listening there. It's unfortunate my dad is buying the bogus theory about the water. I'm not surprised. He doesn't hide the fact that anything but a logical, scientific explanation is pure hooey. Yes, *hooey* is the technical term for all things whimsical. He says my mom cured him of hooey and whimsy.

The doorbell rings. It plays this bombastic little tune that must be audible to the whole neighborhood.

"That would be Reece," I say.

"Does he have to come over tonight? I was going to order a pizza."

I raise my eyebrows. Pizza? That's so tempting. "I asked you earlier if it was okay, and you said yes. You should have stated your objection then."

When he just frowns at me, I lean over and kiss his cheek. "You *said* yes. I'm going to let him in before he rings that doorbell again and wakes up every napping infant in a five mile radius."

Dad grumbles but doesn't stop me. Roger leads the way to the door, tail wagging as if he knows who it is. I follow the dog down the hall, suddenly a little self-conscious. I should have changed. I'm barefoot in purple leggings and a huge, bleach-spattered sweatshirt with the neckline cut out. I tug up the frayed neck, but it slips right back down over my left shoulder.

I open the door to find Reece on the front porch. His hands are jammed deep in his jeans pockets, his shoulders hunched. He looks up, gives me a lopsided grin. "Hey."

"Hey, yourself." The porch light glints off his wet hair. He looks so darn cute standing there. A little nervous. A little eager.

His brows go up. "What?"

I shrug one shoulder and grin at him. "We're eating ice cream."

"About time." He shakes out his rain-soaked hair, reminding me a little of Roger when he does it.

He tucks his arms against his torso and shifts his feet. "Can I come in? It's cold out here."

I lean outside and press my mouth to his. He draws in a sharp breath, then eases into the kiss, slanting his lips against mine. He tastes like cold rain and mint gum—two things that in this moment, I'm sure I could subsist on indefinitely. When I pull away, reluctantly, there's hunger in his eyes that makes my stomach tighten. I drop my gaze, unsure of myself, of these feelings that are intense and unfamiliar. It's a real problem. The more I feel for Reece, the deeper the claws of dread dig into my chest. It's harder and harder to remind myself...*he can't stay*.

Reece's dark eyes hold mine. "Did I do something wrong?" he asks.

"No, I—" *I think I'm falling for you.* "You're a good kisser."

"My gift. My curse." He gives me a shrug and another lopsided smile. "So *may* I come in?"

"Oh. Sorry." I dance backward as he steps inside.

He crouches to scratch behind Roger's floppy ears. "Is your dad going to be mad I'm here?"

I beam a smile. "Not at all. Come. We'll have a pint."

"Mint chip?"

"I can share."

He hangs behind but follows me to the den. My dad is still sitting there, spoon in hand and a scowl on his face.

Reece stops in the entrance to the den. "Hello, Mr. Dovage."

"Mr. Fernandez," Dad says coolly.

The two eye each other for a long, uncomfortable moment. My dad must have a point to make. I plop next to him on the couch and stick an elbow in his side.

Dad shoots me a stern look. "Don't poke me with your elbow."

Reece sighs. "I can go."

My dad huffs out a breath and waves Reece in. "Damn it, come and sit down."

Reece hesitates. It's so obvious that he'd rather not deal with my glowering father, but he comes in and sits down next to me. My dad leans forward and fixes Reece with a hard gaze. "Angie likes you, so you must be an okay kid. But so help me, if I catch you sneaking in the basement with my daughter again, you will leave on a stretcher. Got it?"

Wow. Even as my cheeks heat up, I am a little in awe of this previously unknown side of my dad. It's as fascinating as it is embarrassing.

Reece swallows. "Yes, sir. No basements."

"That's right." My dad settles into the couch. "Have a daughter one day and you'll see. Forget the water," he mutters.

"Kids are what's making people lose their minds."

I can't tell if Reece is intimidated, or if he's pretending for my dad's benefit. I pass Reece a speculative look, which he returns with a quick smile and amused eyes. Only pretending, then. Not surprising. Nothing my dad could do to him would be worse than going through puberty nine times.

"Here." I pass him the mint chip. "You know. Life's too short."

He drops his gaze. "Indeed it is."

"Hey." My dad points at the TV. He looks confused. "I know that guy."

I scan the screen. It's a scene of the crowd outside the college, backed up behind the crime scene tape.

"Who?"

Dad grabs the remote and hits the pause button. "That skinny guy right there, with the wool hat. I *know* him." He rubs his chin. "Trying to remember where."

My heart clutches. I send Reece a look of panic, because we both know that guy, too. His curse may have gifted him one bland set of features for the TV, but *that's* Rafette my father's pointing to.

"Ah!" Dad claps his hands and points to the screen. "Son of a *bitch*. That's the same piece of sh— Oh, sorry for the cursing." He clears his throat, but his eyes are glued to the screen. "That guy used to hang around your mom at the apartment we shared in Pittsburgh, after you came along, Angie, but, well, we were apart for a bit. Something happened and she came home, but when she saw that guy, she really freaked out. I finally confronted him and told him to get lost, which he did, I think. Man, your mom was scared of nothing, but that guy… The guy made an impression on me. I could never forget him." He squints at the TV and circles a hand over his face. "He had a weird kind of face, too, like it wasn't quite… Whatever. I can't explain it."

"That was a long time ago," I choke out. "Are you sure it's the same guy?"

"I know. It can't be, right?" Dad shakes his head, eats a spoonful of butter pecan. "Nah, you're right. Couldn't be. That guy's a spitting image, though. How bizarre is that?"

All three of us stare at the blurred, paused image of the man at the crime scene. I doubt my dad perceives the pleased, satisfied look on the Beekeeper's face. No one else would, either. It's just another face in the crowd.

Reece's lips are so compressed, they're almost colorless. His fingers compulsively rub the scars on his palm. "I should get going." He's trying for lightness, but he sounds as serious as he looks.

Dad looks over and blinks up at him. "That was a short visit."

"I know." Reece gets to his feet. "I just remembered I told my mom I'd be home tonight. To watch the kids. She has a date or something."

My dad sits up straight. "Oh, sure. Is it…um. Is she seeing someone seriously?"

Reece struggles to keep a straight face. "I don't think so. I mean, we just moved here, so…"

"Of course." My dad waves a hand. "None of my business anyway."

Reece covers his mouth with a hand. "Well, okay. I'm gonna go. Good night, Mr. Dovage, Angie."

I get up. "I'll walk you out."

Out of earshot, I grab his arm. "What the *hell* was that?"

He looks away. "Yeah, I don't know. That was weird."

"That was more than weird." My chest swells with anger. "I *told* you there was a connection between my mother and Rafette. I saw her features in Rafette's face that night in the parking lot behind The Strip Mall, and now we learn he was stalking my mom." I jab a finger at his chest. "Which means you lied to me when I asked you about it. Why? What do you know?"

"I didn't lie," he protests. "Remember when I told you how all the Beekeeper's faces once belonged to people who died with their venom in them?"

"Yeah?"

"No one survives that. They just don't. The venom is powerful and shifts reality in a specific way to its victims." He steps close, speaks quietly in my ear. "If your dad saw Rafette stalking your mother back in Pittsburgh, it means she would have been stung just after you were born. Your mother lived for more than a decade after that. The average life-span after a Beekeeper sting is a few weeks, max."

"She *did* take her own life."

"Not violently. She overdosed. Maybe it was intentional, but it was also *many years* later," he counters. "No one lives that long. They just don't. Look what's happening with Corey Anderson, and he was stung only two days ago."

My vision blurs. Officially, no one has heard from Corey Anderson since he was hauled out of PE, but the rumors about him are bad. It's said that he flipped out on his parents, and he went to Pittsburgh for specialized psychiatric treatment.

I cross my arms. "Explain it, then. Explain the connection."

"I can't." He grips my shoulders and leans close. "Angie, we have only a little time left. My family and I are watching you, Rafette, and trying to keep tabs on the people we know he stung. Forget him. Don't dig for answers here," he says quietly, turning the door handle. "Don't forget that you're living in a marked town. There are bigger forces at work here than a Beekeeper playing mind games. Soon, you're going to have to add survival to your list of priorities."

22 from the past

I spend Sunday morning in my studio, trying to finish a half-written song, with varying degrees of success.

Very little success. The violence outside my school made all this Beekeeper, impending disaster business unbearably real. Working on songs feels like a frivolous activity with all the chaos going on around me.

Reece calls me midday to ask if I'd like to come over to watch a movie with him and his family. My dad says okay and although I'm feeling unsettled about Reece, I say I'll go. Six o'clock, Reece tells me. Brooke is cooking.

"Leave your phone on," my dad says at ten to six. "Fair warning. If I call and you don't answer, I'm coming over."

"Fine."

"And stay out of their basement."

"*God*. No basements, Dad. We're going to watch a movie." My teeth grit. "That's *it*."

My dad's brows raise. "Do I sense trouble in paradise?"

"*No*." I say, then sag into a chair. "I mean, I *like* him. He's just very…different from me." To put it mildly, and it doesn't really matter how different or how similar we are, or if he's holding on to secrets, because that whole "murder of crows" is turning into birds and flying away in a short while. My thoughts turn bitter. He wants to focus on *us* until he disappears forever, but he expects me to live with these questions about my mother and Rafette for the rest of my life.

"He's not pressuring you about anything, is he?" Dad asks gruffly. "If he is, I'll— "

"No!" I grab my coat and yank it on. "It's nothing like that. I think his family moves around a lot, that's all. I'm trying not to get too attached."

"Oh," Dad says. "Well, that's sensible."

"Yeah. Hooray for sensible."

My dad smiles gently. Knowingly. "If only the heart knew the meaning of that word."

"If only a lot of things." I force a smile, scratch Roger's ears. The Lab's brown eyes are wide and worried. He lets out an anxious whine. "What's with you, boy? Sorry, you can't come, although Fiona won't be happy with me for not bringing you." I tuck my phone in my pocket and wave to my dad. "I won't be home late."

It's a warm evening. Spring replaced winter so suddenly, the ground is soggy. Tonight, the rain has eased to a balmy mist. My eyes adjust to the dark when I reach the wooded divider between the two properties. I put my hands on the rough pines to keep my balance on the uneven ground.

Halfway there, a shadowy shape moves in the dark trees. I gasp, but it's only my crow. He's alone. None of the others are taking up their perches in the naked branches. The bird lowers its head and caws gently, hopping to a branch in front of me before gliding to the ground. It hops toward me, head bobbing. Something pink is pressed between its beak.

I crouch down, surprised. It doesn't usually get close to me. "What have you got there?"

The crow carefully drops a faded, water-stained bow at my feet, then hops back, as if to ensure I won't touch him. I pick up the bow. It's small. A soft clasp is attached to the back. I smile at this latest gift, a little girl's hair bow that somehow escaped the locks it had been fastened to.

Suddenly, the crow distorts, bloats grotesquely. I back up with a gasp. Fear crawls into my throat, squeezes it shut, as the crow spreads its ever-enlarging wings. A thick, dark mist swirls around the thing's legs and body, enveloping it entirely. The black vapor grows heavier. The acrid smell reminds me of the time I visited a blacksmith's shop at a historic village with my dad. My legs are too rubbery to stand up. I scramble backward until my back bumps up against a tree.

My crow is not a crow anymore. It moves with purpose, seething, growing bigger. *Much* bigger. I don't know what it is—maybe a harbinger. But if that's the case, it isn't transforming correctly. Something is wrong with this creature. My hand covers a whimper as the bird begins to take the shape of a half-human man with a feather-covered torso.

Two legs form, but with claws for feet. Wings spread six feet in diameter from the man's shoulders, just for a second, before one of them shrinks into an arm—*just* one. The other remains a wing. Black feathers cover much of his body. One human eye where it should be, one jet black crow eye, set on the side of his head. His hair is a shock of white in an otherwise middle-aged face.

He looks like something that just crawled up from hell. My back presses against the tree, and I freeze there, too afraid to turn my back on him and run. Tiny tornados of black twist and whirl around his limbs. They migrate upward, toward the man's mouth. The man tilts his head back and hinges his mouth open as wide as he can. He looks to be in horrible agony as the black vapor, or whatever it is, sucks inside his mouth like a vortex. Finally, the last bit of black disappears through his lips. He closes his mouth, looks at me.

I see his face, and my heart stops. Despite the distorted features, I *know* this man.

"I beg your pardon, Angie." His voice is the same low, gentle rumble. It's an easy voice to trust. An easy voice to love. "I hope I haven't frightened you too much."

I can't drag my gaze away from his face. I did love this man once—my mother's favorite and longest lasting ex-boyfriend. "Hank…"

He was my now-and-then father whenever the wind blew him our way. He had been kind to me, taken me to the arcade and took me shopping for clothes. He'd shown me some stuff on the guitar. He'd been so kind. I had learned from my father that it had been Hank who reached out to the private investigator Dad had hired to find me.

He's a harbinger. Tears itch along my jaw and neck. My body shakes with a legion of emotions. Too much of the past intruding on the present. Too much stuff tumbling from boxes. My fingers clench around the bow. "You're the crow that's been…leaving things for me?"

Hank inclines his head. "I had no other way to show you that I meant you no harm. I found these little things and I hoped you would not feel threatened by me."

An earring, a quarter, a flower, a bow. All things he gave me when I was a child. I can't come up with a quick response, not even a thank-you. I just stare at him.

He shifts on his awkward, clawed feet. His knees bend backward, like a bird's. It must be terribly uncomfortable to stand like this.

"I would have brought better things," he says in a rough

voice, "but I am limited by what I can find and carry in a bird's beak."

"No, they're amazing," I choke out. "Thank you. I love them. But you…" I swallow. "What *happened* to you?"

He turns so the crow eye is angled away. "Just a small taste of what I deserve. Punishment for not saving her."

We both know he's referring to my mother. "No one could. She was an addict."

His dark eye seems to sink deeper into his head. From this angle, his face is the same. As a kid, I considered his face the gauge of true handsomeness. I adored his southern drawl and his easy smile. No one compared. Now, I see the sad, downturned edges of his mouth. The white hair that had once been dark brown. The ridges of grief etched into his face. The patches of black feathers covering most of his misshapen body.

He shakes his head wretchedly. "No. I was given a choice. I chose wrong and was punished for it."

"Back up," I say. "*What* choice? What could you have possibly done?"

"Your mom was staying in a marked town. That's when I met her. That's how a harbinger of death meets anyone, you know. Your parents were split up for a while when you were around a year old. I fell for her instantly. It didn't matter to me that she had you and was still in love with your daddy. I was happy to be her rebound guy. I couldn't stick around anyway…"

Hank's human eye tightens with the memories. This reminiscing is costing him, opening old, painful wounds. He swallows with effort. "Your mom was making noises about going back to your dad, settling down. That you needed a stable home. I was all for it. I had a sense that the mark on the town we were in was about to expire, and I wanted her out of there when disaster struck."

"Where was I?" I ask.

"Your dad's parents had taken you for a week, while she was getting her head straight and figuring out what to do. And it was around that time when Rafette noticed how smitten I was and offered to keep her safe—no rules against a Beekeeper saving someone, you know. Only harbingers. Anyhow, in return, he said I had to take the Beekeeper's curse. Thought that would free him. I didn't believe a word of it. Also didn't think he'd keep his word."

He rubs his hand over his face, grief etched into every line. "The mark on that town turned out to be a fire in the motel your mom was staying at, as she was supposed to die in it. There're rules—ancient ones—that forbid us from directly interfering with the dying, but I lost my fool head and pulled her out, thinking no one was watching. No one would care about the fate of one woman. I couldn't stand to let her die like that, to make her baby girl an orphan. But someone *was* watching. Someone who knew the rules and had the power to punish." He shakes his head. "I'm sorry, Angie. I should have gotten her to leave sooner. I should've— "

"It wasn't your fault, Hank," I said, emotion thickening my voice. "You saved her life. But who…'punished' you?" I ask. "Was it Rafette?"

"Something far worse." He smiles bitterly. "Angie, there're more than just harbingers and Beekeepers at work in this world. Quieter, darker entities with far more power than us. One of these beings—one as ancient as Rafette, but more deeply cursed and with darker intentions—twisted my curse, condemning me to this half-life." He spreads his one arm and one wing. "This is what Reece may be doomed to, should he try to interfere with the course of events to come here."

My lips go numb. My heart pounds like a timpani drum in my head. "But my mother *was* stung. I saw her features in Rafette's face."

"He sent a bee to sting her, yes," he says. "Said his bees chose her and not him, but I think he did it out of spite, revenge. Because I refused him."

I drag in a breath and lean against the nearest tree. My legs feel like jelly. I need to sit. I need… "She didn't try to hurt me or anyone. How?"

"Obviously, the drugs dulled that part of her brain. But I believe she had some unique biology that helped—she was a true, gifted psychic, so magic ran through her veins. The bees target those who are mentally unwell, compounding the imbalance already present, turning it into something twisted and dangerous. I don't know, Angie. Maybe your mom was targeted by the bees and not Rafette." His gaze rests on me fondly. He smiles, crinkling the skin around his eyes. "We'll never know, but either way, she found the strength to fight the venom because of her love for you."

"Love for *me?*" I almost choke on that, it's so ridiculous. "She barely knew I was there half the time. We had no home. We lived in that horrible van when we weren't shacked up with some creepy guy. And you think she loved me."

"I *know* she loved you. More than herself. More than anything."

"Then why not let me live with my dad?"

"Well, paranoia is one of the key ingredients in the Beekeeper venom cocktail. In her troubled mind, she believed she was keeping you safe." Hank lowers his head. "It was selfish of me to let you stay with her for as long as I did. You belonged with your dad—he'd been searching for you for years—but I knew once you were gone, she'd have no reason to fight any longer." He drops his head and lets out a shuddering sigh. "My heart died with her."

His words hit me like a fist. I'm breathless, winded as if I just sprinted a mile.

My mother was protecting me. From *herself*.

I feel dizzy just trying to digest this, to change my point of view, after so many years of thinking I knew what happened. Now, following the grotesque lines of Hank's face, I see the stark realization of the harbingers' reality, and it is far more bleak and lonely than I want to admit.

It makes me rethink Reece's every grin, every easy laugh. This is an existence of inescapable despair. There's no way I can cure him of that. I'm not even sure I can stop it from infecting me.

I weakly brush damp hair from my face. "Why did Reece lie to me about Rafette stinging my mother? He knew."

"He didn't know," Hank says.

"How could he *not*?" I demand. "You all live in a family unit."

Hank stretches out his wing, folds it on his back. "I knew my actions were wrong, Angie. I didn't tell anyone about Rafette's offer or that he stung your mother. To this day, all they know is that I tried to save her and was punished by the ancient one for it. They are waiting for me to request the *mortouri*—death by the murder of crows."

It feels like invisible bands are wrapped around my chest. Squeezing, *squeezing*.

"He cares for you," Hank murmurs. "Reece Fernandez—as he's named himself this time around—cares for you very, very much."

"So that's why you're here? To warn me about how Reece and I are doomed." I stagger back heavily against the tree. I sense I'm going to need its support. "You didn't come here to reminisce."

Hank rubs his chin. "Angie, you heard what Rafette had to say about his existence. Harbingers of death can eventually request the *mortouri* by their murder, and their souls are released. The curse finds another human. It's not like that for Beekeepers. Rafette believes the only path to freedom from his curse is for him to coerce a weak harbinger into taking the Beekeeper's curse. He claims to have heard this from one of the ancient ones, but no one can prove it."

"Rafette thinks Reece is weak?"

"Reece *is* weak," he says. "He has feelings for you. He has all but pinned a target on himself."

"No way. We just started dating. Whatever 'feelings' he has aren't something that would weaken him. He's even told me he's leaving after...after whatever is supposed to happen in Cadence, so I don't get too attached." I frown at my lap. "I've been trying not to."

"Angelina."

I look up.

Hank's wing sags to the ground. The long black feathers brush the soggy mud. "This thing between you didn't *just* begin. You were friends as children. You probably don't remember. He's grown a lot since then, has a different name. Reece used to come with me on visits to you and your mom. You were six or so when he stopped. The last time, we spent the day at a park. You wore a blue sundress with little white flowers. I brought you crayons and a Sesame Street coloring book. You shared them with him."

I dig through the dirty boxes of my memories, searching through piles of anxious days and hungry nights for this one day he described. I remember the dress—it was my favorite. I wanted Hank to see me in it—*and there it is!* The prize on the bottom of an otherwise stinking pile of moldering crap. A golden-haired boy with a pretty smile and dark, sparkling eyes. A bright spot amongst all those rotting things.

"His name was..." I think hard. There were so many people around back then. "Steven. Shawn? Something with an S."

"Troy."

"Oh. Well." I swallow hard, trying to piece it together. To connect the boy from my past to the boy I know now. "I remember you set us up at a picnic table. My mom was in the van, and you went to see her." I sound faraway to myself, lost in this memory. "Reece—or *Troy*—colored Cookie Monster green and didn't understand why I got upset about it, but then he laughed and told me we can use any color we want. I thought he was..." *Cute. Sweet.* He'd accompanied Hank on a few subsequent visits to us. How many times did my heart leap at the thought of seeing that kind, handsome boy when Hank would knock on the van door? My mind didn't remember Reece as that boy, but something in my heart must have.

"Reece fell for you back then, and that's my fault, too. When, by awful coincidence, the group found itself in Cadence, he couldn't stay away from you. They couldn't deny him the chance to be happy for a little while, but no one anticipated Rafette's interest in him." Hank's expression turns pleading. "Angie, please. Allowing this relationship to continue could destroy both of you. Reece will do anything to protect you from harm."

"You mean he might..."

"Not might—*would*. Reece would trade himself to the Beekeeper so your life may be spared. Reece has doubts this is possible, but Rafette thinks this is a sure bet. He's picking out his curtains in hell."

My stomach drops, twists into a knot. *Reece fell in love with you, bit by bit...* He was a little older than me. My recollections from before our playdates fade to basic forms, shapes. I was too little, too accustomed to chronic stress, to hold on to memories. I remember impressions, not details. He remembers everything.

"Do you think it's possible?" I ask. "Can Rafette turn Reece into a Beekeeper and free himself?"

"I think he can," he replies. "He wouldn't be so intent on

this course without good reason."

"I won't let a childhood crush ruin his life. Or mine." My words are sluggish, as if my tongue is made of clay. They feel badly constructed because they *are*. The thing between Reece and me is not some flimsy crush. Hank knows it. I know it. It's vital that Rafette doesn't. *Ever*. I press a fist into my palm. "What do I have to do?"

"End it," Hank says, simply. "And get out of this town until whatever is going to happen, happens."

My heart squeezes, painfully. In a different life, under different circumstances, Reece and I would be at the start of something real. Maybe something forever. I've seen enough of the fake stuff to recognize the difference—it was all my mom could handle. I'm not sure what my feelings are for him yet, but ambivalence isn't one of them. I'm attracted to him, and I care for him, too. Allowing him to turn into a monster like Rafette to save me is out the question. Getting out of Cadence is another issue. "Okay. I'll talk to my dad again. See if he'll take me with him on his business trip. And…I'll break up with Reece. I'll try to convince him I don't want to be with him anymore." The words taste bitter just trying them out. They're going to be vile when I say them for real, knowing what a lie they are.

"You'll have to do better than try." Hank gives me a sad smile. "You know, your mother would be proud of you—of your talent, your strong, practical mind. Despite it all, you have a kind, balanced soul. I know you can do this—you will do this, if Reece means anything to you. If you value your own future."

"Hank." I reach out, take his hand. It's solid and warm and brings back a fresh rush of memories. "Will you stay with me?"

His smile fades. Even as my hand falls from his, black vapor curls from his mouth. It doesn't appear to be completely of his own volition, this shift back to crow form. "I can't. And remember that harbingers are cursed creatures. Loving one would only curse you, as well. Best to learn that now, before, well…before."

A knot swells in my throat. Even misshapen and hideous, I want to throw myself in his arms like I used to. He was warmth, safety. A set of clear, focused eyes and steady hands. I hug my arms around myself and stay where I am as he grows smaller and smaller, folding into himself until finally, a bright-eyed crow stands on the ground. It stares up at me before taking flight and disappearing into the trees.

23

the short good-bye

Reece closes the door behind me and frowns. "What's the matter? You look like you're about to be ill."

That's because I *am* about to be ill. My heart aches in a way that feels very much like it's breaking. I ball my hands into fists and choke back a sob.

If I don't do this now, I won't do it at all. And then it will be too late.

The kitchen no longer smells like pancakes and syrup, but dish detergent and cotton. I don't take off my coat.

Brooke breezes in, hand up and eyes averted. "Ignore me. I'm just getting some water."

"N-no problem," I stammer out. "We're just talking."

She slides assessing eyes over me and arches a brow. "Not the good kind of talking."

I glance away as Reece's scowl turns confused.

"What's going on, Angie?" he asks.

"I met a friend of yours in the woods."

"Really?" Brooke's brows raise. "Who?"

"Hank," I say flatly.

Reece's eyes squeeze shut. "Brooke, would you mind leaving us alone, please?"

Brooke lets out a low whistle. "Oh boy. I'd rather not, but…" She shrugs, forgets the water, and leaves with a sympathetic look to Reece.

"You actually…*saw* him?" he asks with a grimace.

"What's left of him, yes." My mouth hardens. "It so happens, he's a friend of mine, too." I take a deep breath and steel myself. "But you know that already."

He shoves his hands in his pockets, expression cool. "So I guess you had quite a talk."

"You should have told me Hank was one of you—a harbinger of death. You should have told me we were friends when we were kids." I swing my arms wide. "Your name was *Troy*. I can't believe you never told me that."

"I was a little surprised you didn't remember me at all. I thought…" He shakes his head. Hurt flashes in his eyes. "Anyway, you didn't. I tried to keep my distance. But I couldn't, obviously. And after, I couldn't find a way to tell you about our past that wasn't weird and disturbing."

My resolve slips, just a little. I cross my arms, determined to do what I need to do. "You want to hear weird and disturbing? That *was* my mom I saw in Rafette's features."

His brows pull together. "Hank told you that? He knows that's not—"

"Possible?" I finish for him. "It is. He declined a bargain with Rafette, who stung my mom. And he was turned into… whatever he is now, by some ancient creature who monitors you all and changed him because he pulled her out of a burning building." My eyes narrow. "You knew Hank and my mother were connected. You can't dole out a tiny slice of the truth and leave out the rest. That's just another form of lying."

Hurt flares in his eyes, but his voice is sharp. "Look, I knew they dated for a while, and I tagged along to see you when Hank visited your mom. He didn't tell me any more than that. Sure, I could have cornered Hank, pressured his already tortured self into sharing his most shameful secret. Would it have made you feel better to know that no matter what Hank chose to do, he was doomed?" He runs an agitated hand through his hair. "I couldn't tell you about how we met without telling a story that wasn't mine to tell. It was Hank's, and he decided to share it with you now."

"It wasn't just Hank's story, but mine and yours, too. We knew each other long before you moved to Cadence, Reece." I turn away, shoving the damp clumps of my hair out of my eyes. "You should have told me the truth. All of it. I deserved to know that you are in real danger from Rafette. I deserved to know what this relationship could cost you."

"I was trying to—"

"If you say 'protect you,' I'm going to belt you in the mouth. I swear, I will."

His lips twitch. "I won't apologize for trying to protect you from the ugly side of what we are."

"I don't want your protection, Reece," I tell him. "I want honesty."

"You think you've seen it all? That nothing can shock you?" he asks, low and menacing. "You're wrong. You think this thing with people getting stung by Beekeeper bees and having psychotic episodes is bad. Let me tell you this—very soon you are *not* going to like what you see around here."

My palms sweat. My heart pounds like a kick drum. My thoughts are not brave. His buildup to this disaster is scaring me, and I'm all full of scary for the week. For a lifetime. "Okay, enough," I rasp out. "I get it."

"You *don't*. That's the problem." Reece sighs and rubs his

palms on his jeans. "Why don't you sit down?" It's a gentle suggestion spoken with a sad voice. His anger has vanished.

"No, thank you." I don't think I can be here much longer. I take a deep breath and look him in the eye. "Reece, Hank pointed out some very clear, very real reasons why regular people and harbingers shouldn't mix. He, himself, was exhibit A." My voice wobbles, but my everything else holds firm. "I don't want us to end up like Hank and my mom. I don't want to get stung by a Beekeeper bee and you…" I won't tell him what Hank revealed to me about Reece's feelings, or the lengths he believes Reece will go to save me. It's a shot to the nuts when I'm already doing enough damage. "I don't want you to become like him. You're going to leave anyway, so we should just… end this now. Before we start to have feelings for each other."

He stares at me, dumbfounded. "We already *have* feelings for each other, Angie. We have so little time left, I don't want to… I thought maybe we could work out something…for after I left." I can see his throat working as he swallows. He knows where this is going. Knows there's no chance of changing the outcome of this conversation, but he tries, anyway, and it hurts so bad to hear it, I can hardly breathe. "I'm not ready to say good-bye, Angie."

"Well, I am." I say it firmly. With a clarity that surprises me. "What do we have, anyway? A week? Maybe two? Good-bye is inevitable, isn't it? You think you can do what Hank did, swing in and out of town in between disasters?" I shake my head. "No, thank you."

"Hank *told* you to break up with me?" Reece doesn't wait for a reply, as it must be written all over my face. A splotchy flush creeps up his neck, into his cheeks. "Let's not forget that this guy is not exactly human anymore."

I jerk back. "And you are? If my mother had stayed away from Hank, neither of them would have ended up the way they did. We should learn from their mistakes."

"If your mom hadn't met Hank, she'd have died in that fire."

"Maybe she should have!" I shout, hating the words, the guilt curling through me. "She suffered. So did I."

He comes forward, removing the distance between us. "We can keep each other safe by sticking together. Beekeepers feed on fear and chaos, and they don't store it well. Rafette can't stay here; that means after the disaster in Cadence, he'll leave." One hand comes up, brushes my cheek. I force myself not to lean in to it. "Don't do this," he says softly. "You're smart enough to know we're stronger together."

"I'm smart enough to know this is a lost cause." I break away from his touch, his warmth. "I'm sorry, Reece. This just isn't worth it. I think maybe…" There's a lump in my throat the size of a small boulder. "My feelings aren't the same as yours." My voice is an echoey hollow. I cross to the back door, not quite feeling my feet on the floor.

This feels so wrong, it shouldn't be real. But this is my voice saying, "Good-bye, Reece."

And this is my body, walking out the door.

Quite possibly leaving my heart behind.

24

definitely for the best

Monday is a grim day at school. The parking lot is quiet, save for the relentless rain. Most traces of last Thursday's violence have been scrubbed away, but a few bullet holes still pockmark the brick of the north wall. Deno sees me getting off the bus and sidles up alongside me.

"Bussing it?" He pulls open the school door and holds it for me.

"Yup." I duck under his arm and go inside.

He smirks. "Reece drive too fast for you?"

"Something like that." I shake the rain off my coat. "We broke up."

"Seriously? Why?"

I force an indifferent shrug. "You know. We wanted different things and all that. It's fine. Definitely for the best."

The vibe in the school is sober, tense. I don't remember the halls ever being this quiet.

Deno's hands make fists, and his lips thin. "Damn it. I *knew* he was an asshole."

"Who's an asshole?" Lacey asks as she joins us in the hall.

"No one," I say quickly, shooting Deno a warning look. Which of course, he doesn't heed.

"Reece," he tells her.

Lacey's eyes go wide. "He is? Oh no. What'd he do?"

Deno interrupts before I even begin. "That asshole broke up with Angie because she wouldn't put out."

"*What?*" Lacey and I say at the same time.

Deno blinks at me. "Isn't that what you meant?"

"*No*," I say, with feeling. "Not at all. I said we wanted different things. Not that he tried to…" I poke him in the chest. "You watch what you say. I don't want rumors floating around school, okay?"

"Yeah, yeah. Got it." Deno rubs his chest. "I should still beat his ass."

Oh, this is *torture*. "No, you should not."

My stomach knots up thinking about seeing Reece in PE, physics, history, *and* lunch. Pretending indifference to my closest friends pushes the limits of my emotional endurance. "Yeah, no ass kicking," I push out in a light voice. "He's a hockey player, Deen."

"So?" He pushes up his glasses as we stop at my locker. "You think I can't take a hockey player?"

I purse my lips and try to find a respectful way to say *no*, but Lacey does it better. She pats his arm. "Angie can handle this herself."

Surprisingly, Deno doesn't argue with her. Maybe he's learning, after all.

Lacey looks past me. Her gaze darkens. "Don't turn around, Angie."

Of course, I do. Reece is passing on the way to his locker. Our eyes meet. His darken to a glower before flickering away.

I turn sightlessly to the contents of my locker. Blood

pounds in my head. This hurts *so much worse* than I expected. "Like I said, it's for the best," I croak out.

Lacey gives me a hug. "I'm really sorry, Angie."

I lean in to her and give myself this one soft moment. "Thank you. Me, too."

"Do you want to tell us what really happened?"

I do. I really do, but I shake my head and give Deno a sharp look. "It's definitely not what you're thinking."

"Sorry." Deno shrugs. "It was a reasonable assumption. You know, considering what happened when we..."

Oh God no, please don't say we made out. I shift my foot and press the stacked heel of my boot into his foot. He grimaces but gets the message. "I'm uh, sorry things didn't work out, Ange. I hope you're okay."

"I will be." *It was for the best.* If I keep saying that, eventually it'll be true.

There's really no getting away from Reece. He's there in history class, two rows behind me. He's there at lunch, at the next table over. In PE, Mrs. Brandt pairs us up for racquetball. It's not a deliberate act, merely the way of the alphabet. *She* certainly didn't know we were dating. I find myself annoyed with a last name that starts with *D*, because it precedes *F*, and there are no *E*s in this annoying class to separate us.

I take my equipment from the bin and take my place on the court without looking at him. The pair of girls we're playing next to exchange glances. My face burns. My first serve bounces straight back and whacks me in the thigh. My hand is so sweaty, it's a miracle I'm still holding the racquet.

"Hey, just relax." Reece's breath brushes my neck, just below my stubby ponytail. He's so close, I could back up one step and lean against his chest. I don't know what's worse—knowing he's close enough to touch, or denying how much I want to.

I can't speak. He wants me to. I can feel it. And I would, if I could trust my words. I step away, letting cool air replace Reece's heat at my back. I drop my racquet in the bin and walk to the locker room. I don't care. I'll take a failing grade for today.

It doesn't get any easier the rest of the week. Every time I see Reece, my heart squeezes. My eyes burn. I find myself wishing this disaster or whatever would just come already so he could leave and I could start forgetting him. And then I feel guilty about that, because I don't want people to die.

I do get through the week without more embarrassing episodes. Friday afternoon after school, I sit at home with my dad, eating pizza on paper plates. He's eyeballing the mozzarella cheese with suspicion, making me think the *you-only-live-once* mood is wearing off. I suspect the dairy-fest we've been having is about to expire.

Dad slants a look at the window. "Read an article that said we're having record rainfall this month. Warmer than usual, too." He shrugs. "Better than snow, I guess."

I follow his gaze to the rain-smeared window and shiver under a ripple of unease. "Hey, Dad, in that article you read, did they say anything about flooding?"

He squints up at me. "You're worried about a flood? We're too high up for that."

We are. Our house is one of many dotting the face of Mt. Franklin. The gentle, sloping mountain was once mined for coal, but now enjoys state park status and fancy neighborhoods like ours. In contrast, there's Mt. Serenity, sitting across the valley and backing up to the lake also bearing the name. Serenity remains wild and uninhabited since mining was halted in the 1960s. It isn't considered stable enough to be granted permits for building.

"I know our house isn't in a flood zone," I say, "but the valley is so low. And with all this rainfall, and how warm it's been, are they worried about...anything else happening?"

"Well, there's not much that *could* happen," he says. "The dam is inspected regularly. You're sounding a little paranoid. Honey, if anything catastrophic was going to happen here, it would have happened years ago when the whole area was being blasted with explosives."

"Okay." I shrug and rip a bite out of my pizza. *Okay*. Then what could it be? Nuclear war? The zombie apocalypse?

"Some of the valley could see some wet basements," my dad admits. "They *are* getting worried about that. Lake Serenity is high, but the dam itself is sound."

Wet basements. Hardly catastrophic, unless something *did* happen to the dam. I shove the last bite of crust into my mouth and push away from the table. "I should go get ready."

"You have a show tonight?"

"Yup. The Strip Mall reopened on Wednesday." The last one for me, maybe. "Have a few things to finish downstairs."

His gaze moves over me. "You're twitchy. Is Reece going to be there?" He knows we broke up. I told him it was because he said they were moving and I didn't want a long-distance relationship, and blah, blah. That explanation is technically true. It's just not the full reason.

"I don't know." Hopefully not. No, that's a lie. I want to see him so badly it hurts. I want him to be there tonight. *Especially* tonight.

"So hey..." It's on the tip of my tongue to ask him if I can catch a bus and meet him in Pittsburgh. Maybe bring Deno and Lacey, if I can persuade them to leave. But the words stick in the back of my throat.

His brows draw together. "What is it?"

This is ridiculous. If I tell him even a sliver of what Reece has told me, he will worry for my sanity. And I *don't* want him to cancel his trip to stay home with me.

Frankly, I'm beginning to seriously think Reece has blown this thing out of proportion. Cadence is not Afghanistan. It's southwestern Pennsylvania. And I don't believe in zombies.

I shake my head with a smile. "Nothing. Just kind of wish I was going with you on your trip this time."

Dad's frown melts away, replaced with something knowing and annoyingly parental. "Wish you were, too, but you can't run away because of a breakup. You have midterms next week." He takes a bite of his pizza. "Frankly, I feel much better about leaving you for a few nights knowing you won't be inviting the neighbor boy over to an empty house. Sorry, but it's true."

He's not sorry at all.

"I know. Okay." A resigned lump settles in my throat. I'm not getting out of Cadence, but my dad is. If Reece's prediction is right, I'm glad he's getting out of here. He'll be safe, either way.

I throw my paper plate in the garbage and head for the basement to put the finishing touches on my set. "See you in a few days, Dad."

I really, *really* hope I do.

25

all good things

Deno picks me up at seven o'clock on the nose. He's extraordinarily punctual. I open a garage door, and he backs up to it so my equipment doesn't get rained on.

He looks me up and down and lets out a low whistle. "Are you sure you want to do this?"

"Yes." I grip my laptop like a shield, feeling as naked as a newborn.

"You don't look sure." He leans against my car. "It's not too late to get changed, you know. Go dye your hair, or whatever you do."

I hand him the laptop. "This is getting ridiculous, Deen. I'm turning eighteen in two months. Graduating in three. This is long overdue."

And I may not get another chance to do this. I swallow and hand him my mixer and a microphone case.

His eyes widen on the microphone. "Seriously?"

"Did you think I'd change my mind?"

"Yes." Deno loads them into his van. "I'm glad you didn't,

even though I just lost another damn bet. Lacey must have hidden psychic abilities. I have to stop betting against her."

"How much did you lose this time?"

"A night of my life."

"What?"

He makes a goofy face. "I have to go with her to her cousin's wedding."

Oh, Lacey, you wily thing. A smile tugs my lips. "Oh, poor you."

"Maybe it won't be so bad." He shrugs. "She's making me wear a suit, though."

"Men wear suits to weddings," I say. "It's the rule."

He tugs his floppy beanie to his brows. "I don't acknowledge the social norms."

"Oh yeah, right." I roll my eyes. "I'll bet you twenty bucks you have fun at the wedding."

He points at me. "You're on."

I smile and tug the blunt ends of my hair. My normal, dyed blond-with-dark-roots hair. The only part of Sparo coming with me tonight is the glasses—my signature giant green sunglasses. The rest is all Angie.

My instructions for Artie, The Strip Mall's lighting guy, are quite specific. His wiry gray brows raise as he reads what I typed out in great detail. He listens to me ramble for a while, then, with a nicotine-stained grin, crumples up the paper and chucks it in the circular file.

I blink at him, a little surprised, but mostly not. Artie sees himself as a lighting artist, far above taking directions from a punk newbie like me. He was once a stagehand for Queen, after all.

"Don't worry, kid, I got you covered," Artie says in his gravelly voice. "It ain't every day I get to do a 'coming out' show. I'll give 'em something they won't forget." He waves me off. "Go kill 'em."

I go back to my booth with glasses off. It's not quite eight o'clock. My set hasn't begun yet, and so far none of the early arrivals have noticed me. Or, if they have, they think I'm just here to help set up. I think.

Deno puts on some music, and Artie lowers the lights. Lacey bustles in, hauling her keyboard and a case of stuff—headphones and extra cables and whatnot. We both do a double take. She's put metallic purple streaks in her black hair and is wearing *makeup*. She's so pretty she doesn't need it, and she's not wearing much. Just enough blush to give her brown skin an extra glow. Her dark eyes look electric in iridescent blue liner, and her nails are tipped in pewter polish.

"What?" she snaps at us. "Aren't we supposed to be setting up?"

"You look…different," Deno says.

She doesn't really. Her hair and makeup showcase what was always there, but Deno stares at her like he's never seen her before.

"I do not," she mutters. "It's just a little— Stop staring!" He continues to do just that, earning him a fierce look from Lacey as she gets to work redoing everything Deno has set up. I bite my lip and turn back to my laptop.

It's cramped in here, with all the extra equipment, and the three of us, and the suddenly charged energy between Deno and Lacey. I sit off to myself, listening to them argue over what should be plugged into what. They sound faraway, like voices calling through a tunnel.

I am nervous. My hand shakes so bad, I can barely control the cursor on my laptop.

I don't look out there, but I feel the press of energy that tells me the room is filling up. It's a heady feeling, knowing they're here for me, for the music I'm going to play for them. The white noise of voices, the shuffle of feet. My heart pounds. Adrenaline spikes. But my euphoria is tainted with pure fear. This is me, tonight. *All me*.

I settle my guitar against my ribs and resist the urge to scan the crowd. My eyes search for Reece. Two minutes ago when I looked, he wasn't here. I try to convince myself that this is *good*. The distance is necessary to keep Rafette away from both of us. But my heart wishes he were here. It's an ache I haven't been able to shake. I can do this. *Just a little while longer, then he'll be gone.*

I put my glasses on my face and signal Artie. I'm ready to begin.

The room goes black. A thousand tiny white lights play on the ceiling and walls, like fireflies. None of the lights fall on me. I adjust my microphone, a new addition to the booth, and a very unnerving thing to see perched in front of me. "This is a special night, kids," I say.

Some guy out there shouts, "I love you, Sparo!" but mostly the room goes silent.

"We're doing things a little differently tonight. I'm going to play some completely new tunes for you."

Whispered voices roll off the crowd. Ice cold sweat trickles down the valley of my spine. Briefly, frantically, I wonder if anyone has recognized my voice and—*oh God, are they going to laugh at me? Boo me off the stage?* Deno pokes me in the arm. He reaches past me, and with slow deliberation, hits PLAY. This isn't a concert, but some music will be performed live. A hypnotic percussion opens up, builds. Other tracks layer on a melodic synth part that Lacey recorded yesterday.

This is happening. *Finally*. All the hiding and shame and

fear that complicate my past was worth fighting through for *this* moment. Fear. Excitement. Elation. Fear, again. It all bubbles through me like a boiling pot. No going back.

I close my eyes. Wait for the right beat. Breathe. Sing.

Fly with me, baby, there's nothing to fear.
Stay with me today, before you have to go.
Be with me, baby, no need to hide.

In the light of the new day, the fire's burning low.
Can't stop searching, for some spark of hope.
Find your way to dry land, the sea will drag me down.

Swimming to the far shore, to the lonely underground.
You'll be gone before I've drowned.
Before I ever make a sound,
I'll never make a sound…

There's an instrumental bit between the two verses, and I glance at my friends during the break. Lacey plays one keyboard part live. Not easy, considering she has to split the keyboard sounds in order to include a little violin bit she added. Deno's head is bent over two tablets. He's manually mixing the tracks of this song we frantically built this week. I'm on the guitar, backing up the track I recorded earlier today.

This is the most "band-like" of my songs, and the difference between my usual DJ set and this semi-live performance feels so… I can't describe it. The music flows, moves around me like a living thing. It's organic, growing. Being created one beat at a time. My voice comes out clear and dreamy, and I don't have to force it. While I'm singing, there're no nerves, no fears. We should be on the stage, not in the booth. It shouldn't surprise me to realize this, but it does.

I launch into the second verse and chance a glance at the crowd. Artie's keeping the lights off me until this song is over. Blue light undulates like water on the ceiling before shifting to purple, then red. Light, made to look like flying birds, plays over the crowd.

Euphoria rolls through me, filling my head with the glorious sensations. I thought I knew myself. I thought I knew what music did to me, but this beats *everything*. Playing my own music is triumph, release, freedom. It's the sun on my face on the first warm day of the year. Cool water in the blistering heat.

A weight shifts, sloughs off like skin from a shedding snake. And suddenly it doesn't matter what my classmates think of this. If they laugh, or never come here again, or beat my ass in the parking lot at the end of the night. *It doesn't matter*. My throat tightens with emotion at the sight of my two friends up here with me. I wrote the words and much of the music, but I wouldn't be here without them. I don't even know how to express how grateful to them I am, for being here, all along.

Then the song ends. Reality returns.

Silence. Dead air.

26

a warning sign

My heart pounds. My hands start to shake so violently, Deno reaches over and turns off my amp to avoid a discordant mess.

Then the boom of applause. Whistles. Feet, stamping for more.

Oh my God.

They liked it.

A white spotlight hits me square in the face. It's hard and honest and renders me completely blind. I push my glasses to the top of my head and try not to squint. "You know me as Sparo, but some of you know my real name." I turn to Deno and Lacey. "This is the ridiculously talented Lacey Taggert on keys." Lacey offers a regal nod as more applause and whistles break out. "My musical partner, my friend, Deno Steinway, on everything else." I turn and bow to them. "Both of you, thank you."

Deno's surprised mouth whips up in a grin. He leans over to the mic. "And let's hear it for Sparo, aka, Cadence's own Angie Dovage," he says, and the crowd erupts again. The energy flows over me, fills me, and none of it feels tainted, contaminated by the darkness of my mother's mistakes. If anything, my experiences have made music the empowering force in my life. The thing I used to do to forget myself is the thing that has made me *more* myself.

Tears prick my eyes. I flick the sunglasses down over them, watery from both emotion and that intense spotlight. I glance up toward Artie, and the light fades. Deno's deft fingers fly over the tablet to start up the next song. It's another one of ours, a faster, older one, recorded on a day long before we considered doing anything like this. The crowd woots. If Kiera Shaw is out there booing, she's being drowned out.

And then I see him.

Reece.

Alone in the center rear of the floor. Arms crossed, feet apart. He looks like he's standing on the deck of a ship. Thank goodness there're no vocals in this song. I'd never get them out. Our gazes meet through the rush of spinning purple light. He doesn't smile. There's an intensity about him that pricks my senses. I push it away. A surge of aimless anger hits me square in the gut. Why did I have to go and fall for a guy like this? Someone unable to stay in one place. Someone who spends his life chasing death. Feeding off it. Having feelings for him has cursed me, too.

My gaze moves to my laptop. To the floor. To anything but him. I've ignored him for the better part of this week. I can do it for a few hours more. From the corner of my eye, I see Lacey pluck Deno's shirt and point as a shadow falls over the booth.

Reece leans over the side, head tilted toward me in a distinctly birdlike manner. His eyes are intensely black, and his irises look bigger than usual. The hair on my arms stands up. My fingers tighten around my laptop. "What is it, Reece?"

He winces at my clipped tone. "The air has changed." His voice is even, but his face is urgent. The skin around his cheekbones appears pulled taut. Shadows dip under his eyes, in the hollows of his cheeks. He looks…tired, hungry. He leans forward and drops his voice. "It's time. You need to get out of here."

I set the laptop down with a quickening pulse. "Are you sure?"

"It smells like it always does right before…" He takes my hand, then drops it like I burned him. Which I kind of did, I guess. "Look, I get that you don't want anything to do with me. I'm not asking you to leave *with* me, but you've got to leave."

"But I've finally done it, Reece," I say, letting his words take their sweet time penetrating. "I'm playing my own music. I'm out here as *me*, and it's so amazing I can't even explain it."

The whites of his eyes flash. "Yes, and I'm sorry the timing is bad, but you need to get somewhere safe."

I look around at the packed room which I don't want to leave. Not tonight. "It's going to happen right now?"

"I don't know the exact second." He takes my hand again and this time, he doesn't let go. "But you need to go. This is your *life*, Angie."

"Whoa, hey. What's up, Romeo?" Deno inserts his bulk between us and plucks Reece's hand off me. "I think you're the one who's going." He signals to Tom across the room.

"Angie, it's *coming*." Reece's voice makes my skin prickle. "I wouldn't bother you for any other reas—"

A strong hand lands on Reece's shoulder and swings him away from me. Tom is still sporting the fading bruises he acquired at my last show. "Hey Sparo, is this one giving you problems?"

"No, I…" My words fade off, along with my musical euphoria. The implications of Reece's warning drain the blood from my head in a world-tilting bout of vertigo.

"Yes, he is," Deno says with a flick of his fingers. "Off you go, sport."

Tom nods grimly. Reece's nostrils flare as Tom jerks him toward the exit.

My stomach rolls with unease. I sink onto a stool and wipe my sweaty palms on my jeans. "We need to get out of here," I whisper to Lacey.

"Um, *no*. You're not going to let your ex derail your show. You're stronger than that." She pumps a fist in the air. "You're in charge."

But I'm not, really. An event outside of my control is. We may be broken up, but Reece wouldn't come here with such an urgent warning unless he meant it. "We *really* need to get out of here."

Deno takes one look at my face and announces a "quick" break. He puts on a prearranged house mix that will run for a few minutes, and we head for the dressing room. The walls and ceiling are painted black, and it's as small as a storage closet—which it probably once was. It's also the only halfway quiet place around here. Inside, I turn to find only Lacey with me. "Where's Deno?" My jaw clenches. We're not leaving without him. My head spins with possible options. Can I get the whole place to evacuate? No way: if I told the room out there—half of which have been drinking—to get in their cars right now and head for the interstate, they'd probably think it was part of my act.

"He stopped to talk to some guy." Lacey hands me a bottle of water. "Angie, you look like you swallowed a fly. What did Reece say to you?"

I hold up a shaking hand. *How* am I going to explain this? "Look, you're not going to believe this, but—"

Deno plows inside, bursting with energy. His smile is

megawatt as he points at me. "You can lose that terrified look—minds are being blown tonight, girl. Shocked the hell out of our classmates, but they're all psyched for you. Katie Long wants to interview you for the school newsletter."

"Deno—" I start, but he holds up a hand and barrels on.

"No, no—wait. I gotta tell you the best part. There's a guy here from a recording studio in Philadelphia who wants to talk to us. Can you believe it? This is really happening."

"I can't—I think I'm going to be sick." I groan and lean forward, bracing my hands against my thighs. When I tell these two that we need to leave—*now*—they're going to want to know why. And if I tell them the truth, they're going to question my sanity. I won't blame them.

"Better not be," Deno says. "We have to be back out there in two minutes." He checks his phone. "More like a minute and thirty. Let's get ready. We don't want dead air out there."

Lacey rests a hand on my back. "What's wrong, Angie?"

I get up too fast and close my eyes against a wave of dizziness. "Look guys, you're not going to believe this, but something much worse than dead air is going to—"

Crack.

Thunder with the power of a hundred lightning bolts.

It's like *nothing* I've ever heard.

Ever.

We go still and silent and waiting. For one horrible, hopeful moment, everything is still. But then, a deafening boom racks the building, makes the floor move beneath our feet. Lacey grabs my arm with a cry. The walls vibrate. Magazines scatter to the floor as the table tips over.

The lights flick out with a spray of sparks. Our small, windowless room plunges into darkness. Shuffling feet and the confused voices of The Strip Mall's patrons, pressing for the exit.

"What's happening?" Lacey shrieks.

"I don't know," Deno says. "*Something*."

In the dark, tears squeeze out of the corners of my eyes.

This is it. The. Big. Thing.

The end.

27

the end of the world

I've never experienced an earthquake, but I imagine this is one. Or we could be getting bombed. It kind of feels like it could be that, too. What else makes the ground tremble? Of course, it could be hell opening up under Cadence to swallow us whole. Dust and bits of the Styrofoam ceiling rain down on us, thickening the air further.

The break room feels like a prison cell with no windows. Deno, who is closest to the door, finds the handle in the dark and wrenches it open. This hallway is dark, too, narrow and not open to the public. And like the back of all strip malls, also windowless, leaving whatever is happening outside a mystery.

Lacey stumbles against me. "Let's get out of here."

Loud, ominous rumbling shakes The Strip Mall again. I press against the wall for support. The surface undulates like a ship at sea. The smell of something burning flicks on all our panic switches.

"Oh! Oh no, no, no." Lacey yells. "Fire. This is bad."

"Stay together." Deno manages to turn on the flashlight of

his phone and shines it into the empty, pitch-black hallway. We stagger through the narrow passage behind the stage, following the emergency lights to the employee exit and the parking lot where the van is parked.

We plunge into the rain and dash for the van. The air is dense and acrid with smoke. We still can't see much, enclosed by The Strip Mall on one side, thick trees, and dumpsters, but can't miss the pillars of smoke billowing lighter gray against the night sky. Deno drags his keys out of his pocket and repeatedly hits the unlock button. All three of us climb in the front seats, with Lacey and me crammed together in the front passenger. We're practically sitting on each other, but I don't care. Neither does she. We hold each other tight, breathless with fear.

"What about our equipment?" Lacey cries. All our stuff is still in the booth.

"Later." Deno stabs the key in the ignition, after missing a few times, and throws the van in reverse. His glasses go askew. He rips them off and chucks them to the back of the van. "Hold on."

He spins the van around and jerks it into drive with a squeal of tires. The van rockets out of the parking lot and onto the road. We're not the only erratic cars out here. Traffic laws are *not* being observed. Deno skids around a fender bender and hits the gas, zooming down Dredge Street in the general direction of his and Lacey's neighborhood.

That horrible, deafening rumbling has eased to the sound of rolling thunder. My fear still rides high. Something is terribly, terribly wrong. We just can't see what, yet.

I brace a hand on the dash. "Where are we going?"

"I don't know. Home." Panic sends Deno's voice pitching high.

"Wait. We don't know—" *what happened.* And then we round a curve and the trees clear and the valley comes into view. We can see exactly what happened.

Any normal night, we would see Mt. Franklin to our left and Mt. Serenity to our right, with the dam branching off the side of Mt. Serenity, holding back the lake waters beyond. But tonight is not normal. Even in the dark, through a rain-splattered windshield, the huge, inverted *V* scar stands out on the side of Mt. Serenity. The mountain appears to be halved in size.

My limbs go rubbery as the implications start to dig through my mind. "Half the mountain is gone."

"It's…it's a landslide." Deno's foot slips off the gas, sending the van drifting to the shoulder.

There are moments when a thing is too impossible to the eye, too surreal to be true, that all you can do is stare as your extremities slowly go numb.

The mountain, which has been a constant fixture of the landscape since I moved here, is no more. Lights dance at the edges of my vision. There is no air in here. What happened to the air? Nothing. I'd forgotten to breathe. What is causing these sharp pains in my rib cage? It's my heart breaking for these people, my neighbors, who have lived their last day frightened and suffering and dying in ways my imagination refuses to show me.

My fingertips splay on the glass. The van is too small—*why am I always stuck in a van?*—to contain this torrent of emotion. I'm all the way across town, and the impact of this horror is crushing me. *What must it be like for the harbingers to experience this up close, time and time again?*

Deno slams on the brakes a moment before rear-ending an uneven backup of stopped cars. Dozens of headlights point toward a slope of rock and debris covering the road.

"My dad said this could happen. The old miners have always said the mountain wasn't stable. They said…" Deno's bottom lip quivers before he sucks it into his mouth and bites down. "My parents— " His voice cracks. He covers his mouth, but the sob slips through.

"Th-they don't live over th-there." Lacey is right. But both of their homes are on the other side of the debris field. Hopefully, clear of it. Her body shakes as she holds out a hand. "Cell phone," she says to me, and I pull it from my pocket and hand it to her. She places a call, and begins to cry as the phone rings and rings and finally goes to voicemail.

My throat clamps shut. Guilt twists my guts like a twirling fork. My house, my family, is safe, all because my dad makes a lot of money and bought a house in the Estates. I press away the need to call *my* father. By now, he's in Pittsburgh or almost there. Safe.

"Where…uh, where should we go?" I shouldn't ask this. Asking any question to my friends, who do not know if their families are safe, is a cruelty right now, but we can't remain *here*. The huge fall of rock and earth looks at least twenty feet high. A narrow stretch of it spans straight through the valley, spewing debris nearly straight across to the base of Mt. Franklin. We can't pass through any of these streets to the other side of the slide, to where Lacey and Deno's houses lie.

Deno squeezes through a gap in two cars and turns around in a hair salon parking lot. "I think I know a way around."

"Around to *where?*" Lacey wails. "Does the van suddenly grow wings?"

All three of us turn around. Behind us is a backed-up Tetris screen of stopped cars. Several are overturned. People are getting out, running erratically. One car is halfway up a telephone pole and on fire. The highway is impassable.

Lacey takes a death grip on my arm. "What if the rest of the mountain goes?"

Deno pins her with a look of pure determination. "Screw

the mountain." He reaches out, squeezes her hand. "We're finding our families."

The fight goes right out of Lacey. I hug her as Deno maneuvers the van away from the slide and along the side of the road. He jumps the sidewalk and cuts through another parking lot, into a residential neighborhood. Visibility is crap. The wipers swipe mud and rain and whatever else the wind feels like throwing at the windshield. It doesn't help that the speed limit is twenty-five and he's blasting through at fifty.

My face is wet with tears, even though I'm not aware that I'm crying. Reality feels like a thin, insubstantial thing. There is a small, self-preserving slice of me that desperately wants my head to believe we are actors in an action movie. Because the alternative pushes my sanity to the brink. "Do you know where you're going?" I ask Deno.

"There's a dirt road up here that leads to one of the old mine entrances in Mt. Franklin." His jaw is set. "We can get close to the edge of the slide and go the rest of the way on foot. I think I remember where it is. It will hopefully bypass most of the debris."

I don't mention how very unsafe this sounds. How much I hate this plan, because, if it were my family down there in the valley, I'd take unwise risks, too. Nothing could change Deno's course, now, anyway. We bust through someone's hedges and plunge into the forest. There *is* a road here. Sort of. It's full of ruts and rocks and small trees, and it slopes distinctly upward. The aging minivan bounces violently. I drag the seat belt over Lacey and me and click it. Not that it's going to help us if the van goes tumbling.

"Slow down, will you please?" I grind out, clinging to the handle above the window. "Losing a wheel isn't going to help."

Deno expels a harsh breath but slows down. Not a lot, but enough so each bounce doesn't render us airborne. He nurses the van to a rocky area where the slide pushed debris clear across the valley to the foot of Mt. Franklin. Here, he comes to a stop, unable to go farther. I gaze at the blocked road ahead. If we could continue, we'd wind up in the general area of my development. I'm nearly 100 percent sure the north face of Mt. Franklin—where I live—is unscathed.

"We walk from here." Deno opens the door and jumps out. "If we just skirt the edge of the slide, it should take us to the center of town. To our...homes." He doesn't say *families*. "Angie, if you don't want to go..."

Where else would I go at this point? Trudge home alone to an empty, dark house? Roger's automatic feeder and water bowl will keep him fed and hydrated for at least a few days. And, in any case, I'm not leaving my friends now, when we need to stay together. When *I* need to stay with them. I look behind me, not for the first time. For something moving in the dark forest. For the Beekeeper who vowed to keep me "safe." No, I don't want to be alone.

For an answer, I start walking. So do they.

28

into the ruins

Within moments, we are soaked with chilled, dirty rain. Grit crunches between my teeth and burns my eyes. Sirens scream in the distance, from all directions, and Serenity is still making more rumbling sounds. My nails dig deeper into my palms with each tremor.

My crow—*Hank*, I should remember to call him—is nowhere to be found. It's strange and…lonely, after being followed by him for all this time, to walk without his dark, papery-winged presence in the trees above me. But even he can't deny the call of fresh death, I suppose. Even misshapen and twisted as he is, he is still a harbinger of death. He still needs to feed on the dead.

Lacey and I struggle on the wide trail of debris strewn out before us. It's not just rock. There are whole trees and sections of brick walls, probably from the buildings on Main Street. We are now walking on the disgorged bulk of a mountain that is likely still unstable. I suck air through my teeth and try not to think about that. About what would happen if the rest of the mountain gave way. Twenty feet away, part of a roof protrudes from the rubble. There're bound to be people, too…or what's left of them.

Oh, Reece. Is *this* your reality? He's here, somewhere, feeding on all this death. I imagine him crouched over the broken bodies, eyes that horrible red-black, an expression of suppressed ecstasy on his tortured face. Slightly more animal than human.

The image isn't romantic. It's as alien and unnatural as the Beekeeper's changing face. I should be repulsed. I should be sickened by his true nature, and I suppose I would be if that *were* his true nature. But right now, he is probably suffering as he takes in all this death just to keep his soul alive.

Unless he was in the path of the landslide. In which case… *No*. I won't think that.

Deno stops and waits for us to catch up. There's impatience in the line of his body, but he says nothing. We're on an incline with about a half mile of loose rock and debris to cross before we reach the area where the center of town is—hopefully, will still be. We're in the dark, shivering in the rain. In the worst shoes imaginable.

Lacey scowls at her four-inch wedge-heeled sandals and mutters something about poor fashion choices. I'm in no better shape with lace-up platform boots.

"I know. I didn't expect to go hiking tonight, either." I hug myself and rub my numb hands over my arms. "Left a perfectly good jacket in the break room."

She looks at me, wide-eyed. Mascara runs tragic black rivers down her cheeks. "What are we going to do?"

"We're going to go slowly and not bust an ankle." I glance back in the direction of my house, then to the dangerous path before us. "We'll get there."

Lacey and I pick our way over the debris field. The loose

rocks are slick and unstable. Serenity still growls in the night. At one point, another chunk of rock face breaks free. We hear the crack and freeze as a few boulders tumble down the mountain. Nothing nearly as big as the first slide, but it sends another plume of dust and dirt into the air.

My dad calls. I nearly double over with the comfort of hearing his voice. My phone is wet from being in my jeans pocket, but I cup my hand over it and try to talk. The noises that come from my mouth are garbled fragments and aren't comprehensible to my own ears, but he's just happy to hear my voice. He's so choked up, I can barely understand him, too.

"I'm sorry, Angie," he says, panic cracking his voice. "I should have taken you with me on my trip. I should have— They won't let me come back. All the roads are closed. I don't know how to get to you. I can't *find* you." The hysteria coloring his voice is about more than just this particular event. His pitch and frantic tone are the same as they were five years ago, when distrustful, twelve-year-old me was first returned to him. *I couldn't get to you, I couldn't find you...* This is bringing back years of searching for a missing child for him, and I can't stand it. I want to be strong for him, explain to him exactly where I am, that I'm close to home—and make a joke that will defuse his terror—*See, Dad? An ice cream a day keeps the landslides away*, but I collapse in tears on a pile of rocks and tell him that I love him and that I'm safe and that I wish he were here. And then the rain works its way into my phone, because it cuts off abruptly with a dead screen. I tuck the thing in my bra—I don't care—dig my fingers into my scalp, and let out a wrenching cry that's stolen by the pattering rain, the sirens, and that infernal growling mountain that has just torn apart my town.

Lacey and Deno remain silent and waiting while I am on the phone. I imagine they are thinking of their own families. Lacey's parents didn't answer when she called. Deno didn't even try. I get up. We keep moving in the dark—Deno's phone flashlight stopped working a while ago.

We know we are closer to the center of town, because the debris is thicker and smoke pours from between the rocks. It wouldn't be so terrible if it smelled like a campfire, but it's not just wood burning. Chemicals. Plastic. Something else, utterly nauseating. Smoke chokes our lungs and rain splutters over our mouths, noses. I pull the front of my soaking shirt over my nose and pull in air, but breathing is hard.

There are sounds. Noises that make bile climb up the back of my throat and whimpers escape my lips. People moaning, crying. Calling for help with far-off voices. Dogs howl just like Roger did when the Ortleys were killed.

"Look!" Lacey points to open pavement ahead. We get clear of the debris and look around to get our bearings. "We're getting close."

We are? This section of town is comprised of blocks of near-identical houses laid out in a grid. The destruction has upheaved the landscape. A number of homes are on fire, filling the air with smoke and ash. Our location is indistinguishable to me without street signs, and I can't see any of those. Not in the rain in the middle of the night.

Up ahead, people huddle together on the corner of an intersection. Some buildings are perfectly intact, while others are flattened, buried, or just collapsed during the tremors. People are frantic, calling names, crying. Some lie on the ground, injured or dazed. Some lie on the ground, not moving at all.

The three of us start to move apart, scattered, overwhelmed. I don't want to be alone—not with Rafette out there, possibly watching me. I don't want them to be alone, either, depending on what they find at their homes. "Hey guys," I call out. Deno and Lacey come over, and I put an arm around each of them. I draw them into a huddle, momentarily blocking out the upended world surrounding us. "Do either of you know where we are?"

Lacey hesitates, but Deno nods, pointing behind him. "The corner of Winkel and Dunn Streets. I sold candy for The Boy Scouts all around here— What?" he says when Lacey raises her brows. "I was like nine years old."

"Okay." I look at each of their faces. "How close are we to your homes?"

Neither of them answer right away, even though both of them can. They don't have to tell me they're afraid. I am, too. "We have to do this," I say. "We have to find your families."

"I know." Lacey looks at the ground, eyes glazed. "I know."

Deno pushes her hair back from her face. "We're only two blocks away," he says. "Come on. We can cut through some backyards."

We break our circle but keep our hands linked. Deno leads the way, as he demonstrates remarkable skill at maneuvering through other people's yards, over and around fences, avoiding the properties with panic-stricken dogs. Avoiding the homes that are on fire. It takes us no time to arrive in front of the Taggert home. Deno has led us to Lacey's first.

Her house is still standing, but obviously empty. A group of residents congregates at the corner, talking, trying to comfort one another and figure out how long it will take for help to arrive. All are dirty and injured and appear absolutely terrified.

My pace falters at the sight of several men holding weapons. When they see us, they turn, brandishing their baseball bats and other blunt instruments. I try to hold on to Lacey's hand, but she rips away from us and bolts straight for them, her neighbors, who maybe think we're a threat.

"Where're my parents?" she cries. "Suzanne and Bill?"

"Lacey!" Deno sprints to catch up with her. The people recognize her—thankfully—and part to reveal six people sitting or lying on the ground. They all appear alive, but not necessarily for long. My stomach clutches at the amount of blood on everyone. A strangled sound wrenches from Lacey. Injuries forgotten, she collapses next to a woman. It's her mom. Her leg is bent at a strange angle. Blood smears over her cheek, but her face lights in surprised relief.

"Mom," Lacey cries. "You're okay. Oh God, you're okay. Where's Dad?"

"Lacey! I was so worried!" Mrs. Taggert grabs Lacey's hand and squeezes it. "Your dad went with a few others for help." The group closes around them, sheltering the injured from, well, whatever they're afraid of.

"Are you kids nuts, running around like this?" one of the men shouts at Deno and me. He's holding a crowbar in white-knuckled hands. "It's not safe out here."

"Why?" I back up instinctively. "What's going on?"

"We've been attacked twice tonight since Mt. Serenity went down." His gaze narrows and sweeps the streets, which are still. "They're setting fires to homes, looting, attacking anyone they can get to. Whole neighborhood would be ablaze if not for all the soaking we've been getting these past weeks."

"Who would do that?" Deno asks.

"People," another man replies. "Sick, demented people. No one I recognize, but..." He shrugs. "Look, I don't know. We ran a few off. We...did a number on one guy who just wouldn't leave us alone. He's locked in Murphy's bathroom." He nods toward a yellow house. "Don't know what shape he's in."

"Why aren't you inside?"

"Can't see who's coming. They're setting fires. Can't signal for rescue." His body goes tense as his gaze sharpens on something across the street. "Get behind us, kids. I think we have company."

I spin around, heart pounding. Unsure of what to do. The

whipping blades of helicopters sound in the distance. Rescue is on its way. I can just sit tight and wait to be airlifted out of here.

My senses prick at a sweet, familiar scent on the air: honey.

No. Not here. Not now.

A disorganized smattering of people darts down the street. They're whooping, of all things. A rock wings past my shoulder, strikes one of the men standing guard. He curses, grabs my arm, and propels me into the group. My gaze sweeps the chaos, the terrified people. It snags on a man standing on a darkened porch, watching. He's not someone anyone would notice. Not someone who would stand out. He's an island of calm in a sea of fear. My heart pounds hard and heavy, even as my stomach sinks. I hope I'm mistaken.

A beard slides over the man's face, then disappears.

I can feel it, the moment our gazes meet. It's like a rocket locking onto me. My breath chokes off.

Beekeeper.

He nods, so slowly. Acknowledgment.

Run. It's my first thought. My only thought.

I break free of the group and into a flat run, away from the people throwing rocks, away from the group protecting themselves. I only make it a block when a woman crashes into me. I land on the shattered panes of a window. The impact jars every inch of my aching body. Glass scrapes against pavement, digs into my palms. The woman scrabbles over me, clawing at my hair like it's smothering her. An incomprehensible stream babbles from her mouth. I catch a glimpse of bare teeth, feral, rolled-back eyes.

A red welt on the side of her neck with white, vein-like striations twists up her jaw.

Fresh panic squeezes my chest. How many people are running around right now with Beekeeper stings? How many infected people are roaming the ruins of Cadence?

The woman uses my back as a stair tread and darts off. I lurch to my feet, hurting everywhere. This is like playing Modern Warfare…on the *wrong* side of the screen.

My gaze flicks back to the porch. It's empty. The Beekeeper could be anywhere.

Run, damn it!

My thoughts devolve to the primal. Fear is the only thing.

There's a commotion behind me, and the sound of a stampede, and something hits me over the back of the head. Hard.

I hit the ground again. My head spins. My vision darkens at the edges, slowly swallowing my sight. Dismay is a lead blanket.

I could have gotten away. I was warned. But no…

People are yelling: *Put it down… I don't want to hurt you… You don't want to hurt anyone.*

Hysterical laughter peals through the sounds. *Devils are among us… I do, very much, want to hurt you.*

I shudder, carefully pull myself up to hands and knees. My head pulses with a dizzying headache. I close my eyes as tears slide out, mixing with this hateful, never-ending rain. I must have hurt my ankle, because it feels like it's dangling from a tendon. My hands are numb, but throbbing. Whatever's wrong with them will hurt later.

The pavement swings like a pendulum under my face before fading out completely. I can't think of a single reason to haul myself upright. I'm so tired of upright.

Several pairs of feet pound toward me. I recognize Deno's green Converses, but not the black army-type boots next to him. There's a brief, heated debate above me that sounds like Charlie Brown's teacher, *mla-mah-mah-mla,* then powerful arms slide under my legs and around my back. They gather me against an alarmingly hot chest. "Go on," says a garbled voice to Deno. "I've got her."

No! I can't go with Rafette. I twist and buck, but he's strong, and I'm so freaking *done*.

"Please, don't." But my words are little more than air.

"Shut up," he growls in my ear. "This will be easier if you don't fight me."

29
mountain view gardens

Soft. Warm. Dry. Oh yes—*dry*.

Hmm…nice.

I awake in a bed that is not mine.

It *is* a bed, though. Not the sidewalk, or someone's lawn, or under a fresh pile of rubble. That's a comforting thing. I drag my mind back in time to the last thing I remember.

Rafette.

Oh hell.

I crack open one eye. Pale light seeps through a dirty window, illuminating what appears to be a small studio apartment. It's a real classy place. Strips of duct tape hold a broken windowpane together, and a thin yellow sheet is tacked up halfway over it. My gaze moves to the recliner next to the bed, which looks as if it was acquired from a curb. Only the massive, wall-mounted TV looks like it was purchased in the last decade.

And then there's Reece.

Wait. *Reece?*

I lift my head off the pillow, then think better of it and ease back down. This could be a trick. A magic Beekeeper trick. Or Reece might not be *Reece* anymore.

He's hunched over on a kitchen chair with his back to me. *Shirtless*. I swear, the boy forgoes shirts just to gain the advantage. My eyes follow the muscled curve of spine from his bowed head to the waistband of baggy jeans that hang too low on his hips to be his. He sighs and shifts the hand propping up his head, holding his cell phone in the other.

I spy my sodden clothes, draped over kitchen chairs. *My clothes.* I close a hand over a nearby body part—my hip—and flip both eyes open. I'm in a big T-shirt. Someone *else's* T-shirt.

Clutching the covers, I sit bolt upright, then sway forward with a groan. Pain shoots through my eyes, down through my teeth.

He gets up, startled, then immediately backs into the shadowed kitchenette. His head stays down. His hair is a curtain of dark tendrils over a face he's clearly trying to hide.

"Hey, easy there." His voice is a quiet rumble. "You were hit in the head."

Right. Forgot about that. "How long was I out?"

"About six hours."

My eyes are gritty and sore. I rub them with a groan. *Six hours.* My dad must be stroking out. "Where's my phone?"

"Gone," he says. "You must have dropped it."

"Can I borrow yours? To let my dad know I'm still alive?"

He flicks it on the table. "Happy to, if it was working."

Fantastic. I run my fingers over my head and find a small bump. "You changed my clothes." My voice is accusatory. I don't even know why. Tears burn my eyes, because I don't have words for how glad I am to *see him alive*.

He leans back, arms crossed. "You were unable to change yourself."

Why is he staying so far away? What is wrong with his face?

Teeth flash in his shadowed features. "Don't tell me that's your big concern right now," he says.

"It's not. I mean… Forget it." I don't know what I mean. Him seeing me naked is, by far, the easiest thing to worry about.

"I didn't do anything to you while you were unconscious." He turns away, bracing his hands on the counter. "Do you think that little of me?"

"Of course not. Sorry, this is all really…alarming."

"You were freezing and in shock. I had to get you warm and dry." His voice is rough. "I'm not sorry."

There's an open window in the living room area, letting in a sharp breeze. I don't see how that is part of getting me warm, but that is a question so far down the list, it's not worth the air. I pull the covers tighter around me. "So where are we?"

I'm not sure I want to know. Everything about this place screams of unhappiness, from the duct-taped window to the stink of unwashed everything.

"They're trying to evacuate Cadence, with varied success," he says. "The owner of this apartment has left, along with most of the residents of the Mountain View Gardens. You remember this place."

I do, unfortunately. I can't suppress a shudder at the memory of the last time I was here.

"You should have stayed away from me," I say.

His shoulders hunch. "I couldn't."

"The helicopters were there," I say. "I would have been rescued."

"You would have been butchered."

"But—"

"The helicopters would not have gotten to you in time. When we left, your friends' neighbors were battling the Beekeeper's infected army. And if you'd gotten past them somehow, there's Rafette to contend with. He wouldn't have let you out of Cadence so easily."

"So you rescued me."

"Didn't feel like a rescue." Muscles flex up and down his arms as he twists his palms together. "You put up a fight. You acted like…" He grimaces. "Like you were afraid of me."

"I thought you were him."

He turns back to face me but stays carefully in the shadow. "How could you mistake me for him?"

"Your voice," I shrug. "It sounded…not quite human."

He nods. "These are the times when the curse has the most control over me. I'm at my least human."

My breath suspends as a pause sucks the oxygen from the room. It grows heavier as the seconds tick by. His words feel like a warning and an apology. And a plea.

"I was—*am*—afraid for you," I say.

"You shouldn't be." His voice is harsh. It scrapes through me like sandpaper. "I can handle Rafette."

But I'm not sure he can.

I start to curl my legs under me. The movement startles a pained gasp out of me. I forgot about my injured ankle. I reach for it and find it wrapped in a snug bandage. My hands are clean and bandaged, too. My heart gives a little squeeze. He did more than undress me. He tended my wounds. *Damn you, Reece.* I can't push him away. He's making it impossible. Nearly.

I tilt up my chin. "Rafette wants you, not me. *You.*"

"I said, I can handle Rafette." Reese's mouth compresses. "Please, don't act like I'm—" He cuts off, rubs his eyes.

"Reece, I *saw* what happened to Hank. Just because he and my mom were close…"

"Doesn't mean I'd be turned into that, too."

"Doesn't mean you wouldn't. Or something worse." My words come out sharper than I meant. "Why take the chance,

Reece? You were only going to leave, anyway. I wanted to protect you. I don't want to be your weakness."

His body goes tense. I realize too late that "weakness" was, perhaps, a poor word choice.

"Three or four lifetimes ago, I lived for five years after an explosion left me with one arm and third-degree burns over most of my body. My face was pretty much gone. Then later, in the Vietnam War, my legs got shot up, and I lay in the jungle for what felt like an eternity until I finally died from a parasitic infection. I've endured horrors, Angie." He rakes his fingers through his hair. "So don't talk to me about weakness. I'm stronger than Hank was, and I've been around a whole lot longer. You're the one who gets only one life. That's over the moment you get stung by one of Rafette's bees."

I lower my head. "Fine. Rafette *thinks* I'm your weakness. Hank said Beekeepers are relentless. And the ancient creature that turned Hank into this twisted thing could be here, waiting for you to mess up."

His hands clench at his sides, but he can't hide his shudder. "He was talking about a Strawman. No one has spotted one of them here. And I didn't do anything wrong. I didn't pull you out of the rubble, just got you out of the path of a Beekeeper mob."

"Are you sure those creatures will catch the nuance there?" I ask gently. "It would destroy me to see you end up like Hank. It would destroy me to see you becoming a Beekeeper. That is a hell you can't die and be reborn from. It's forever, apparently, and I put distance between us because Rafette thinks I'm important to you." My voice cracks over the words, the only indication that they are important to *me*.

Reece goes perfectly still. "You *are* important to me," he says finally. "More important than anything any cursed creature thinks he could do to me."

Blood sings through my body. My heart stumbles behind

my ribs, but I manage a messy reply. "Well then. That's a problem."

"It is. A bigger problem than you think." He slowly walks toward the bed, all lean muscle and sun-kissed skin. He keeps the hair over his eyes. "I don't know if you're ready for this, but I can't hide it any longer."

Ready for what? My breathing goes wonky. I clamp my arms tighter over the sheet, but all he does is take a ratty throw blanket from the foot of the bed and pull it around my shoulders. Such a simple gesture, and so tender, it almost cracks me. Reece perches on the edge of the bed. Tense, as if he's ready to bolt.

I close my eyes against the threatening tears and bow under the light weight of the blanket. "Thank you." I relax, as there's nothing wrong with his face. It's the same handsome one I've been looking at for the last month or so. But then, his hair shifts away from his eyes, and a gasp tumbles from my lips. I barely stop myself from jerking backward. My fingers tremble against my lips. "Reece…your *eyes*."

His eyeballs are solid dark red—the color of congealed blood. Because it's his *whole* eyeball, it makes him look dead, at best. Demonic, at worst.

He lowers his gaze to the bed, keeping his lids low. "I'm sorry. This is…what I am."

"I just…" I choke off. There's no reassuring thing to say. "*Why* are your eyes like that?"

He flinches, body curling away from me. "Harbingers of death not as pretty as you thought?"

"Stop it." I swallow. "It's a reasonable question."

His shoulders slouch wearily. "You're right. I'm sorry. I hate that you're seeing me like this. I can usually control the eyes, sort of, but not when I'm this…charged."

"Charged?"

He shrugs. "I've taken in a lot of death energy. My body is telling me it's time to change into a crow and leave." He brushes his fingers over the back of my hand, then quickly draws back. "You aren't... You must be disgusted by me."

"I..." *Am I?* I'm totally overwhelmed. Shaken, for sure. Scared, oh yes, but that's more to do with the danger at hand, not him. Disgusted isn't a word that came to mind. My gaze traces over him. The familiar tousled head, high cheekbones. Other than those gruesome eyes, he's still Reece, just a little more...otherworldly, for lack of a better word. His features are sharper. The way he moves is a little more birdlike, as if the boy and the crow are not entirely separate anymore.

With a deep breath, I reach for his hand and thread my fingers through his. "I missed you, Reece."

He closes his eyes, lets out a shuddering breath. "I missed you, too."

That's when I notice the heat. It radiates from him. I don't mean normal body heat, either. The room is chilly. Suddenly, I notice the light steam coming off his skin—the same coming from my mouth when I speak. It feels like I'm sitting next to an attractive, boy-shaped wood stove.

I pull my hand from his and press it to his forehead. "Reece, you're burning up!"

"No, it's normal." He keeps his head low. Hair shadows his eyes. "I mean, normal for *me*. I get warm when I..." He trails off. And there's a tightness to the way he's holding his body. It's like he's struggling to sit still.

"So your eyes and your body heat are like this because you just...ah, fed?"

His lips thin into a grimace. "You don't have to find pretty words for it. My eyes change and my body gets hotter the more death I absorb." He tilts his head to the ceiling and closes those gruesome eyes. "How can you *not* see me as a monster?"

Granted, I am still disturbed by his eyes, but a monster, he is *not*. "Oh yes. You saved me from a dangerous mob, brought me someplace safe and dry, bandaged my cuts, and wrapped my ankle. Very monstrous of you."

A smile flickers over his lips, but he ducks his head. "Rafette told you a story. I have one for you, too. It's also short, and one I know only because it's been passed down from harbinger to harbinger. It started long before the curse found my wretched body."

"Where the curse came from?" I've wanted to know this for a while, but getting information out of Reece has never been easy. "And nothing about your body is wretched."

That surprises a hot flush out of me and a smile out of him. "Well, some of the story is the same as Rafette's—there was a time when magic *was* real and the people who wielded it were powerful. It was science, really, but different from today. This magic-science was used across all social strata—peasants to kings—but the most powerful sorcerers worked in service to the great queens and kings of the time. Harbingers of death were created to scout for potential disasters in a kingdom. If an earthquake, or a hurricane, or an invading army was coming, harbingers could scent it and inform the king, who could then prepare." Reece slouches forward, resting his forearms on his thighs. "But merging a human being with a scavenger bird had an unintended side effect. The crows' need to feed on carrion manifested in the harbingers' need to consume the thing they were sent to help prevent—death. It kind of made them a failed experiment. They couldn't just report back, they had to stay and consume the energy of death to survive. They frequently died, making them unreliable scouts." He looks at me, and it's all there—his expression is flayed open and exposed. Raw, vulnerable in a way I'm not completely sure how to handle. I feel like he's as fragile as thinly blown glass.

I deliberately spread my fingers over his jaw, his flushed cheek, letting his heated skin warm my chilled flesh. I tilt up his face, look him straight in those red-black eyes, and I do *not* flinch. "Thank you," I say. "For telling me that story."

He leans forward, resting his forehead against mine. I feel his breath on my skin as he exhales a deep breath.

"I'm sorry." His voice is slurred and rough. "But you see, I should have been dead for nearly two hundred years. Instead, by chance, I was found by a curse and was turned into *this*. Not human, not immortal, but some cruel melding of the two. I endured two centuries of horrors, and maybe it was all so I could be here with you. If my unnatural existence means nothing else, it means this. I get to be here, now, with you."

My heart pounds so hard, I can feel it beat in my toes. "I don't understand your life. I'm only just beginning to understand my own, but I *do* understand having to pretend to be normal, even though the events of your past have made you into something that will always be different."

My hand slides down his neck, over his collarbone. He holds his breath until my palm stops on his chest, where his heart beats as hard and fast as my own. The moment hangs, an unanswered question, until I pull him forward and press my mouth to his.

Reece makes a small sound in his throat, and his arms crush me against him. Desperate, fierce, as if he'd been starving for the contact. As if he's been waiting for me to accept him, all his flaws and impossibilities included. I draw in a breath as his skin infuses mine with searing heat. It's almost too much.

Almost. A trill of fear and nervous anticipation moves through me. Suddenly, I don't know what to do. Or what *not* to do. Kissing him like this is like teasing a starving, wild thing, shot full with strange power. His hand finds my thigh under the blanket and slides toward my hip. He's barely human right now, but rather something wild and dangerous and uncertain in a way that should terrify me, but doesn't.

I slip my arms around his neck and tangle my fingers in his hair.

His tongue slides against mine as his mouth slants deeper. The heat of his skin turns mine feverish. The taste of him—bright and effervescent—turns my thoughts soft and tangled. The aches of my body are a distant echo. We press together so close, the combined pounding of our hearts beat like riotous drums.

When I pull back, my hands tremble on my throbbing lips—lips swollen and foreign-feeling. His gruesome red eyes are hot and intense and a little afraid.

"The world reeks of death and pain, and you smell like life and joy and everything I can never have." He rests his forehead against mine. "I hate this. I hate what I am, that I can't stay with you, Angie."

I gulp back a wave of sadness. I know he can't stay, and hearing it again sends an ache through me worse than all my injuries. "We're together right now."

He runs a hand down my arm. "Promise me, what little time we have left together, you won't push me away again." He sighs against my neck. "I'm not your enemy. I can't bear to be treated like one."

A promise I can make. His hair sifts through my fingers. "Okay."

His lips replace breath against my skin. I let my fingers slide down his back. The hot cage of his arms tightens, and I stop thinking in sentences. I want—*oh*, how I want…

Reece's head snaps up. He cocks his head in a sharp, lightning-fast way, just like a bird.

My reeling head struggles to compose itself. "What is it?"

His own breathing is harsh, labored, but he eases back, a

finger pressed to my lips. Silently, he slips away and edges to the door. He stands there and listens, then returns to me with a pinched expression on his face. He shifts to the wall and peeks out the open window.

"What's going on?" I ask. "Is Rafette here?"

"No, another one. He's curious, maybe." He crosses the room, tosses my clothes to me. "Get dressed, just in case. I have to go."

I clench my still damp jeans. "Go where?"

Without a word, he scoops me into his arms—covers and all—and holds me close. His pulse pounds in perfect rhythm with mine. "I want you to stay right here," he says. "I'll be back as soon as I can. It's important that you stay as high up as possible."

I rear back, goose bumps erupting over my arms. "Why?"

He sets me back. "I'll lead him away from here, even though he's probably going to leave soon, anyway. To catch the rest of it."

"The rest of *what?*"

He pins me with those red-black eyes. "The landslide damaged that hydro dam. Lake Serenity isn't stable. We could see it from the air—it's likely to go, and it's going to do so magnificently. The landslide was part one. Part two is going to happen at any moment, and you must keep to high ground before it does."

"High ground? That would mean…" *No, no, no.* My blood turns to ice. "But my friends are down there, in the valley."

"Hopefully, most of it will be diverted to the highway, and the lowest lying areas, but…" He glances at the window, conflict flexing in the muscle of his jaw. "I'm sorry, Angie, people are going to be in the way of this."

"What are you going to do?" I ask.

The worst thing about Reece's eyes like this, is I can't tell exactly where he's looking. With no whites, his eyes appear sightless. Right now, however, I know he's looking right at me, trying to decide something. He glances out the window and makes an impatient sound. "I'm sorry about this," he says. "I don't want you to see this, after Hank, but…"

"See wh—" But black, oily mist is coiling out of his mouth before the words finish. I stand, transfixed, as Reece closes his eyes, and the black vapor envelops his body. His transformation is smoother, faster than Hank's was, but no less dramatic. Reece's arms stretch smoothly into sleek, jointed wings. His fingers splay into long black feathers and for a moment, he looks every inch the dark tortured angel. His face is a pained grimace, then it's gone, engulfed in that black stuff. In a sudden rush, his body collapses, folds into itself. Compressing down, smaller, smaller. Then, the mist is gone, and standing in the circle of Reece's ill-fitting jeans is a sleek black crow. He studies me with dark red eyes, and I get now why those jeans didn't fit and why he didn't bother with a shirt. Every time he changes back into a human, he has to find new clothes. Sometimes, other people's clothes.

The crow—Reece—hops to the windowsill. No mystery now why it was kept open. He gives me a long, last look, spreads his wings, and glides from the apartment.

I tug the blanket around my shoulders and rush to the window. The lone crow glides low over a figure in the parking lot below. That other Beekeeper, I'm assuming. I can't see his faces from this distance, but his head turns as Reece flies on without looking back, banking sharply to the west. To the center of town. The figure turns away from the Mountain View Apartments and follows him.

But shortly afterward, a man walks into the parking lot. He tugs his wooly hat low over his forehead and looks up, slowly.

Rafette.

I shift away from the windows and slam against the wall, breathing hard. A million bucks says there aren't too many open windows in the building, making it pretty obvious which apartment I'm in. And he *does* know I'm in here. Trapped.

Footsteps crackle over the broken pavement. The door squeaks as it turns on its hinges. Rafette is inside. Coming for me—the one he believes can persuade Reece to take on a curse worse than the one he already has.

30

part two

I've never dressed so quickly. My aching body complains about the haste, but my bruises haven't gotten the memo that this hellish adventure isn't over yet. I dash to the window and haul myself onto the fire escape—my only way out, with Rafette inside somewhere. I step over a dead houseplant with a few dozen cigarette butts stuck in the soil and hurry down the zigzagging steps and landings. It's not quiet business. The rickety setup rattles under my feet like a metal skeleton. But slowing down isn't an option.

Keep to high ground...

My feet hit pavement. The ankle hurts, but I run on it anyway. The alternative will hurt more. I would give anything to trade these miserable boots for something practical.

The only advantage here is that the rain has *finally* stopped. I run-limp across the parking lot, feeling absurd anger toward the handful of parked cars I don't have keys to. I run straight over the spot where I watched that drunk guy crash his car—suddenly a lifetime ago—and scramble over the flattened chain link fence. It hadn't been repaired, thankfully. The bloodstains are long since washed away, but as I race across the empty highway, the doomed driver's skid marks are still visible on the pavement. That would have completely freaked me out a week ago. Now, I pass with barely a glance. The memory of that night is nothing in comparison to the past twenty-four hours, or what I'm likely to see in the next twenty-four.

I dart across the four deserted lanes. The *whip-whip-whip* of helicopters is constant, but they are too far away to see me. They come and go, circling the epicenter of the landslide. The only thought in my head is to get away and get to higher ground, but my options are pitiful. If I had headed toward town, I'd run into the other Beekeepers, and this way, it's just the southern foothills of Mt. Franklin. I look back at the Mountain View Apartments and choke back a cry.

Rafette stands in the open window of the apartment I just came from. I throw myself behind a shrub and try to be still. It's a good distance, but I can't be sure he didn't see me. Probably watched me the whole way. My stomach drops like a stone, and the thought invades: *he's stronger, faster than you. You stand no chance.*

Rafette spreads his arms and tilts his head back. He looks like he's worshipping a god, but then, all of a sudden, his body bursts apart in what looks like a cloud. I stare, mouth gaping, and wondering what the hell just happened, when that little dark cloud writhes in a weird way and begins moving toward me.

Wait. This isn't a cloud. It's a swarm of bees. Rafette just *turned into* a swarm of bees, and he's coming for me. Just when I thought I'd seen it all. I cover my head with a whimper and hope the pain isn't too bad. There's no escaping *this*.

Suddenly, a chorus of *caws* fills the air. I look up to see several dark shapes diving toward the bees. The swarm breaks up as the crows swoop at them. They're creating confusion.

They're giving me a chance.

I look up at Franklin and steel myself. People hike this mountain. The view's amazing, from what I hear, but they do it from the *other* side—where there's a managed trail, a gentler slope, and pretty trees to walk through. Here, it's just loose rock layered on a slippery incline. No one hikes this, but I don't have time to trek a couple miles around to find the trailhead. I need to go up. *Now*.

I scrabble over a section of mud and stones and attack the steep slope. Behind me, the crows still battle the bees. The crows' calls have grown desperate. I can see a ledge trail cut into the bank above me—maybe one used years ago by miners or currently by animals. It's only about ten feet away. If I can get to it, I'd make up some ground and possibly find someplace to hide. It's a long shot at best, but the crows are back there fighting for me, so I can't give up. I shed my disguise and played my music for a crowd. I can climb a damn hill.

Slivers of wet shale slide out beneath my feet, and my knees crash on the rocks for the umpteenth time. I land on my belly, panting. *Again*. I don't have the footwear for this, or the strength. My arms shake with fatigue. My stomach lets out an empty howl.

Then, for the second time, the sound of thunder cracks through the valley.

The crows go silent. The buzzing quiets to a dull hum. It's as if they are waiting…

A terrible thundering unsettles the rock beneath me. It vibrates, shifts, with tremors as frightening as the crack of the landslide. The loose rock and soil beneath my fingers gives way. I slide down a few hard-won feet.

I wait, ribs heaving against the rocky surface. Nothing happens. My view of Cadence is limited from here. I can't *see* anything, and for a second, my body sags with relief. It's beautiful and brief, wiped away by a sound both unfamiliar and terrifying. It is a roar, quiet and relentless. It's the sound of water.

I look to the bend in the highway, and a cry rips from my throat. A frothing tumble of water unrolls down the four lanes like a dark, filthy ribbon. The road is a deep groove cut into the landscape, making it act as a perfect funnel. Debris I can't identify tumbles with it, and the water is deepening, thickening with each passing second. Reece was right—the water ran for the highway—but I don't know what else it's hitting. Whether it's moving through the valley or found a path over and through the rubble. Either way, Lake Serenity is free of her restraints, and she's moving fast.

I dig in my hands and feet and scrabble upward with desperation. My feet find a slippery patch of loose rock, and I slide down more. The water is not deep, but it surges up the base of the slope and tugs at my feet. I can't climb up the muddy mess I'm clinging to. It's like climbing up mashed potatoes. I am no match for the water's power. Ice cold fingers pull my legs, yanking me with terrifying force.

The swift current jerks me into its turbulent rush. In an instant, the mountain is gone. Gravity is gone. Sky and earth, shaken senseless. I'm capable of swimming, but not in *this*. I am nothing. A small, breakable toy being tossed around by nature's force.

I *won't* survive this. I grab one last lungful of air before being sucked under again, bumping and scraping against rocks and earth and things once owned by people. *This is how I'm going to die*. It's a neutral thought. I can't even summon emotion. It's just simple fact.

Something big and solid slams against my back. Pain shoots up my spine, around my ribs. I gasp in a lungful of water and reach back for the rough, layered thing against my spine. Shingles. *A house?* With the last of my strength, I haul myself onto the object behind me. It *is* a roof—part of one, anyway. It's buoyant enough to stay steady in the rushing current. I drag myself as high as I can and collapse against the peak, gasping, coughing up filthy water from aching lungs. The pain in my ribs makes me retch. Or maybe it's all the river I choked in. Hard to tell. Harder to care.

How long did that whole thing take? Five seconds? Fifty? It felt like an eternity. I open my eyes and see a woman, facedown, being pushed along by the current. I shut my eyes and don't open them again. That could have been me. It *should* have been me. At this moment, Reece should be very thankful of his ability to turn into a bird. *I'd* rather be a bird right now.

The ride slows. Lake Serenity is large, but it isn't an ocean. As the water spreads out, the urgent push of it eases. The roof grinds to a halt, and now, for some reason, I feel like crying. And I would, if I had anything left. But I do have to open my eyes. Face whatever post-apocalyptic hellscape is waiting for me on the other side of my lids.

So I look, half expecting to see fires, destruction, a sea of corpses. But no. The air isn't thick with grit here, but clear. The body I saw before is nowhere to be found. In fact, there are no bodies anywhere in sight. I push myself to sit and blink in confusion. Am I having a delusion? There's no piles of rubble or ruined buildings. I'm not on the highway anymore. At some point, the water changed course, eased around Mount Franklin, following gravity's pull, spreading out and dispersing. Aside from the six-or-so inches of gently moving muddy water, this cross street is intact—houses, trees, everything is as it was before the landslide. I know this because I know precisely where I am. My roof has run aground in the parking lot of Reilly's Gas and Variety on Route 12. My heart stutters off beat. I'm close to home. I shouldn't be surprised. Cadence is a small town. I'm not too far from the entrance to Mount Franklin Estates.

Walking a few miles uphill is unthinkable, but oh...*home*. I wondered if I'd see it again. I climb off the roof and stagger to my feet. My body is unevenly heavy, as if different weights are tied to my limbs. I try to take stock, figure out what might be broken. Pretty much everything hurts, but not so terribly that I'm debilitated. I'm standing, after all.

I eye the front door of Reilly's and begin to slosh toward it. There's food in there. Water. My throat feels coated in sand. I'm dragging my left foot a little, reducing my progress to a plodding shuffle. A hysterical laugh shudders out of my belly, unbidden.

I climb the step and push open the convenience store's door, admitting a thin spread of water. A sour smell hits my nose, making my spirits drop. Someone's been through here. A glance to the right shows empty refrigerator cases with doors hanging open. A smashed gallon of milk spreads sticky and white over the floor. So much for water. That was surely what was looted first. My thoughts focus on the aisles. *Food*. Something must still be left.

I turn at the sound of a light moan. A girl around my age lies on the floor, folded into a ball, her back to me. Her hair is caked with blood and dirt. I hurry to her side and lay a hand on her shoulder. The girl whimpers and curls tighter. There are bruises up her bare arms. Her hands clutch at her torn T-shirt, printed with the words Reilly's Variety across the chest. She must be a worker here.

"Shh," I soothe. "I'm not here to hurt you. Can you sit up?"

The girl hesitantly rolls. Both her eyes are swollen—one is blackened—but she can open the other one a bit. "They're still here," she whispers. Her eye turns toward the back room.

A loud crash sounds from there, followed by rowdy, feverish laughter. At least two males, as far as I can tell. My heart races. Fresh fear sweeps adrenaline into my wiped-out system. "They did this to you?"

The girl just closes her eye. The rest of her face is streaked with dirt, puffed and purpled with bruises. A gash runs from her eyebrow into her hair. The men in the back room laugh again. It's a high, demented sound. Not sane. I would bet good money that they have been stung.

I slide an arm under her and gently lift her to sitting. "Can you walk?"

Her brow knits. "If I could walk, do you think I would still be *here?*"

Her reply is so snappish, I pause. Then it's so familiar, I almost drop her like a rock. Only one person has that voice. "*Kiera Shaw?*"

31

a murder of crows

"Oh hell. Angie *Dovage*?" She tries an eye roll, fails. "Of course, it would be you."

My grip on her loosens. I didn't know she worked here. I never stopped at this gas station because the gas was more expensive than anywhere else. Still, I can't imagine the queen of Cadence High behind the counter, selling lottery tickets and potato chips. But this isn't high school—this is survival. I give her a little shake. "Get up, Kiera."

She sighs. "I don't expect you to help me."

My stomach coils with something cold and ugly. It's not my job to help her. I'm wounded, too—and weak and hungry and dehydrated—and Kiera Shaw has made my life hell since I arrived in Cadence. No one would blame me for walking away. No one but *me*. I couldn't abandon her and live with myself.

Glass shatters in the back room, and one of the men lets out a howl. Loud banging ensues. I cringe at the sound of fists hitting flesh and the screams of a man who is not going to win. My senses fly into high gear. One of them is going to come out of there shortly, maybe looking for another body to beat on.

Kiera drops her head and waves her hand. "Just go," she rasps out. Her mouth stretches into a bloody smirk, exposing a dislodged eye tooth. "I'll get what I deserve, right?"

"Shut up." I hook my arms under her armpits and heave her back up against my chest. "No one deserves this."

Using my last scraps of adrenaline, I drag her toward the door. I'm not gentle about it. Maybe she *does* deserve that. I back into the door, grateful beyond words the bell isn't working.

Breath coming in labored puffs, I haul her to the side of the building and pin her against the wall. I'm not trying to be mean, but carrying a girl with five inches and twenty pounds on me isn't something I can sustain. "You need to walk."

Her face is surprised. That one eye is open as wide as she can make it. "I told you, I *can't*. It's broken."

I wince at the sound of things smashing inside the convenience store. The man is out of the back room and probably looking for Kiera. We're in a really bad spot here. Reilly's Gas and Variety hugs a curve in the road, leaving only asphalt to our sides and a wedge of thick forest to the rear. Our only hope lies on the other side of the street. It's a neighborhood. The houses are small and closer together.

We could hide in one of those small houses until the guy forgets and moves on. At least, we could find a way to defend ourselves. But we have to cross the wide-open space of gas pumps and parking lot before we even reach Route 12. And then we'd have to cross *that* two-lane road. A lot of ground to cover by two wounded girls.

A bottle of liquor explodes against the inside of the plate-glass window, startling muffled shrieks from Kiera and me.

He's going to see us if we run. But he's going to see us if we stay here.

I grab Kiera's arm and pull it over my shoulder. "We're

going. You *have* to walk. It's going to hurt."

A pained gasp wheezes from her. "But—."

"I don't care." I *don't*. My entire body is a throbbing knot of pain. Plus, I'm pretty sure I've got a cracked rib from my ride in Lake Serenity's water slide. I yank her forward as another bottle smashes on the window. "You will hurt more with *him*."

Kiera starts walking, and I know it hurts her. Her face is gray, and she whimpers each time she puts weight on that broken ankle. But she does it.

We make it all the way to the pumps before the door smashes open, banging against its frame. I glance back to see a wide-bellied man in a bloodstained T-shirt shout at us. I can't tell his age. All I see is rage and clenched red fists, trembling at his sides.

He sees us and starts running. Not fast, but faster than us.

I jerk Kiera forward, and we're able to pick up the pace slightly. Not enough. I don't see the curb through the water, and we both tumble into the street.

"What are you, suicidal? Leave me and *go*," she gasps, holding her face out of the water with trembling arms. This time, there's nothing snide behind her words. She means it. The chase is over, and she knows it.

The truth is, even without her, I wouldn't be able to outrun him. "When he reaches us, we fight," I tell her. "Nail him in the crotch. I'll go for his eyes."

"Where you going, girlies?" the man gasps. He's closer than I thought, closing the gap fast.

Kiera's mouth opens in surprise, then firms. "Crotch. Got it."

Suddenly, the sounds of flapping papery wings and feverish *caws* fill the street. A cloud of crows heads directly for our pursuer. The man flings his meaty arms wildly as the birds descend on him.

This scene is *very* different from the one at the bus stop

when I met Reece, all those weeks ago. Different from the skirmish they just had with the Beekeeper swarm. This is a serious attack. This is *mortouri.* The harbingers of death are dealing it themselves this time, and although I know little about this magical system, I think this is probably against the rules. Either they know it and hope their dark watchers aren't seeing this, or they know it and don't care.

Unlike Rafette, this man is no match for a murder of supernatural crows. There are more of them this time—more than a dozen. The crows easily dodge his clumsy flailing. I flinch as their talons dig into exposed flesh, ripping, shredding. Their skilled beaks aim for eyes, the skin just below the ears. The man drops to his knees with a howl, hands covering the ruined remains of his face. Blood streams through his fingers, down his filthy T-shirt.

Kiera squeezes my arm as one of the crows breaks away from the rest and turns sharp red eyes on us.

Reece? I can't tell. They all look the same. Its beak is shiny. Drops of red drip from the tip into the murky water. My throat goes dry. If this is Reece, I can't imagine the boy on the other side of this gore-spattered bird. He hops forward and lets out a low *caw*.

Kiera moans, dragging her arms over her head.

"They won't hurt us," I murmur, but she's crying so loudly she doesn't hear.

The crows peck and dig until the man goes still. Until the water around him turns rust-colored.

Some of the crows perch in a gruesome row on the man's body. Others fly to the gas pumps. They begin to run their beaks through glossy feathers. All except for the one standing on the curb, watching me. It dips its head and blinks at me. I mouth the words, *thank you*.

Satisfied, it hops back to the others, perched on the dead

guy's back. They shift to make room for it, and it lets out a long, mournful *kraaaah* before cleaning its feathers.

I turn away, feeling a little light-headed, and I climb to my feet. "Come on," I croak, pulling Kiera upright. "Let's break into that house."

Kiera points and blubbers at the crows, but I tug her away. Together we limp to the closest house, a neat little yellow number with window boxes. They're all abandoned around here, of course. Inconvenient. It would be so much easier if someone would just open their doors and let us in. Two beaten girls, filthy and drenched in foul water, hobbling across the street. Kiera might be in shock. She's making weird little mewling sounds.

"Zip it, will you?" I mutter. "You're creeping me out."

She rolls that swollen eye my way. "*I'm* creeping *you* out? We just saw a man get pecked to death by crows. *Crows*, Angie, and you're not even fazed." She shakes her head. "You *are* a freak."

I glance over at the blood-caked wreck of a girl next to me and grin. *Yes*, I grin, when just a few weeks ago, her words would have had me pushing back tears. When did this girl cease to have power over me? I wish I could pinpoint the precise moment. To feel the before and after and know if it happened because of something I did, or because of something that happened to me. My grin turns into a chuckle. "I actually feel sorry for you right now."

Despite the bruises, Kiera's face pulls in a well-worn expression of disdain. "Oh please. You are so full of it."

I'm not interested in being her friend, but maybe there was a part of me that once did. Maybe that's why it used to hurt when she was so cruel to me. "Yes, I am," I say, "and maybe that's the thing. You're just…*empty*. Like, there's nothing there. It's like you're waiting for a train or something. Being mean to kill the boredom."

Kiera looks away with a faraway frown. The front door is locked, of course, so I leave Kiera on the front stoop and move to try the rest of the doors and windows. Her mouth moves like she wants to say something, but she closes it and turns away.

I shuffle off and try the other doors, but they're also locked. Luckily, there's an unlocked living room window. I open it and carefully hoist myself inside, being mindful of my ribs and ankle and, oh, everything. The only furniture is a leather couch, a large TV on the wall, and a game system sprawled on the floor. Games and their plastic boxes float in an inch of water on the floor. I'd bet money that a single guy lives here. Hopefully he won't mind if we borrow his house for a bit. I lean out the window to Kiera. "Go around to the front door. I'll unlock it."

Kiera does as I say and limps through the front door. She collapses on the couch. I rifle through the homeowner's kitchen for something to eat and drink. I know I'm desperate when the not-so-clear water on the floor is starting to look good. In the fridge, I find a six-pack of water bottles shoved behind a case of beer. The cabinet is stuffed with junk food. I return to the living room, hand Kiera a water and a tube of Pringles.

She accepts them, but instead of opening them, she presses her loose eye tooth upward with her thumb and shudders in fresh pain. "Why are you still helping me?" she asks around her thumb.

I stare at her for a minute. "Because it's the decent thing to do. You should try it sometime."

She scoops up a Madden NFL box and shakes the water from it. "Do you think I owe you something now?"

I look out the bare window. I'm restless but unsure where to go. "No," I say. "Just try to… Oh forget it." I shrug and rip open a bag of Doritos. "We're graduating in a few months then we'll never see each other again. Hopefully."

I'm surprised to see hurt flicker over her bruised features.

"You're right, you know," she says in a small voice.

"About what?"

"I am…empty. Waiting, or whatever." She waves a hand. "You said it better. You say everything better."

I struggle not to roll my eyes. In the scheme of things I'd like to do right now, playing therapist to Kiera Shaw is ranked way, *way* low on the list. I scarf down several handfuls of Doritos and shove the rest in a plastic grocery bag I found in the kitchen. "You'll figure it out," I say. "Or not."

"You know exactly what you want to be, always have." Her eye goes steely on mine. "You came from shit, you know, just like me. You think I work at Reilly's for fun? Watching you fancy people up there in the 'Estates' gas up your Beemers…" She trails off with a hiss. "Anyway, you're doing what you love. What took you so long to reveal yourself, anyway? Never mind, don't answer that. I don't really care." She releases her tooth and delicately touches her fingertips to her swollen eye, pretending not to notice my flinch.

"And you're *good*. That makes it worse. Now I'm going to be the girl who was mean to the super-talented musician who's going to go and be *famous*." There's a compliment buried in there, and clearly it cost her.

"Who *cares?*" I ask. "It's *high school*. Four years that are almost over, thank *God*."

"Yeah well, I get full-time shifts at Reilly's after graduation. What will you be doing?" She holds out a hand when I start to say something. "No. *Stop*. You are *so* lucky, you don't even know."

"I'm not lucky. I lived with a mother who—" I shake my head. "I am *not* lucky." I say it again because she's made me realize that she is *right*. All I have to do is think of my dad to realize just how fortunate I am. I admit, I know nothing about Kiera's life. If she's dealt with anything near to what I did with my mom, I truly feel awful for her. It doesn't make her bad treatment of me okay, but there's comfort in knowing the origin of her bitterness. I got out of my bad situation and was dropped in the arms of a wealthy, adoring father. She didn't.

A tap at the window snaps our heads to the sound. A black crow flutters against the glass. He gains footing on the sill and tosses his beak in impatience.

Kiera squeals and shrinks into the couch. "Oh no, not again! Get it away."

Reece. It's got to be him this time. Both wings are jet black—no white feather marking it as Hank. I bite my lip to keep from grinning and stuff two water bottles in my bag. "Okay, I'm going," I say to Kiera. "You'll be safe here."

Kiera sits upright. "You're leaving?"

I nod. "I'm sure the National Guard or someone is checking the area for survivors. Sit tight until they find you. If I see any rescue personnel, I'll tell them where to find you." I pause, as she's staring at me like I've just sprouted wings. "There's food, three bottles of water, and well, there's beer in the fridge if you want it. You probably do."

"You're leaving with that *bird* out there? We just watched them peck a guy's face off."

"I know, right? Well, I am a freak, after all." I sling the bag over my shoulder with a smile. On my way out, I glance back at her. "By the way, Kiera, some luck is the type we make ourselves. So don't write yourself off yet, okay?"

And that's all the goodwill I have for her. I open the door and head outside, leaving Kiera glowering after me.

Outside, I tilt back my head and smile. An ink-black wing brushes my cheek in a feathery caress. Talons gently pluck at my hair, and I laugh in delight. The crow lands on it, then hops down to my shoulder.

"Hi there," I say.

The crow nuzzles my cheek with his beak. He's clean and smooth. Gone is any gory evidence that he helped kill the man who tried to attack Kiera and me.

Reece leaves my shoulder and flies ahead, landing farther up the street. He lets out a low *caw* and hops impatiently. He wants me to follow him, but the road is an uphill one. It also leads someplace wonderful—home.

"Okay," I say with sudden enthusiasm. I'd forgotten that we have a generator. Water. Lights. Clean clothes. Such *luxuries*. "Let's go home."

32
home

Reece stays ahead of me, sometimes moving from tree to tree, sometimes circling above, but never straying far. I eat most of the food on the way. It's total crap—chips and various puffed things—but it fills the void in my belly and keeps the feet moving. My stomach is a churning, greasy mess by the time I reach my driveway, thanks in part to partially hydrogenated soybean oil and pure, giddy relief.

Reece stays in a tree as I dig out the key hidden under a solar light and open my front door. I'm greeted by an eager wet nose shoving through the opening. *Roger*. His whole body wiggles in welcome. I drop to my knees and bury my face in his coarse fur.

I've never been so happy to see him. *He's* never seemed so happy to see *me*. "Hey there, boy," I croon. His fur is warm and smells wonderfully familiar. I rest my cheek on his neck and hug him tighter than he'd like, taking his enthusiastic kisses square on the face without even a wince. If I have to endure his slobber, he has to endure my vulnerable moment. "I wasn't sure I'd see you again, handsome."

Someone "shushes" from the direction of the kitchen. I freeze. *Someone's here?* My body goes tense, but Roger doesn't seem concerned. "Hello? Who's there?" I call.

Two heads poke around the corner. *"Angie?"*

Who? Oh, that's me. And that's… "Lacey? Deno?"

Maybe it's the surprise of seeing them. Maybe I just used up all my mental energy on Kiera. Spots of black appear at my peripheral vision. I sway, dropping my bag.

Lacey and Deno jump forward. Deno grabs me and lowers me to the floor. "Angie, are you okay?"

I sag against him, vaguely wondering why he's clutching one of my dad's fancy carving knives. "Yeah, I'm…" I feel my brows knit. "How did you get in here?"

"You gave me a key and the security code. It was a few months ago when you and your dad went to visit your grandparents and I watched Roger. Remember?"

I do remember, but I can't organize a response. I just sort of stare up at him. His brows draw together in sudden concern. "Did you hit your head?"

"I hit just about everything." Relief and joy and something akin to love move through me. I'm really, *really* happy to see them. I'm so glad they thought to come here. I could kiss both of them. I grin at Deno. "You look different."

His eyes are hard, haunted. Thick hair mats around his face, which is dirty and sports a bruise on his forehead. His clothes are…my dad's, except for his haggard-looking army jacket hanging from his shoulders. It's strange to see Deno in this package.

"Yeah, well, you look like an extra from *The Walking Dead*." He winces. "Smell pretty bad, too."

"That bad, huh?"

"Not *good*," he says, half carrying me to the living room.

"We didn't shower because we didn't want to use up all the propane in the generator, but maybe you should make an exception."

He eases me to a couch. Roger trots over and heaves himself practically on my lap. Lacey hands me a half-filled cup of tea. I accept it with a grateful sigh. Ah, something *warm*.

Lacey sits on the cushion next to me and tosses back her long hair. Long, *clean* hair. She doesn't have any visible bruises. She's wearing my clothes and looks better in them than I do. "How the hell do you look so good after surviving a landslide and a flood?" I ask her.

She flashes a smile and a sly shrug. "I look where I'm going."

Deno snorts, and I burst into giggles. It's better than crying, which is the release my emotions are pushing for.

"Oh Angie, we were so worried about you." Lacey pauses, then speaks gently. "Do you know what happened to Reece? He carried you off…that's the last we saw of either of you."

Oh man, how do I explain *this?* "Reece and I…got separated. He's okay, I think."

Well, considering he's outside right now, I'm *sure*. There've got to be times the boy is thankful he can turn into a bird. I only wish he'd utilize his one and only superpower and get himself to safety.

"I can't tell you how glad I am to see you both." I set aside the empty cup of tea with a sigh. "But what are you two *doing* here? I thought you'd be evacuated. There were helicopters everywhere."

Lacey and Deno exchange a tense look.

My hands, stroking Roger's silky ears, go still. "What's going on, guys?"

"We didn't get on the rescue helicopter." Lacey's lips compress to a line. "There wasn't room for everyone, and there were people who needed to get to a hospital worse than us. And then we ran."

"What?" I ask. "Why not wait for the next one?"

"The next helicopter wasn't coming for another hour." Deno scrapes his hands through his grimy hair. "There were bees. A *lot* of bees."

"I have a hunch," Lacey says in a quiet voice, "that they are not normal bees at all."

33

the birds and the bees

"We headed for your place. It was the only safe place we could think of. It's high and dry, and you have a generator." He glances at me sheepishly. "I hope you don't mind."

"Are you kidding? Of course I don't mind." I'm so glad they came, it's all I can do to not sit here and cry at them.

He swallows hard. "I'll never look at a bee the same way. They seemed to go after certain people. And people were acting sick, breaking things, attacking for no reason. It was like a horror movie."

"You must have been really scared." I work to keep my voice even. "This is a long way from town. Five miles or so."

He feels the bump on his forehead, winces. "I don't know how to explain it. You probably think we overreacted."

"I totally don't. *At all.* I agree with you about the bees," I reply.

"I was probably being paranoid," Lacey says, "But I wanted to get away from there as fast as I could. They got my mom on the helicopter. My two little brothers, too."

"Good. You're not being paranoid." *Eyes on floor.* I'm *so* bad at deception. "You did the right thing."

"Uh-huh." Deno's eyes narrow. "What are you not telling us?"

I slowly get to my feet. "I need some water."

They watch me hobble to the kitchen in silence. I check on Roger's food and water, even though I know they took care of him already. At the sink, I pour a large glass of water and force myself to drink it slowly. How much should I tell my friends? I could answer all their questions, but telling them anything opens me up to the whopper of *how* I know about all this stuff, and that's not my story to tell. They already know I know more than I'm saying. They already know there's something abnormal with the bees.

There's a shout at the front door. A thud and some cursing. I drop my cup and hurry to the foyer, where I heard the sounds. Deno and Lacey are backing away from the closed front door. There's a commotion on the other side in the form of scratching and squawking.

Deno points. "I think it's a bird," he says, eyes wide. "One of those crows."

It's Reece. I don't think about it. I ease past them and open it.

"Ack! No! What are you doing?" Deno holds out his hands, stumbling backward.

The crow hops inside and delivers Deno a loud, offended squawk. Long black claws click delicately on the marble floor.

Deno sputters at the bird. "What the *hell*, Angie?"

"Close the door, will you?" I ask, ignoring him. "You're letting in the chill."

Lacey squats down and studies the crow as if he were a rat with an ear growing on his back. She doesn't appear to share

Deno's fear or repulsion. "What are you, you interesting little guy?"

"*That's* a good question." Deno pins me with a hard look, fury blazing in his eyes. "What *is* it? What the hell is going on around here?"

Reece jumps, flaps his wings, and alights on my shoulder.

"You made friends with a crow?" Lacey raises her brows. "That's so cool. How did you do that?"

I smile weakly. "He's not exactly a normal crow."

Deno rubs his hands over his face. "You *think*?" He stares at me with a blanched face and bugged-out eyes. There's a weird, unstable look to him. It sets me on edge.

"Angie. I'm at the end of my rope." He presses his fists to his temples and squeezes his eyes shut. "I need a rational explanation, because I can't take any more weird shit. I really can't."

Reece sinks low against my shoulder and lets out a low growl.

I try, but I can't find any decent words. Yeah, I get how *not* normal this looks. Deno must be feeling kind of like how I felt that first day at the bus stop with Reece. The day my life changed. Deno may never look at me the same. I suppose that's okay, because *I'm* not the same. And neither is he.

"Just calm down." I say to him, wincing at the dig of talons in my shoulder.

Lacey's brows knit in a rare scowl. "Angie, we deserve to know *why* there is a crow on your shoulder."

"All right." They do. Plus, I simply lack the energy to pick and choose truths and lies that I'll have to recall and repeat later. I sit down, rest my back against the wall. Reece hops off my shoulder and settles down next to my knee.

"We're listening." Deno says when I hesitate to say more.

I give him a hard look. "Are you sure you want to know?

The things I tell you are going to sound insane."

His gaze slides to the dark bird sitting beside me. "Seriously, nothing you say could shock me right now."

"I doubt that, but..." I shrug and tell them the facts I know about the Beekeepers. I tell them about my first encounter with Rafette in The Strip Mall's parking lot and his many shifting faces. Deno and Lacey listen in silence, growing stiller with each word I utter.

I go quiet when I run out of things to share. I'm holding back, still reluctant to include my friends in Reece's secret.

Lacey touches my knee. "What about the bird, Angie?"

I look down. "It's not my secret to tell."

"Is it evil?" Deno asks, but the heat is out of his voice. "Is it the same sort of creature as the Beekeepers you described?"

"No," is my quick reply. "But they have similar origins." Absently, I run a hand over Reece's sleek back. He lifts his beak in the air and closes his little red eyes. "The crows are harbingers of death. They can tell where bad things are going to happen. They travel to these places, absorbing the energy of the dying and recently dead. They don't cause the problems. It's just how they survive."

"Harbingers of death. Like the legends. But real." Deno eyes Reece with less hostility. More curiosity. "And this one has befriended you?"

Um. "You could say that."

"How come?" Lacey asks. "And why you?"

I open my mouth, then close it. She *always* asks the squirmiest questions. My hand stroking Reece goes still. We're getting to questions I don't want to answer—not sure I *can* answer. As if sensing my dread, Reece shakes his feathers and hops into the living room. Black mist curls around him. My nostrils flare at the acrid bite of a blacksmith's shop.

"What's it doing?" Lacey asks.

I think I know. We can still see him—he's just on the other side of the archway—but far enough away that anyone who might be afraid won't feel too threatened by what they're about to witness. Reece tucks his head low and goes very still. More ribbons of black vapor pull from his feathers. His body expands.

"Oh." I breathe in awe and dread and fascination. "Well, he can show you himself."

My friends stare, open-mouthed as bird legs stretch and thicken into human legs. Wings morph into arms. Bird features soften, transform into a familiar human boy's face.

The black mist looks sinister, evil. I would like to know why he smells of smelting metal. The mist snakes around Reece's body, then gathers in a dark rope and forces itself down his throat.

Reece is on his knees, arms braced on the floor. Naked and sweating and choking in deep, shuddering breaths. He keeps his gaze to the floor. His eyes are shielded by a damp curtain of his hair. "Please don't be afraid," he gasps, eyes wide. "I'm not going to hurt you."

34 the beekeepers

Deno backs up slowly. His back hits the wall hard, and he sinks into a crouch, brow shiny with sweat. "This is not happening," he says. "This is not fucking happening."

Lacey stares, too, but she does not seem frightened to see the crow recently hopping around the foyer transform into my boyfriend. Her face is oddly relieved, as if *finally*, it all makes sense to her. All she says is, "Deno, your language has been coarse lately. It's making you sound ignorant."

For the first time in recorded history, Deno doesn't have a smart retort. Ironic, because *now* would be a perfectly appropriate time to use coarse language.

"I apologize," he says quietly, not taking his eyes off Reece.

I cross to Reece, snagging a throw blanket off the back of a chair—a brightly colored number knitted by my grandmother. He tucks it around his waist like a kilt. I doubt Grams envisioned *this* use for her handiwork.

Reece heaves himself upright and leans close to me. "How are my eyes?" he murmurs. "I don't want to scare them."

A smile curves my lips. "If they're still standing after your little Crow-to-Boy Transformation Show, I think you're okay."

Reece winces. "I guess so, but..."

I brush the hair out of his eyes and gaze into black irises and white whites. My own relief must be palpable. *I'm* happy to see Reece looking like Reece again. "You look like you."

He lets out a breath. His expression is still worried. "For now, at least. I don't have full control. It was *so* hard to take this form."

"It's okay," I say with a pang. Just another reminder of his impending departure. "Thank you. Thank you for staying. It's selfish of me to say that, but I'm glad. You should have left. The unselfish part of me wishes you did."

He leans in to my palm. I feel his cheek fold into a smile.

"I told you I wouldn't," he says, tilting my chin up. His head bows. Warm lips brush mine.

"Um. Oh dear. We're still here," says an awkward voice from the doorway.

We turn, remembering Lacey and Deno. I don't know what's more shocking—that Reece turned from crow to boy in front of my friends and I'm standing here kissing him moments later, or the fact that they're composed about it. A normal person would be climbing the walls. "Oh. *Very* sorry about that." A blush heats my cheeks. "I don't even know where to start explaining all...this." I gesture to Reece, who rolls his shoulders.

Lacey shifts her gaze from Reece to me. "A portion of our town is destroyed. There are creatures running around with bees in their mouths, stinging people and infecting them with some sort of psychosis-inducing venom. Speaking for myself..." She points to Reece. "*This* is the least of my worries."

Deno narrows one eye. "Aside from my coarse language."

"I always worry about you, Deno." She gives him a blinding smile. "Or I should say, *Daniel*."

Deno blinks at her as if she just said all that in a foreign language. "What's with you?"

"My God, you cannot be that dense." Reece rakes a hand through his damp hair. "She *likes* you, and if you have half a brain, you'll like her back and do your best to not screw it up. Later, though. Let's survive the night first."

Lacey's cheeks pinken, but she appears pleased with Reece's assessment. Deno still looks vaguely confused.

Reece reinforces the throw blanket around his waist and stretches. His spine pops and crunches with each bend and twist. He groans, with pain or relief, I can't tell. His grimace could mean either.

"Easy does it, man." Deno's pained gaze swings from Lacey to Reece. "Does it hurt when you…do that?"

"What? Change into a person? It's excruciating." Reece rolls his shoulder, unleashing another series of grinding pops. We *all* groan at the sound. "It's still the least awful aspect of my curse." He looks at me, an apology pulling down his brow. "We can't stay here. Rafette has enlisted the help of a few other Beekeepers who have arrived. It won't take them long to look for us here."

"I thought they didn't work together," I say.

"They don't, usually. Maybe they want to see if his plan can work. If there is a way to break the Beekeeper curse," Reece replies, and for the first time, there's worry in his eyes. Perhaps he's no longer certain that Rafette's scheme is impossible.

My heart drops. "How long?"

He shrugs. "They checked here a few hours ago. They will circle back when they've exhausted their efforts elsewhere."

"Who is coming here?" Lacey asks. "The Beekeepers?"

Reece nods.

"Okay." Deno scrubs his hands over his face. "What do they *want?*"

Reece sighs. "Me."

Deno blinks at him. *"You?"*

"That's what I said."

"Why you?" Deno smirks. "One of them have the hots for you?"

Reece raises his brows to Lacey. "You seem like a smart girl. Are you sure about this guy?"

Lacey bites down on a laugh, but Deno's face goes red. "Yeah, ha-ha. But it's a real question. Why are they after you? And what does that mean for us?"

Reece sobers instantly. "Rafette believes his curse is transferrable to harbingers. I have no clue about the mechanics of this, but he's convinced that if he can force me to accept his curse, his own soul can be set free. It doesn't mean anything to you and Lacey. You both got caught in the middle."

"And what's Angie's role in all this?" Lacey asks.

Reece's jaw clenches. "Rafette thinks that if he can get his hands on Angie, I'll go along with his plan in return for her freedom. Frankly, I'm more worried about him stinging her. I don't plan to let Rafette anywhere near her. I'll protect Angie until Rafette leaves—and he'll have to leave—and then I'll depart with my harbinger family."

Deno lets out a breath. "So you didn't break up because he tried to—"

"*No*, Deno," I snap. "Ugh."

"Tried to what?" Reece's brows knit in confusion.

"Nothing," I grind out, sending Deno a killing look.

"That's just so *sad*." Tears brighten Lacey's eyes. "You really can't stay, Reece?"

"No," Reece says. "It's a struggle to stay in human form as it is. The curse is fighting me, pressing me to fly."

"That's terrible." Lacey frowns at him, as if any of this were his choice. "That's the most tragic thing I've ever heard."

"Yeah. It totally sucks," Deno says. "But like he said, we're being hunted by Bee-guys right *now*, and Lacey and I are not going to let them win here. So how do we defeat them?"

Reece looks amused. "We don't. They're more powerful than harbingers. And they're true immortals. They can't be killed by any known means."

"What are their weaknesses?" Deno persists. "Do they have any?"

Reece tilts his head, thinks. "Well, after a disaster, they leave quickly. They can't tolerate the change in energy. They can't go underground, either. It bugs them out for some reason. They have no mental abilities that we know of, like telepathy or anything. We can sense when they're near, but it doesn't go the other way, as far as we know." He shrugs. "That's it, I think."

"So we wait them out," Deno says. "All of us. We stick together."

Reece studies him for a moment, then nods. "But we can't stay here. If they choose to attack, their bees *will* find a way inside. I'll know if Rafette is on his way, but we need to keep moving, find someplace better hidden."

"No." I wag my finger between Deno and Lacey. "You two are getting out of here. On the first rescue helicopter we see."

Lacey's eyes widen. "We won't leave you."

I shake my head firmly. "I appreciate that, but I need you two to be safe. This isn't your fight."

Lacey's eyes narrow. "How exactly is it yours?"

I don't like this question. I bite my bottom lip and search for a way around it. There isn't one, and I won't start lying to my friends now, after all this uncomfortable truthfulness. I won't insult them that way. "My mother was stung by a Beekeeper." *Breathe*. It's not so bad, saying it out loud. "It's what killed her, ultimately."

Deno's gaze goes sharp. "But she never hurt you. She never acted like the people out there, setting fires and attacking for no reason."

"She became addicted to opiates." I rub the dull ache in my ankle. "We lived in a Volkswagen van, and she told fortunes for a living. She died of a drug overdose."

"But she never *hurt* you, did she?" He leans forward. "She never beat you or anything."

Lacey gives him an odd look. "Deno, what…?"

"It's okay," I say to her. "No, she never beat me, but her behavior was abusive. You can't use drugs like she did and give a kid a healthy life. You can't—" I drag in a knotted breath and close my eyes. Let my heart rate ease back to normal. "Look, if they sting me, I'll make sure I'm not a danger to anyone. I'll check myself into an institution or something." I don't want to think about the "or something."

"They're not going to sting you," Reece says.

"You keep saying that," I say. "How do you know?"

He studies me with tired eyes. Eyes that have seen so many terrible things. "Because the last time Rafette stung a harbinger's loved one, it did not achieve the desired result."

Loved one. My heart bumps around under my ribs, painful and thrilling and, as Lacey so aptly put it, tragic. "What do you mean?"

Reece's voice goes gentle. "Destroying your mother's mind did not free the Beekeeper of his curse. Hank didn't take on Rafette's curse." He rolls a shoulder, and the joint pops in place. He lets out a relieved sigh. "Rafette may be sociopathic, but he learned from his mistakes."

I swallow through a suddenly parched throat. "So what are they going to do to me instead?"

"Nothing. They're not going to get near you."

"But if they—"

"I don't know what they'd do, okay?" he says. "*I'm* not a sociopath."

"Are you *sure?*" Deno tosses out with another smirk. "You feed off the *dead*."

Reece turns to Deno, eyes hard and black. He looks ferocious, even with a rainbow throw blanket knotted around his waist. Deno shrinks back.

"I'm a lot of things, *Daniel*," Reece enunciates each word through his teeth. "Feeding on death energy is not a choice for me any more than eating food is for you. I don't know what that makes me, but I'm *not* a sadist. I don't hurt people." He turns toward the stairs. "Don't compare me to a Beekeeper again."

Reece lopes up the stairs. The instant he's out of sight, I turn to Deno. "What was *that* about?"

Deno rests his head in his tense fingertips. "I don't know. I'm sorry. I guess I'm overtired."

"Fine, be overtired," I say. "But don't be an ass, too."

"That wasn't nice, Deen." Lacey shakes her head. "Come on. Let's pack up some food and water. If Beekeepers are coming, we need to move."

Deno gets to his feet and follows after her like a scolded child.

I look at the stairs and sigh. *Reece*. It's important we don't drag Deno and Lacey into this game of manhunt. We can't "stick together," as Deno said. I don't understand why Reece agreed with that statement.

I find Reece in the upstairs bathroom, scrubbing water over his face. He looks up. "Hey."

"Hey." I lean a hip against the doorframe. "You okay?"

"Yeah, I'm fine." He braces his hands on either side of the sink. Droplets drip from his wet hair into the water with rhythmic plops.

"I don't remember Deno being so provoking," he says.

"Me, either. He says he's tired."

"Yeah." Reece lets the water drain and pulls a towel off the rack. He dries his face, then loops the towel around his neck.

I raise a brow. "That's my towel, you know."

Of course he knows. It's *my* bathroom. And if he wasn't sure, the dozens of skin and hair products crowding the sink would give him a clue. Although, in fairness, my dad's collection rivals mine.

A smile curves Reece's lips. He crowds me against the doorframe. "I know. It smells like you."

My heart trips over itself, picks up the pace. "Ew. Before or after a shower?"

"After, of course." His hands encircle my waist. Heat emanates from him, still abnormal for a person, but it's not the intense burn of earlier.

"I, uh… Hmm." My thoughts unravel. What did I come up here to talk to him about? It was important. Really…important.

Oh, right. I let out a frustrated groan. "Reece, Lacey and Deno need to get out of Cadence with some human rescuers, and *you* need to take off. Go back to your group and disappear." My throat threatens to shut down around the words. He can't know how hard they are to say. "If they think we broke up and you don't care about me, they'll give up pursuing you."

"It's too late to make them think I don't care about you." His hands slide around my waist, trace up the bumps of my spine. "I will *always* care about you."

I suck in a sharp breath, inhaling the scent of woods and earth and my cucumber-melon cleanser he must have washed his face with. "Don't say that."

"Why not?" His voice is husky. "I fell in love with you when we were six. No matter what happens, that's the truth. You should know it."

My heart swells and knots, pushes so hard against my ribs I fear they'll snap. "I can't *take* it, Reece." The words rip out in a rasp. "When this is all over, you'll be gone. *Forever.* And

I have to go on. Finish high school. Go to college. *Hopefully*, make a life."

His gaze slides over my face. Pain tightens his features, quickly disguised. "Yes. All those things and more."

A tear slides down my cheek. He wipes it away with his thumb. "Right. Well, how am I supposed to do that if I can't stop being in love with you?"

His hand stills. "You're in love with *me?*"

Seriously? I press down the urge to hit him. "And you called Deno dense?"

"Deno's right—I *do* feed off the dead. I'm unnatural. Disgusting. An abomin—"

I shut him up by closing the space between us and pressing my fingertips to his lips. "Say one more nasty thing about yourself and I'll clobber you."

Reece pulls me up against his bare chest. There aren't even words for this feeling. It's need and longing and a hearty dose of desperation. Thoughts spill away as he lowers his head. His lips brush against mine in the whisper of a kiss. It's different from any other. It tastes of certainty and sadness and promises that can never be made. It drags me under, like floodwaters from a broken dam.

Too soon, he eases back, breath harsh against my cheek as his hands slide to my hips. Then, with what looks like colossal effort, he pushes himself away from me.

"What's wrong?" I ask, shivering with rejection.

He rests his forehead against mine. "Everything. Your friends are downstairs. Rafette is on our heels and I—" He leans back, rubs tense hands over his face. "I'm up here kissing you like we have all the time in the world."

I draw in a deep breath. Downstairs, I can hear Lacey playing the piano. A long, plaintive melody rising above the hum of the generator.

I should be thankful he's so flipping considerate, but with my heart beating out of my chest and my head spinning like a top, I can't quite manage it. "Right."

He edges past me, into the hall. A flush rides high on his cheeks, and he doesn't meet my gaze. "Go ahead and wash up. I'm going to borrow some of your dad's clothes."

My lips move and sound comes out. I'm not sure how. "Yeah. Sure."

I close the bathroom door and dunk my head under cold running water until my face is numb. Now, with water burning my sinuses, I see his wisdom in stopping our kiss. It just pisses me off that there is never a good time for Reece and me. Probably never will be. And I'm so tired of remembering that little fact.

I peel off my filthy clothes like they're a layer of rotting skin. I ball them up and stuff them in the wastebasket. I definitely *don't* smell like my clean towel. The shower beckons me to blow through the fuel in the generator and take a long, hot one. Instead, I use a washcloth and cold water to scrub off what filth I can.

After, I pad down the hall in a towel to my room. Reece isn't in there. I look around my room in a state of disorientation, but not because it's different. It's so much the same, I don't know what to make of it. The pile of laundry lays half in, mostly out of the hamper. A knotted mess of headphone wires and power cords I've been meaning to untangle sits next to my bed. Necklaces hang off my cluttered vanity mirror. It's all so very much the same.

But the owner of this room is *not* the same.

I put on clean underwear. Jeans. A black sweater. Warm socks and the hiking boots I wear on the trails. I lay back on the bed, sighing as my body sinks into the mattress and exhaustion smashes me across the head. The bed is a cool purple paradise, and I'm so tired. The thought of crawling under the rumpled covers and sleeping for a week makes my body ache with a very different kind of longing than it had a few minutes ago in Reece's arms.

He appears in my doorway, composed and dressed in a pair of my dad's designer jeans and a snug thermal shirt. "I didn't stop kissing you because I wanted to. I hope you know that."

I gaze at the ceiling. "I know."

"Maybe one day…" He shakes his head. "I don't know—"

I hold up a hand. "Stop. Just…*stop*. Don't pretend we'll ever be together. You know we won't."

He comes forward and sits on the mattress next to me. His hands close on mine, tightly. "I remember those times we spent together when we were little kids. I thought—no, wished so hard it hurt—that I could be a normal boy and see you every day. That I could walk to school with you and sit with you at lunch. Watch you change. Grow up *with* you." His lips curve gently, at the corners. "I'd give anything to be a normal guy for you, Angie."

"You did get to go to school with me," I say.

"That's true," he says with a smile. "I'll carry these memories with me for the rest of my existence, however long that is."

I sit up with a strangled sob and wrap my arms around him. His arms loop around me and pull me close, and his heart beats firm and steady against my cheek. The rise and fall of his breathing, so ordinary. So *human*. But he's not. I must not pretend otherwise. Not when a short while ago, I watched a crow transform into this boy I'm embracing.

This boy *I cannot keep*, no matter how much I want to.

With effort, I sit up and shift away from him. I wipe at an errant tear with rubbery fingers. "Let's go. We need to go."

Downstairs, the piano stops abruptly. Outside, a chorus of crows begins to shriek.

35

the bus ride

"Angie!" Lacey yells. "Someone's here!"

Rafette is here.

Reece and I practically fly downstairs. My ankle gives out, and I trip on the last step, but he catches me and swings me to the floor. "Kitchen."

"Wha—?" My question turns into a yelp as glass shatters somewhere in the house.

He grabs my hand and yanks me forward as the security system screams to life. The alarm is ear-splitting and pointless. The alarm signal won't reach dispatch with all the communication lines down. Even if it did, no one would come. Not to an evacuated town with a whole bunch of other alarms going off everywhere. Figures make shifting shadows at the windows. I don't know how many, surrounding the house like a pack of wolves. A swarm of bees.

Surrounded. I stumble after Reece, stomach sinking, into the kitchen. Deno holds open the door for us, and Reece slams it behind us. Lacey trembles, clutching a stuffed backpack to her chest. Roger leans against my leg, looking like a predator. He barks, teeth bared to the gums.

Reece wedges a step stool under the knob. "That won't be enough," he calls over the wailing alarm.

There's pounding at the front door. A slow, relentless thud that sets my teeth on edge.

Reece looks at me. His chin is high, but fear glints in his eyes. "Their patience has run out."

Lacey slings the backpack over her shoulder. "We need to get out of here."

Another window breaks. The smell of honey seeps into the kitchen. I grab for something—anything. A butcher knife from the wood block, even though it won't help me against a Beekeeper.

There's only one other way out of here. "Follow me!" I dart for our only exit, bursting into the dark garage. "The door locks from the kitchen."

Reece jams a folding chair under the door. The alarm noise is muffled here, but still loud. The waning sun leaks through the narrow garage windows.

We group in the space where my dad's car is usually parked.

"What are we waiting for?" Deno opens the door of my car. "Let's *go*."

I stare at my car, mouth dry as a desert. "I don't have the keys."

"*What?*" Deno shrieks. "Where are they?"

"They're in my backpack, at The Strip Mall." I yell back at him. "With the rest of my stuff."

"Why did you leave them there?"

"You were *there*, Deno." My fists ball at my side. "You tell me why I wasn't thinking about keys to a car I wasn't driving!"

"You don't have a spare?"

I throw my hands up. "Yes! On my dad's keychain."

"What about *that?*" Reece nods toward my mom's beautifully restored Volkswagen Bus.

My insides turn to ice. Cold, unmeltable ice. "No way."

Reece raises a brow. "You said it runs. Are the keys in it?"

"Yes, but no. I-I…can't."

The doorknob rattles. All of us jump. Roger's nails click nervously on the cement floor. The chair Reece put there holds. For now.

Suddenly, Lacey is in my face. *Right* in my face. Her fingers clamp on my shoulders.

"Angie, sweetie, we've fought through hell to make it this far. I know you have personal issues with that vehicle, but we are going to get in it and drive out of here. Right now." Her voice is mild, but her nails dig painful half-moons into my skin. She doesn't smile. "Now get in the damn van, or I'm going to use your dad's nine iron on your hard head and drag you in."

I back out of her unnerving grip, nodding. "Hell. Okay, fine."

"I'll drive it," Deno offers.

"No!" No one's sitting in that seat but me. "The gearshift is tricky. I'll do it."

The thought of doing this makes me want to curl into the fetal position, but I'm not making up that part about the gearshift.

Reece runs a warm hand down my hair. He cups the back of my head and tilts it up to his dark eyes. "It's only a van, Angie. Your mother left it a long time ago," he says, gently. "I *can* drive if you want."

"I got this." The words are sluggish, like I'm underwater, drowning in all the lonely voices in the dark places of my mind that insist I abandoned my mother. That if I had been *more*, she would have been okay. I know better than that now, but a few revelations can't overturn a lifetime of thinking a certain way.

The knob is no longer rattling. Something hard smashes against the door.

"Angie!" Lacey's voice is shrill. "I will use that nine iron!"

Deno and Lacey are already inside the van, Lacey in the back, Deno in the passenger seat.

Seeing them inside punches the breath right out of my chest, but not with that tired, well-worn grief I am so used to. It's a decision, clear and resolute. A single thought burning in my chest—*no one else will die in this vehicle.*

I run to the van but the dog stays at the door. "Roger! Come on, boy!"

Reece climbs into the seat behind me, but the dog doesn't budge. He's rooted at the door, fur up and snarling, looking as ferocious as I've ever seen a yellow Lab.

"I can't leave Roger!" I yell.

"Just *go*. The Beekeepers want us, not the dog," Reece shouts back. "We'll lead them away from him."

I bite my lip. Every shred of my being wants to run over there and haul my dog into the van, but it would take three of us to carry a thrashing, snarling Roger inside.

My fingers find the key and turn it. The engine rattles to life, momentarily filling the interior with a puff of exhaust. My stomach clenches at the familiar smell. Memories crowd my head. I lock one hand around the steering wheel and the other around the knob of the gearshift.

Reece looks at me, then hits the garage door remote button. "You got this."

I nod, but my heart pounds in my throat. "What if they grab on as we're driving away?"

"That happens only in movies," Reece says. "Just drive."

The garage door isn't fully up before I tromp the clutch and put us into reverse. I've driven this beast many times—illegally, of course. I was eleven, twelve, but tow-away zones wait for no mother to regain consciousness.

The Bus feels clunky and old compared to my automatic

Honda. But I still remember how to finesse the sticky gearshift and the weird timing required to work the clutch.

I set my jaw and ignore the two Beekeepers who jump out of the way. Roger clamps his jaws on one of their ankles. A powerful arm swings down, sending him skidding across the garage with a pained yelp.

My throat squeezes tight at the sound, but the Beekeepers are already outside. They spread their arms and burst into two massive swarms of bees.

Lacey lets out a muffled scream. "Oh my *God*, did you see that?"

I hit the brake, turn the wheel, and slam the Bus into drive. The smell of burned rubber mixes with honey and exhaust and the bite of my own fear.

A roiling wall of bees rolls toward us like an angry storm cloud. And it's gaining on us.

"Where are we going?" I call out to anyone in the van. "Directions!"

"Turn right at the T," Deno replies. "Follow it to the old mine road."

I go sightless for a split second. "Are you sick? We're *not* going there."

Deno stabs a finger toward Reece. "*He* says they won't go underground. There's an old mine entrance back there somewhere. It's—"

"Burnham Mine," I cut in. "I know where it is."

"Good. That's where we're going."

Reece nods. "They won't follow us into the mine."

I glance at the rearview mirror and let out a whimper.

"You'd better be right." I grit my teeth and yank the wheel toward the right at the crossroads.

The van pitches to the left but doesn't tip. Tires squeal. I hit the gas and steer through the winding road as the paved drives of my neighbors' homes flash by. The road ends in a tidy gravel parking lot and a big sign about proper trail conduct and a dog poop bag dispenser. I never took note of these civilized things before on my many walks out to the mine. The world right now is not civilized at all.

I blow past the trail entrance to the lovely hike up Mt. Franklin and turn left down the maintenance road, flattening a sign that says Official Vehicles Only.

We bounce horribly over rocks and roots, but I can't slow down. The bees are behind us. I can hear their furious drone over the noisy engine and the branches whipping against the windows. I remind myself to thank my dad for putting new, all-weather tires on this thing when he had it restored. This ride would be over at the first bump if the van still had the bald, cracked ones my mom drove around on.

Then I find the side path to the mine. It's perilously narrow for a bit, but then the road widens and the entrance to the mine comes into view. So does the eight-foot-high chain link fence that I'm used to squeezing through.

My heart stops. I swear it does. "Reece!"

He grips the back of my seat. "Keep going. The fence is down around the other side, behind those trees."

This is suicide. The bees must have discerned our plan. They divide up—half follow us, the other half break off and appear to swarm at the entrance of the mine.

I ignore Deno's frantic pointing and swing around a stand of trees, downshift, and brake in a spray of dirt and rocks. Sure enough, a section of the fence curls away from the rest. I hit the gas and burst through the opening. It's not wide enough. The sides of the Bus screech as clipped chain link scrapes teal paint, but we take down what is left of the fence and cross to the mine entrance. *Yes*, the one we're heading toward. That's when I understand—the bees are swarming there to disguise the precise entry. Maybe they are trying to make us crash so they'll have us injured and surrounded.

I bite my bottom lip and line the van up with the domed entrance as best I can, working on memory and instinct and hoping for a bit of luck.

"Oh crap!" Deno yells. "There's a wall up there, Ange!"

"I can take it down," I say, not that anyone's listening.

I'm beyond the point of questioning myself. I couldn't if I wanted to, and I do *not* want to. I hold my breath. We're being sandwiched—a swarm ahead and a swarm behind.

A mine entrance that I may or may not be lined up with.

"Headlights!" Reece bellows.

I fumble for the knob and yank the headlights on. I gulp down air and hit the gas pedal again, propelling us into the swarm. Bees splatter on the windshield in sick thuds, immediately followed by the wooden barrier and gate. The windows darken with bees, then darken completely as we plunge into the pitch-black mineshaft. The buzzing eases off, as does my foot on the gas.

My breath comes in long wheezes as I slow the ailing Bus down the shaft. The tunnel was designed for trucks to get inside, but I don't know how far I should—or *can*—go. It narrows and snakes off in different directions into the mountain.

Despite the high ceiling of the tunnel, Volkswagen Buses were not intended to drive through such places. I come to a full stop, hands shaking so badly, putting the Bus in park comes only after an epic fight with the gearshift. The sudden quiet and darkness is disorienting. I swivel in my seat and look back. I can't judge the distance, but the tunnel opening is a prick of dim evening light, pretty far back there. The bees coil in a huge, furious knot at the entrance. But they don't follow us in here.

I turn off the key and sag against the seat. I—and the Bus—let out rasping sighs of relief.

The smell of honey is replaced by cool, damp earth and overworked engine. With reluctance, I switch off the headlights. We may need the battery. The dark corridor ahead plunges into darkness. The only light comes from the opening far behind us. And that is fading by the second. Night will arrive soon.

Deno slaps my seat. "I can't *believe* we just did that. Good thing I knew about this mine, eh?"

I'm too exhausted to respond. But if I wasn't, I'd remind him that his role was limited to a lot of pointing and yelling in my ear. Getaway drivers are underappreciated.

Reece reaches over and finds my hand. "Nice driving."

I sit still, listening to my heart hammer away at my ribs. "I never want to do that again. *Ever*."

"I hope you never have to."

I will, probably. We have to leave the mine at some point. There's really no telling how long the bees can—or will—lay siege to us.

Deno lets out a loud, maniacal whoop. He flings open the door and jumps out.

"What is he doing?" I ask.

Lacey lets out a startled noise as we hear the sound of Deno's feet crunching on gravel. A vile stream of profanity flows from his mouth. He's *walking* somewhere, but it's too dark to see anything.

"He's gonna get lost out there." Lacey grabs Reece's arm. "Stop him! Please!"

Reece lets out a curse himself, and slams out of the Bus. "Lights, please, Angie."

I pull on the headlights. Lacey and I watch, faces pressed to the glass as he rushes to Deno. I'm not worried about Reece. He's a hockey player, which I assume means he's used to being in fights. Deno knows more about digital mixers and obscure bands than throwing punches. Hopefully Reece won't actually *hurt* him.

The boys' voices are muffled, but I can see Reece trying to reason with Deno. There's a brief, heated discussion, but it does no good. Deno waves his arms and tries to take a swing at Reece. Lacey lets out a yelp as Deno misses by a mile and winds up taking Reece's right fist neatly on the jaw. Deno goes down, and Reece catches him in the midsection with one arm, knocking the wind out of Deno.

Reece returns to the Bus, dragging a mumbling, semiconscious Deno. He hauls my friend onto the floor of the back of the Bus and begins fiddling with Deno's clothes. "Did you pack a flashlight?" he asks Lacey.

"I think so." She climbs in the back to dig through the backpack and returns with my dad's small mag light.

Reece takes the flashlight and shines it on Deno's neck. He purses his lips. "Help me pull up his shirt, please."

Lacey blinks in confusion but untucks Deno's shirt from his pants. "What are you doing?"

"Checking for something."

She yanks Deno's shirt up his back. "*What,* exactly?"

Reece sweeps the flashlight over Deno's lower back. His breath hisses through his teeth. He aims the beam on Deno's lower back and an angry red spot with white striations curling from the sting like frayed lace. "*That.*"

Lacey leans forward. "What is that?"

"Exactly what I was afraid of."

Panic knots my gut. "It's a Beekeeper sting."

Reece rubs his hands over his face and nods. "I suspected. It's why I wanted us to stay together—to keep an eye on him. He's dangerous. You remember that nice young man who came to the college parking lot with a gun?"

I jerk back. "No. Deno could never do that."

"He's been stung by a Beekeeper," Reece says grimly. "He's capable of far worse."

"*No*," I say again. "How can we fix this?"

He flicks off the flashlight. "We can't."

Lacey shifts around next to us. "Are you saying he was stung by one of *those* bees?" Her voice goes shrill. "And now he's going to go homicidal maniac on us?"

Reece wisely takes his time with a reply. He turns the flashlight on again and shows Lacey the sting. "See those white marks fanning out? They tell me this sting didn't just happen. It's at least a day old. By now, the infected person is usually out of control, psychotic."

"But Deno wasn't like that," Lacey says.

Neither was my mother. But look how she ended up. I wrap my arms tight around my middle and breathe through the chill rattling me. It's unthinkable that Deno will spiral slowly into psychosis or that he'll snap and try to kill us.

"Deno was sane," Reece agrees. "He just got kind of…nasty."

Lacey's lips compress at the description, but she doesn't argue it. "That's a good sign, right? He could end up okay?"

The hope in her voice is painful to listen to. *Oh Lacey, I've seen how this ends…*

Reece pulls down Deno's shirt. He snaps off the flashlight again, plunging the van into darkness. "It's unlikely he will be okay, Lacey," Reece says gently. "His control *is* unusual, though. Beekeepers can sense people who are unstable, just like harbingers can smell impending death. *That's* who they typically sting—the unbalanced. People who are sick to begin with."

"Which Deno isn't," Lacey says. "So why sting *him?*"

Reece's brows pull together. "That's a good question. Maybe because of his connection to Angie. Maybe—" He breaks off and shrugs. His mouth hardens, and his eyes take on a faraway look. He's thinking something. Something he's not going to tell me. Or maybe just doesn't want to say in front of Lacey.

I bite my tongue and turn to Lacey. I'll quiz Reece later, when we're alone. "You've been with him this whole time. Any idea when or where Deno may have gotten stung?"

Lacey's eyes flutter skyward as she thinks. "Well, um. The only other time we were around bees was yesterday. When we almost got on a rescue helicopter, there were bees around. Deno didn't say anything to me about getting stung, though." She looks to Reece. "Do they hurt? Would he have even known?"

Reece makes a humorless laugh. "Oh, he knew. It's terribly painful, so I've heard. He may have kept it to himself so he wouldn't worry you."

"My mom didn't have a sting like that," I say quietly.

"The stings fade," Reece replies, head close to mine. "They disappear completely upon death."

"So what do we do?" Lacey demands. "We *have* to do something. There must be a cure—a way to reverse whatever this sting is doing to him."

"I'm sorry, Lacey." Reece's voice is empty. Devoid of hope. "There is no known cure for a Beekeeper sting."

36

under the ground

Our eyes adjust to the darkness. We have a debate about it, but decide against tying up Deno, even though Reece makes it clear that it would be smart if we did. He even offers his belt—which came from my dad's closet—for the job.

When Deno is lucid again, we ask him about the sting. He knew, of course. Afraid to scare Lacey, he kept it to himself and tried to deal with his increasingly negative impulses.

He doesn't ask about a cure. He doesn't ask about anything.

Lacey and Reece take the flashlight and go to check the mine entrance, to see if the bees are still there, and I stay in the Bus with Deno. He sits on the floor, a dark shape in a dark place.

For a long time, we are still and quiet. I count my own heartbeats. I wait for Deno to talk, which usually doesn't require a wait, but he falls silent and stays that way. Deno, who for as long as I've known him, has been the schemer, the planner, the hopeful one. This time, he seems to be the one who needs a plan and some hope.

I sit across from him. The rear seats are long gone, leaving the back open. When I lived with my mother, this was packed with our stuff and *us*, when we weren't living with some guy. My fingers pluck at the matted floor carpet. My dad had the Bus thoroughly detailed, but a bit of *her* scent lingers—hair spray, ramen noodles, pot. The industrial cleaners have scrubbed away the smell of unwashed bodies and general life apathy. Still, I'm afraid to breathe too deeply.

"That's where I used to sleep," I say to him. To the dark quiet. "Right there, where you're sitting. I had a purple sleeping bag and a Barbie book bag that contained all the pilfered goods I'd lifted from the assholes we shacked up with. It was mostly silly stuff, but things that would annoy them. Sunglasses. One sock from a pair. Packs of cigarettes. Remote controls." I grin in the dark. "I took a lot of remote controls."

"What did you do with all that crap?"

He's talking. He sounds normal. My shoulders unfold from my ears and relax. "I usually kept it for a while, then found some place to throw it out. I didn't really *want* the stuff. I just liked messing with those guys. I blamed them a little bit for why we lived like that—the reason my mom wasn't much of a *mom*. I'd look around and see these nice families and wonder what I'd done to deserve living in a van, in dirty clothes." I rap my knuckles lightly on the floor. "*This* shouldn't be a kid's home, but it could have been worse. My mom did her best to take care of me," I say, and I surprise myself by meaning it.

He makes a disgusted sound. "Sounds awful, Ange."

I close my eyes as faces of other children I'd met swim behind my eyelids. Children with addict parents who were not as scrupulous as my mom. In all those years, I hadn't been touched by the men she was involved with. Some had tried. Some had offered her money and drugs in exchange for time alone with me. She'd laughed in their faces and threatened to cut off their balls if they so much as looked at me too long.

"She wasn't a *good* mother," I say, voice thick with emotion. "I could spend a lifetime recording her mistakes. But, to her unwell mind, she was protecting me."

"You're generous. She should have let your dad take you."

I laugh, remembering what my dad said about himself and his youthful days. And Mom's paranoia. "Yes, but I can't do anything to change it now." My smile slides away. "And neither can she."

I can sense, rather than see, him nodding. He doesn't press the issue. "This is the most you've ever talked about yourself," he says quietly. "After all these years of us being friends, it takes me being on the verge of psychosis for you to open up."

"Yeah well, now if you tell anyone, no one will believe you."

He laughs. It's a good sound—familiar and real. It makes my heart warm to hear it.

"I'm curious how you knew this place was here," I say. "I've never known you to muck around in abandoned mines."

"Why not? If there was a mine anywhere in the county, someone I'm related to worked it. We're not like Lacey's family, where everyone has attended some fancy music school in Switzerland or whatever. I'm not related to anyone who's been to college. Most never finished high school." He shifts around, and suddenly I get it—the reason he's uncomfortable with Lacey's interest. He thinks she's a class above. Too good for him.

I smile in the darkness. Interesting how despite my dad's money, *I'm* not in this category. My druggie mom apparently leveled the field. That, and my dad's family were miners, too.

"And before I found music, me and some of the other low-valley kids had bush parties out here. Never underestimate the powerful combination of boys, intense boredom, and the allure of signs that say 'No Trespassing.'"

I smile. "You could have been hurt."

"That was the point." His clothes rustle in a shrug. "If there was no danger in it, there'd be no point in doing it. Just like you stealing your mother's boyfriends' remote controls. Bet they would have been pissed if they'd caught you."

"Yeah."

"Angie? I don't feel homicidal. Just…angry sometimes. Like Lacey gets when she can't get a chord progression right."

My reply is immediate. "You're not homicidal."

"But you all said—"

"Beekeepers typically sting people who are unstable to begin with," I say. "We've established that you weren't unstable, but…" Ah, hell. I shake my head in the dark. "You *have* changed, Deen. You're kind of…jerky. Reckless, too. Whatever is in that venom will continue to change you."

"Unless…?"

"Unless nothing." I reach for a bottle of water. My throat is *so* dry. "Reece says there's no undoing a Beekeeper sting."

"And you believe him?"

My thoughts spin, pulling distant memories, stitching them to recent events. "He knows more about them than I do."

"Maybe he's wrong."

I wince at the hope in his voice. "Yeah. Maybe."

Suddenly, I can't bear to be alone in here with him. I feel like I'm running out of oxygen. I hate telling him that magic bees are corrupting his mind, that nothing can stop it. I stick my head out the open rear door and gulp in a breath. "Hey! Where are you guys?" I call to Reece and Lacey.

"We're here." Reece's voice is close. The side of the Bus dips and groans as Reece and Lacey climb inside.

"We were eavesdropping," Lacey states. "It was wrong. A shameful breach of privacy and I apologize for it."

"Refreshing, not to be the one apologizing for a change." Deno murmurs.

Lacey's sigh of relief is audible. "Oh good. You're talking."

"Never thought you'd say that, did you?" There's a smile in Deno's voice.

"We didn't want to interrupt your conversation," Reece adds. "It sounded…important."

Maybe it's the darkness, making me hypersensitive to the voices around me, but there's an edge to Reece's words. It pricks my attention, making me think of the smell of milk left out too long in the sun. Maybe Reece would have liked me to share all that ugly stuff about my childhood with *him*, but Deno needed the honesty. He needed to be trusted with something important. To know he still *could* be trusted.

The Bus falls into silence. Except for the rustle of a bag of chips being opened and then the sound of someone crunching.

The smell of salt and oil and processed potato fills the space. Not a particularly alluring odor under most circumstances, but I grope for the backpack and pull out a random snack bag.

Pretzels. Eh. Figures. I resign myself to my least favorite snack. "Maybe the magic affecting harbingers and Beekeepers is changing. Maybe you *aren't* screwed, Deno."

Reece smiles, I can sense it. "Angie, you're turning into an optimist. Is this a new hat for you?"

I stick out my tongue at him, and he laughs as if he saw it. "Can you see in the dark?"

"No," he says, but I'm not sure I believe him. "Who knows? The magic *is* changing. I can feel…" His voice fades off to a hush. He rubs his hands together. "I've soaked up more death than this and not burned so hot."

My brows knit. "Are you worried?"

"About myself? Never," he says matter-of-factly. "My whole life is a worst-case scenario. Honestly, I'd welcome an opportunity to die—*really* die."

The Bus falls quiet once again. No one knows quite how to respond to that. Not when the rest of us are desperate for a way to live.

"Okay, so I think we need to form a plan," Lacey says. "I don't think Deno should stay here, considering his…what happened to him."

She was going to say "condition." It was right there on her tongue. It's still hanging in the air, as dark and sharp-edged as the death sentence Reece thinks it is. I'm just not as ready, or maybe as hardened, as he is. "What do you think we should do?" I ask her.

"I think we should split up." Her words are quick and defensive, like she expects an argument.

No one says a word. There's only the quiet crunching of potato chips and pretzels.

Lacey clears her throat. "The Bus is so visible now, the Beekeeper will instantly recognize it. Earlier, when Reece and I were watching the mine entrance, we noticed that only Rafette was there. The others had left. And for whatever reason, Rafette left frequently—like once an hour he'd go somewhere."

"It's hard work to stay in human form after a crisis is over," Reece puts in. "I imagine he's returning to a place where there's still fear and chaos so he can feed off it. The rescue site, is most likely."

"Right," Lacey says. "So there are times when the entrance is empty—only breaks, but we can use them. If Deno and I were to take the Bus, we could lead him away from here. He'd probably figure it out that he's following the wrong kids pretty quickly, but you two would have a chance to split. You'd be on foot, but it's better than staying in here, in case he decides to wait it out."

Silence again.

I don't *want* to split up. My body reacts at the mere thought of not knowing what was happening to them. "Where would you go?" I ask.

"The school," she says. "That's where the rescue operation base is. We could try to meet up there. There will be people there. *Real* people." She makes a little noise. "No offense, Reece."

"None taken," he replies.

"That sounds dangerous," I say. "The valley is flooded. And most of the roads are blocked. Where do you expect to drive?"

"As far as we can," she says. "We're not the ones that Rafette guy wants. We'd be safer on our own."

Safer is not *safe*. "You can't drive the Bus. The gearshift is— "

"Sticky, I know." Lacey sighs. "Angie, my Dad's truck is a stick shift. Every old car has a funky gearshift. I can drive it, if you'll let me. If it's the Bus you're worried about— "

"I don't care about the *Bus*," I burst out, cutting her off this time. "I've spent enough time worrying over this vehicle. I care about you and Deno and *not* going to your funerals."

"No one wants to die, Angie." Deno clears his throat. "Well, *most* of us don't. I agree with Lacey. We should split up. First thing in the morning, when we have light, we'll make for the school. I'll find myself a padded cell before this stuff in my veins really kicks in." He says it like a joke, but no one laughs. "Right. So you two find someplace else to hide, or find another route out of here." Deno shifts around. The sound is restless, jerky. He inhales, sharply. "It's hard to...keep my head together in here. I'm starting to feel...well, I can't stay closed up like this. I can't stay *here*, Angie."

Reece shifts, then I hear the sound of long fingers dipping inside the pretzel bag and withdrawing with a handful. He's been quiet for a while. His breath brushes my neck, shivering along my skin as he says, "Neither can we."

37

through the low valley

Deno and Lacey's exit is the exact opposite of our entrance. Reece and I watch them ease out of the mine, just as the dawn's pale rays put color back in the sky. No clouds today, just the watery blue of morning. And no bees, as far as I can see.

"Maybe Rafette knows we aren't in the Bus," I say.

We're standing only ten feet back from the entrance. Not far.

Reece doesn't answer. He's listening, head cocked. "Rafette isn't here," he says at last.

"You can tell?"

He nods. "I don't smell him."

Sure enough, there's one distant *caw,* though not from any self-respecting crow—it's Deno's butchered interpretation—and we let out twin breaths. Of relief and anxiety. As we planned before Deno and Lacey departed, one caw meant no sign of bees. Two caws meant our enemies were out there, waiting to ambush, and we should stay where we are.

One caw means it's time to run.

"The other Beekeepers are moving on," he says. "They're limited by how long they can stay away from their energy source. They helped Rafette, probably out of curiosity, but they won't deplete themselves for his mission." He holds out his hand with a crooked smile. "Ready to hike?"

I roll the sleep from my shoulders and take his hand. "No, but let's go."

We have a long way to go. Downhill, while better than uphill, is still lousy. The ground is uneven and rain-soaked, making my ankle throb and my ribs ache. Our ultimate goal is to get to the school, find emergency personnel, and get out of Cadence. By splitting up, Deno and Lacey take the van and hopefully get any watchful Beekeepers to follow them. This would give Reece and me a chance to evade Rafette by taking the direct, overland route straight to the spot where the helicopters seem to be coming and going from. However, that plan is subject to change depending on a multitude of factors I simply refuse to think about. Really, all we know is that we have to *go*. It's the crappiest plan ever, but it's what we have.

Gnawing at my mind is the knowledge that if Reece would just turn into a crow and leave, he'd be safe. He could rejoin his family, wherever they are, and be free. I suggested it, *again*, but he refuses to leave me until he knows I'm safe.

During the night, we worked through ideas, searching for the perfect plan, but there wasn't one. Lacey had suggested staying in the mine, but Reece made the point that if Rafette decides to wait us out, we could be days or weeks without food and water. The facts were this: The next town is eighteen miles away, and we have no clue how to find a road to it. With Deno and me—but especially Deno—needing medical attention, the decision was to go.

It's a harsh walk through the woods, not a trail, through brush and thick stands of trees. The wet leaves buffer some of our sounds, but we're not stealthy. Eventually, we find ourselves in the backyard of a little blue house. I don't know whose. This is not my neighborhood. My directions are all messed up. Behind the house, an uncovered grill sits on an empty deck—a reminder of easier times in the town of Cadence. We walk alongside the house to the front and stop. The street is quiet except for the omnipresent whir of helicopter blades. The street and front yards of all the houses on this side are flooded. Trees and mailboxes poke out of the thick brown water like forlorn survivors.

Inside the house, a small dog has detected us and starts up a hopeful barking. I think of Roger, and pluck Reece's jacket. "There's a dog trapped in there."

"I hear it," he replies.

"We can't leave it."

"We have to." His voice is hard. He takes my chin between his fingers and tilts my face up to his. "Look, as we head down into the valley and into town, you're going to see things. Terrible things. Don't feel bad if you need to look away. Forcing yourself to look doesn't make you a better person or anything. It just leaves you with memories you can't erase." He turns away from me. "That little dog is safer inside than out." My hands curl into fists. The cuts on my palms hurt, but I do it anyway. I've seen enough in this short life of mine. Enough suffering, enough death. But this time, he's right. If Roger had come when called, he'd be here with us. And that wouldn't be such a good thing. He'd be afraid and hungry. He'd be one more thing I'd be worrying about.

"Are we going through *that?*" I ask, pointing at the water.

Reece eyes the route ahead with distaste. "Looks like it. Prepare to get cold and dirty."

I steel myself to the dog's cries, but take note of the house number and street name. Maybe I'll have the chance to tell someone about the dog.

Reece sets his jaw and strides forward, into the water. I follow, letting out a hiss of discomfort when the ice-cold liquid curls around my shins. In no time, my teeth are chattering. It feels like I'm chilled from the inside out. We're three houses away before the dog gives up and falls silent. I try not to think about it.

We forgo the streets and cut straight through peoples' yards. The houses become closer together and smaller the lower into the valley we go. Yards turn into small, fenced-in rectangles, and we're back to streets, as the fences are not worth climbing over. Evidence of the landslide comes into view. A layer of dirt and gravel coats everything in brown—cars, trees, homes. We turn a corner, and the devastation comes into clear view. It looks like a bomb hit. But it's the randomness of it that is truly disturbing. Some homes are destroyed, others stand untouched, as if spared by a divine hand. And, looming behind it all, is the sad remnant of Mt. Serenity. Not a mountain anymore at all.

The water comes up to our knees here, and it's thick with all the mud, making it feel like we're slogging through peanut butter. A house with a duck mailbox comes into view, and suddenly, it all looks familiar.

"We're near Deno's house," I spin around and stumble toward where my friend's house should be.

"Angie, wait," Reece says, but I don't listen. I need to see if his house is still there.

I fumble with someone's chain link gate and pry it open, cutting through their yard to the street on the other side. Relief turns my knees mushy. This section of street was spared serious damage. Deno's house still stands.

I half expect the front door to slam open and Mrs. Steinway to come out in a billowing housedress, yelling at me to get out of the cold and have some pie. But the door doesn't open. The windows are dark, like all the rest. I don't know what happened to Deno's parents, but I do know that Cadence will never be the same. It's as scarred as the mountain behind it. I stand here in the ruins of this neighborhood, built so many years ago by the company that mined the broken mountain. I can't imagine people living here again. Of civilization returning to this silent, drowned town. I think of my mom's Bus, wherever Lacey and Deno took it, and it strikes me how, once again, the world I knew has been torn apart, obliterated.

A sound comes from behind me. Reece is across the street, standing inside a house that has the front ripped off. Smoke wafts from the wreckage. I can see his head and shoulders above the jagged opening, in what was probably the living room. I open my mouth to call out, warn him to get out of there. It looks horribly unsafe. Smoldering beams teeter above him, where a roof used to be. They could fall any minute, but I hold my tongue. The way he's standing there is so strange. Still and placid, like a meditating monk.

"Reece!" I call out. He doesn't so much as twitch, and that alarms me. It's not like my voice is competing with any other noise. I splash my way over to him, but when I reach him, he's still zoned out. And then I see why.

There's two dead people in there. A young couple, is my impression, and that's based on the clothes. I can't look away. Blood is everywhere. The shallow water he's standing in is oily dark with it. I glimpse twisted limbs and a severed arm, floating. Fingers curled slightly. An open mouth. Eyes wide open, staring at the sky. My gaze swings and holds on living, breathing Reece. Red-black eyes are fixed on the gruesome scene before him. He breathes through his teeth. A wild flush darkens his cheeks as he absorbs the fleeting, lingering energy of the semi-recent dead. That's definitely what he's doing. I shudder and turn away, feeling oddly embarrassed, as if I am witnessing a private act. It's so easy, sometimes, to forget that Reece is different. That he's not quite human, and all this horror is not quite as horrible for him.

"Reece." I touch his arm, tentatively.

He turns abruptly, and I snatch my hand back. He's searing hot again.

He blinks at me slowly, but I'm not sure he sees me.

"What are you doing?" I ask, like I don't know. Like I'm trying to be polite or something. "Are you okay?"

"Yeah." He rakes shaky fingers through his hair. "These were…there's so much energy here—way more than I need right now—it's overwhelming."

I put a hand over my mouth and stifle a gag. My voice is a hoarse whisper. "I don't know how you can—"

"I wish I could explain it to you, Angie," he says. "It's like being ultra alive and completely dead at the same time." He grabs my sleeve and tugs it with a weird urgency. "We have to stay together. Whatever happens from now on, we can't be separated."

"Okay, okay." I pry his hand off my sleeve and twine my fingers with his. His grip is almost painful. "So don't go running off to every dead person you come across." *There're bound to be more of them.* I sneak another quick peek at the deceased couple—or what's left of them under the collapsed section of their attic—and bear down on another wave of nausea. "Let's get out of here."

"*Yes*. How far is it to the school? I'm getting you on the first heli—" He breaks off, gaze narrowing on something beyond my shoulder.

"What is it?" I whip around, and I see. "Oh *no*."

Across the street and two houses down, a man stands on the peak of a roof. His posture is easy, completely unconcerned with falling. His head swivels slowly, scanning the street. It's

Rafette. I recognize the hat. That puffy coat I've grown to hate.

Reece grabs my jacket and yanks me down, below the shattered window frame and hopefully out of sight. His hand burns against my spine. "Don't move."

"Do you think he saw us?" My heart pounds so loud, every living thing within two miles must hear it.

"Don't think so." He lifts his head to peek out. "We have to go before he does."

A crow suddenly cries out, and five dark birds streak over the rooftops. They fly low and make noise. Rafette turns away, watching the birds.

Reece whispers a thank-you to his family for the distraction and tugs me forward. We slip out of the gaping opening in the front of the house and move to the rear, flattening ourselves against vinyl siding. It's hard to move in water and not make splashy sounds, but we're not the only things disturbing the water. All sorts of things float around, liberated from peoples' homes. A child's plastic Big Wheels. Half-empty gallons of paint. The bloating corpse of a cat.

We hug the side of the house and slip through the rear neighbor's backyard. We sneak up another few streets, moving from house to house. Reece ducks into someone's open garage and pulls me in behind him. We press against the wall.

"Have we lost him?"

He puts a finger to his lips and points to the garage window. The view shows a sliver of the street we were just on, between two homes. Rafette turns his head back and forth with clear frustration, then heads up the street. Away from us, again. We wait until he's out of sight before sinking to the floor.

A wave of dizziness forces me to drop my head to my knees until it passes.

"Are you sick?" he asks.

"No." Frightened out of my mind, hungry, hurting, yes.

Reece rubs absent circles on my back. There's a frown in his voice. "How far are we from the school?" He asked me this before.

"Not far," I say. "About a quarter mile east of here." Not in the same direction Rafette went, but not the opposite, either.

He rubs his eyes with a frown. A light sweat gleams on his forehead. "How bad do I look?"

"You have the scary eyes."

"Damn." He closes them. "I'm not going to be able to go with you when we reach the school. I can't let them see me like this."

I give a slow nod. He definitely *shouldn't* let himself be seen right now. The truth is, it's more than his eyes that's scary. I've never seen him look quite this…inhuman. "Hey." I touch his heated cheek. "Are you all right? You look really strange."

"I'm fine." But he turns away. "My body is fighting the urge to change. The crow wants to take over so badly. It's taking some effort to not do that." He catches my gaze and holds up a finger. "But I am *not* doing that. Don't worry."

I bite my lip and hold back from telling him how much he *should* change and fly away, but we're past that conversation. Even if we weren't, *now* would not be the time to have it.

38

stronger than this

We continue moving from house to house. It's slow and nerve-wracking and unbelievably exhausting. Every one of my senses is tuned in. That effort alone is delusion-inducing. The farther we go, the less I see why we're bothering to be stealthy. My gut tells me the reason we've managed to evade Rafette is *not* because we're so flipping clever, but because he knows exactly where we are. He has a legion of bees at his disposal. Depending on how they work for him, he could be *everywhere*—sitting on tree branches, watching from rooftops. My bet is, he's waiting us out—something Rafette knows a lot about.

I suspect Reece knows this, too. It's an unspoken thing neither of us wants to say, because if we do, we may lose the will to keep walking.

There would be no hope of getting away.

Besides, we're getting closer to the school. The sounds of human activity are muted but *there*. Voices, the hum of generators, the now-and-then wail of a siren. My head throbs. No, my *everything* throbs. Reece doesn't appear affected by our conditions. He keeps going at a grueling pace, as if moving forward is the only thing keeping his head straight. We are slipping around the side of a house when he suddenly stops dead.

I bump into his back. "What's the matter?"

He doesn't answer, but his body goes perfectly still.

"Is Rafette there?"

"No," he says softly. "Someone's dead in this house."

"Oh no, you don't. We talked about this." I tug his arm. "We *have* to keep going."

He squeezes his eyes shut. Sweat trickles down his temple. "Angie, I don't know how to *not* go in there."

Dread coils in my throat. He's already kind of out of it. His skin is so hot, I almost can't keep holding his arm. It can't be healthy for him to absorb more death energy. "You just *don't*," I say firmly. "You fight it. You are stronger than this."

He turns to me, and I know I've lost him. The look on his face is one of defeat, agony. "No, I'm not." His voice is empty. "You don't understand, Angie. I have to go in."

He breaks away from me, walks up the front steps. Like a zombie. Like a drone. And disappears into the house.

I stand there, breathless. Hurting. Every ache and pain and sore spot, magnified. I won't follow him. I will *not* step foot in that house. I wrap my arms around my sore ribcage and shudder against the chill in the air and the ice in my bones. I had warded off the cold by constant movement, but standing still, it slices through me.

All those times Reece told me we can't ever be together, a part of me clung to the hope that we'd find a way to make it work. But standing here, the truth of it finally hits home. There is no way this relationship will work. After all is said and done, I will lose Reece to this curse that defines his existence. No amount of love or willpower or compromise will change what he is. I have no choice but to let him go, and the thought of it makes me want to put my fist through a wall. Not that I *could*, but…

A hand clamps over my mouth, cutting off my quiet sob. Another wraps around my torso, pinning my arms, and jerking me against a male chest. Wearing a puffy coat.

Honey. Panic explodes in my chest. I buck and twist with the force of a seizure. I scream, even though it's muffled against the warm, sweet-smelling hand.

"He can't hear you." A voice laughs into my ear. "Even if he could, he's in no condition to help you."

Rafette.

No. My heart sinks but I fight harder, flush with adrenaline. This is my life. My *life*. It's no use, of course. Reece said Beekeepers possess great strength, and Rafette is demonstrating that with terrifying accuracy. His grip is effortless and unyielding.

"Please stop struggling," he says mildly. "You're damaging yourself."

Like he cares. Like *I* care at this point. Surely he plans to damage me far worse than the bruises my squirming will cause.

The arm around my battered ribs tightens, pushing the air out of my lungs and sending blinding pain straight through the top of my skull. I go still, and the pressure instantly eases.

"That's better. No reason to fight. No point in it, really." Rafette's mouth touches my ear as he speaks—accidentally, I think—but bile spikes in my throat.

The hand on my mouth slides down to my neck. His fingers start probing around. I draw in a breath to scream.

Rafette says, "Ah, there it is," and squeezes something deep in the side of my neck.

I never get the scream out. Time stops. The world goes black.

39 the bitter sting

I open my eyes to a colorful honeycomb grid set against a blue sky.

A puffy cloud in the shape of a penguin reshapes into an elephant.

And then a dog. And then…

Despair.

Rafette brought me here, which means I'm going to die soon. I may already be dying. I should be more upset about this, but whatever Rafette did to my neck has given me the mother of all headaches and a weird tickling all over my skin. I couldn't run now if I wanted to. Just turning my head is a chore, as if my spine has rusted solid.

I recognize my viewpoint from the underside of the monkey bars dome in the playground of Cadence Elementary School.

The cloud turns into a leering clown face.

I sense someone to my left and spot Rafette. He sits on the ground, knees up, back resting on the metal bars. "You can sit up, if you like." His shaky voice is gentle. "But do it slowly.

You don't want to make them nervous."

Make who nervous? I roll to my side and prop myself on an elbow. Then I see them.

Bees. Dozens of them. No, *hundreds*.

And they are silent. They crawl along my arms and legs. That explains the itching sensation. I feel them now—in my hair, between my fingers, crawling around under my pant legs. A whimper slips from my lips. I make my body go still. I'm afraid to open my mouth, in case a bee should crawl inside. I'm afraid to do *anything*.

"You have been stung only once." He touches a fingertip to my right wrist. "*Here*. But they will deliver more stings if you move suddenly."

Stung? I convulse at his words. My mind feels intact, but the sting is fresh. All I feel is bone deep weariness and a sickening dip in my stomach. I've been stung, like my mother. I can't even process the sharp, profound sadness rolling through me. It leadens my limbs and fills my eyes with tears. I let out a sob and the bees buzz nervously.

"Relax, please," Rafette urges. "They can sense your agitation."

Relax? Is he on crack? There's no way to be *not* agitated in this situation. "So I'm doomed, then?" I rasp out. My mouth feels like it's filled with cotton balls.

"No." Rafette rests his forearms on his knees. "Your harbinger may choose to save you. He may choose to let the venom destroy you. It's up to him, really. Personally, I am hoping he chooses to save you. My bees don't want to sting you. They sense, as do I, that your mind is strong. We don't like to hurt strong people."

"He won't." My voice is slurred. "You're wasting your time."

"I don't think so." A bee spirals from Rafette's mouth and lands on his eyebrow. He closes one eye as it crawls over the lid and down his cheek. "You know, I learned something from what happened with the last harbinger. You sting the loved one *before* asking them to take the curse. The motivation is so much greater that way."

I shudder at sudden stabbing pain behind my eyes. My mother had headaches. So it begins: the breakdown of my mind. "You're sick. Cruel. Hideous. Sadistic. Disgusting."

"I know," he says. "Can you now see why I am so eager to be rid of this curse?" He looks…tired. The features of his face shift sluggishly. His shoulders hunch. It's hard to imagine this creature is exhausted, but he appears to be. "Centuries ago, you would not have called me hideous. I had a beautiful face," he says. "I was more beautiful than your harbinger. Everything I once was became swallowed up by all *this*." He gestures harshly to his face. "If you were me, would you not do anything to end it?"

"Not like this." But I have no idea what centuries of living like this would do to me. Maybe I would be that desperate, but it doesn't matter. I'm on the wrong side of this equation.

He sighs again, rubs the back of his neck in a very human gesture. "If your harbinger accepts my queen bee, all those who have been stung will be released from the effects of the venom. You and your friend will be saved."

Saved? Am I hallucinating? A bee wanders over the curve of my ear. I stifle another whimper. "How is that?"

"I have it on good authority that the magic in the bees dies with me. Anyone stung would be restored to normal." He closes his eyes—pale green with red lashes—and bares his teeth in a terrible smile. He turns slowly, hearing something behind him. "Ah, it appears your hero has arrived to rescue you." His faces shift furiously, changing so fast they blur together. The bees on me suddenly beat their tiny wings and let out an angry hum. It's a terrifying sound. Like imminent agony and inevitable death.

Reece stalks across the playground, all fury and clenched fists. A crow keeps pace above him, flying in agitated circles as if trying to make him turn back. It lets out distressed squawks, plucks at his shirt with those sharp talons. It's him—Hank. I can just make out his white feather.

Reece waves a hand, brushing off the bird, and pins hot, red-black eyes on my captor. "Rafette." His voice is menacing.

"So nice to see you, harbinger." Rafette folds his arms. "You are late."

"Let her go," Reece snarls.

"I would be pleased to," Rafette replies. "But as you can see, you must offer me something in order for her release."

"And what's that?"

"You must accept my queen bee into yourself," Rafette says. "I will be free."

"You're delusional if you think that would work," Reece sneers.

"It *will* work. One of the ancient Strawmen gave me the secret." The Beekeeper presses a finger to his temple. "He put it all right in here, without saying a word."

This sounds like made up nonsense to me, but Reece visibly pales. His entire body deflates. When I first met Reece, I remember glimpses of profound grief. Desolation so deep it made me shudder. It eased as we spent more time together, but I see it now, stripped down and exposed, in the lines of his face, the curve of his body. He hunches with the weight of loss. The burden of every death and horror he's witnessed. With the truth in the Beekeeper's words and the magnitude of the choice before him.

I sit straight up, fingers digging into the soggy earth. The bees drone in disapproval. Another stinger sinks into my flesh, making my ankle jerk. "Don't even *think* of it, Reece."

Reece does not look away from the Beekeeper. His lips

thin, then turn down at the edges.

"Thank you, harbinger," Rafette says gently. "After a millennia of this torment, I will finally be allowed to die."

My heart smashes against my ribs. The bees buzz faster in distress, but I don't care what they do. I'm already stung. Their venom is moving through my tissues, sending it deeper, to my bones. Soon, to my mind. "Not him!" I beg Rafette. "Don't do this to him."

Rafette finally turns to me. He has the nerve to look apologetic. "But it *must* be him. Only another creature of the lost magic can accept the curse. I've waited a very long time to find a harbinger with something to lose." He turns knowing eyes to Reece. "He wouldn't walk away now, even if I begged him. Isn't that right, scavenger?"

Reece stares at the thick red welt on my wrist. He shakes his head.

"Do *not* become one of them for me," I say, willing him to listen to me. "I'm not worth losing your soul over."

Reece's gaze turns to me, all blazing eyes and determination. "You're worth all that and more."

"*No!*" Tears streak from my eyes. *What is wrong with him?* "Do *not* do this. *Please*."

"I can't let you die, Angie."

"He's going to kill me with these bees either way," I shoot back. "He told me so."

It's a total lie and I feel zero guilt about it. I will say anything, at this point, to get him to leave.

The Beekeeper raises his brows. "My word is true, and he knows it." He turns to Reece. "Now, harbinger, shall we get on with it?"

40

the queen

Reece and Rafette exchange a look that sends blood pounding in my ears.

It's done. Decided. If his soul wasn't about to be forfeited, I'd be flattered that this didn't appear to be a difficult decision. He may think he's saving me from death, but I don't think he's considered what his choice will do to *my* soul. I won't just get on with my life as if nothing happened. I won't be able to live with this.

"Let's get this over with," Reece says roughly, walking toward us. "Before I'm too late to save her."

Rafette smiles, wide and pleased. "A wise decision."

"No!" I surge to my feet and lunge for the side of the monkey bars. Reece stands on the other side. "You *can't*. I won't let you!"

Eyes wide, Rafette holds out a hand. "No, *don't*—!"

The stingers of a hundred bees pierce my skin, release their venom. Pain pours over and through me like liquid fire. White and hot and engulfing me in an unnamable agony. Breathing is out of the question. I drop to my knees in a gasp.

"Angie!" Reece is at my side, kneeling down next to me. "What have you done?"

His eyes are gentle and worried. And any remaining conflict about his decision is gone. He brushes a hand over my face, brushing off a few bees. "You can call the rest back now, Rafette," he says quietly.

The Beekeeper stares at me in open astonishment. The few bees who didn't just kill themselves stinging me fly off me and return to his mouth. Revulsion squeezes my heart. Reece *can't* become this. Not because of me.

Reece's trembling fingers curl around mine. His palm, despite being so hot, is clammy.

"Don't do this, Reece," I plead. "Please. This will destroy me, too."

"No," he whispers into my hair. "You'll go on and live your life. You'll find a guy who *can* be with you. Who can give you everything you deserve."

Everything I deserve. What is that, exactly? And who gets to decide? Not him, I think.

"It's time." Rafette's voice quavers with eagerness, but with a touch of fear, too. He wasn't expecting this. "Open your mouth, harbinger."

Reece looks up at him. I can see the whites of his eyes and the stark paleness of his skin. I can feel the trembles going through him. The effort of swallowing makes his Adam's apple bob dramatically. He's scared. No, he's terrified beyond belief.

But still, he is doing this.

He looks at me, blinks, and a tear slips down his cheek. "I love you, Angie." His voice sounds like broken glass.

And it cuts through me, shredding everything. I croak out a response. Maybe I tell him I love him. Maybe I babble nonsense. I'm not sure what I say with the venom starting to dig into my system and swell up my tongue. Every emotion I've ever known is struggling for supremacy within my overwhelmed mind.

Through the chaos, one thought holds, fixes in place:

I cannot allow Reece to take this curse. I hold on to this, my anchor in a sea of fracturing thoughts.

Reece parts his lips, and Rafette opens his mouth. He lets out a whimper of relief as a fat bee floats out. The queen. Her flight is clumsy, heavy.

I grab Reece's arm. "You listen to me," I grind out through my tears. "Do this and I will never forgive you."

"But you will live," he says. "You *will* live." Reece firmly peels off my hand. His eyes stay glued to the bee, even as tears leak from the corners of them. His breathing goes rapid and short.

A shrieking *caw* snaps the air, followed by a cacophony of squawks. More crows darken the sky. Dozens of them swarm the playground, wings flapping, beaks snapping. They fly in agitated circles, then land on the metal rungs above us. It makes sense now, why Rafette chose this spot. Not easy maneuvering for a crow. But clearly, they aren't pleased by what's going on.

Hope expands in my chest. My ribs ache with it. Surely *they* will stop this. His family will show him how horrible a mistake this is.

But they don't. They remain perched on the rungs, screaming their disapproval down upon us. The noise is maddening, but Reece doesn't waver.

"I'm sorry," he whispers to the crows, before squeezing his eyes shut to his fellow harbingers. The crows scream as if they are the ones who are dying.

"Open your mouth wide, harbinger," whispers Rafette.

With a quiet sob, he opens his mouth. The meandering bee spots her destination and aims for his mouth. She's fast. Faster than she appeared.

She's an inch from Reece's lips, and all I can think is, *I cannot allow this to happen!*

I reach out. My fist closes around the queen the second before she enters Reece's mouth.

I don't hesitate. I'm already ruined, after all.

Frantic wings beat against my palm. Delicate legs scramble at the seams between my fingers. The world looks featured, like stop-action frames. I see Reece's shocked wide eyes, the "no" forming on his lips. The gasp of surprise from Rafette, who falls to the ground and convulses.

The queen stabs her stinger into my palm, and my vision turns spotless white. My hand feels like it's been plunged into a bucket of acid. This is blinding, obscene pain, beyond description. Worse than anything I could have imagined. It is the type of pain that makes one wish for death.

Every instinct in my body wails at me to open my hand. To release her. Instead, I close my eyes and squeeze.

Reece's voice cracks over a broken, "No!" He realizes what I've done. The queen's venom is an instant death sentence.

She stings me again and again. But I keep squeezing until there is nothing left of her. I glance down at the sticky mess between my fingers and stiffen as pulsing waves of agony double me over. My hand is no longer *my hand*. It's an appendage of indescribable burning.

I drop to the ground as a bitter taste erupts in my mouth. The crows fall silent.

The inexplicable scent of fresh hay mixing with rotting flesh fills my nostrils. A shadow falls over me, cooling my fevered skin, turning the color filtering through my closed eyelids from red to gray. There is a strange sound next to me, like straw snapping, then a sigh. I sense, in that moment, that someone else is at the playground with us. Someone ancient. Someone far more dangerous than Rafette. And a voice in my head that is not my own: *Well done, child.*

Then the presence is gone, and everything slows down. I feel the sharp prick of talons on my arms, the brush of feathers on my cheek, and then the wings are *inside me*, beating frantically under my ribs. It's as if a bird is trapped there, scrabbling for escape. It must be my heart, throbbing unevenly, struggling to keep blood pumping. The erratic beat gets louder, bigger, thunderous, until it takes over all the sensations in my body.

Then, the fluttering rises up. I can almost feel dry feathers on the back of my throat, surging up and out of my mouth, taking all the air with it. My lungs gasp in a breath. My heart settles back into rhythm. Another breath. More beats. The pain returns, filling up my extremities like a bucket filling with water one spoonful at a time. I'm fearful of what I'll have to endure next, before this misery ends, but I want to hold on to every moment I have left with Reece. I open my eyes and look.

Next to me sprawls a young man dressed like Rafette. His eyes are open, sightless in death. His head is turned toward me, one hand outstretched as if reaching in my direction. My vision doubles a bit, but even my addled, pain-eroded brain perceives the shocking beauty of him. To call him handsome would not do him justice. His face is one in a million. Impossible to look away from. A genetic lottery winner of strong, elegant, masculine bones, over fine golden skin. The man's vacant gaze is frozen in what appears to be complete bliss.

The realization hits me—this is Rafette—the *real* Rafette before he was cursed—and for the first time in a millennia, his beautiful features don't change. Thousands of dead bees carpet the ground around him, like a wreath. A burden of incalculable weight, finally set aside. I've experienced something I can't fully understand—don't *want* to fully understand.

Suddenly, Reece's terrified face is in front of mine. He shakes my shoulders, calls my name. He sounds frantic, but his touch and his voice feel so far away, off in the distance. He's talking to someone, arguing. *Too many stings,* someone says. *A queen has never stung someone before…*

Once again, the pain subsides. It's like a lapping tide, slowly ebbing away. My senses switch off, one by one. Reece's voice fades out. Everything fades out.

Is this it, finally? That precious, pendulous tipping point of life into death? How absurd that I'm wasting my last few moments *thinking* about such a thing. *I'm so sorry, Dad.* A different kind of pain twists my heart. I didn't get to say goodbye. I feel so terrible about leaving him.

But I saved Reece, Deno, so many other people—even Rafette, who needed saving more than any of us. And I had to sacrifice only myself. My body seizes. I guess the toxins have reached something important, at last. A burning sensation creeps up my neck, then detonates in my skull. I'm flying apart. Breaking into pieces, one molecule at a time.

Bright light burns my eyes. A ripple of heat rakes over my burning skin. I'm being lifted, moved.

And then, nothing.

Blessed, glorious, painless *nothing.*

41

just a boy

It's raining again. I can hear it on the roof. A cup of tea is getting cold on my nightstand. A pile of at-home schoolwork is piling up in my inbox. I snuggle deeper under my purple comforter and hug my right hand against my chest. It's still red and painful and a constant memory of what happened in the playground nearly a month ago. The queen's stings had become infected. I'm still being treated with antibiotics.

The house next door is empty again. The windows are dark. A fresh, new For Sale sign swings hopefully next to the street. It's as if the Fernandezes were never there. I would seriously consider that maybe I imagined the whole thing, if my dad hadn't regaled me with tales of how Reece carried me nearly a mile to the safe hands of paramedics. Or if Deno and Lacey hadn't come over and made me relive every single moment. They're a couple now, and I admit, it's a little weird seeing them that way. Weird in a good way.

I wasn't awake for any of my rescue, unfortunately. If I'd known that day would be the last time I'd see Reece, I would have made an effort to remain conscious.

I thought for sure he'd at least stop in at the hospital. To say good-bye, like he promised. To say *something*.

But he didn't visit. Not once in the two days I was a patient there. Not once in the two weeks we stayed at the hotel while power and road access were restored to our neighborhood. Not in the week since my dad and I came home. I thought we went through something remarkable enough to warrant a good-bye, at least, but what happened in Cadence was probably just another day at the office for a harbinger of death.

Knuckles lightly rap on my bedroom door, and Dad pokes his head in. "Hey."

Roger shoves through the open door and does a running leap onto my bed. He sneezes, then flops onto his back in a demand for belly rubs. Of course, I comply. He's fully healed from the blow he took from the Beekeeper in the garage.

"How are you doing?" Dad comes in and perches on the edge of my bed. He smooths the hair out of my eyes. "Want me to reheat your tea?"

"No thanks," I say. "I'm good."

His brows draw together. "You very clearly are *not* good."

"Yeah, I am." I struggle to an upright seat with a wince. "Healing is hard work."

"It is, but the body isn't what's bothering you right now." Dad's face softens. "Kiddo, you survived a landslide, a *flood*, all the insanity that ensued, and nearly died by stumbling on a colony of bees. Yet somehow I think *heartache* is causing you as much pain as that cracked rib."

I shake my head and hold up my stung palm. "This still hurts more."

"They sure did a number on you," Dad says. "Over a hundred stings is a lot for a person your size."

I smile weakly. "Sure. Remind me how short I am."

"You're not that short."

My heart flips over in my chest. Those words didn't come from my father. Roger's tail starts up a rapid thumping.

I pęek around my dad with dread and hope and the sudden urge to cry, and see Reece in the doorway. His arms are folded tight over his chest. He wavers at the jamb, as if unsure whether or not to come in. "Hi Angie."

"Oh yes. By the way, you have a visitor." My father clears his throat and gets to his feet. "Well. I'll just give you two a moment." He crosses to the door and pauses before Reece. "She's still supposed to be resting," he says. "I'll be downstairs."

"Yes sir," Reece replies, a picture of deference. "Thank you for letting me see her."

"Yeah, yeah. I made you wait long enough." Dad mumbles something, then retreats, closing the door behind him, but not clicking it.

Reece looks healthy and handsome, in a blue T-shirt and jeans. He watches my father leave with a gentle, inscrutable expression. His gaze shifts to the floor and stays there. The room is so quiet. *Too* quiet.

I scrape my hair back and wish I had washed it recently. I don't want to know what I look like right now. *Thanks for the warning, Dad*. I'm wearing Hello Kitty pajamas, of all things.

No wonder he won't look at me. Wait...why *won't* he look at me? Why is he still all the way on the other side of the room? It isn't because of how I look. Or smell.

The answer slams into me. Burns worse than my hundred bee stings. *This* is good-bye. He's leaving. Finally.

I close my eyes and ignore the burn behind my lids. At least he kept his word. This is just one more thing I'll have to survive.

"How long do you have?" I manage to keep my voice even.

His head comes up. "How long for what?"

"Before you leave, of course."

He rolls his shoulders in a tense shrug. "I don't know."

So we're playing the vague game. Fan-freaking-tastic. After all we went through, we're back to *this*.

"Fine," I say. "You just let me know, then." Somehow, I managed to infuse ample snottiness in my words. Even as my stomach slowly knots. Even as I bite my lip to keep it from quivering.

"I don't know when I'm leaving," he says hesitantly, "because I don't know *if* I'm leaving. That part is up to you."

As if my head wasn't pounding enough. "What does that mean? I thought you were here to say good-bye."

He comes forward and stands next to the bed. Finally, his eyes turn to mine. I tilt my head, confused by what I see. The lights are low, but I swear it looks like…

He blinks. Long, dark lashes sweep over crystal-blue eyes.

Not black. Not red. Not any other shade.

I rise up to my knees and lean close. Those blue eyes blink slowly, gaze at me with an inscrutable expression.

"Reece, your eyes are *blue*." My voice is a reverent whisper. "What does this mean?"

He holds up his hand. The three scars running the length of his palm are gone. His lips turn up in a crooked, uncertain smile. "It means you—what you did—ended it for me. The crow is gone. You released it. I have a life—*one* life, one death, like everyone else. No more curses. No more changing into a—" He cuts off with a shaky indrawn breath.

"You mean you're not a harbinger of death anymore?" I ask. "You're just…you?"

His mouth moves into a wavering smile. "Yes. I'm just me." His voice is low and rough and aching with deep emotion. His gaze shifts to my sore hand. "I don't have the words. They just don't exist—*thank* you, Angie. You…freed me. Rafette, too. And everyone who had been stung by Rafette, as you know."

He lowers his head. "I owe you everything."

"You don't owe me anything," I say roughly. "You were going to become a Beekeeper to save me, remember?" My heart pounds. I can't stop staring at his eyes. So *blue*. If it weren't for them, I'd wonder if this was a latent bee sting-induced hallucination. "You don't look happy."

He rubs his palms on his jeans and lets out a breath. "I am, it's just… My family has left. They're all excited that there *is* a way out of this curse, even though what happened with us can't be replicated. But it's given them hope."

Hope. Such a powerful emotion. I glance over at my dresser, to the small glass bowl sitting there. Inside are Hank's gifts, untouched, and the amethyst Reece found in the mine. "How is Hank?" I ask.

Reece sighs. He reaches into his pocket with slow movements and comes out with a long white wing feather. He takes my hand and reverently places it in my palm. "After it was confirmed that you would recover, he requested the *mortouri* and it was granted." He looks away, brow creased. "I wasn't present for it. I didn't…"

"It's okay." My throat tightens. I close my fingers around the stiff white feather. "He suffered enough. Maybe his curse will die with him, too."

"I hope so." Reece's gaze flickers back up to mine, then away.

"Thank you for this." I hold the feather to my chest. "I'll never forget him."

"Nor will I. He tried to save himself and your mother, but wound up damning them both. But with us…" He runs a hand through his hair. "I don't know what happened after you grabbed Rafette's queen bee. I was incapacitated for a while, as the curse worked its way out of my body. I couldn't see what happened. My family thinks it was our willingness to lose ourselves, to save each other, that cracked the curse. We may never know for sure what did it. I still can't believe you survived the queen's venom, too."

Yes, there are things we'll never know about that day. Maybe my mom's final gift to me was whatever magic allowed her to survive so long with Rafette's venom. In the end, I'd like to believe my mom saved me.

I think back to my fleeting memories, just before I passed out in that playground. Of Rafette's shockingly beautiful face. Of the smell of decay, the sound of snapping straw. Of the quiet voice in my head saying, *Well done, child*. I can't be sure any of it was real and not the byproduct of pain, venom, and fear. Maybe I'll tell Reece about them sometime, but I may never have the chance to.

"So what are your…plans?" I ask, unsure where this is going. If this is *not necessarily* good-bye, what is it?

"My family has put me in charge of their estate, since I'm, well, all human now. For the first time in more years than I can remember, I don't know what happens next. I'm…scared."

"Good." I force myself to sit still, even though I want to jump off this bed and dance. I want to sing at the top of my lungs. I want to kiss him breathless. "It's life. It's supposed to be scary."

He sobers, eyes turning serious and watchful. "So I have to ask, because I have choices now, and so do you." He swallows with effort and shifts his gaze to the blue twinkle lights draped above my headboard. "Do you want me to stick around or not? I found an apartment in Summit, the next town over. I can live on my own, since I'm eighteen, but if you'd rather I leave the area, I will." His hands are restless, tracing designs on my comforter. "I'm afraid I'm never going to be completely normal. The things I've seen and I… Well, you never really recover from it. I'd understand if you want to go separate ways. You're not obligated to—"

"Oh, shut up, Reece." I reach out a hand and he steps toward me. "Of course I want you to stay."

His face brightens. "Are you sure? I know you have plans to go to college, and if you don't want me to go with you, just say so. I wouldn't blame you."

I'm grateful my left hand doesn't hurt. I use it to grab the front of his shirt and pull him toward me. He stops rambling and peers down at me, a smile spreading slowly over his lips.

My mouth finds his and his eyes close and we kiss. A first kiss. A kiss of beginnings and possibilities and impossible dreams.

acknowledgments

If you're reading this, that means my book has become a real thing. It's a big deal to see the messy story idea from your head turn into a solid object you can hold in your hand. I wish to express my deepest gratitude to everyone who helped make this happen.

One sentence isn't enough to express my thanks to my editor, Jennifer Mishler, whose insights made this a better book and me a better writer. And to Liz Pelletier and the amazing team at Entangled TEEN, who go above and beyond for their authors.

Thank you to my literary agent, Beth Miller, at Writers House, for her guidance, expertise, and patience.

Thanks to Pintip Dunn for more than I can begin to articulate. *Seriously.* So much.

Thanks to Stephanie Winkelhake for her support and feedback and to Wanda Thomas, for always pushing me to write it better, to dig deeper.

I'd like to thank the DoomsDaisies and the 2016 Mermaids for being the supportive communities you are.

Thank you to my mentor, Brenna Yovanoff, for answering all my baby author questions.

Thanks to Michelle Libby and Judi Phillips for taking in a stray Jersey girl all those years ago and teaching her the ropes. And to the talented women of Maine Romance Writers for the encouragement and support they so generously give.

Thank you to my YA girls, Mariah, Jess, and Heather, for

the late night, fast food, deep talks.

Thank you L.J. Anderson, at Mayhem Cover Creations, for this stunning cover.

Thank you to the folks at the Falmouth Memorial Library, for the "quiet area" in the back, where I wrote and revised a good portion of this book.

A big thank you to my wonderful family: Karen, Jack, and Evan, for thinking I'm better than I am and never letting me forget it.

Finally, thank you to my husband, Pete, who never, ever doubted me. And Poppy, who reminds me every day of the importance of having fun.

Grab the Entangled Teen releases readers are talking about!

27 Hours
by Tristina Wright

ZERO HOUR MEANS WAR

Rumor Mora fears two things: hellhounds too strong for him to kill, and failure. Jude Welton has two dreams: for humans to stop killing monsters, and for his strange abilities to vanish.

But in no reality should a boy raised to love monsters fall for a boy raised to kill them.

During one twenty-seven-hour night, if they can't stop the war between the colonies and the monsters from becoming a war of extinction, the things they wish for will never come true, and the things they fear will be all that's left.

Remember Yesterday
By Pintip Dunn

Jessa Stone's psychic abilities may make her the most valuable citizen in Eden City, but she'd much rather break in to their labs and sabotage their research—starting with Tanner Callahan, budding scientist and the boy she loathes most at school.

The past isn't what she assumed, though—and neither is Tanner. When his research opens the door to the possibility that Jessa can rectify a fatal mistake made ten years earlier, she'll do anything to change the past—even if it means teaming up with the enemy she swore to defeat.